PROSPERO'S LASS

Parts One & Two

Part One: *Prospero's Lass*
Part Two: *Beyond the Joke*

Alwyne Joseph Kennedy

CALAMITY BOOKS

CALAMITY BOOKS
PO BOX 12843
LONDON
SE13 7XS

Part One first published by COCKaSNOOK BOOKS, 1993.
Revised for Calamity Books, 1995.

© ALWYNE KENNEDY 1995, 1996

All rights reserved. No part of this publication may be reproduced, stored in a retrieval system, or transmitted, in any form or by any means, electronic, mechanical, photocopying, recording or otherwise, without the prior permission in writing of the publisher.

British Library Cataloguing-in-Publication Data.
A catalogue record for this book is available from the British Library.

Typeset by Calamity Books in 10pt. Garamond.

ISBN 0 9529670 0 6

*To the unimpeachably wonderful SUSAN AULT, flower of Finsbury, whose birthday it is this very day of January 6th, I dedicate this humble labour. Susan — a diamond in the dirt of my life. Susan — a gleam in the gloom. Susan — a goddess to me.
Her sister's not bad, either.*

Part One

Prospero's Lass

1.1

Love's Cruel Darts

Lisa was the first big love of his October.

And Pross was forever falling in love.

Result: misery.

Pross fell tragically in love seven to seventy times each month. Acute and agonizing nympholepsy was to blame.

Nympholepsy: the despair arising from being tantalised by glimpses of unattainable nymphs.

And nymphs lay in wait for him everywhere, ready to tear his heart to pieces.

After what seemed like a thousand years of suffering, he leaned over the side of the bed, awaiting the inevitable. And after several unproductive retching motions, he spewed forth, his abdomen straining and heaving painfully.

His head throbbed, his stomach was in painful spasm, he was semi-delirious, and, unknown to him, his long brown hair was dangling into his own vomit.

Later, in that precious, merciful calm that often follows vomiting, he slumped back on to the pillow, eyes closed... only to become aware that his cat, which had been on the bed all the while, was trying to eat his hair. Investigation revealed that his hair was garnished with the former contents of his own stomach.

Holding the drenched tresses out of the cat's way as best he could, he commented upon his own condition. 'This is insane,' he murmured weakly. 'I can't go on drinking and puking like this.' A few seconds later he found the solution: 'I'll have to cut my hair.'

He pushed the cat away, tucked the savoury part of his hair under the pillow for protection, and closed his eyes, hoping for sleep.

Moments later, a crashing thud jarred his eyes back open. His cat, peculiarly lacking in many of the essential cat skills, particularly climbing, had, in an attempt to scale its heights, toppled over a bookcase, spilling volumes of science, literature and poetry over the bedroom floor.

Many years' dust billowed from the texts.

Leaving the books fallen, he managed an hour's fitful but dream-packed sleep before being woken by the sound of his doorbell. Lifting his head from the pillow, he immediately wished he hadn't bothered, for it throbbed and pounded so violently he was compelled to wince and pull in his shoulders sharply. 'No way,' he said to himself, 'can't be done.' Then adding ruefully, 'Might be the blonde one from Abba, though.'

Puzzled is what he was when he heard his flatmate answer the door. It was only eleven o'clock — Ron should have been at work.

Brought back into full consciousness, Pross began to feel like throwing up again, and he leaned over the bucket once more.

The bedroom door was slightly open, and coming from the hall he could faintly hear the caller speaking. More than once he discerned his own name in the muffled dialogue.

The talking stopped.

Footsteps sounded outside his bedroom.

After a single loud tap, the white-painted wooden door of the bedroom opened and Ron stuck his sandy-haired, dark-blue-eyed head into the room.

'What are you doing home?' asked Pross, viewing him sideways.

'I was given time off to sort out some travel arrangements,' was the brisk answer. 'What happened to the bookcase?'

'Cat knocked it over. Where are you going?'

'Told you yesterday. Iceland for two weeks. Business.'

Ron rolled his eyes when he saw the bucket. 'Christ, have you been puking again? Were you drinking last night?'

'Lilith treated me. Kings Arms,' muttered Pross.

'You're your own worst enemy, you. You know you can't take it,' said Ron, viewing Pross with a 50:40:10 mixture of contempt, despair and pathos, in that order.

Pross half-wondered why Ron was being so twatty. Lifting himself completely back on to the bed and lying down sideways, he moaned, 'My head feels like it's in a clamp. A hot one with spikes dipped in witches' curses.'

Ron was unmoved. 'There's a couple of mates of yours out here wanting to see you,' he said.

But the inevitable was about to happen again, and Pross didn't particularly want an audience. 'Tell them to...'

Too late: he was already over the bucket, retching.

Ron didn't care, and he beckoned the visitors into the bedroom.

Ron led a young policeman and an even younger policewoman to the bottom of Pross's bed while the latter was gulping, snorting and sniffing into the bucket, like some great dying beast.

The policeman was carrying a large, bulging manilla envelope.

Once within the darkened room, the coppers eyed the toppled bookcase and Rolf Harris posters adorning the walls.

Then they eyed Pross filling a bucket.

Ron spoke to them in a hushed voice. 'This is him. Prospero Pi-Meson.'

'It's Melanie's fault,' groaned Prospero Pi-Meson.

'It is Melanie's fault,' agreed Ron equitably, speaking to the officers.

'What is?' asked the policeman.

'Why he's called what he's called. Try not to tire him out, he's very sick.'

In deference to Pross's condition, the policeman took off his helmet and spoke in softened Geordie tones to Ron. 'What's the matter with him, like?'

'Progressive melancholia,' answered Ron. 'You're lucky to catch him lucid.'

The copper looked at Pross, then at Ron. 'Serious, is it?'

'Killed Van Gogh,' groaned Pross.

'That's right,' agreed Ron.

In the medical dark, the copper asked, 'What is it?'

Pross, head still over bucket, sickly provided his stock answer. 'It's a debilitating spiritual condition that afflicts the clinically lovelorn. You'd be this way too if you'd seen Lisa.' Lifting his head, which pounded in violent protest, he looked at his visitors for the first time. 'Aw, not coppers again.'

Ron couldn't help laughing at this point, and the policeman began to strongly suspect he was having the piss taken out of him, as he saw it. He became a getting-to-the-point copper and took out from the manilla envelope a letter and a pink T-shirt, which looked like this:

'What's all this about, like?' asked the policeman firmly. 'And what's all the stuff about death in this letter you sent? The poor lass who got them's absolutely distraught.'

'Lisa,' pined Pross, stretching the two syllables for miles.

It soon became apparent to the officers that nothing was to be gained from questioning Pross and Ron, and since fear of a tricky television documentary investigation dissuaded them from radioing their colleagues for help in pounding some respect for the uniform into these two cocky bastards, they decided to retreat. As they left, a firm warning was issued. 'Look. The girl doesn't want to have anything to do with you, so you'd better just keep away from her if you know what's good for you.'

'Exercise,' said Pross.

'What?'

'Exercise. That's something I know's good for me.'

Becoming angrier, the policeman pursued his warning. 'Send her any more letters or go anywhere near her again, you'll be in big trouble.'

The officers left, forgetting the T-shirt, which Ron picked up.

Observing stealthily from behind the curtain in the bedroom, Ron watched the officers as they drove off. Once satisfied that they'd really gone, he gave Pross what he deserved, in the tone he deserved.

'Moron.'

Pross sank down into his bed. 'Aw, Ron, I'm too ill. Tell me off later.'

'You need your fucking head examining.'

'Save it till tomorrow.'

Tomorrow wouldn't wait.

'Why don't you grow up?' Ron wanted to know.

'I've outgrown the childish pursuit of maturity,' replied Pross, a retort which secretly impressed Ron, forcing him to change his angle of attack.

'Do you want me to get bust? Why don't you tell me when you've done something that might attract cops? What if they'd seen a joint? Or the plant in the garden?'

Seeing the plant in the garden was unlikely, since someone had stolen it the previous week.

'There isn't a plant in the garden,' remarked Pross, unwisely.

Ron glowered at him.

'Rab C. Scoones would have every excuse he needed if I ended up in court on a dope charge. It's all right for you, you've got nothing to lose.'

'Aw, how was I to know she'd freak?' groaned Pross. 'It was actually a bloody flattering letter. My latest. Proud of it.' Turning over on to his side, he muttered, 'I was only playing around.'

Ron's response was heated. '*You* know you were playing around. *I* know you were playing around. But how was *she* to know?'

'Because she's seen my eyes,' said Pross, and a particularly moony expression came over him as he angled his face towards Ron, showing him his eyes. 'All who observe my eyes know poetry and gentleness. She's been insensitive to my sensitivity.'

Ron didn't agree.

'You think that everyone else alive exists just to provide amusement for you, don't you?'

Pross nodded, if only because he knew it would set Ron off.

'You're arrogant, that's what you are.'

Pross agreed. 'I'm supercilious too. Often bombastic.'

'You'll get your comeuppance one day, I'll wager,' predicted Ron, then turning his attention to the T-shirt, which he unfurled for dismissive examination. He shook his head and quietly said, 'One of the most cunning minds ever devised by nature.' He shook his head again. 'Who would believe it? Who *would* believe it?'

Pross looked at him.

'That's what Tony said about you last night,' continued Ron. 'A consultant psychiatrist, no less. *One of the most cunning minds ever devised by nature*. But I wonder. Sometimes I really do wonder.'

'Thought Lisa would have been proud to wear it,' muttered Pross.

'Who is this Lisa, anyway?'

'A memory of Beauty once glimpsed.'

'Aw, for fuck's sake, she's not that bimboish one you've been ogling down the Kings Arms, is she?'

'Might be.'

It was now time for Ron to pass sentence: 'If you and that word processor bring any more cops around, I'll thump you. Christ, that's the third time in as many months.'

Pross seemed to be genuinely sorry. 'Ok,' he said, 'I promise that next time I send a love letter, I'll tell you first.'

'That's better.'

'In fact I'm going to send one now — that policewoman was rather lush. Switch it on for me and take dictation.'

Ron cracked. He took hold of the bottom of Pross's bed and tipped the whole thing, together with panicking, protesting occupant, vertical, resting it upright against the wall. Being six foot six and naturally built to match, this was no hard task for him.

Ron made average sized men feel runty when he stood next to them.

'I knew I shouldn't have got you that thing,' growled Ron, 'you're supposed to be writing a novel on it for fuck's sake. I want my money back for it. Give me my money back, you talentless fucker.'

And he started shaking the bed.

'I've already finished a novel!' claimed Pross desperately.

Ron ceased the shaking.

'What?'

'It's finished. I finished it the other day.'

'Don't believe you. Show me.'

'The manuscript's on the table.'

Ron looked at the table, and saw only the slimmest of documents: three pages, to be exact, and that included a title page.

The title page read: *GODFREY, ALIEN PHYSICIST (My First Novel)*.

Admittedly, upon examination, the second page revealed itself to be crammed with text, and the third was well over half utilised (counting the large *The End*), but Ron couldn't help suspecting that novels were supposed to be just a little more *substantial* than this example.

And so he cracked again.

'Get up and get a job,' he ordered, kicking the underside of the bed.

'Ow, don't hurt me.'

'Why not?'

'Because it's my birthday.'

Ron was taken aback a little by this intelligence. 'It's not, is it?'

'Fucking well is.'

Ron sat down. 'Why the fuck do I share a flat with him?' he wanted the gods to reveal.

'Because I get Housing Benefit and it covers the whole rent,' answered Pross from behind the upright bed.

'Oh, yeah, remember now,' said Ron. Cooling down a little, he picked up one of the science books from the floor — *Entropy: The Leveller of the Universe*. 'You ought to sell these fucking books. I haven't seen you read anything for years.'

'Can't be arsed any more.'

Ron began reading.

'What are you in such a twatty mood for, anyway?' asked Pross a short while later.

Becoming angry again, Ron said, 'You'd be in a twatty mood too if you'd had to bite your tongue this morning while being given a pathetic warning about being too informal at work.'

So *that* was it, realised Pross. It was that Scoones dwarf with the jam jar glasses and the Rab C. Nesbit haircut again.

Pross hated Rab C. Scoones. Scoones made his life a misery.

'I wouldn't bite it,' he said.

'And you wouldn't get paid,' said Ron.

'Then I wouldn't get paid.'

'Bastard Rab C. Scoones!' shouted Ron before leaving the room, taking the book with him.

Pross's cat entered.

It investigated the new furniture lay out.

'Well, cat,' said Pross, 'twenty-four years ago today, my unhappy heart began its labour of senseless bumping.'

Half an hour later, his head throbbing slightly less, Pross crawled from the wreckage of his bed, making for the bathroom.

After washing and dressing, viewing himself in the mirror in his bedroom, dispiritedly pushing his damp hair around, he decided that today he really would say goodbye to the unintentional Crusty Traveller look that his hair seemed determined always to confer upon him, despite his recent new clothes acquisitions.

'Right, it's definite: proper haircut for me today,' he declared to his reflection, like he'd just resolved to climb Everest or die in the attempt. 'I'm sick of puking on it.'

A little while later, just after midday, headache tolerably diminished, he was closing his flat's inner door and walking across the tiled hall towards the outer door. Harry, the occupant of the attic flat, was sitting on the bottom step, his door key (which he always kept on a thick cord around his neck) jangling against his lager can.

'Morning Harry,' said Pross as he passed by. 'How's the political career going?'

Harry muttered something incomprehensible in Geordie.

Harry was an alcoholic of around sixty, with little hair, three teeth, and one dirty green jumper.

Opening the outer door, Pross found himself face to face with a postwoman making the day's second delivery.

'This you?' she asked, showing Pross a junk mail envelope.

'Uh, huh,' said Pross, taking the letter and tossing it into the hall. 'Anything else? Anything looking like a birthday card?'

'No, sorry.'

The cat appeared in the doorway.

'Aw, what a lovely cat,' said the postwoman, bending down to give it a stroke. 'What's he called?'

'Spock. And he's a she.'

'Whatever did you call her Spock for?' asked the postwoman, as if it were an action that warranted a police investigation.

'Because she's got pointed ears,' answered Pross as he set off walking down the garden path on his haircut mission, wearing his favourite black boots, faded blue jeans and black leather jacket.

In the hairdressers, a nymph smiled at him and said her name was Joanne, and Lisa was consigned to history.

'How short do you want it?' asked Joanne.

'Shorter than a bucket's length,' answered Pross.

Later in the afternoon, Pross drifted into the estate agents where his friend, Lilith, worked.

Pross didn't have a wide circle of friends. Less than ten, actually, and often that figure seemed extravagant to him. There were less than ten people he ever bothered with, and who reciprocally bothered with him, and months could go by without him exchanging so much as a single word with someone additional, excluding the odd "thanks" uttered in supermarkets.

This growing tendency for social isolation had not gone unnoticed by Ron, who maintained that Pross was becoming an eerie recluse. Indeed, he had taken to predicting to people that his flatmate would go completely mad one day soon if he didn't get out into the world a bit more.

Ron had even tried to organise a sweepstake on the event.

Lilith was a disaster area. No nymph was she. Nothing about the poor girl seemed to match. Her hands were tiny and almost not worth having (Pross had once cruelly joked that she would be better off just sharpening her wrists to useful spikes), yet her arms were long. Her eyes were different colours. Her breasts were also quite disparate, one being about the size of a fried egg, the other being the size of about four fried eggs. Her semi-circle of upper teeth were rotated so much to one side, her two large incisors pointed thirty degrees away from dead-ahead, and her lower teeth were chipped badly. Her legs were stout, yet she was generally slim; and although she *was* generally slim, her face was round and large, and she had a definite second chin, but, bizarrely, her first chin was notable for its absence. Her shoulders were rounded, so that she always appeared to be slouching, yet she was energetic and effervescent. Her small mouth was turned down at both corners so that she always appeared to be miserable, yet she was quite a comic by nature. And when she moved, all her limbs, as well as the other, less extreme parts of her, seemed to have an independence of not only rhythm, but also of direction.

And twenty-year-old Lilith had never had a boyfriend.

Lilith was busy totalling some figures and didn't realise Pross was in the office until he suddenly slumped face-down on to her desk.

Lilith bolted upright and emitted a little shriek.

Lilith's colleague at another desk cast a look of disapproval. Customers turned around.

'Wrists like I've never seen before. Such maddening wrists.'

'Pross... hello,' said Lilith. 'You've cut your hair the way I suggested!'

'Coincidence. Was puking on it too much.'

Lilith extended a tentative hand and began fingering his locks. 'It's curling a bit now that it's shorter. Told you it would.'

'Each curl individually sucked into shape by a supermodel.' Sitting up, he waved a lock, slightly shorter than a buck is deep, in front of Lilith. 'See this one? Claudia Schieffer.'

But the strain of sitting up proved too much for him. 'Oh my hungover head.'

'Hangover? You only drank as much as me.'

'Poet's constitution, dear girl.'

'It's cut very well. Did you go to a hairdresser's?'

Pross nodded, embarrassed for it to be known that he cared enough to have gone to such lengths over his image. 'Uh, huh. Cost me twelve bastard quid. Only got a quid left to last me until my giro comes on Wednesday.'

'Money well spent,' declared Lilith. 'You look dead raunchy.'

'But it cost me my peace of mind too.'

'How's that?'

'If you'd seen the hairdresser, you wouldn't need to ask,' said Pross, adding dreamily, 'Such wrists. Such maddening wrists.'

Lilith gathered her papers together and took them into the back room, reappearing a few moments later with a carrier bag, a glass of water and some paracetamols.

'For your headache: painkillers,' she said, offering the tablets and water.

Pross took them from her. 'Are they effective against the sting of love's cruel darts?' he asked.

Lilith smiled, then handed Pross the carrier bag.

'Happy birthday, Pross. Was going to wrap it, but you might as well have it now. I bought it for you when I was in London.'

Pross felt uncomfortable accepting presents and tokens of affection, and sometimes his defensive reactions could offend. 'How did you know?' he found himself asking as a diversion from the awkwardness he was feeling. 'I've never told anyone.'

'I made the effort to find out,' returned Lilith. 'Well, take it out,' she said, a little tersely.

Pross retrieved from the bag a fancy, multi-coloured silk shirt.

'I can't wear this,' he protested, 'it's too cheerful. People will think I'm shallow. They'll think I don't know all happiness is doomed.'

Wandering home in the late afternoon of his twenty-fourth birthday, now wearing his new shirt, Pross turned off the main road and into Devon Road, which, considering his philosophies, was just about the worst place he could live in Durham. Pross was a ranting, militant atheist, and Devon Road, short though it was, had *two* churches. One was a Catholic church, just off the main road, and the other was a modern evangelical eyesore, right opposite his flat.

Approaching the Catholic church, and knowing that confession was in progress, Pross felt some long-fancied mischief coming on, and he passed through its hallowed portals.

Although it was thirteen years since he'd last indulged in the confession absurdity, he still knew the ritual, knew the ritual that he considered served only to lessen the burden of guilt for the admittedly guilty, helping wife-beaters and burglars to sleep better at night.

Kneeling in the box, speaking to a priest through a translucent screen, adopting the standard penitential tone, he began accusing himself.

'Forgive me, Father, for I have sinned since my last confession.'

'Tell me, in what way have you sinned?' replied the priest, with a practised air that oozed comfort, support and understanding.

'I have committed the sin of fornication.'

'Ah,' sighed the priest, 'that's a sin many young people are tempted by these days.'

'But I've done it worse,' said Pross, laying on the gravity.

'And how might that be?' asked the priest, now more attentive.

'I've fucked a nun of your parish. The one with big tits.'

It was time to leave.

Feeling like he'd just struck a major blow for both sanity and comedy in an absurd world, rounding the bend that led to his flat, Pross was annoyingly reminded that madness was ubiquitous.

The evangelical church right opposite his flat had acquired a large hoarding since he'd walked past it last, four hours earlier. A workman, being overseen by a young man with born again eyes, was just finishing pasting a day-glo orange sign over the new hoarding, which read, in huge black letters, *JESUS WILL ANSWER YOUR PRAYERS!*

Annoyance tinged with despair was the expression on Pross's face as he paused to ingest the message.

The born-againer effusively thanked the workman as he carried his ladder away.

The born-againer was wearing a T-shirt which read: *MORRIS CERULLO WORLD EVANGELISM*.

The happy-clappy born-againer was brimming with self-satisfaction over the successful completion of the job. So carried away was he, he turned to Pross and blurted joyously, 'Jesus will answer your prayers!'

'After two thousand fucking years of fucking calamities and fucking atrocities, you'd think that even someone as dumb-looking as you would realise that prayers are never answered,' was Pross's cruel return.

The born-againer was taken aback, and taken even further back when Pross tugged at his T-shirt and said, 'Morris has got you fooled, hasn't he? How much has he had out of you so far?'

The born-againer was not up for a discussion. Instead, he employed what he considered to be saintly restraint. 'Jesus loves you,' he said, turning to walk into the church.

'You said that like a threat,' called out Pross after him. 'You said that like watch your step because Jesus loves *me*.'

The born-againer retreated into his shelter, and Pross crossed the road to reach his flat, a Victorian terrace conversion. Lifting the latch of his front gate, he glanced only briefly at the hole in the overgrown garden that showed where a fair-sized dope plant, grown and loved obsessively by Ron, had existed until its theft last week.

Beside the house's front door were positioned three bell-buttons, one for each of the house's flats. The ground floor flat was Ron and Pross's. The attic flat was the province of Harry, and the middle flat was occupied by Mrs Brown. The button for her flat bore her name in a spidery hand, but had been hanging off the wall for as long as Pross could remember.

Mrs Brown was a thin, drawn, wretch of a woman. It was hard to guess her age. She looked to be in her seventies, but that figure might be two decades high. Her body amounted to little more than the skeleton beneath the skin. She gave Pross the heebie-jeebies. It was something about her eyes. Her eyes were dead.

No one ever came to see Mrs Brown.

Or Harry.

Kicking open the outer door with his foot, Pross walked across the tiled hall where the dustbins were kept, and then slid his key into his own inner door. Closing the inner door behind him, he walked into the drab living room he shared with Ron.

Ron was sitting on the sofa, pen in hand, pondering something.

Largely ignored by Ron, Pross stomped over to the window to glare at the sign across the road.

'Seen the fucking monstrosity they've stuck up over the road?'

'No.'

'Why are people allowed to spread lies? I was thinking today how every schoolkid has the lie of religion drummed into them by law. It's crazy. It shouldn't be legal to promote thinking that conflicts with the evidence. Why isn't it illegal?'

'Don't know.'

'One day soon there'll be enough of them Evangelical mental cases to fight a war at the whim of one of those deranged tv preachers. Scares me shitless. It'll be people like me they'll come gunning for. You know, the free-thinking pretty people with sexy haircuts. You'll be all right, though.'

'Is that so?'

Pross continued to glare at the sign. 'What this world needs is a leader who'll eventually show even the thickest of his followers that they've been duped. Might put an end to religious mentality for good.'

'Maybe it's your calling in life,' suggested Ron, if only to get him out of the flat more often.

Pross now realised that Ron was far more interested in doing whatever it was he was doing than in the conversation, which wasn't unusual.

So he turned to see.

'What are you doing?'

'Picking my lottery numbers,' answered Ron.

To Pross, the national lottery wasn't far off being a religious movement in itself: it gave unrealistic hopes of salvation to the masses. He'd never even considered entering himself. Not once.

'Not again,' he said. 'Every week you fall for that fool's dream.'

Ron was tiring of Pross ranting. 'Get out of bed the wrong side of twenty-three today, did we? Smell the stench of aged decay?'

'Put the money on the horses, idiot, at least you'll occasionally win. Anyway,' he added, 'I was tipped out then beaten, remember?'

Ron was too absorbed in his numbers selection task to rise to any bait. 'Do you think fifteen's lucky?' he asked, offering his own bait.

'Do we have to go through this paranormal numerology ritual *every* week? I've seen enough religion for one day. Astrology, UFO's, it's all religion. Anyway, why should fifteen be lucky?'

'Got my first shag at fifteen,' answered Ron, then nostalgically realising that it was almost ten years ago to the very day.

'Ones with your dad don't count.'

'What about nineteen? That's how many different girls I've done it with.' Throwing a sideways look at Pross, he added, 'Beats your two, doesn't it?'

'Never told me it was a competition.'

Viewing Pross for the first time since he'd returned, Ron was struck by the new shirt being sported by his usually drab flatmate. 'When did you get that shirt?' he asked, more than a little jealous.

'Lilith gave it to me this afternoon.'

'Bloody hell, you've done all right by her. First the jacket, then the boots, now that shirt. If I didn't know you better I'd guess she fancied you. Do something about your manners and you could get your next shag with her. She wouldn't get the police on to you, either.'

The suggestion that Lilith might be attracted to him felt like an insult, and Pross was greatly inclined to defend himself. 'Lilith couldn't fancy anyone. She'd need oestrogen to do that.'

Ron was next struck by Pross's hair: it looked good.

He gaped insultingly.

'Had it cut,' explained Pross.

Ron quickly realised the possible implications of this. 'You better not have spent the rent money on it. Fuck it, I wish they'd send it straight to the landlord.'

'Haven't touched it,' said Pross.

By virtue of Pross's unemployed status, Housing Benefit was obliged to cover his rent, Ron not being officially an occupant of the flat. Ron, in turn, took care of the bills.

Ron continued to be fascinated by Pross's tonsorial transformation, and he moved in nearer for a better look, and a better look soon necessitated him forcefully pulling Pross over to the window to view the haircut in the light.

'Ow, don't hurt me!' complained Pross.

'Why not?' said Ron plainly.

'Because it's still my birthday.'

'It's not still, is it?'

'Fucking is. Has been all day.'

Ron released Pross, saying, 'Marginally better than your usual clinically depressed feudal peasant look.'

Ten argument-filled minutes later, the pair were sat at the table beside the front window, with the cat up there with them. Ron was still pondering lottery issues, and Pross was trying to interest Spock in a speck of his own blood that had welled up on his finger after he'd accidentally pricked himself.

The cat just looked at him as if he was stupid.

'What about...'

'Look,' cut in Pross, 'how many times do I have to tell you? Exact knowledge of the future is specifically outlawed by Heisenberg's Uncertainty Principle. There is absolutely no way of knowing due to the inherent randomness of quantum events, therefore all so-called predictive arts are clearly bullshit.'

'So what about twelve, then?' asked Ron.

'Heisenberg's Uncertainty Principle,' retorted Pross.

'Twelve's the number of signs of the zodiac.'

'Say anything astrological and I'll hit you.'

'What about twenty-two?'

Pross threw his arms in the air. 'Scientist in state of fucking anger! No truly random event can ever be predicted. The Quantum Theory, the most successful scientific theory ever, states it so.'

'That's the number of cards in a tarot pack.'

Pross had news for Ron there. 'There's seventy-eight cards in a tarot pack.'

'Twenty-two in the pack I bought the other day, mate.'

'Look,' said Pross truculently, 'I'll bury your claptrap once and for all. Using my supposedly cunning mind, I'll devise the best possible conditions for predicting the lottery numbers using the so-called supernatural. And when I don't win, and I've convinced even you of Heisenberg's Uncertainty Principle, you have to promise never to torture me with superstition again.'

Ron thought for a second. 'OK. A deal,' he said.

Half an hour later, with the curtains closed and candles and incense burning, Ron and Pross were presiding over a magical incantation. On the floor, amid badly drawn pentangles, astrological signs and tarot cards, were arranged in a circle the numbers one to forty-nine. In this circle was Spock, bemused.

'O blackest of cats,' moaned Pross magically, 'reveal to us the last lottery number.'

After a few seconds, Spock approached a number and sniffed it.

'Seventeen,' observed Ron. 'It's seventeen.'

He scribbled the number down on a scrap of paper bearing the five other numbers Spock had selected.

Pross began kicking the magic paraphernalia around. 'Right, that's it. If a black cat in a fucking pentangle can't pick lottery numbers, then you'll have to admit for all time that the supernatural doesn't exist. Right?'

'Right,' agreed Ron, putting his jacket on. 'Let's have your pound and I'll catch the shop before it closes.'

Pross, with some muttering, relinquished the last of his cash.

'And don't pick on the landlord if he comes when I'm out,' nagged Ron before leaving.

1.2
A Delicate Flower

Sitting at the table, Pross viewed Ron through the window as he lifted the gate latch, on his way to make their lottery entries at the corner shop. At the same time, pulling up outside the flat in a battered Ford cortina, was the landlord, wearing his usual dark suit. Ron exchanged a few words with him, then continued on his way. Soon the landlord was knocking on the flat's inner door.

It was rent day, and Pross moaned with displeasure as he got up to get the money from under the mantelpiece clock.

The landlord was a man in his late twenties who lived in a neighbouring town, and that was all Pross knew about him, except that he was an opportunity for sport. Every month when he came to collect the rent, Pross would complain straight-faced to him that the shower was still working and would ask when he was going to get it broken so that he couldn't start taking showers again.

It had become a bit of a stupid ritual.

And every month, the landlord would say nothing in reply, simply taking the rent money, marking the rent card, then leaving. All done with the minimum of words.

A curious thing about the landlord was that in all the four years Pross had lived in the house, he'd never known him go up the stairs to collect rent from the house's two other tenants. And his visits were never more than five minute affairs, performed no more often than the necessary twice a month.

With his rent card and cash in hand, Pross opened the inner door.

'Evening,' he said.

The landlord said nothing in reply, just made an awkward nod as he took the rent card and money being held out.

'One hundred and twenty. Two weeks' rent,' said Pross.

The landlord quickly counted it, then began marking the card.

Over the landlord's shoulder, Pross saw that Mrs Brown was standing in the hall, beside the dustbins. Standing like mental patients do, no purpose apparent, lost in some private nightmare of forlorn distress, eyes cast towards the landlord.

The landlord, done with the card, handed it back, then turned to leave, but Pross, mischief beginning to glint in his eyes, reached out and took hold of his arm. 'Hey, that bloody shower's still working.'

The landlord pulled his arm back, walking away down the hall, passing Mrs Brown without so much as glancing. Mrs Brown had seemed about to attempt, or at least want, to reach out and touch the landlord as he passed by, but also seemed to be inhibited from doing so.

'Now there, sir,' said the shopkeeper. 'Just in time.'

Ron made an appropriate reply and picked up a lottery playslip.

Peering over the shelves into the street, the shopkeeper viewed Ron's vehicle. 'How's that car of yours going?' he asked.

'Not bad, mate. Needs a polish.'

Ron began filling in the playslip, firstly with Spock's numbers, which were written on the scrap of paper he'd brought with him.

Behind the counter, beside the shopkeeper, a little girl of perhaps ten summers was amusing herself.

'Any of my magazines in yet?' asked Ron.

The shopkeeper, a balding blonde man in his early forties, looked under his counter. 'Let's see now.'

While the shopkeeper was checking this, Ron began filling his own numbers in. Right then, he almost thought out loud, first shag at fifteen... he crossed off fifteen. Done it with nineteen girls... he crossed off nineteen. Nineteen, er, that's thirty-eight breasts... he crossed off thirty-eight.

And so on.

The playslip completed, Ron approached the counter, seeing that the shopkeeper had two magazines for him: *Classic Cars* and *Autocar*.

The shopkeeper took the playslip and ran it through his computer terminal.

'Here you go, mate,' said the shopkeeper, handing Ron the lottery computer receipt, playslip, and his two magazines. 'Any chance of you settling your account today? It's two months now.'

'Can do,' said Ron. 'How much?'

The shopkeeper viewed his accounts book, which was open at the relevant page. 'Let's see now. Eight *Autocars* at one pound fifty...'

Ron began totalling the sums in biro on his playslip.

'... Two *Classic Cars* at two pounds fifty. Eight motor sports at one twenty. That's...'

'Twenty-six pounds sixty,' said Ron.

'Plus two pounds for the lottery, making twenty-eight pounds sixty.'

Ron proffered adequate cash and received his change.

But then he saw a magazine on the shelf beside him that he thought

Pross might like.

He bought that too.

Taking his lottery receipt but leaving behind his playslip and scrap of paper, Ron said goodbye and went out to his car.

As Ron was leaving, the shopkeeper handed his daughter Ron's playslip. 'Here you are, little angel, another one for you.'

The little girl smiled and added Ron's playslip to a bundle of some three hundred other slips that she was holding.

Browsing through the magazines, Ron sauntered to his car, which was parked right outside the shop. Behind him, the shopkeeper was now pulling down shutters for the night.

Ron tossed his magazines and the lottery receipt on to his car's backseat and drove off.

Upon returning to the flat, Ron found Pross in the kitchen, eating. He had a small mirror propped up against a sauce bottle on the table so that he could admire his hair.

Ron sat down on the other side of the table. 'Paid the rent?' he asked.

Pross nodded while continuing his self-admiration.

'One day soon, the face in the mirror will be old, then you'll regret every wasted day.'

'Happy birthday, Pross,' said Pross, laying guilt on to Ron.

'Fancy going out tonight?' suggested Ron after a short while.

'Got no money left.'

'I'll get them in tonight.'

Pross didn't hear. He was too obsessed with his new haircut, which apparently made him look "dead raunchy". No one had ever said that before. Dreary, yes; raunchy, no. Although he wasn't quite sure whether Lilith's opinion on raunch counted for anything at all.

I wonder if it's peaked yet? he thought, examining his reflected image with particular closeness.

'Well?' pursued Ron impatiently. 'Coming out tonight or not?'

Pross said he would, and promised to ask the cat for some of its lottery winnings next week to pay Ron back.

'Why don't you get a job,' said Ron, 'instead of sponging off the cat all the time?'

'Why should I? The cat's never complained. Besides, I have an occupation. I'm a novelist of great distinction.'

'Hah,' scoffed Ron, moving over to the sink, 'that's a laugh. Some novelist. It's two years since you said you were going to write a book and I got you that computer and printer, but you still haven't written anything.'

Pross, making a show of dignity, held a spoonful of his meal poised a strategic two inches from his mouth. 'That's not exactly true now, Ronald, and you know it isn't,' he corrected in a measured voice. 'You've seen my novel with your own eyes.'

He spooned the food into his mouth.

'Not even two pages long,' said Ron, filling the kettle.

But then he suddenly cracked.

From behind, pushing Pross's face down on to the table, he menaced, 'If you haven't written a proper novel by the end of the month, I'm going to sell that computer.'

'I'll write one! I'll write one!' said Pross, food spluttering out with his words.

'You'd better,' said Ron, releasing him. 'End of the month, or else.'

'I need longer. Writing's harder work than you think.'

'You're just lazy and useless.'

'Anyway,' said Pross, 'I haven't always sponged off the cat. I had a proper job once.'

'Yeah,' ridiculed Ron, now plugging the kettle into a socket, 'a poxy newspaper delivery job years ago when you were at school. And you were sacked.'

Pross, making a show of restraint, slowly said, 'A paper round is a worthy and laudable vocation, and I was sacked only because my poet's constitution proved too sensitive for early rising. Delicate flowers are not meant for toil and drudgery.'

The arguments continued for some more minutes until Pross retreated to his room, bringing a cup of tea with him.

To reach his bed, he had to climb over the fallen books.

He sat on the bed, picking up a book from the floor to read.

A minute later, he let it fall, attention drifting away to nowhere.

A magazine article was about his limit these days.

It was generally agreed by the few friends Pross had that, although obviously some sort of genius, he was in a serious slump, but not one of those friends had yet been able to get *him* to take the slump seriously. 'Who cares?' he would say, 'I'm just one of five billion all destined to die.' It was also generally agreed that to advance his life from the current standstill, he should change his name back to what it had been and have at least *some* part of his head examined, neither which suggestion he ever listened to. 'You never listen to anything anyone ever tells you, do you?' Ron had said to him the other night. 'Not really,' he had replied, cunningly adding, 'Try inferring things instead. I enjoy the thrill of the chase.'

An easterly breeze that had blown throughout the day had now petered out. High pressure had pushed its way over the north of England, promising a clear, frosty night. Tomorrow, that high was forecast to move away, allowing a rain-laden warm front to move over the country. But for now there was not a cloud in the Durham sky to obscure the evening sun, a sun which offered Ron the opportunity to polish his car one more time before the week was over.

Ron's car was an eye-catching 1960 Ford Consul. Thanks to countless hours and pounds lavished on it, it appeared to be in no worse condition now than the day it had rolled off the production line.

While Ron was devoutly polishing invisible rust blemishes from the chrome bumper, Pross idled up to him.

'Nice evening,' observed Ron.

'I was going to say that, but I decided it would be too vacuous.'

Ron stopped polishing and drew in a breath, as if to speak... 'Nah,' he eventually said, 'it's too vacuous.'

'What is?' inquired Pross keenly. 'Go on, tell me. Go on. Please.'

Ron would not be drawn, and resumed polishing. After a few minutes, Pross asked, 'What kind of a dickhead devotes his life to overcoming bits of rust on a piece of metal?' Ron didn't answer. Pross remained there, absently following the action of Ron's polishing cloth with his eyes as it moved in small, fast circles over the surface of the bumper. Reflected in the shiny bumper, he could see his hair. Even when grossly distorted by the curvature of the metal, the image given back was still enough to impress him.

He continued to regard his own reflection. The more he looked, the more he realised that Lilith was right — he *was* raunchy. It was definitely the haircut, he decided, that was making the difference. It put him in another league. Yes, he had a certain something, he decided.

In a fit of narcissism, he began assessing his own raunchiness.

His hair was surely perfect.

His eyes were an attractive greyish-green, sensitive and sensuous.

His nose was a sensible one.

His lips were well-shaped and kissable.

And his body was pretty good too. Five feet eleven-and-a-half, not thin, not large.

'I'M SO FUCKIN' HANDSOME!' he suddenly shouted.

'It's deeper than you think,' said Ron, not interrupting the rhythm of his work.

'What?'

'Why I polish my car so often.' With a snarly grin of power, he revealed: 'The universe decays but my car endures.'

'Really?' drawled Pross, not at all convinced.

'It's all to do with entropy,' explained Ron. 'I'm reversing its effects. *That's* why I devote my life to overcoming bits of rust.'

'You're not really understanding that book you stole from me, are you? The universe decays *faster* because of your car. You've got tunnel vision. You don't see the global picture. You only accelerate entropy by doing what you're doing. The metal on your car reacts with oxygen, releasing energy. Appalled by this local entropy, you then go and release many times more energy to counter the rusting. Coal was hewn out of the ground to provide the energy to make that chrome cleaner stuff you're using.'

'I was only on page ten,' said Ron, beginning to polish harder.

'And it's not just your car that destroys the cosmos,' Pross further commented a little later, 'it's you as a person as well. You're a twat, that's what you are.'

'Oh aye?'

'Yeah. You eat compounds all day long, robbing them of energy. Then you squander that energy in twatty heat and motion. You're a little valueless pocket in space-time where entropy is neutralised at the expense of the rest of the universe, that's what you are.'

Ron looked at Pross.

'Do you want a lift to the pub tonight or not?'

'Wouldn't say no,' answered Pross baldly.

Ron got on with his work, and Pross continued to admire his own reflection. 'Just think, it'll look even better when it peaks.'

'What?'

'My hair.'

'Peaks?'

'Yeah, peaks. Haircuts always peak sometime after they've been done. Lilith told me.'

'Oh.'

Pross admired himself some more.

'If you see it starting to peak, tell me so I can nip out and impress girls with it. Mind you, knowing my luck I'll be in bed asleep when it happens.'

Ron pointed to the church sign. 'Then just pray to Jesus that you're not alone, that's all. You could pray for a sensible name while you're at it as well.' Here Ron's voice became particularly patronising. 'Silly names aren't conducive to achievement, you know. Astronauts didn't reach the moon by giving themselves silly names whenever they felt like it.'

'It was Melanie's fault. She drove me to revenge.'

Ron nodded his head towards their flat. 'Go and write a proper novel.'

'Not on my birthday.'

1.3
Drunk Again

The Arts Centre is where they usually went. The Arts Centre being a large building dedicated to housing local arts and crafts: a gallery, a dance studio, two theatres, a cinema, a small restaurant and some photographic workshops. Pross had once or twice availed himself of the workshops after catching an expensive photo bug a few years earlier, a bug that had almost led him into attempting to forge some sort of career out of taking snaps.

He was over it now.

Unfortunately, he was still lumbered with hundreds of pounds worth of gear he'd somehow managed to accrue, since none of the local papers would ever accept his classified advert: *Imminent Suicide Forces Quick Sale...* He absolutely refused to change the wording to get an ad printed. It was a matter of high principle.

The Arts Centre also boasted dozens of other activity rooms. But more importantly now for Pross, the Arts Centre had a bar, which tonight was crowded. It was crowded because an in-house theatre performance had just come to an end. It was crowded with little groups of theatre goers ensconced around tables, cleverly debating in deliberately loud voices subjects such as the role of abstract painting in western society, mortgage tax-relief, and the performance figures for their respective hatchbacks.

Pross stepped through the door.

Then he slowed to a halt.

'Look at all these bastards,' he complained.

'Never mind all *those* bastards,' said Ron, 'look at *that* bastard. Who d'you think he is?'

Ron was indicating a short, overweight, grey-suited man, one of four similarly clad men stood around a cluster of briefcases.

Pross didn't have to think long: the jam jar glasses and ragged haircut gave it away. 'Rab C. Scoones,' he said with a snarl.

'The one and only,' said Ron. 'Should have known he'd be here. I heard him say he was going to see a play tonight. Said it loud, he did, so everyone would know he's an intellectual.'

'I'm going to get him,' said Pross simply, and before Ron knew what was happening, over to Scoones Pross went.

'Pross! Pross!' called Ron in desperate whispers, too scared of being spotted to risk going any nearer to his manager. 'Don't. Come back.'

Pross didn't come back. He went straight over to Scoones, standing before him.

Ron slinked away to the car park, peeping through a window. His whole career was now subject to Pross's whim and discretion: he didn't hold out much hope.

Scoones looked at the stranger now standing before him.

'Stop it,' said Pross, with a trace of menace.

'Stop what?' asked Scoones apprehensively.

The three men with Scoones ceased chatting and looked at Pross, wondering what his business with them was.

'You other bastards better stop it too,' added Pross.

'Stop what?' said Scoones, becoming braver now that his companions were involved.

'Contributing to entropy,' said Pross. 'Accelerating the decay of my universe, that's what. Every bastard one of you is oxidizing feverishly, messing things for me. I'll get you for it one day.'

And he left them, going off to find Ron.

He found him hiding in his car.

Ron was livid.

Really livid.

'I was only pissing around,' said Pross.

'You didn't get me involved, did you?'

'Course not. He hasn't a clue who I am.'

'Are you sure?'

'Positive.'

'Get down!' ordered Ron suddenly. 'They're coming out.'

Pross got down, and didn't get up again until they'd driven off.

It wasn't long, however, before Ron calmed down over the issue. 'So what did you say to him?' he asked as they re-entered the Arts Centre, threading their way through the crowd.

'Just had a go at him for contributing entropy-wise to the decay of my universe. Bewildered and crapping himself, he was.'

'Whoever said it's *your* universe?' asked Ron when they reached their destination, making one end of the long, L-shaped bar their temporary home.

'It must be my universe,' Pross retorted, leaning on the bar. 'I'm everywhere I ever go in it; and everywhere I've ever been, I was there too. As far as I've ever been able to tell, I completely pervade this universe. I'm fucking omnipresent. The Earth is flying through space at thousands of miles an hour, and I'm everywhere it ever gets to. It *must* be my universe.'

Ron bought a beer for Pross, who propped himself up against the wall beside him to drink it, casting an eye around the room. 'I wish these other bastards would fuck off out of my universe too,' he said.

'If it's your universe,' said Ron thoughtfully, 'then you'll be able to tell me where that UFO I saw last week came from.'

'What UFO?'

'The UFO I saw over the cathedral last Saturday.'

'Bullshit,' said Pross, taking his drink up and gulping some down. 'Scientist in state of pugnacity.'

Ron smirked with malicious satisfaction. 'I know what I know and I saw what I saw,' he said.

'Scientist in state of annoyed exasperation,' declared Pross.

'I'm telling you,' insisted Ron, poking Pross's shoulder painfully, believing this assault to enhance the force of his argument, 'I saw a bloody huge spaceship hovering over the cathedral.'

'So what did this so-called spaceship look like?'

'It was immense,' said Ron reverently, 'and it hummed and throbbed with light, and it was in the shape of a giant flying teacup.'

'Flying teacup my arse,' sneered Pross.

'No, really, that's what I saw. But maybe the hyper-advanced, spoon-bending, tarot-bearing, horoscope-wielding aliens that built the fucking huge teacup thing I saw have a sense of humour? Maybe they're cosmic jesters? Maybe they...'

Pross suddenly blurted, 'Look at her.'

'What?' puzzled Ron.

'Her,' Pross said, becoming excited, pointing to a young lady alone at the other end of the long, L-shaped bar, the end where no serving was done. She was almost, but not quite, out of sight. Perched on a high stool, she was seemingly absorbed in the reading of a thick paperback book. 'She's the one I've been looking for all my long, lonely Friday.'

Ron peered in the direction of Pross's digit.

'Who?'

'Her.'

'Where?'

'There.'

'What, the dark-haired girl with the book? Do you know her?'

'Course I do,' he said with eyes devotionally affixed, 'she's Helen... she's Cleopatra... she's Juliet.' Then Pross fell into a reverie, a mesmerised silence as he realised with pain and pleasure that his list of identities for the vision he was beholding in awe had been quite remiss and quite, quite unfair to her.

In a low enchanted murmur, Pross proceeded to correct the identification, as much to convince himself of the possibility of it as for his companion's enlightenment.

'No, she's... she's... she's...'

'Who?' inquired Ron, sharing Pross's fascination with the angelic bar-stool bibliophile.

'Can it be?' murmured Pross.

'Can it be who? Tell me.'

'Can fate have finally delivered her unto me?'

'And me,' added Ron.

'Is it true? Is it her?'

'Who?'

Pross again fell into silence, his eyes never straying from the face of the girl he was daring to think of as being the incarnation of his greatest ever love.

He gazed.

And he gazed some more.

Now he was completely convinced.

'My God, it *is* her,' he murmured in agony and ecstasy. 'It's her. It's her. It's bloody her.'

'Who?'

Pross became speechless.

'Who?' Ron demanded to be told, gripping Pross by the shoulders and shaking him in an attempt to disperse the reverie into which he had fallen. 'Who? Who?'

Pross told him: 'Only bloody Tess of the d'Urbervilles, that's all. Only bloody Tess of the bloody d'Urbervilles. Only my most yearned-for literary babe.'

Ron was sceptical: this wasn't the first time Pross had claimed a person to be Tess. He studied her some more, though little of her was actually visible, just her head and shoulders, the rest being obscured by the bar.

'Tess of the d'Urbervilles? Are you sure?'

'Of course I'm sure,' Pross snapped. 'Anyway, what do *you* know about Tess? You haven't even read the book.'

'I saw the film, though,' countered Ron.

Pross made some retching motions to show that he considered the Tess in the film to be a travesty of the Tess in the book and his imagination. 'Chalk and cheese,' he said. 'Chalk and cheese.'

'So you think she's the real Tess?'

'Of course she is. All the hallmarks are there.' He rested his hand on

Ron's shoulder and, both of them looking keenly in the same direction, argued his case. 'Look at her eyes. Do they not bewitch and inflame the heart?'

Ron had to agree that they did.

'And look at her mouth. Has there ever been such a maddening mouth since Eve's?'

'No, I don't think there has,' decided Ron after a little contemplation.

'Then,' Pross said simply and cockily, his argument conclusively proven, his claim wholly justified, '*ipso facto, ex silentio*, she must be Tess.'

'Is that what makes a Tess then?' inquired Ron, a transport of love beginning to carry *his* heart away. 'Bewitching eyes and the most maddening mouth since Eve's?'

'Certainly is,' said Pross. 'Bloody hell! Did you see that?'

'See what?' asked Ron.

Pross was becoming elated. 'She looked over towards me. She's smitten. It's my haircut.'

'Rubbish. She glanced at the clock on the wall behind you.'

'No, she looked at me — lingeringly.'

'You sure?'

'Positive. She wants me, Ron. She wants me. It was me she was looking at.'

Ron thought for a few seconds. 'Maybe she's an anthropologist?' he said. 'Or a talent spotter for Crimewatch.' But his gibes went unheard.

'I'm going over to mingle my soul with hers,' announced Pross, standing up. 'I owe it to my haircut.'

Ron now became alarmed, and gripped Pross's wrist. 'No you're not. For fuck's sake, Pross, you used to be just a quiet, shy trouble maker who never left his bedroom, now you're a brazen one. What's got into you lately?'

Twisting free from Ron's grip, Pross declared, 'Raunchiness.'

That claim was more than Ron could bear to hear without laughing derisively. 'Hah! Raunchy? You?'

'Yeah, raunchy, me. That's what Lilith said I was this afternoon. Honest.'

'So that's it,' derided Ron. 'One compliment from a sad virgin and you imagine you're irresistible all of a sudden.'

Pross was too involved with Tess to bother with Ron. He had just decided that she would look even better if she was wearing his *Prospero's Lass* T-shirt.

He took it out from his jacket pocket.

Ron saw it, and grabbed it from him.

'Give it back,' demanded Pross.

'Not a chance,' said Ron, keeping it out of Pross's reach.
'Give me it back,' said Pross, making grabs for it.
'Why don't you just ask her if you can buy her a drink?'
Pross stopped trying to get the T-shirt. 'What, chat her up, you mean? Proper, like? Maybe ask her for a date if we hit it off?'
'That's it,' said Ron with happy relief, 'you're beginning to understand.'
'I could never be so audacious or presumptuous,' declared Pross, resuming his attempts to snatch the garment.
'You'll get yourself arrested,' said Ron, stuffing the T-shirt into his pocket.
'Never mind,' said Pross, beginning a slow drift in the direction of Tess, 'with my haircut, kissable lips and general overall raunchiness, I'll have my soul mingled with hers faster than she can say *contraception*.'
'Please, please, don't go over to her,' begged Ron, 'you'll get the both of us arrested. You know what you're like.'
Pross was single-minded.
Over to her he went.
Ron stayed where he was and worried.
Pulling a stool up next to Tess, Pross settled tipsily on to it.
By a slight movement she made when he sat down, Pross knew Tess to be aware of someone being at her side, but she did not look up from her book. Pross let his eyes drink in her appearance; and the most striking thing about her was her attire. She was clad in a long black dress of a very antiquated type — Victorian, he guessed. It looked well-worn and a little dusty, as if it might degenerate into its constituent threads at any moment. It had many folds and pleats, with a low front revealing cleavage. Over this dress, she wore a silk-lined waistcoat of a similar design. Black stockings covered her legs and disappeared into black leather shoes which seemed to be as old as the dress.
There was no doubt about it, thought Pross, this was Tess all right.
But the really strange thing about Tess was her hair-slide, which appeared to be a section of human skull. Her hair was lush and plentiful, very dark brown, almost black, and the section of skull she wore in it served to draw long tresses from the back of her head, casting them forward and to the sides so that her face was amid a luxuriant tousled mane. The piece of skull was made from a section incorporating the eye sockets and half an inch of forehead. It was cut so that it resembled a pair of thick-rimmed spectacles without the lenses. It looked very old.
Curious, Pross lifted her book slightly so that he could read the title. Even as he did this, she gave him no regard or acknowledgement.

The book was Dickens' *David Copperfield*.

In keeping with the Victorian theme, Pross spoke formally to her. 'Tess, I am extremely out of heart. I have been so tormented here beside you, by my love for you, that should you choose to vex me with your indifference for but another moment I fear it would make an end of me.'

Tess appeared to be both intrigued and unsure, and she looked up from her book, her eyes meeting Pross's.

'Excuse me, did you call me Tess? Did you think you knew me?'

Her voice was cultured, but still discernably north of England.

'I know you all right. You're Tess,' said Pross.

'I'm sorry, I'm not Tess. You're mistaken.'

She resumed reading.

'You are,' asserted Pross, 'You're Tess... of the d'Urbervilles. Tess, Tess, Tess. You're Tess, and I love you.'

With a resigned manner, she put her book down, and for a moment seemed poised to move towards anger. Turning to face Pross, with a single finger she swept her hair away from her eyes. She looked at him, but then actually laughed.

Ron was astonished, and immediately made his way over to them. He stood behind and between them, placing his hand on Pross's back, saying, with an innocent air, 'There's a table free over here, Pross. Why not bring your friend over too?'

Pross was fully aware of Ron's sly game. Nevertheless, he followed Ron over to the table, taking Tess's book with him so that she would have to follow. 'Come on, Tess,' he said.

Once seated, Ron courteously offered Tess his hand. 'The name's Ron, by the way.'

'Sarah-Jane,' she replied.

Pross began shaking his head in brokenhearted despair. 'No. No. You're Tess. You're Tess.'

'I'm not,' smiled Sarah-Jane.

'Oh, no,' groaned Ron, 'he doesn't think you're Tess of the d'Urbervilles, does he?' Pross glowered at Ron, who continued nevertheless. 'A couple of years ago, after reading the book, he was forever pointing out Tess-a-bloody-likes in the street. Mind you, it was worse after he read *Lolita*. It was all I could manage to stop him hanging around the schools all day long then. Hope the stupid fucker never reads *Watership Down*.'

Sarah-Jane laughed greatly, and Pross began sulking.

Taking pity on him, she asked, 'What made you think I was Tess?'

'The evidence of your appearance,' answered Pross. He gently brushed some wayward strands of her hair from her face, and she bent her head down slightly as he did this, sharing the *Mills and Boon* scene joke. 'Your eyes and mouth told me.'

Not moving her head, but lifting her gaze to meet Pross's, she asked quietly, 'How's that?'

'Bewitching eyes and the most maddening mouth since Eve's.'

This bizarre scene between Sarah-Jane and Pross was becoming too intimate for Ron to bear, so he interrupted them with an inquiry concerning her skull hair-slide.

She took it from her hair, tossing her tresses back with a flick of her head. 'Do you like it?' she asked, showing it to Ron, who studied it with great curiosity. It had long metal prongs glued to its back so that it would stay firm in hair.

'Is it real?' he asked.

'Hope not,' she answered. 'I got it from the props department here.'

'The props department?' asked Ron.

'And why are you dressed like Tess?' cut in Pross, accusingly. 'Imposter.'

'Well,' she began slowly, ordering her reply, 'I'm doing a Ph.D. in music at the University. I'm wearing this gear because I attended a dress rehearsal here this evening for a ridiculous presentation that's coming up next week in which all the performers wear period costume. And I put the bone in my hair simply because I took a fancy to it when I was rummaging around in the props room.'

'You're a proper musician?' said Ron.

'If that's what you want to call me, yes. The cello's my instrument.'

Pross was by now almost dead from the torment of his love for Sarah. Ron, however, was clouding the picture, so he connived to get rid of him for a while by announcing to Sarah that Ron desperately wanted to buy her a drink on his behalf.

Sarah-Jane perceived that Pross might be broke, and said as much.

'Flat,' bemoaned he.

'Concave,' sniped Ron.

'Spent the last of my cash on a lottery entry for my cat this evening,' explained Pross with a look of regret.

Although Sarah didn't understand this lottery and cat reference, she did not pursue it. 'I don't want a drink,' she said, 'I haven't finished this one yet.'

'That doesn't matter,' said Pross, 'you can stockpile them. I just want Ron to go to the bar so he'll buy me a drink too.'

Sarah-Jane delved into her bag for her purse. 'Then let me get you one,' she offered.

Ron stayed her hand. 'No, don't get Pross one,' he urged, 'he has to limit his drinking. It sets off his psychopathic disorder.'

'Ignore him,' said Pross, 'he's just upset because we're going to sleep together.'

Sarah glowered at him. 'Are we?'

'Maybe twice,' stated Pross, 'if you can be moved at all to pity.'

Sarah-Jane laughed again.

Ron insisted on buying the drinks, perhaps hoping to impress Sarah with his generosity. He lumbered over to the bar while she asked Pross about his name. 'Why did Ron just call you Pross? It's not your name, is it?'

'Because it's short for Prospero,' he returned.

'Oh, I see... how's Miranda?'

'You're my Miranda,' he replied, contemplating incest for the very first time.

'Ron seems to be your Ariel,' she observed.

Pross smiled a little. 'I think you mean Caliban.'

Sarah-Jane took a slow sip of her drink. 'So, Pross, what do you do for a living?'

'Paper boy — retired,' he said with a shrug.

'I see,' she said, thankfully not pursuing the issue. 'Your friend's very sweet, what's his story?'

Hearing Ron being described as sweet was quite upsetting for Pross: it was time for some negative p.r. Without showing his disgust for her opinion, he leant on the table with both elbows and spoke casually. 'Sweet? Yeah, I suppose he can appear like that at first. Prison improved him a lot. He only got out this afternoon, by the way.'

A look of concern crossed the face of Sarah-Jane. 'Prison? What was he in for?' she asked in a low voice, although Ron was nowhere near being within earshot.

'Manslaughter,' answered Pross, also in a low voice, repeatedly looking over to Ron as if fearing his words to be overheard. 'He killed his wife because she'd constantly taunted him about the diminutive size of his penis.'

'Really?' she said, glancing towards Ron, who caught her eye and smiled. She didn't smile back.

'Yeah,' continued Pross, 'it was murder really, but he had a good lawyer. That's why we're out drinking tonight. We're celebrating his release. I don't really like him, but I'm afraid to let him know. He's got a rotten temper.' Further negative p.r. was on its way. 'He thinks you're quite sweet too.'

'Does he?'

'Yeah. He said you're the best bit of gash he's seen since he was banged up two years ago.'

'Gash?' said Sarah-Jane, with a look of imminent revulsion.

'It's his word for women he fancies,' explained Pross. 'Horrible, isn't it?'

'Horrible? It's the most revolting expression I've ever heard!'

Believing he was getting somewhere negative, Pross went in for the kill. 'You've obviously never heard his word for little girls he fancies.'

She grimaced in anticipation.

'Slit.'

'Ugh! That's even worse!'

'I know,' agreed Pross, 'should we call the police?'

Sarah-Jane laughed. 'I don't believe any of this, by the way,' she said, touching his arm.

The moment she touched him, Pross resolved to entwine his life with hers, no matter what. Ron didn't appear at all in his picture of romantic bliss. If Ron loved her too, then that was his hard luck: he'd just have to work out his sexual frustration on a consenting Alsatian.

Sarah-Jane was beautiful. She had long, sultry, marvellously tousled dark hair; large, intelligent brown eyes; a slender, lissome body with a generous bosom; and lips the likes of which Pross had never seen before outside his imagination.

Pross now found himself too love-struck to speak, and simply gazed at her in a dreamy sort of way, breathing the occasional feeble sigh, and blinking comically with affected coyness whenever her eyes met his. The spoony's transport of misty-eyed adoration continued this way until Sarah-Jane, finally exasperated, picked up *David Copperfield* from the table and resumed her reading, trying to ignore the blatant attention she was receiving from her companion.

'Where are you up to in the book?' he asked, regaining the power of speech as Sarah-Jane leafed through pages to find her place again.

'Oh, Copperfield's wife is dying,' she answered.

'That bit's all about the Victorian guilt Dickens felt over his own sexuality,' he informed her.

Sarah-Jane was delighted with Pross's knowledge of Dickens. She wanted to hear more, but, satisfied with having impressed her so succinctly, he relapsed into his adoring silence, from which she could coax no conversation.

Ron returned with the drinks. 'You'll be sick tomorrow,' he said patronisingly as he deposited a pint in front of Pross.

'No I won't.'

'He probably will be,' Ron said to Sarah-Jane with a patronising tone, 'he usually is. Gets spazmoed easier than anyone else I know. Gets the worst hangovers known to carousing. Anything more than two pints and there's a good chance he'll spend the next day in bed with a bucket, moaning the name of whatever female he took a shine to the night before.'

In response to this slur on his manhood, Pross began quaffing his drink as if there would be no tomorrow, and Sarah-Jane asked him why he was doing it if he always got sick the next day.

'Poison to my body, but medicine to my soul. Got to drink myself into a state of emotional amnesia every night. Been told to do it by doctors. You see, I suffer from progressive melancholia: every day, in every way, I get more and more sad. It's a debilitating mental condition that affects the clinically lovelorn.'

'Who are you so lovelorn for?' Sarah-Jane wanted to know.

Pross turned sad eyes to her. 'I couldn't bear to talk about her yet. I'm not nearly drunk enough.'

'I still yearn for her,' he lamentably informed Sarah-Jane out of the blue, two pints later into the evening, before slumping down in his chair. 'I'll never know happiness again without her, and every pint is an attempt to swill her from my memory. She hurt me bad.'

'Aw, you poor victim of love, who did?' asked Sarah-Jane, grinning to Ron.

Pross answered, 'Susan Murray. She done me bad.'

'Aw... tell me all about it.'

Being now sufficiently drunk, he began his woeful, oft repeated tale of unrequited love. 'She was the first and greatest love of my life,' he explained. 'I was still in junior school and in the same class as her. She was utterly beautiful — and I mean beautiful — and I decided there and then to make her mine. Now, the teacher had a policy of making boys who were naughty sit next to cissy girls as a punishment, and it eventually came to pass that the only vacant seat next to a girl was beside Susan. I resolved to occupy that seat or die in the attempt. So for days on end I performed every act of mischief short of homicide, and my efforts were eventually rewarded one glorious Friday afternoon, whereupon I was moved next to the divine Susan. I was blissfully happy for almost a whole hour until school broke up for the weekend. I hadn't made much headway in wooing her in that heavenly hour, but I had the rest of the term to win her and plan our elopement. But would you believe it, during assembly on the following Monday morning the teacher announced that Susan had moved halfway across the country with her family that weekend. I'll never get over that heart-breaking tragedy.' He raised his head and apostrophised heavenward: 'O Susan, last seen as a coy nine-year-old, the hole you left in my heart still gapes. Where are you now? Why did you leave me?'

'It was probably something you said,' muttered Ron.

Sarah-Jane had something to say about the tragic tale too. 'She moved away just after you sat next to her? That was a bit of a coincidence, wasn't it? Sure you're not taking a little bit of poetic licence?'

'I'll say it was a coincidence,' agreed Pross, 'but I swear it's true.'

Pross continued with further recollections of lost content until he was jerked to a halt by the unholy clatter of the last-orders bell. And very soon afterwards he was quietly following Ron and Sarah-Jane as they walked to the car park.

True to the weather forecast, a frost lay on the ground; the first of the year. The sky was clear. Ghostly white emanations from chimneys floated upwards without sideways movement. To the east, Orion loomed bright and large behind Pross as he wandered idiotically around the car park, considerably under the deliriant effects of alcohol. Sarah-Jane had bade her two new friends goodnight, but Pross hadn't realised it. He walked aimlessly about, first following Sarah-Jane until she disappeared some place he knew not where, then trotting over to Ron, slipping once or twice on what he didn't realise was ice. Ron guided him — well, shoved him — into the back of his car, where he lay on his side, head spinning.

Ron started the engine, the activity rousing Pross, who sat upright and leaned forward to talk. 'Where's Sarah-Jane gone?' he demanded to be told. 'Where is she?'

'She's gone home,' answered Ron. He tapped the rear-view mirror. 'That's her car leaving now.'

Pross twisted around to look through the back window, which was annoyingly misted. Using a little piece of paper he found lying on the back seat, he wiped the mist away. Now kneeling on the seat, he watched in agitated regret and frustration as the tail-lights of Sarah-Jane's car diminished in the distance. 'Shit! I'll never know who she is. I'll probably never see her again. I've never met anyone like her. I don't even know her second name.'

Ron smirked, though Pross didn't notice. 'It's all right, I'll ask her tomorrow.'

Pross began to whine, frantically rubbing condensation off the back window so that he could see the dwindling lights of his love. When they finally disappeared, he slumped down on to the seat, partly in woe and partly because Ron had put the car into reverse and set off backwards, unsettling his distraught passenger.

They pulled out on to the main road, going off in the opposite direction to Sarah-Jane.

Now it began to sink in...

Pross sat up and spoke to Ron. 'What do you mean you'll ask her tomorrow?'

'I mean,' answered Ron, trying hard to be seen trying hard not to gloat, 'that I'll ask her what her second name is tomorrow... when I go out somewhere with her.'

Pross was momentarily confused.

Then he was furious.

'You sneaky bastard. And just when did you arrange your sordid little evening out with her?'

Ron could restrain the gloat no longer. 'During your pathetic Susan Murray oration. I wish I could have a pound for every time I've had to sit through that little tale. Anyway, you ought to forget about Susan, she's been nothing but trouble to you.'

Pross pressed his forehead against the cold, dewy rear window and looked forlornly in the direction that Sarah-Jane had taken.

A low moan began.

As their car rounded a corner, Pross suddenly shouted, 'Stop! I'm gonna throw.'

Ron hit the brakes, stretching over to reach the back door handle and pushing it open while the car was still coming to a halt. Pross desperately slid over to the open door and puked pints into the road.

'Stop showing off,' said Ron. 'She can't see you. She's long gone.'

After a minute or two, Pross, becalmed, wiped his lips with the damp paper he'd removed the window mist with, and threw it outside.

Ron got the car moving again, and they went home.

1.4
In The Blues

It was another morning after.

Pross had a bad head.

A very bad head.

And nausea.

He was making an unsteady crawl to his kitchen.

He was seeking liquids.

Sat in just his underwear on the cold, greasy floor, wedged in a corner between cupboards, he downed a pint of orange squash.

'I'll never drink again,' he muttered to Spock, who was expectantly pacing about the cupboard where the cat food was kept.

Dubious of recovery, he collected a bucket before returning to bed on all fours.

Back in bed, suffering a headache he reckoned could floor a charging elephant, he closed his eyes and regretted every drink he'd had the night before, especially the last one: he was certain he would have been all right if it hadn't been for that last one.

After an eternity, he vomited curdled orange squash.

I bet my hair'll peak while my head's in this bastard bucket, he thought.

By one o'clock, although his headache was only slightly diminished, Pross was confident of recovery, and he pulled himself out of bed to face another day.

By four o'clock, he was starting to feel hungry.

By six o'clock, he'd actually got around to cooking something.

But it was starting.

Gathering the cutlery, Pross knew it was starting. He was slipping *out of sorts*, so to speak.

His life was a waste and a monotonous bore.

He was getting nowhere.

He was getting a fit of the blues.

In silence, he took his meal into the living room and sat near to the window in the fading light of another lost day.

'Did you hear that?' he asked quietly after a minute or so.

'Hear what?' replied Ron, not lifting his eyes from a tv guide.

'The sigh of the dying day.'

'No.'

'That's because your life is but a roar of coarse interests that drown out the voices of the elfin sprites that sing their low-toned miserere in poet's ears. You're fucking lucky, you are.'

'Get a stupid job and a stupid car like me then, then you won't be able to hear the little elfin bastards,' suggested Ron, still reading the tv guide.

'Can't,' said Pross, toying with his food. 'I wish I could be like you, but I can't. I'm a poet, you're not. My world belongs to Melancholy — a quiet, thoughtful, deep-eyed maiden who shuns the hurly-burly of day-to-day life.'

Ron said nothing.

About another minute elapsed.

'When the light thickens, she oft comes to me, you know, Ronald, and her enchantment sinks deep into my heart. It's then that I hear the sigh of the dying day in the rustle of branches or the call of a blackbird. And as the light dims more, she allows me soft visions of the Great Sea, and I fancy I hear its distant murmur in my ears. *Do not linger*, she gently tells me; *hasten down, for the shadowy ships are spreading their sable sails.*'

Pross looked at Ron.

Ron returned the look, seeming, for a moment, almost moved. 'Punch the little bitch next time,' he advised.

Weary of his meal, Pross left the table and moved over to a threadbare armchair.

He felt bored and unsettled, and decided to take a walk outside to help clear his still-hungover head.

In his bedroom, he quickly shaved with an electric razor. This done, he pulled on his boots and jacket and headed for the front door.

'Where are you going?' inquired Ron.

'To the sable ships.'

Pross was virtually incapable of ever leaving the house or going to bed without making at least a veiled hint at suicide.

He decided to head towards the city centre.

The high pressure had indeed slipped away, and the predicted warm front was already manifesting itself, the air now being many degrees warmer than it had been the day before. The sky was overcast, threatening rain. Walking down his street, he noticed Mrs Brown coming along from the opposite direction. It was unusual for her to be out at this time of day. Lost in some painful world of her own, she didn't see Pross. Had she noticed him, an awkward attempt at a smile of recognition would have been all she would have given. But she didn't see him, and shuffled past; a small, frail, bony figure in a shabby coat, staring at the pavement as she went by. Mrs

Brown walked like a bird, her head jutting forward with each step taken. Even though her eyes were dead, her face showed a torment that perhaps originated in her own thoughts.

It was heebie-jeebies time.

Pross's journey into the blues continued, and soon it came to be crammed with morose reflection upon his life and times.

He'd been ill-used from the cradle was the conclusion.

Then he found himself thinking about Sarah-Jane, the biggest and deepest love of his life, with the possible exception of Susan Murray, whom he hadn't seen since he was nine. Thinking despondently about Sarah-Jane and his boundless love for her led Pross to think about all the other girls he had, or had had, boundless love for. There must be hundreds, he thought. Yes, there must be hundreds. There were so many it was hard for him to bring them all to mind.

He decided to get his love life in order by forming an alphabetical list.

Thirty minutes later, he had only reached M; and even though he knew the names of only a tiny fraction of the nymphs he'd fallen for in his life, there were still lots of M's on his mental list. There were at least seven Maureens (only one of whom would even so much as talk to him); there was particularly callipygous Melanie, Lilith's older sister, whose fault it was he was called what he was called (although he wouldn't ever openly admit to adoring her, since it would be viewed by her as a personal triumph and vindication); a Mandy (who wouldn't talk to him); a Melissa; another Melanie (who wouldn't talk to him); and surely many other M's, talking or reticent, he actually knew the names of but couldn't recall just then.

Presently he gave up on his mental list. There were just too many to cope with without a filing cabinet.

He began musing upon how much different his life would surely have turned out if he hadn't spent so much of it pining over Susan Murray and her successors. That was when the rot set in, he decided: the day he first saw Susan Murray. On that day, contentment was forever lost. But if he'd never seen her? Well, then he could have achieved wonders with the time saved, he reckoned, wandering through the drizzle that had begun to sift down. He could have done most anything: could have won the Nobel Prize for detecting gravity waves.

His stroll had taken him over a mile from his home. Proper rain began to fall, starting with large, well-spaced drops, like the heralds of a summer thunder storm. He was now crossing one of the bridges that spanned the river Wear in the city, heading towards the cathedral, where most of his strolls seemed to take him.

Some while later, still bored and blue, Pross found himself drifting homeward, fantasising about his own death.

Suicide was something he hadn't thought seriously about for days now.

His first resolution to kill himself had been made at the age of eighteen, with death on his nineteenth birthday being the intention. He had come to regard death as desirable because life was, as he saw it then and more so now, absurd — a *disease of matter*, as he had once heard it described. Life was a disease of matter, he had understood, and life is that thing attributed solely to organisms. What is an organism? Just the vehicle DNA uses to drive itself on into the future. And what is DNA? Just molecular cancer, that's all. So, at eighteen, he had decided that he would die by his own hand on his next birthday.

In the years since his first death-date, Pross had made numerous other resolutions to end it all. And here he was again: musingly contemplating the end of mortal strife. Devising methods of committing suicide was his chief form of relaxation. He believed he had a great and prolific talent for it, and the method he was now fantasising about was a complicated affair involving helium gas.

In a little while, he was back in his flat.

Mentally reliving his own death, as he had done a thousand times before, cheered Pross, and he started coming out of the blues. He checked the rooms to see what Ron was up to: Ron could not be found. Looking out of the window to see if his car was still there, Pross witnessed Ron hunting for something within the vehicle.

A few minutes later, carrying some magazines, Ron came into the flat, agitated. 'Did you pick up our lottery ticket off the back seat of my car last night?'

'No,' answered Pross.

'You must have, it's gone.'

'Didn't touch...'

A pause.

Then, 'Oops.'

'You wanker,' groaned Ron.

'Sorry,' said Pross, 'might have been what I wiped the window with last night.'

It transpired that it *had* been what he'd wiped the window with... and the puke from his lips. And when Ron heard that he'd then tossed it away, he was none too pleased. 'That was important, that was,' he bellowed. 'You can't claim a prize without that. Brilliant. Absolutely fucking brilliant.'

'Sorry, didn't know what it was. Thought it was a sales receipt, or something.'

That defence was meagre in Ron's mind, so all Pross could do to save himself was to say sorry a few more times and point out that the chances of a major prize were fourteen million to one.

A few minutes later, Ron switched on the tv to watch the lottery draw. Being able to remember his own numbers, he soon knew he would not have been a winner, but Spock's numbers were not in his memory.

'I can't remember, either,' admitted Pross.

And that was that.

Switching the tv off, Ron unceremoniously threw a magazine over to Pross. 'Here, bastard. Bought this for you yesterday. Birthday present. Forgot to give it to you.'

It was *New Scientist*.

Ron began putting his jacket on, saying, 'I'm off out. I'm not taking my car, so keep an eye on it for me.'

'Dream on. Where are you going, anyway?'

'To meet that gorgeous babe you chatted up for me last night.'

Pross had to think about suicide again to cope.

1.5
Bored Again

Never again, was still the resolution, although his headache was now reduced to just the occasional castigatory twinge of pain to remind him of the previous night's stupidity.

He felt hungry, but nothing in the kitchen interested him, so he brewed some tea and slumped down to watch whatever the television had to offer. Consequently, by the time nine o'clock arrived he was bored once more.

Very bored.

He was so bored, he began watching a programme celebrating an air show. The television commentator was rapturously detailing the virtues of the latest Plane of Death, truly a reason for national pride — the new one that flies at a million miles an hour and can napalm at once a thousand babies while they're still in the womb without damaging the mothers' maternity dresses.

Pross detested the arms industry. Every single person employed by the Companies of Death, from tea ladies to chairmen, made him wrathful. How could they sleep at night? How, knowing that at armaments sales jamborees, representatives from their company impress mirror-shaded generals from nations the world over with clinical sales patter about their product's "battle effectiveness".

How?

He switched over to Channel 4, hoping for something more gentle but finding something infuriating: a documentary on crackpot millennium religious nonsense.

There were millennium armageddonists; millennium conspiracy-theoryists; millennium return-of-the-Buddhists; millennium prophecies-of-the-Virgin-Maryists; millennium let's-arm-ourselves-to-the-teeth-and-distrust-the-United-Nationsists.

And there was even a look at a cult called the Aetherius Society, whose robed followers maintained that Jesus and Buddha are Cosmic Masters currently living on other planets in our solar system, often sending telepathic messages to their cult's spiritual leader.

According to them, the other planets abound with such Masters.

The followers of the cult were shown dramatically praying into small metal boxes with aerials attached, boxes which they claimed were actually spiritual energy storage batteries. They also claimed that Cosmic Masters in flying saucers are secretly visiting Earth all the time, waiting for the right moment to introduce themselves to the population in general.

And that right moment would be after a Master leads the world into a Golden Millennium of peace and enlightenment.

But first, the bad people would be sorted from the good.

They also said that, after many progressive reincarnations, a human who is goodly enough would be allowed to "graduate" to higher planets in the solar system.

The sun's planets are like classrooms, they said.

Earth was the dunces' class.

And although the other planets appear to our telescopes and probes to be uninhabited and uninhabitable, highly advanced beings actually abound on them, except that they exist on different spiritual planes, only adopting physical form when deliberately showing themselves to us, like Jesus did.

The sound of a bottle dropping to the floor and then rolling some distance echoed in the house's bare entrance hall. Feet could be heard shuffling, together with some cantankerous muttering.

It was Harry, pathetically chasing his supper.

Pross wondered why Harry bothered to cling on to life.

Harry had been the victim of a burglary earlier in the year. He'd gone out one day, leaving his door unlocked, and had had unwelcome visitors, and when he'd got back things were missing.

Since that day, Harry had taken to locking his flat whenever he left it, keeping the key on a loop of thick cord around his neck so that he could never misplace it.

Still bored.

What could he do? He couldn't visit friends since most of them did things on Saturday nights, things which he simply couldn't afford to do, although sometimes he suspected he secretly welcomed the excuse not to involve himself in everyday life.

He switched off the television and turned on the gas fire, which was the only heat source in the flat. The other rooms, notably Ron's bedroom, could get awfully cold in winter, and dampness was a perennial problem, with wallpaper peeling off in the corners and black mould establishing itself in places. None of this bothered the young tenants because they both considered themselves to be only temporary residents. Ron was stashing away cash for the day when he got a permanent place of his own, and within Pross there existed a fuzzy belief that soon he would begin doing something gainful. Something really gainful. Something to elevate and free him from day-to-day considerations.

Pross wanted big money, not the trifling sums paid to workers for getting out of bed early each morning for years on end.

But, apart from an undeveloped idea of his for a more energy efficient saucepan, the only thing Pross could realistically imagine earning big money from without leaving his bedroom, or even getting dressed, was writing. That's why he'd persuaded Ron to buy him a computer. Unfortunately, his literary output so far was just one *micro*-novel. But he felt he could manage a full-length novel if only he could knuckle down to it.

And he'd have to, soon, wouldn't he? he reminded himself. Ron was going to sell the equipment if he didn't hurry up.

Bearing this in mind, he reckoned that this, finally, was the time to start working on a proper, full-length novel.

Yes, now was the time, he declared to himself in thought.

Now was the time.

And so he began thinking about a plot for it.

Actually, he managed nothing more than *thinking* about thinking about a plot for it.

His concentration dissolved.

He became appalled with his own laziness. 'Come on, make a start on it,' he whispered sternly. 'Nah, tomorrow,' he said out loud.

And still he was bored.

He tried, for a short while, to play with Spock, but Spock was in a particularly serious mood and would have none of it.

He picked up the science magazine Ron had bought him, and read half an article about an American professor who was in trouble with his university faculty for claiming to have found solid evidence for mind over matter in electronic experiments.

And he read half of an article about a Nobel prize-winning physicist who had spoken out *against* the construction of the Superconducting Super Collider, the most ambitious particle accelerator ever proposed. This opposition was curious because it had been the very same scientist who had laid the theoretical groundwork that had made other scientists believe such a grand laboratory experiment was needed.

Many of the other scientists now shunned him.

And one was even rude to his wife.

Next, he read almost a whole article about evolutionary psychology. Articles about evolutionary psychology usually annoyed Pross. They annoyed him because whatever discovery or theory they were expounding, Pross felt he could have easily proposed it himself if only someone had just had the sense to ask him for his views. This territory was his *forte*. Pross often looked at life from an evolutionary psychologist's point of view. It made sense of murders and wars... but it sadly cheapened love. And without love, there was no special, saving reason to go on at all. So whenever he looked at life from an evolutionary angle, he left love to transcendent romance.

But suicide — that really *was* transcendent. Had to be, for it was utterly unexplainable evolutionary wise.

He let the magazine drop, feeling more bored than surely... surely just about anytime since he'd last been forced to go to church.

He'd been eleven then.

And that was the day when, to show his contempt for religious mumbo-jumbo, he'd slyly poured water he'd drawn from a toilet bowl into the church's holy water font.

He decided to take another walk, the rain having abated.

His walk took him past a kebab shop. A kebab could lift his spirits a precious little right now, but he had no money. Not even enough in his pocket for a kebab, he ruefully thought. Being so hard up that he was sometimes unable to feed himself was finally beginning to get to him. The lack of material things, or even the inability to go out most nights, bothered him not. It was the never-ending *petty* miseries of his hardupishness that were finally beginning to grind him down.

He found himself toying in a defeated, half-hearted way with the idea of getting a normal job. Getting a job would present a greater problem for him than most other people: he knew that he was virtually unemployable.

He was psychologically unsuited to employment.

There were many things he knew he *could* do, but there was little he knew he *would* do. People were forever telling him that he had more talents than he deserved, saying also that he could get ahead in a dozen different directions if he could just rouse himself from his torpor. But the only job he could realistically envisage doing, without being dismissed in the first half hour, was one offering zero scope for subversion. Maybe a job limited to a single action, such as tightening one bolt on an assemblage as it passed before him on a conveyer-belt. Administrative work was out of the question: nothing gave him greater scope for silliness than a form to fill in.

Actually, he did get a proper job once. Just after leaving school he'd been accepted as a labourer on a building-site, but it was drizzling on the morning he was due to start, so he'd remained in bed.

Pross was now wondering if the time had come to suppress, or even try to abandon, his silliness. But silliness, as far as he could tell, was his reaction to a world of absurdity and cruelty. Of course he wanted the comforts that money could bring, but acquiring the money would mean bottling-up his instincts, and acting like he was taking something seriously for once.

He couldn't ever imagine treating something seriously.

He saw people do bad things when taking things seriously.

Arguing. Joining armies to defend arbitrary nations. Banding together to hooliganise for football teams, elect savage governments and fight wars.

O that mob instinct!

Pross was fond of considering the human mind to be a two-storey structure, with the ground floor being the province of atavism in all its various guises; armies, racialism, hooliganism, nationalism, patriotism. In the upper floor dwells a greater power, and from the upper floor the ground floor can be viewed and examined.

Unfortunately, he considered most as lacking the imagination or the courage to climb the stairs for the overview.

Yes, Pross thought, wandering past another fucking evangelical church, how easily could so many of the world's ills be cured if only most people could accept that *all* minds carry a legacy from the past. For once recognised, the redundancy can be examined and, when necessary, overruled. But no, people still gather stupidly in arbitrary groups: Catholics & Protestants; Muslims & Christians; Spurs & Millwall.

Football: now *there* was material galore for the evolutionary psychologist within him, reckoned Pross. All those feelings of reflected glory in the sporting successes of others were screaming out for examination. Why should anyone follow a team? Or celebrate a team's, or nation's, sporting success? How could people, sitting in their armchairs in front of a television, joyously say "*we* won a medal?" or "*we* won the cup?". That's not to say he himself never felt twinges of pride and joy when a British team triumphed somewhere in the world: he did, as strongly as most. Everyone did, he supposed. But, he concluded, those feelings were surely the abstract equivalent of an animal pack's frenzy at a successful kill by some of its hunters. Just like in everyone else, the evolutionary primitive ground floor of his mind delighted in abstract pack success — gold medals, war victories — but, climbing the stairs and looking from a greater height, he recognised such joys to be only the modified leftovers of redundant behaviour programs.

He saw these leftover programs as being the initiators of conflict and the deaths of children.

He saw these programs make men openly proud of their nation's armed forces, armaments and arms industry.

Thinking these thoughts, walking down the street, Pross made a vow to himself never to work for anybody in any capacity that might possibly contribute to killing. And the more he explored the consequences of his vow, the more, albeit often tentative, connections he could make between any occupation in the world and the manufacture of guns. He even managed to dismiss a career in the Health Service by arguing that he might one day unknowingly save the life of an arms dealer.

Making sure he didn't save the life of an arms dealer was Pross's new, conscientious excuse for lying in bed all day.

His walk soon took him back home. Noisily kicking open the house's outer door, he stepped into the bare entrance hall. The light was on. Mrs Brown, dropping a bag of rubbish into her dustbin at the bottom of the staircase, straightened up with a start.

It was heebie-jeebies time again.

He tried not to look at her.

He looked at the red tiled floor instead.

The inner door to his flat was in a direct line from the outer door, some five yards distant. Sliding the key into the lock, soon he was sitting by the gas fire again.

He became unsettled and abandoned the fire, slumping into an old, high-backed armchair.

Boredom began to swell again.

Time was slowing down, so it seemed, just to piss him off.

The minutes felt like hours.

His brain was playing with the clocks.

He began thinking about time for a time, then decided not to believe in it any more as an independent entity. Time, he knew, was just that thing measured by clocks, and clocks go as fast or as slow as the observer's mind perceives them to, especially on a wet Saturday night when the observer is hard up and all his mates have gone out.

Time is illusion, he thought. Merely another facet of entropy.

He thought some more.

Time is merely that thing measured by clocks, and all clocks, from a burning marked candle to a quartz watch, operate by seeking to rate and regulate entropy. He realised that except as a measure of the inconsequential dissolution of atomic order — order he termed *arbitrary order*, like, say, the atoms that make up a cat — time is non-existent. That's all time really was, he perceived: the dissolution of arbitrary order. In time, the cat might die and decay, and we say that time has passed. The atoms that made up the cat disperse. The order that they once formed, the arbitrary order that made up that thing once called cat, is lost. But what has really happened? Nothing, Pross realised. The matter that made up the cat is intrinsically unchanged. It still exists. Some of it may have undergone nuclear decay and become energy particles, but that process is reversible. Everything in the sub-atomic world is reversible. It is a world of frictionless see-saws. And one sub-atomic particle is completely indistinguishable from another of the same ilk. Therefore, he decided, time was simply an invented human expression to commemorate ongoing atomic disorder; the march of entropy, measured *with* entropy, *against* entropy, and a measure *of* entropy.

Therefore, realised Pross, when entropy has run its course and the universe is energetically homogeneous, that is to say, when there are no hotspots left and deep space is the same temperature as the exhausted stars, time would cease to exist as a measurable thing.

But in the meantime, he was still bored shitless and the seconds still dragged.

It was beginning to rain heavily again. And, unusual for the season, rumbles of thunder could be heard. He was so bored, he wondered in awe about the immense energy released in storms, each thundercloud forming a giant electrostatic cell, positive charge at the top of the cloud, negative at the bottom. He wondered how much energy was being released with each stroke. Enough to heat a room for a year, he guessed roughly.

He opened the curtains and sat back in the armchair to watch the spectacle.

He was so bored, he imagined thousands of electric fires hanging on the underside of the cloud, briefly pushing out heat instead of lightning flashes being violently ejected.

He was so bored, he wondered about the people privileged and lucky enough to have their houses struck that night.

The rain lashed against the window. How much water would fall on his roof? he wondered. If a half-inch of rain fell in the storm and his roof had an area of eight hundred square feet, then that would make two hundred and eight gallons, enough water to sustain, perhaps, two hundred and eight people for a day in a drought stricken country.

Just the waste run-off from his roof could sustain two hundred and eight lives.

Eventually, he drifted into his bedroom, and found himself *so* bored he resolved to *really* begin his full-length novel.

Yes, he would.

He *would*.

He would begin another novel. Any novel, if only just to distract and tire him out for bed.

He was desperately bored.

And so he *did* begin another novel, a novel inspired by the articles he'd read in *New Scientist*: that *real* engineering dean claiming to have discovered true mind over matter evidence, and that *real* Nobel physicist who had spoken out against the building of the Superconducting Super Collider.

Before turning in for the night, Pross's *second* novel was complete. And this one was *long*.

He printed it, and found that it covered nearly eleven sides of A4 paper — maybe enough to fool Ron, especially if he double-spaced the type and concluded it all with a large *The End*.

This was his second novel:-

```
In the city of Washington, Congressional hearings
were taking place to decide the fate of the
Superconducting Super Collider, the largest, most
ambitious particle accelerator ever proposed. Already,
many hundreds of millions of tax payers' dollars had
```

been sunk into the project, and it was still a very long way from being operational. The *raison d'etre* of the SSC was to verify the existence of, and to explore the properties of, the Higgs boson — the particle assumed to precipitate the breaking of high energy symmetry, thus recreating the conditions of the very early universe.

Called to testify at these hearings, to justify the further expense, were many scientists working in the field. All American Nobel Prize winning physicists were requested as a matter of course. Also requested was the Indian Physicist, Rasheed Shankra, who twenty years earlier had become a Nobel laureate for work which had directly led other physicists on to the trail of the theoretical Higgs particle.

Those scientists familiar with Shankra's work were surprised and heartened to learn that he had agreed to travel to Washington, for Shankra, now white-haired and in his seventies, no longer belonged to the academic world. Not long after receiving the Nobel prize, he had unexpectedly resigned his Princeton Professorship, moving back to India, where he had lived since. He had not contributed a single thing to science since that day, or involved himself in any discussion or project. He had virtually disappeared for twenty years.

The scientists supposed that, feeling so strongly that this line of fundamental research should continue, Shankra had come out of seclusion to add his considerable weight to the cause.

High above the lobby of the Flamingo Astoria Hotel, Las Vagas, overlooking serried ranks of slot machines, a gaudy neon sign flashed 97.4 — *THE HOTTEST SLOT PERCENTAGE IN TOWN!*

Thirty-eight-year-old Alaister Dashwood, a dean of engineering at the University of Nevada, there in Las Vagas, was in the hotel to meet with an associate who was in town.

Dashwood and his associate, named Johnson, were having breakfast, discussing their current work: the

Superconducting Super Collider. The dining area had a viewing window which overlooked the slot machines. While talking leisurely about the forthcoming Congressional hearings which they were due to attend, Johnson looked across to the neon sign and wryly said: "*97.4 percent return — we've adjusted our machines to cream off only 2.6 cents of every dollar you give us*. God, if ever any proof were needed against the existence of psychic power, this city's gambling halls is where to find it."

"Maybe you're wrong," suggested Dashwood. "These machines aren't good experiments."

Johnson was surprised by Dashwood's response. It was almost as if Dashwood were defending the existence of the paranormal influence of the human mind.

"Come now," laughed Johnson, "look at those gamblers' faces masked in concentration — it can hardly be said that they're not exerting every psychic effort to influence the random, yet still the cash flows into the casino owners' pockets in an even, predictable stream."

Dashwood looked at Johnson. "Suppose someone *had* devised a reliable laboratory test for the existence of mental powers?"

"You?" asked Johnson.

"The very same."

"And?"

"I believe I've found evidence."

Johnson laughed and shook his head. "Well don't go public — you'll lose your deanship faster than those guys are losing their money."

Dashwood became earnest. "I'm serious. I've been running some private electronic tests, and the evidence is there: the random can be influenced."

"What about those guys?" said Johnson, looking at the gamblers.

"Bad test. My powers are vanishingly small..."

"Your powers?" cut in Johnson.

"My powers. I did better than anyone else. A tenth of one percent I managed. You see? A tenth of one percent is swamped by the 2.6 percent chance of losing here."

"Don't go public," urged Johnson. "You'll be ridiculed."

The hearings were in progress. Every scientist called gave effusive support to the Collider, saying how necessary it was to the quest for fundamental understanding.

Then Shankra was called. Looking weary and sad-eyed, he took position on the podium. As with everyone else, he was to be questioned by advocates and objectors. Advocates were mainly particle physicists, objectors were mainly politicians.

The advocates had been heartened by the defence put forward by their ranks so far, but now they were in for a shock, for the very man whose work had first suggested the existence of the Higgs particle was to reject the whole direction of fundamental science.

"Gentlemen," he began with quiet nobility, "I, as the person largely responsible for beginning the quest for the Higgs particle, have been called here to give my opinion, and I shall say things that have been manifestly true to me for many years now: I do not believe that this proposed collider will address issues of uniquely fundamental importance, nor will it yield anything of practical value. I urge the Congress of this powerful nation to withdraw funding and to direct the money and effort to reducing human suffering instead. Just half of this money could immunise every living person against a host of diseases which currently kill millions each year."

The other scientists were dumbstruck.

An economic advisor to the President, who was opposed to the Collider, leapt at his chance, asking Shankra to explain his doubts.

Shankra seemed reluctant to elucidate, merely saying, "the very precepts of modern physics are wrong, that much I have learnt since I set the world looking for this particle. It exists, I am sure, but we must stop looking under the street lamp for the answers, and venture away from known territory. Please do not let me live the remainder of my days knowing I have sent the world on a foolish errand. The billions of dollars can and should be better spent. Again, I state that just half of the money would be sufficient to immunise the world."

Having recovered from the shock a little, one of the advocating scientists jumped in with questions.

"What have you told this hearing that has any substance? We need to know reasons and facts."

Shankra answered, "Gentlemen, I have never been one to boast, but now must. When I was eleven, a mere schoolboy in Bangalore, I submitted a paper to the scientific community which proved Goldbach's conjecture that every positive even number could be expressed as the sum of two prime numbers. That proof had eluded mathematicians for two centuries: it was child's play to me. As an adult, I was professor of quantum mechanics at your Princeton University, where Einstein taught. Like Einstein, I was awarded a Nobel prize. I say to you now, and hope that you'll value and respect my opinion: do not waste so much on a pointless journey."

"But you haven't explained your objections!" boomed the scientist. "Why are the precepts of physics wrong? Tell us."

Shankra obviously wished not to elucidate, but felt he must. "Consciousness," he said quietly, "has a fundamental role in the cosmos. It creates the universe, forcing reality into being out of a quantum mechanical haze of possibilities. It is we who make the microscopic world real: a little bit of God operates in us all, and that is what should be explored."

"What is consciousness? Who can answer that?"

"Consciousness is many things. The awareness of time, for one," said Shankra. "Consciousness can look forward or back — when back we call it memory, when forward you call it impossible."

"Metaphysical claptrap," scoffed the scientist.

"Has it never once occurred to you," responded

Shankra, "that human thought processes might be affecting the results of quantum events, and that your machines might be measuring what is within, not what is without?"

"And now he's talking mind over matter!"

The scientists laughed mockingly... except Dashwood, who was intrigued.

"Gentleman," said Shankra with dignity, "I was invited to offer my opinion, and that I have done. Good day to you all."

"Traitor," said someone.

Shankra left the stand and exited the hall through a convenient door. He seemed intent on avoiding people.

Dashwood now had a burning desire to learn more from Shankra. Only Dashwood had seen solid proof of the intervention of thought processes in sensitive experiments. Dashwood trusted his own results.

Dashwood made it his business to find out where Shankra was staying, and soon he was outside his hotel room.

He knocked on the door.

Shankra, who had been reading, courteously admitted Dashwood.

The curtains were drawn, and incense was in the air.

To Dashwood's surprise, Shankra said that he was aware that his guest was the dean of engineering at the University of Nevada. "I have not removed myself *so* far from the academic world I once inhabited," he explained.

Apologising, Shankra told the dean that he was hungry, and asked him to postpone telling him the object of his visit until he had eaten. Dashwood said that he was not hungry himself, but would wait until Shankra had satisfied his own appetite. Shankra contacted room service and requested his meal.

Shankra began to talk politely to the dean about how much America had changed since he had seen it last, twenty years before. "So much technology," he said. "So many computers talking to other computers."

He explained that he had been living the simplest of lives in India, and was more given to meditation than to keeping abreast with the pace of change."

Dashwood was unable to restrain his desire for information and found himself raising a question concerning one of Shankra's comments earlier that day at the Congressional hearing.

"Ah, you were there?"

"I was," confirmed Dashwood.

Shankra smiled gently, and explained that although he was hungry, he would listen to what the dean had to ask while he awaited room service.

The dean eagerly jumped at his chance. "You said that consciousness could work forward as well as back."

"I believe I did," answered Shankra, "although few were listening."

"And you said that when it looks forward, *we* call it impossible."

"That I believe I also said."

"Which implies that *you* don't consider it impossible."

"I do not consider it impossible. You are correct."

The dean looked ardently at Shankra. "I *know* it's not impossible. I've done experiments, experiments which gave results I couldn't explain, but I think you can."

Dashwood described his experiments to Shankra, and Shankra offered brief explanations, "What we call the present is shaped by consciousness. Each single moment the cosmos unfolds by consensus from a chaos of possibilities. Every conscious entity works to shape the chaos. Some, however, learn to peer further into the chaos than others. They see the moments unfolding."

Dashwood thought hard. "You said that consciousness can work forward as well as back. How can you mean that awareness of the future can exist if the future unfolds from a chaos of possibilities? Chaos, by its very nature, is unpredictable."

Shankra said nothing. He didn't have to, for the dean rapidly drew his own conclusion. "Probability!

That's it. The collective consciousness shapes the probability for each moment. In the distant future, all given event outcomes are possible. As the present draws closer, certain conditions become more probable, until the actual real event becomes inevitable. A person who could cast his consciousness into the chaos of the future, could become aware of the seeds that might grow into firm outcomes."

Shankra looked kindly at the dean. "You have arrived, almost by chance, by the eye-opener of your benchtop experiments, at the understanding I came to many years ago through pure cerebration."

The dean was now hungry for more knowledge. "How far into the future can useful awareness be cast?"

"The chaos becomes total beyond half a second. The moment begins to significantly crystallise almost as soon as it is upon us."

"That would explain my results!" said the dean. "My mind was unconsciously occasionally able to view the dice of uncertainty far enough into the future for me to predict outcomes better than even chance. I've managed a tenth of a percent above even. The electronically produced randomness of my experiments, generated in only microseconds, was sensed by me once every thousand times on average."

The dean then fell silent, gazing at Shankra with growing awe. "You said a person could learn to work harder at projecting their consciousness into the future — how much harder? I can only manage microseconds with a success rate on one in a thousand. How much is possible?"

Shankra was unwilling to answer.

The dean pursued the issue. "I need to know what you know."

"I am wary of divulging such knowledge."

"If you promise to show me all you know, I'll promise to help stop the construction of the Super Collider. I'm an engineer on the project. I can say I think it's technically impossible."

"Can you also say where the saved money will be

spent?" asked Shankra. "Can you direct half of it to freeing the world's poor of disease?"

"Of course I can't."

Shankra fixed him with a look. "Would you if you could?"

"Of course I would."

"If you speak out against it, you will be vilified by the academic world. The ranks will close and you'll never get a position again. They want this toy badly."

"I need to know what you know more than anything else."

Shankra seemed to be acquiescing, and the dean leapt at the open window of opportunity. "Half a second, you mentioned. Is that *your* limit. Can you cast your awareness that far with a measurable success rate? You can, can't you?"

"Do you promise to help stop the Super Collider?" asked Shankra.

"Yes," said the dean emphatically.

"Half a second is indeed my limit," answered Shankra. Laughing a little, he added, "But it is so very tiring! And I am old now, and my will fades so quickly."

"How? Tell me how."

"It arrives after many years," answered Shankra.

"What does it feel like?"

"Like being in a misty dream. You may have experienced the hallucinatory effects of LSD. I understand now that part of the LSD experience arises from having one's consciousness expanded chemically ever so slightly into the future, and glimpsing the ever unfolding chaos overwhelms the mind. Learning not to be overwhelmed, but to recognise the probable outcomes as they unfold from chaos is the task. The majority avoid and deny the chaotic mist, instinctively fearing the uncertainty. The gurus of the east abandon themselves to the mist. I, perhaps the only person ever to have done so, comprehend the mist. To teach you my methods may take years. The gurus spent years leading me into the mist, and only then after years of gaining trust in me. It is so very sacred what we do:

to have so much of God operating within us."

"That's how I felt doing my experiments, ever so slightly. Like I was half a step into a misty realm. So that's where I was — unconsciously skirting the fringes of a chaos of possibilities. If I could learn to consciously wander in that mist, who knows what I might achieve?"

"Who indeed?" said Shankra quietly.

"Don't you realise what kind of power you could wield — having an early grasp on all moments?"

"I have never contemplated the power," replied Shankra.

"And all one has to do is let one's consciousness seep forward from the moment," rambled Dashwood.

"It takes years," said Shankra.

"But I already do it," countered Dashwood.

"A little."

"Becoming aware of time unfolding before it arrives...," said Dashwood, taking a seat, awed by the hugeness of the notion.

Shankra moved nearer to him, and began talking in a gentle, even voice. "Consciousness is all, and all is consciousness. And time, so long held by western science to be inviolable, is merely consciousness condensing, for convenient, palpable examination, the foggy chaos of the microscopic world. To behold creation in its entirety, one must explore the fog..."

As Shankra continued speaking, Dashwood found himself unconsciously attempting to enter the fog, and indeed, as if now that he was aware of its existence, he began to feel the world melt into a dreamy mist, much more overwhelmingly so than he'd felt when performing his psychic experiments... until called to a fixed moment by Shankra, who was gently telling him something.

"Alaister, you appear to have drifted away. Wake up and answer your telephone."

Dashwood realised that the mobile phone in his briefcase was ringing. It was Johnson calling. Johnson said that the Collider's chief engineer, due to speak to the Congress that very afternoon, had taken very ill, and that he should return at once.

The news was very upsetting to the dean — for one thing, because of his colleague and friend's illness, for another, because he would be forced to interrupt his talk with Shankra. He told Shankra he would have to return to the hearings, but begged him to avail himself in the near future.

"I will avail myself," Shankra assured him.

Crossing Washington by taxi, Dashwood lay his head back and contemplated all that had been said to him. He tried to enter the altered state of mind again, and soon found himself experiencing a dreamy sensation. Looking out of the window, things appeared not just to happen, but to quickly settle into a happening. Each moment seemed to be suspended in a weak fluid of moments. The feeling, although fleeting, was even stronger than in the hotel room. "Years?" murmured Dashwood, "I'm nearly there already!"

In the Congress building, Dashwood was met by Johnson, who looked grave. "He's very ill," said Johnson. "Heart attack. This project was his life. Guess the stress of having to defend it was too much for him."

Many of the project's engineering coordinators and administrators were there. They were desperate: the chief engineer had been due to speak that very afternoon. "You'll have to speak in his stead, Dashwood. You know more about this project than anyone else. You're chief engineer now."

Later, Dashwood was called to the stand. When asked to defend the project, he felt he could not let his colleagues down. Speaking out at this moment, with his friend lying gravely ill, would be a monstrous thing to do, he thought.

The audience applauded when he spoke of the exciting challenge the project represented.

After his speech, someone came to shake Dashwood's hand. Over the person's shoulder he was surprised to see Shankra. After meeting his eye, Shankra turned and walked away. "Wait!" called Dashwood, running to catch up.

"I came to hear you speak out against the wasteful folly," said Shankra, "yet you did not."

"I couldn't," explained Dashwood. "Not now. Not with him lying ill. Besides, if the government didn't spend the money on it, they'd spend it on some other project — maybe even something military. It wouldn't go to help the poor, that's for sure. I can't say where the money would go."

"Would you if you could?" asked Shankra once more.

"Of course I would," replied Dashwood.

Another gushy colleague came up to Dashwood. Distracted for a moment, upon looking back, he discovered Shankra had disappeared into the crowd.

Dashwood made his way over to Shankra's hotel, but was informed that Shankra was not there, although a message would be conveyed.

That night, Dashwood, alone in his own hotel room, began experimenting with his aptitude. On his laptop PC, he devised a program to generate at random one of two symbols. Entering into his expanded state of consciousness, he found that, in a dreamy way, he very, very briefly saw — no, experienced — both symbols fade up on his screen before one would fade away again to leave a solid image of just one of the shapes to persist into reality.

He was seeing events under construction.

Knowing which was going to fade was the crux.

However, exhausted, he soon fell into a deep sleep, from which he did not awake until the morning, when SSC officials telephoned him. They informed him that the chief had died in the night and that he was now head of the engineering team, and that Congress seemed likely to continue the project's funding. Dashwood was now the leader of the biggest technical project in the world.

During that day, Dashwood was inundated with visitors and messages.

Late into the evening, when the last visitor had left, a knock sounded on his door. It was Shankra. Shankra expressed his dismay at the likely funding of the project, and asked that Dashwood honour his promise before it was too late. Dashwood, embarrassed, said that he would do it as soon as he could.

While Skankra was there, a fax came through from the SSC administrators informing Dashwood that his salary was now doubled, and that his engineering budget was secure: Congress had funded the project.

Although saddened, Shankra acknowledged that it was now a *fait accompli*. "Well, at least you will be able to donate half of your increased salary. Is not that so?"

Dashwood said that it was so.

Shankra left, saying that he had business to attend to.

Many weeks passed, and, back in the University in Las Vagas, Dashwood, whenever he was free, continued to explore his abilities. More and more he was now able to penetrate the future mists. He found that many seemingly random events were his to predict, and his success rate was ever increasing. Soon he was scoring a success rate of five percent above even. It was then that he realised that such a power could be turned to profit: casting his awareness into the unfolding chaos of the future, and seeing it condense into events, he could cream every casino in Las Vagas.

Knowing slightly more often than not which button to press on those fast-moving win / lose chances, on average he would win 105 times every two hundred.

Dashwood did just that, although the sustained effort exhausted him daily.

As the weeks passed, he grew to become a fluent winner. And he grew also to be obsessed with his power. Obsessed with the profit. He was earning many thousands each day.

He was too obsessed with this to continue his SSC work, and resigned his position.

The roulette tables, however, proved too tricky: not enough time after sensing where the ball had probably settled to place a corresponding bet. Too physical.

After some months of this activity, now a millionaire, Dashwood hit upon a greater challenge: the biggest casino in the world — financial speculation. He knew that much trading now occurred electronically. If he could sense with reasonable accuracy half a second in advance whether a commodity was going to go up or down in price, he could hit the buy or sell button in time to make the profit. Do better than fifty percent and he'd be earning big time.

Dashwood did just that. Using his gambling profits, he set up as a financial speculator, trading electronically. Employing a small team of advisors who followed market trends and informed him of potential areas for his attention, he watched computer screens for opportunities, able to hazily predict which way figures were going to go: up or down. If he thought they were going to go up, he hit the buy button a fraction before; down he sold. Slightly more often than not, he was right.

But it was enough.

He began risking moderate amounts: thousands rather than millions. Months later, he was in a position to speculate in the millions, and he made his first million dollar investment.

He lost.

But he was used to encountering losses. Statistically, he was winning.

His first big killing came with Magnetic Industrial. Tipped off by his advisors, who had reckoned on some possible movement in this company due to it being rumoured to have been awarded a large contract, he later sensed the share price rise on his screen and bought half a million shares quarter of a second before they began a rise of fifty cents in but a few minutes. He later discovered that they had risen after the marketplace had learned that Magnetic Industrial had been awarded the contract to supply the SSC with superconducting magnets.

He laughed.

A year later, locked almost permanently into a hazy semi-reality, Dashwood, atop a New York office complex overlooking Central Park, now operated a technically offshore, unregulated and very secretive trading business. He was now dealing hundreds of millions of dollars each day, speculating mostly against currencies. Monthly profits were growing almost exponentially.

It came to pass that one day an opportunity arose to speculate against the dollar in favour of the yen. Sinking billions into the opportunity, Dashwood made nearly thirty billion dollars profit in one day: he had profited at the expense of the United States by as much as the SSC was set to cost.

Dashwood was now the wealthiest person alive by a long way.

Turning around in his office chair, he was momentarily unnerved to see Shankra right in front of him.

"You're a very clever man," said Shankra. "Living the simple, you would say backward, life I have lived in India this last twenty years, I had never realised how my learning could benefit me. So many computers in the world now. Seconds split up so importantly these days. I see that today you made a profit more than equal to the cost of the Collider which you promised to help me have stopped. Can you not now give half of that profit to remove so much of the world's suffering?"

Dashwood said, "You too must be a clever man to have entered this office without my permission."

"Remember your promise to me, Dashwood. I am sure that from this desk you could send billions to the World Health Organisation who would put it to good use. Do it now, Dashwood."

Dashwood said that he was weary of Shankra's requests, and that, anyway, he had developed his abilities on his own, not under any tutelage. "Persist in importuning me and I shall have my security men throw you out, fakir that you are."

Presumedly summoned by secret button, a security man appeared in the room.

Shankra could only answer that he would go, but said this also, "Much of my Nobel prize money I long ago gave to the poor, so that I also became a poor man, and the very last of my money I spent coming here to your country. I now have not even enough for a meal. Can you not give me enough to feed myself today?"

"Do as I did," said Dashwood. "Use your powers, if you have any."

"Maybe I am too old and slow to perform such tricks," sighed Shankra, "and so might you be too by the time you had learnt the knowledge."

"Learnt it!" exclaimed Dashwood. "I am master of it."

"You have learnt nothing," said Shankra, whereupon Dashwood perceived his face changing in a strange fashion, as was the whole room. "Since you will not give me food, it seems I shall have to have the meal I ordered earlier." And the guard, who had now become a room service man, came forward with a platter of food.

Dashwood, who was utterly taken aback to find himself returned to the hotel room, was also taken aback with shame, and did not know what to say.

Shankra very politely saw him to the door, saying that he was surely due back at the hearings.

"How?" asked Dashwood, as he shuffled in confusion. "Hypnotism? Telepathy? How?"

"It takes years," said Shankra. "Now, if you will excuse me, I must eat."

After his meal, Shankra picked up the *Yellow Pages* and looked under Investment Advisors.

In the small hours, with Ron still not returned from his night out with possibly the greatest love of Pross's life, he, bleary-eyed and much out of heart, retired to bed.

1.6
Tess's Younger Sister

Sunday. The Sabbath. The Lord's day.

'I fuckin' hate Sundays,' moaned Pross to Spock as he fell depressingly awake, the cat's intrusion into his room having been responsible for the termination of his dreams. There was only one sort of day Pross hated more than a Sunday, and that was a bank holiday Monday. A Sunday followed by a bank holiday was just like having two Sundays in a row, except the second one was even more boring than the first: it had compound disinterest.

It wasn't until just past two in the afternoon that he felt able to face another Sabbath.

He bequeathed the warmth of the bed to Spock and set about dressing.

'Give up again?'

'OK, give up,' said Ron, becoming grumpy. 'But it's not fair. It's your room and you know everything in it.'

Sarah-Jane laughed, pulled the duvet over their heads and bit Ron's ear. Ron yelped.

She laughed again, and lifted the duvet. 'OK, then, we'll make it fair. I *don't* spy, with my little eye, something beginning with J.'

Ron felt even more handicapped, but gave it a shot.

'Jerusalem?'

'No.'

'Japan?'

'No.'

'Jodrell Bank?'

'No.'

He heaved a sigh and gave up again.

'Jennifer,' said Sarah.

'Jennifer who?'

'Jennifer, my sister. Well, my half-sister.'

'That's not fair again,' complained Ron, stroking Sarah's hair, her head resting on his broad chest.

Sarah had become quiet, and Ron soon perceived that she was contemplative. 'What are you thinking about? You look worried.'

'My sister. She does worry me.'

Encouraged by the intimacy of their position, their warm, naked bodies pressed comfortingly close, Sarah went on to explain her sister's history. She told of how, nearly two years earlier, their parents had died in a crash with a drunken driver. Sarah had been in Durham completing her degree at the time, but Jennifer had only just turned sixteen. Since then, it had seemed to Sarah that Jennifer had become more and more dispirited and insular. 'I can't help feeling responsible,' she confessed. 'I should have spent more time with her instead of sticking college. She went to live with our aunt afterwards, and that couldn't have helped much.'

'Maybe she's just shy,' suggested Ron.

'No... she is shy. Very shy. But it's more than that. Now she hardly takes any interest in anything. Like, I buy most of her clothes for her. She doesn't bother. And she never goes out when John's not home. Just sits in with the tv. But she never says anything's wrong if you ask her. I try to get her to come to Durham for weekends, but she always declines. With the money we got after the accident, she could travel the world for years, but it just sits in the bank.'

Ron gently kissed Sarah's hair, which was spilling over his pillow.

'Who's John? Her boyfriend?'

'Uh, huh. I don't like him. He's stupid. And she's so sweet and thoughtful. He was her first boyfriend. She'd been out with him a few times just before the accident, and they've been together since. Fortunately he's in the navy so he's hardly ever home. When I see them together, sometimes it's like she's getting some kind of satisfaction out of giving herself to someone she... no, it's like she gets some sense of suffering from... Oh, I don't know. I really don't know. I don't know my own sister. Maybe she loves him. Maybe that's it.'

Ron gently kissed her hair again, and Sarah gently squeezed his hand.

'I've never slept with anyone so soon as I slept with you,' she said. 'Not that I've had that many partners.'

Again, Ron gently kissed her hair.

'You know what made me trust you so soon?' continued Sarah.

'Tell me.'

'Pross. The way you let him pick on you.'

Ron smiled. 'I'll tell him,' he said. Then he gently pulled the duvet away to expose Sarah's breasts, which he began kissing. 'He'll be delighted to have helped me.'

'The bastard,' said Pross, 'the big twatty bastard.'

Looking into Ron's bedroom, Pross had just determined that Ron had not returned home last night, which suggested he'd stayed with Sarah-Jane.

So, much depressed by this, this particular Sabbath proved to be an interminably slow one, structured around cups of tea with biscuits and tv channel hopping, then, come seven o'clock, lying on his bed and staring at the ceiling.

But then the telephone rang in the living room.

'Hiya, Pross,' said the voice in the phone, 'Pete here. Is Ron about?'

Pross lay on his back to speak lazily to Pete. 'Yeah, but he's unavailable. He's masturbating in the shed. I can hear him moaning my name even from here.'

At this moment, Pross heard Ron's key working the lock.

Pete was confused. 'You haven't got a shed.'

'We have now,' explained Pross to Pete as Ron appeared in the living room. 'Ron built himself a shed especially to wank in, even though I've warned him about that habit of his. He'll only end up getting emotionally involved with himself.' Dispiritedly, Pross offered the receiver to Ron. 'It's for you, dream defiler. Pete.'

When taking the phone, Ron said, 'Evening, Pross. Gone mad yet?'

'Not yet. Been busy.'

Ron was hoping that this phone call would be the one he'd been waiting days for. Pete was Ron's dope supplier. The call was much awaited because Pete's own wholesale supply had run dry a few weeks earlier, creating a local dope famine.

Ron had not been stoned now for five days.

The phone call told that relief supplies had arrived.

Pross never bought dope himself. He didn't have to, for Ron was prepared to bestow endless quantities upon him. Ron gave him dope, and encouraged him to get stoned, solely to keep him sedated. When Pross was stoned, he was only a fraction as talkative as when he was straight, and that was Ron's way of getting peace and quiet. However, Pross indulged nowhere near as often as Ron would like. To Ron, dope was a way of life, but to Pross, dope was simply an occasional treat, to be enjoyed late at night as an entertainment. As a way of life, Pross thought that dope stank.

After the ten-second call, Ron sported a grin.

'Good news?' inquired Pross, trying to sound glad about it for Ron's sake.

'Fabulous news, Old Boy,' said Ron, mimicking W.C. Fields, 'quantities of fine Moroccan Black await me at Pete's. Glad times are upon us once more.'

Driving to Pete's place to pick up his drugs was now paramount in Ron's scheme of things, and he began looking for his car keys.

With Ron in a good mood and distracted, Pross decided to give him the news about his second work of literature.

'I wrote another novel last night, like you ordered me to.'

'Oh yeah?' said Ron with lashings of suspicion, searching under cushions.

'This one's long.'

'How long?'

'Eleven pages.'

'Not long enough,' said Ron, forcing his hand down the back of the sofa.

'Twenty-two if it's double-spaced,' tried Pross hopefully.

Ron shook his head.

Pross lost his equanimity. 'Well how long do you want? Tell me. Give me some boundaries.'

'Hundred pages.'

Pross heard someone walking into the flat. It was Sarah-Jane. She had first come back with Ron, but, on the doorstep, had nipped back to her car to fetch her bag. Dressed in a billowy silk blouse and a sweeping skirt, Sarah-Jane looked quite the Pre-Raphaelite beauty. The voluminosity of her clothes paradoxically emphasised her slender frame. But Sarah's eyes held the real key to her allure: they could tame lions.

Sarah smiled at Pross, then draped herself over an armchair. She was a person very confident of herself. 'Grotty flat,' she said, observing her surroundings.

'Don't look at me until I've done my hair,' whined Pross, holding his hands over his head.

Off to the bathroom to get himself looking good he went.

But a few steps on, he came back. 'This doesn't mean I'm shallow, you know,' he insisted to Sarah-Jane.

'It never crossed my mind,' said she, and Pross went away again.

Ron was still hunting for his keys as Pross emerged from the bathroom, hair dripping, going to his bedroom to use his hairdryer.

A few minutes later, bored with watching Ron's search, Sarah sought out Pross's whereabouts, tapping gently on his open bedroom door.

'Come in and sit down,' Pross impatiently said as Sarah stood with annoying politeness on the threshold of the room.

Coming in proved a little difficult since a heap of books spilling out from a fallen bookshelf blocked her way. 'What happened here?' she wanted to know.

'Cat knocked it over the other day.'

'And you haven't picked them up yet?'

'One day, maybe. Anyway, it's the cat's responsibility.'

Sarah lifted the large bookshelf up herself, then began replacing the texts.

Knelt on the floor, drying his hair, Pross watched her actions without comment.

When finished, Sarah sat on the chair next to Pross's word processor. 'I keep meaning to buy a computer,' she said, tapping the machine's keys. 'Ron says you wrote a novel last night?'

'That's right.'

'What's it about?'

'What all novels are about: sex and death. Except I didn't bother about the sex bit — gets in the way of the death. I didn't bother much about the death bit, either, come to think of it. Didn't have time.'

She looked at him, saying in gushing admiration, 'Gosh, a whole novel in one night. It must have been terribly exhausting. How many pages?'

'Eleven.'

'Gosh, that's a lot.'

Pross was modest. 'For normal people it would be,' he said, 'but luckily I'm what we writers call *fuckin' prolific*.'

'Gosh again,' she said. 'I get a tingling sensation being in the presence of such genius.'

'I'm going to write another one by the end of the month. Over a hundred pages.'

A whoop of delight came from Ron in the kitchen. 'Found them! See you soon.' And the front door slammed.

Sarah-Jane had told Ron she'd rather remain in the flat than make the journey across town again. After a little while, she began to wander around Pross's bedroom, picking up things to look at. The Rolf Harris posters amused her a little. When over by the window, she tried to part the curtains to sample the view, but discovered that they were stitched together in the middle. 'Don't you ever open your curtains?'

'Never.'

'Christ, you're as bad as my sister. She's always sitting in the dark.'

Sister! Pross was almost certain he'd heard her say sister.

He beckoned Sarah-Jane closer, indicating that she should sit at the bottom of his bed. She did, suspicious as he slinked over to her, devilment burning worryingly bright in his eyes.

On his hands and knees on the floor, he looked into her eyes. 'Did you just let slip that you had a sister?'

A little disconcerted by Pross's intense interest, Sarah answered, 'Er, yes. Jennifer.'

It was love.

'Tell me more,' he said in a low, demanding voice.

'Er, she's just turned eighteen, and she's a Veterinary Assistant.'

'More.'

'She's just moved into a flat with a girl in Richmond, where we come from.'

'Richmond down south or Richmond North Yorkshire?'

'North Yorkshire.'

Overwhelmed, Pross moved on to the bed, slumping down on to his back. 'Tess has a younger sister,' he murmured.

Sarah-Jane looked unbelievingly at him as he gazed heavenward in a transport of love. But suddenly, he jumped up to face her, demonically obsessed.

Sarah recoiled with a start.

'Describe her. How tall is she?' he asked.

'About an inch shorter than me,' she answered.

Gripping Sarah's wrist, he demanded more information. 'Mimic her voice for me. Ape her walk. Describe her face. Kiss me like she kisses.'

Closing his eyes tight, he drew Sarah's face towards his by her hair and offered his puckered lips for kissing.

Sarah shook him off and moved away. 'For God's sake, Pross,' she complained, 'Ron's right, you do need your head examining. She's just my sister. Anyway, she's already got a boyfriend.'

Pross fell heavily from elation.

'No, no, no,' he almost sobbed. 'It can't be.'

'I wish it couldn't be as well,' muttered Sarah, for her own ears... but Pross heard her.

The way Sarah-Jane had spoke revealed to Pross that she disapproved of her sister's relationship with her boyfriend.

Opportunity for opportunism.

In the course of the next few minutes, Pross actually managed to fake a sensible conversation. It was an effort, but the potential rewards kept him going. A few sympathetic noises and expressions, and a few concerned questions, coaxed Sarah to reveal many of the things she had told Ron that morning.

A sidewards tilt of his head, coupled with appropriate expressions, led Sarah to elaborate even further.

'I don't know,' she said, with an air of vagueness, 'sort of distant. She used to be quite outgoing, but after they died she withdrew a lot. But sometimes I wonder if she changed just because she got older. Maybe she would have been like that anyway? I don't know. It must have come at a bad age for her, though. She became very disillusioned with life, I think. She would stay in all day and just sit in her room with the television, and she only ever went to school when she was forced to. Missed her exams. Walked out on some.' A cloud seemed to pass over Sarah's face. 'It was all very sad. I should have spent more time with her, but I had my studies to do here, didn't I?' Sarah was pensive for a moment. 'She never went to the funeral. She was ill on the day. Vomiting. But she hasn't visited the grave once since. She says she doesn't want to. It's only a stone, not them, she says.'

'What about her boyfriend?' asked Pross.

Sarah's expression changed to one of muted disdain.

'He's twenty-one and a jerk, though she must think he's all right. Actually, she's not my full sister, she's my half-sister. Same mother, different fathers. I was the result of a night of passion at a music festival. I've never met my real father.'

'How long have they been seeing each other?'

'Over two years. He's the only one she's ever had.'

His name was John, Pross learnt, and he was in the navy, and as far as Sarah was concerned, long absences were his most appealing quality.

A deep dislike for John being evident, Pross set about discovering its roots, questioning Sarah further.

'John? I don't like him at all. She deserves better. He's on leave with her now, so I won't be going to see her until he pisses off back to sea in a few days. I keep asking her to come to Durham to stay with me at weekends when she's alone, but she never wants to. I think she's nervous about it. Or maybe she just isn't interested.'

'What's so terrible about this John jerk, then?'

'I just don't like him. He's horrible. Odious.'

'Odious?' echoed Pross, re-employing the tactical tilt of his head.

'Odious,' repeated Sarah, and after a slight hesitation, she said, 'Once — I never told Jennifer this, by the way — he turned up on his own out of the blue at my flat here in Durham and asked if I could put him up for the night. He'd been out drinking with some navy pals. I didn't want him to stay, but I was tired and I couldn't be bothered to argue.'

Sarah stopped there.

'Is that all?'

'No it's not,' she said. 'He kept me up talking till all hours, then started trying it on with me. I was really scared at one point, but he backed off when he realised how much he'd frightened me. I got to bed eventually, only to wake up later to find him about to get in bed beside me. I had to really give him hell before the message got through. In the morning, when he'd sobered up, he acted as if nothing had happened.'

'Makes me ashamed of my sex,' said Pross. 'Men are big and strong, and wouldn't the world be a nicer place if they acted small and weak?'

'Too right. Voltair had it right when he said that the sum of the world's evils would be greatly reduced if men could just learn to sit quietly in their bedrooms.'

'That's what I do,' said Pross, straightening up with pride. 'I'm philosophically advanced, me. Be sure to tell your sister.'

There was no response from Sarah. She was apparently still brooding over John.

Pross decided to help. 'Don't worry about Jennifer,' he said, having now exhausted his entire supply of sensibleness, 'I'll stab this John character in the head and marry her for you... as a favour, like.'

Sarah's reaction was swift and curt. 'She doesn't need a loony like you in her life.' In fact her reaction was so swift and curt, it upset Pross a little. 'Aw, I'm sorry,' she said. 'I'm a bit protective about her.'

Pross was going to milk Sarah's penitence for as much as he could. 'Can I have her phone number?' he asked meekly.

'Not a chance,' said Sarah firmly, without any hesitation or diplomacy.

'Please,' begged Pross.

'Absolutely not.'

Ron was heard coming up the garden path, and he was not alone. Pross could hear the voice of Melanie, Lilith's sister, among others.

This was the Melanie whose fault it was he was called what he was.

Sarah stood up, meaning to leave the room, but Pross also stood up. 'Take me to her now,' he said. 'Come on, you've got a car. I saw it on Friday.'

Sarah had other ideas. 'No way, Richmond's thirty miles away, and I'd never drive anywhere with you in a car. Anyway, she'll probably be going out with John tonight since he's home on leave.'

This intelligence crushed Pross, and he made quite a show of falling to the floor and wrapping his arms clingingly around Sarah's lower legs.

'I love her. I love her,' he whined. 'Go to Richmond without me then, but bring her back here. Tell her it's a party.'

'And what about John? Do I bring him too? And let go of my legs.'

'But my whole existence revolves around her.'

'Don't be silly, Pross, you've never even met her.'

'So what?' he said. 'The pope's never met God, but he still reckons to love him.'

Sarah tried to reason with him. 'My sister's not like me. She's a lot more innocent.'

'Innocent? Right on — she'll have nothing to compare me with.'

She tutted in disapproval. 'I don't mean sexually. I mean that she's not as confident as me. You'd scare the life out of her. And let go of my legs, will you?'

'No, never. You're from the same gene stock as Jennifer.'

'Let me go.'

'No.'

'Yes.'

'No... all right, maybe. OK, yes, then — if you'll compromise. If I can't have her, I'll settle for you. Let's make love.'

Sarah began pulling his hair. 'Pross, will you please let go of my legs.'

'No,' he declared, enduring the pain. 'You have to make love with me in lieu of your sister.'

'No I don't.' Sarah gave up pulling his hair and, as best she could with her legs held tightly, sat down on the edge of the bed. 'I thought you said you sit quietly in your bedroom?'

Letting her go, Pross answered, 'I am in my bedroom.'

'Oh, so you are,' she conceded.

But with a sterner voice, Pross said, 'I'll ask you only once more. After all, I do have *some* pride you know. This is your last chance. I'll never ask again. Will you make love with me in lieu of your sister?'

'No, I won't.'

'That's it,' he said resolutely, 'you've blown it.' His resolve lasted something under three seconds. 'Aw, come on,' he whined, completely without pride, clinging to her legs again, 'make love with me. It won't take long, and you'll hardly notice anything happening.'

Ron appeared in the doorway. Behind him were Melanie and Tony, her husband, and her sister, Lilith.

Sarah-Jane appealed to her new lover.

'Ron,' she said, exasperated, 'can you please stop Pross hassling me for sex.'

'Can't,' said Ron. 'Wouldn't know how. Just stay calm and he'll probably tire himself out in a few days.'

The newcomers laughed.

Still trying to free herself from Pross's grip, Sarah said, 'You can. You're big enough, use violence.'

Pross looked at Ron.

Ron looked at Pross, then at Sarah, then back at Pross. Then he began a menacing walk over to him. But before he'd managed three steps, Pross made noises of pain and submission, let go of Sarah and rolled up into a ball, whimpering.

Sarah-Jane was disgusted. 'Aw, get up will you, he hasn't even hit you yet.'

Pross began crawling away, insisting that it hadn't been fear of Ron that had brought him so swiftly to his knees. 'My socks started pinching,' he told her.

Sarah laughed.

Ron and the others, whom he'd met at Pete's, left for the living room while Pross took the opportunity of Sarah's elevated mood to get some more pleading done. Sitting, rather sadly, on the bed, he said, 'Please give me her phone number. Me and Jennifer are soul mates.'

Sitting down beside him, Sarah now seemed almost sympathetic. 'You've never even met her, Pross. You don't even know what she looks like.'

'She looks like you,' he said, 'except more virginal.'

'No she doesn't,' countered Sarah, ignoring the insult.

'Yes she does. Lots more.'

Also ignoring the further insult, leaning over to reach her shoulder bag, which was on the floor beside the bed, Sarah asserted, 'No she doesn't. This is what she looks like.' Delving into the bag, she retrieved a wallet, and from the wallet, she retrieved a photograph, handing it to Pross. 'Well, it's what she looked like last year. Her hair's different now.'

It was a devastating transaction. Pross was transfixed, able only to murmur, 'It's her. It's her.'

Sarah-Jane soon gave up on him and went to join Ron and the others.

1.7
Stoned Again

Other people had now arrived, and a sort of party was happening in Pross's living room. Ron had been so excited about getting a new load of dope he'd bought some beers and invited people around to celebrate. But it had taken a full half hour for Pross to recover sufficiently from the initial mesmerizing effects of Jennifer's photograph for him to rejoin reality, by which time the party was in full-slump.

Eventually he wandered into the living room, playing the fool, gazing at the photo, still murmuring, 'It's her... it's her...'

'Who?' asked Pete as he peered over Pross's shoulder. Pete looked like Ringo Starr on hunger strike.

'It's her.'

'Who?'

'Her. My dream. My dream walks the Earth.'

Ron came over to determine what the fuss was all about.

He inspected the photo.

'Oh God, you've done it now,' he told Sarah with a heavy tone of foreboding.

'Done what?' she asked.

'Disturbed the peace for the next six-months, that's all,' he complained.

Although the photo was a little blurred and grainy, Jennifer's looks did seem devastating. Her eyes were as blue as the Caribbean in summer. Her hair was blonde and long, with gentle ringlets. Her lips were full and sensual.

The photograph had been taken by Sarah on Jennifer's seventeenth birthday. Even though she appeared quite happy in the photo, Pross nevertheless felt he could discern a certain quality in her mien; an enchanting, pensive sadness that suggested and hinted at a mysterious inner sorrow. A far-away, melancholy look. A waiting for a prince look, he romantically decided.

He was now lost in a world of silent grief. He knew that life without Jennifer would be sterile and impoverished. He lay on his back on the floor near the gas fire, holding the photo at arms length above him. He lay that way until Ron took pity on him and insisted he partake of a pipe.

'Fuck off, I'm in love,' growled Pross. But almost immediately he realised what he'd turned down and snatched the pipe from Ron, taking a long draw on it as if were nepenthes itself.

Handing the pipe back to Ron, Pross resumed his adoration of Jennifer's image.

'Fancy her, then?' asked Ron.

Pross turned his melancholy eyes towards Ron and answered, 'Lots and lots, Ronald. Lots and lots.'

'Never mind, you'll be bored with wanting her this time next week. You always are.'

'Not this time, Ronald. Not this time. The search is over.'

Ronald snidely chuckled. 'I've heard *that* before.'

Pross sighed feebly. 'You don't understand, Ronald. She's my life. Without her my existence will be but a mechanical thing. A spiritless animation, cold and without heart. She's...'

'Well, that's a twat, isn't it?' Ron cut in rudely, then wandered off to speak with Melanie.

With her long brown curly hair, pixy-like face, deep brown eyes and ballet dancer's physique, Melanie, Lilith's older sister, was fortunate enough not to look much like Lilith at all.

Over the years since first encountering her at school, Pross had fallen in love with Melanie more than two hundred separate times, but had never once given her the satisfaction of knowing .

She used to tease him when they were young.

Melanie was now married to Tony, a psychiatrist.

It was generally agreed that Tony should apply his knowledge and training to sorting out Pross's peculiar head, something which Pross himself found rather insulting. 'Tony couldn't even analyse my arse,' he would say, if he ever deigned to say anything at all.

Soon Pross, too, was slumped: the pipe, plus three or four more, had got the job done. A calm had descended upon him, and the music playing in the background — Mike Oldfield's *Ommadawn* — filled and cloyed his senses. He lay back to quietly enjoy the evening, like everyone else was doing. Anywhere else, dope tended to make him anxious and paranoid, but not when he was at home with his friends. Here it made him serene.

Closing his eyes, he began to imagine he was in a soft fresh wind beside a mountain waterfall.

Everything was light and airy.

Opening his eyes after what seemed a long while, he found Sarah to be near him. She looked more alluring than ever. Softer, lambent and dream-like.

Sarah caught his eye and smiled. 'Stoned?' she asked.

'Stoned? Fucking fossilized.'

He continued to gaze with appreciation at Sarah-Jane.

'Why do you keep looking at me?' she asked amusedly after a little while.

'Aesthetic reasons,' said Pross.

'Aesthetic reasons?'

'Yeah. Mind you,' he warned, 'I think you ought to know that if you get just the slightest bit more beautiful you could explode.'

'I shouldn't wish to explode,' she said.

'Well you will,' warned Pross, 'if you don't do something to make yourself ugly. Be very careful, you're borderline.'

'Why should I explode?'

'Don't you keep up with the discoveries of science? Nothing perfect can last, you know. It's been proven. Only at the big bang were things mathematically perfect and symmetrical. Then the symmetry broke down and the imperfect evolved. Eventually we got Ron.'

Sarah cast him a look.

'Get any prettier,' he continued, 'and you could be the next big bang. I'm scared shitless my hair'll detonate.'

Pross suddenly messed his hair up a bit, just in case, and Sarah pulled a twisty face, just in case.

They smiled at their shared joke.

Melanie unsteadily lifted herself out of the armchair beside which Pross was lying. From the kitchen, where her husband was, she could hear a high-spirited commotion developing, and she was off to investigate.

Sarah capitalised on the seat vacancy, sprawling out in the chair just deserted.

Ron also went to the kitchen.

Pross sat up, still mumbling fearfully about the big bang and exploding babes. He looked at Sarah: she pulled another face to stop him worrying. He smiled gratefully, and settled back against the side of the armchair holding her.

A minute passed during which Pross stared pensively at his own hands. Eventually he revealed what was on his mind. 'Are you sure you're not Tess,' he asked without looking up.

'Cross my heart,' she said.

'I thought I'd finally found her when I saw you,' he sighed. 'I've made mistakes in the past, but I was certain you were really her.'

'I'm sorry,' she said tenderly, wondering if he actually *was* mad.

He put a brave face on it. 'I suppose I'll just have to keep on searching.'

Then he twisted around to look inquiringly at Sarah. 'Would you like to hear a short story I read once?'

Sarah lightly touched his shoulder. 'All right,' she said.

Pross made himself a little more comfortable, ready to recite the story he knew by heart.

'Once upon a time,' he began in the traditional style, 'there was a brilliant physicist called Godfrey who succeeded in producing the Equation of Everything. He was a white-haired, kindly old professor, and, like many of the people working in his field, he had grown old, weary and sad-eyed trying to develop the elusive theory that successfully unifies all the forces of nature into a single one.'

Pross held up a single finger and said, 'Just one.'

'I'm with you,' said Sarah, also holding up a finger. 'Just one.'

He continued the story.

'After years of work, inspiration and collaboration, one night, in his study at home, Godfrey realised he was finally getting somewhere. The previously accepted unification of electricity and magnetism was wrong, he sensed. It was an erroneous and misleading theory. It had seemed to work before, but that was only coincidental, like the old belief that the sun revolved around the Earth each day.'

Pross swung his left arm around in a wide arc to graphically illustrate the sun seemingly traversing the sky.

'Godfrey swept aside the old theory of electromagnetism and replaced it with one of his own. He felt full of wonder. As the night wore on, working without rest, he pulled into his new theory other forces... gravity... the strong nuclear force... the weak nuclear force: they were all methodically slotted in turn. All forces were now at the behest of Godfrey's powerful mathematics.'

Pross meaningfully cupped his hands together to symbolise this unity.

Sarah listened with interest.

'The resulting single equation was a sprawling monstrosity, tens of dozens of pages long with hundreds of variables, but it *felt* right. The more Godfrey reflected upon his discoveries, the more phenomena he realised they explained. Matter was easily explained: it was just a special manifestation of energy. Time, he realised, was merely an illusory symptom of entropy — the decay of the universe as an ordered system. He realised that, except as a measure of the inconsequential dissolution of atomic order — order he termed 'arbitrary order,' like, say, the atoms that make up a cat — time was non-existent. And as for space, it became a simple function of the effect of forces upon dimensionality. Yes, he was getting close to the universal truth. All parts of the jigsaw fitted, but the picture was far too large for him to be able to see it all at once. 'The equations must be simpler,' he told himself, 'they must reduce.' Throughout the next day he worked with perfect precision on the piles of formulae — integrating; cancelling like terms; amalgamating different aspects — and as each action brought him closer to a complete understanding of the discovery, he felt a growing "oneness". He was performing a sublime, mystical act, he felt. A sacred act.'

The story teller took a sip of beer from a can that Sarah proffered.

'Finally,' Pross continued, 'the complexities dwindled entirely away, and he began to apperceive the whole. His last mathematical act brought him complete comprehension of all the laws of nature. He hurriedly cancelled the remaining terms of the ultimate equation, and found that he was left with only $x = x$. And at that moment, the moment of understanding, his mind became one with all, all with one; and for as long as it pleased him to behold it, all was formless and symmetrical in the mind of Godfrey. Then He said, 'Let there be light!' and there *was* light, a mighty *explosion* of light, such was the glory of Godfrey. And when He eventually become lonely, He simply made some friends.'

Pross looked at Sarah; she at him.

'That was nice,' she said. 'Is there any more?'

'The rest is history,' he returned.

'Who wrote it?' she asked.

'I did, last week,' answered Pross.

Sarah thought for a moment.

'I thought you said you'd *read* it?'

'I did read it,' he explained. 'I wrote it first, then I read it back to check for spelling mistakes.'

Sarah laughed and draped her hand over Pross's shoulder. 'You're crazy,' said she.

'Lend me a fish,' said he, and Sarah laughed again.

He looked up into her eyes, and said quietly, 'Tell me your sister's address so I can send her flowers and stuff. And orientate my prayer mat. And visit her in my dreams.'

Deliberating for a moment, Sarah said, 'She'd like flowers. 94 Dene Terrace.'

'And her phone number.'

'Not a chance.'

Pross called out, 'Ron, lend me twenty quid so I can send Sarah's sister some flowers.'

'Piss off, pervert,' was the return call from the kitchen.

1.8
Blue Again

As the evening wore on, Pross became unusually subdued. A cloud of gloom, named *For want of Jennifer*, had descended upon him, and he could not shake it, nor even see a way forward through its impenetrable, beguiling mists.

Love had laid him low.

In fact, he looked so sad that Sarah-Jane actually volunteered to introduce her sister to him under strictly controlled conditions. 'She's not very confident,' she explained, 'and quite shy.'

'When?' asked Pross, pitiful yet hopeful.

'After I get back from holiday with Ron.'

'Holiday?' he said, jolted.

Sarah looked surprised. 'Didn't Ron tell you? He asked me to go away with him. We're setting off early tomorrow.'

'Holiday?' he again said. 'You can't, I need you here. I love your sister.'

'I'll be back on Friday,' she consoled.

'Friday? Just think of all the suicides I'll face.' Sighing heavily, he slumped down in his chair, staring into the distance.

Many moments passed.

With his focus still set at infinity, he resignedly asked, 'Where are you going?'

'Iceland,' answered Sarah.

'Iceland? What in the fuck is there to do in Iceland?'

'Don't know,' she said, 'but Ron has to go there for a fortnight to work. He asked me to go along for the trip, so, seeing that it's reading week and I won't have any lecturing to do...'

'Reading week?'

'Half-term break, to you, Pross. Seeing that it's reading week, I said yes. But I've got to be back by Friday to play in that production at the Arts Centre. It's being staged that night.'

He continued to stare demurely into the distance, and, feeling sorry for his lovelorn plight, Sarah offered some solace. She knelt beside him and spoke kindly, holding his limp, lifeless hand in hers. 'Oh please cheer up, won't you?'

'Cheer up? Cheer up?' said Pross. 'How can I cheer up without Jennifer?'

Sarah once again gave up on him, returning her attention to Ron. Soon they were billing and cooing in the armchair they were sharing, discussing their Iceland plans. Ron, if he got time, wanted to look at volcanos, and Sarah wanted to look at glaciers.

Near to midnight, the guests began leaving.

Presently, Sarah announced that she, too, was going, explaining that she had to get back to pack her things because they were catching an early flight.

'Don't go,' Pross suddenly said, sitting by the gas fire which was giving the only light in the room, 'you're genetically similar to Jennifer.'

Sarah patted Pross patronisingly on the head. 'I like you very much,' she said, 'even though you're a bit mental. I'll see you next Friday, maybe, if you're down the Arts Centre. The performance ends at about ten o'clock.'

'I'll come earlier to see you play.'

'You can't. It's only for people connected with my university faculty.' She kissed him goodbye. 'You can keep the photo for a while, since it means so much to you.'

And then she was gone.

Sarah's unexpected gesture charmed Pross, for it has to be said that Northerners of the opposite sex seldom kiss each other goodbye, even the closest of friends. Where Pross came from they're more likely to *punch* each other goodbye. Twice if they're family.

A few minutes after she left, Pross raised the Iceland subject with Ron. 'I hear you're going away tomorrow.'

'Yep,' Ron replied happily. 'Anyway, what do you mean you *hear* that I'm going away? I told you myself loads of times.'

'Did you? To Iceland?'

'Yep. A fortnight in Reykjavik installing a computer system for my firm.'

'With Sarah?'

'Yep, until she leaves for home on Friday. Romantic, ain't it?'

A short silence.

'I may not be here when you get back,' said Pross.

'Oh, is that so? Where will you be?'

Pross's answer came in the form of a dejected shuffle to his bedroom, mumbling something about injecting himself with *Domestos* and how everyone would miss him when he's gone and wish they'd been nicer to him while they'd had the chance.

Having withdrawn to his room, he set about getting some serious pining done over Jennifer. He removed from a frame a signed photograph of Rolf Harris (a photo which Ron had bought for £1.50 at a charity auction the month before and had given to Pross as a surprise present, initiating his crush on the Aussie), replacing it with the photo of Jennifer. He then set

Jennifer on the table, next to his computer, lighting a candle to illuminate her reverently.

He sighed loudly while putting a Nick Drake album on his record player. There must be more to life than being me, he thought. Nick's guitar began to weep. To the sound of the sobbing, he switched off the main room light and lay on his bed to gaze at Jennifer's highlighted image. Under the influence of Mr Drake's plaintive songs and Jennifer's painfully beautiful likeness, Pross soon began to feel therapeutically suicidal.

Despairing suicidally about the Jenniferlessness aspect of his life led Pross to despair suicidally about his life in general (although this sort of grim and sober life-assessment was standard despondency for the night before he had to get up early to sign on). Jennifer might be a new and lancinating pain in Pross's life, but signing on was a chronic ache. He was now suffering routine fortnightly pre-signing-on blues, suffering routinely marginally outweighed by Christ-I-actually-managed-to-get-up-and-do-it-post-signing-on relief and giro-arrival-day giddiness.

Every other Sunday night, Pross would resolve to get his life in order. To Pross "order" meant being dead and (hopefully) lamented by thousands of beautiful, weeping nymphs. These thousands of nymphs would be clad in black lace, standing solemnly in line, awaiting their turn to adorn his grave with flowers. In his imagination, having made a pilgrimage to his tomb, each nymph would then go sadly away, brokenhearted, to devote the rest of their chaste lives to writing endless volumes of sentimental poetry that bemoaned his demise and pointed out what an exceptionally nice bloke he had been and what great hair he'd had.

His imagination soon took him to realms of even greater unlikeliness.

He now pictured Sarah-Jane, half mad with grief, clad in her Victorian garb. Heedless to time and inanition, she is intensely and wildly playing requiem cello for her lost love beside his Gothic tomb in some lonely, time-forgotten English country churchyard. He pictured a sorrowful Jennifer, her face drawn, ashen and pale, veiled in diaphanous black lace. He pictured her china-blue eyes suffusing with tears as she kneels down to his grave to tenderly brush away with her gloved hand the fallen autumn leaves. And as Jennifer weeps, Sarah's plangent threnodies fill the still air. And all about in the moody welkin above, wet-eyed clouds gather in mournful solemnity to darkly veil the sky summer knew blue.

He didn't picture Lilith at all.

After having adequately indulged himself with lush, therapeutic visions of lamenting nymphs, Pross set his clock-radio for 7am before slipping in-between the sheets. It was now almost 4am, and he suspected that getting out of bed only three hours after getting into it might prove to be beyond his powers.

Once in bed, he reflected sadly on summer's passing.

Autumn never failed to strike at Pross's heart and imbue him with melancholy.

He began to compose a bad poem lamenting Summer's death:
In me thou mayst perceive a sadness
That springs from that which undoes spring...
But he fell asleep.

1.9
Signing On

Morning.

Strictly a thing of science fiction to Pross.

An eerie, weird world where an unfamiliar sun hangs low in the sky, illuminating alien thralls trudging grimly to their places of toil.

Pross's clock-radio went off. *Welcome to the planet Morning*, it said.

He reached sleepily for the flex and yanked the plug out of the socket. 'Sod off, Morning,' he muttered.

He fell asleep.

Lying in bed doesn't get the rent paid when there's signing on to be done. No one knew this better than Ron, who had a vested interest in Pross's unemployment: Housing Benefit.

Whenever Pross exhibited a determination to sleep rather than to sign on, Ron would take it upon himself to rouse him.

A quilt pulled off and thrown out of the window...

A firework tossed into the bedroom...

Or, like today, a dousing with a cup of ice cold water.

'Aaarrrrggghhh! You bastard!' screamed Pross, leaping up in shock.

'See you in a fortnight,' laughed Ron, fleeing to his car.

Might as well sign on while I'm up, thought Pross.

After a cup of tea and a bowl of cereal, he took a shower and then made a special effort with his hair until satisfaction was achieved. He was now ready to show himself to the sort-of-cute girl he sort-of-fancied at the dole office.

The time at which he had to sign on was nine o'clock.

The October morning air was heavy, saturated with the smell of damp autumn decay. A persistence of morning mist added extra beauty to his half-mile walk along the river bank into town.

The dole office was crowded. Pross used to take a magazine with him to read while he was in the queue, but of late had just looked at the floor. Today, however, he'd brought along the picture of Jennifer to gaze at while the queue shuffled and inched forward.

Unfortunately, the sort-of-cute girl wasn't anywhere to be seen. Regrettably, staffing the claims counter was the DSS's answer to Heinrich Himmler. Most of the office staff were pleasant and polite to the public, but not the woman on signing duty this day.

Her name was Richardson. Richardson was her surname, and Pross doubted very much if she had a first name: she just didn't look like she'd suit having one.

Today, Richardson, for an unknown reason, had her neck supported in a plaster collar. Pross wondered if it might be because someone had tried to hang her. And why not? He knew that every doley in Durham hated her. Often, while waiting in the queue, he had therapeutic, fanciful visions of furtive, skulking groups of depressed doleys (the more desperate, down-market types) meeting within tumbledown derelict houses to plot the old bag's assassination in hushed but vengeful voices.

To say that Richardson was an "old bag" was not exactly correct. She certainly was a bag, but she was far from being chronologically old. She just looked it. In actual fact, Richardson was probably no more than three or four years older than Pross himself, but since she looked and acted old, then that's how he thought of her: as old.

This day, she was being particularly haughty and superior. The office system had just been computerised and, as part of the new way of doing things, she got to ask each person if their circumstances had changed in any way since they'd last signed. If the answer was no, then the computer files needed no updating and the claim was speedily dealt with by the machine.

As each claimant arrived at the front of the queue, Richardson asked, 'any changes?' The answer was no each time. It was procedure, but Pross could tell that for Richardson it was a way to bring home to the claimant their unchanging poverty, state of joblessness and inferiority to her.

'Any changes?' said Richardson.

'No,' replied the miserable claimant quietly.

'Any changes?' Richardson said to the next person.

'No.'

Pross's turn. Richardson knew him by sight, and entered his annoying name into the desk-terminal.

'Any changes?'

Pross looked up from the photo. 'What?'

Richardson spoke to him as if he was retarded. 'Any changes since you last signed?'

'Of course there have been changes,' he returned, 'nothing sublunary endures...' He held out the photo for Richardson to see, 'except my love. Only my love endures. Only the immortal love of a true poet like me is immutable.'

Richardson was annoyed. She hated smart doleys.

'I meant,' she said crossly, 'have there been any changes in your circumstances?'

He thought for a few seconds.

'I've had a haircut. I suppose you noticed my magnificence in that department straightaway, though.'

Richardson wasn't going to bandy words any longer. With inadequately concealed relish, she said, 'Right. That's it. If you don't give me a proper answer this time, I'll disqualify your claim. Any changes?'

'No. No changes,' he said with a smirk, though he was feeling slightly miffed with himself for having just capitulated to society.

Richardson retrieved Pross's claim file from the drawer below the desk for him to sign. Opening it, she discovered a note inside that gave instructions to suspend all payments to him until he'd been interviewed by the inspector.

Pross was told to wait.

He waited.

And waited.

The inspector appeared.

Pross inspected the inspector. He was young, with a thin face and square, gold-rimmed glasses. He was wearing a grey suit which he didn't fill.

The inspector led Pross up a staircase and into a room that contained only a table and two chairs. The walls were painted an insipid yellow. The rushed brush strokes had set hard and visible in the emulsion. The table was unadorned except for a trapezoidal paperweight about four inches long that bore the name *John Booth* in stick-on letters.

He invited Pross to take a seat.

Booth explained that he had to get some papers from another room.

He was gone a long time.

When he returned to the room, he placed himself down in the chair across the table from Pross.

Half a minute of silence passed while Booth arranged some papers on the desk, glancing through them to refresh his memory. Eventually he looked up.

'Good morning, sir,' the inspector began in an officious manner. 'My name's John Booth and I'm an inspector for the DSS. The reason we've called you in is to determine what efforts you've been making to find employment. This is necessary because firstly you failed to attend a compulsory Restart interview at the jobcentre, and secondly, when you were given another interview date, you attended but were uncooperative with the interviewing officer, refusing even to complete the form that helps them to decide your claim eligibility.'

'But I did fill in the form.'

'Yes, you did,' conceded Booth, 'but not to their satisfaction.'

'It's not my fault they're so fussy.'

Booth retrieved the contentious form from a cardboard folder in his briefcase, holding it gingerly by one corner, as if fearing some suspected miasma, some contagious insanity, maybe. He spread it out on the desktop, cast a disapproving eye over it, then spun it around with a fingertip, presenting it to Pross as conclusive evidence of his uncooperative nature. He then spun it back around again and began reading selected parts in a disdainful voice. 'Name: Prospero Pi-Meson...'

'That's Melanie's fault.'

'Age: weary. What type of job are you looking for? peadriatic gynaecologist. How far are you prepared to travel daily to get to work? no further than the 18th century. What type of work have you usually done? paper round. Do you have any health problems that affect your ability to gain employment? progressive melancholia and poet's constitution...'

'The melancholia's a lot worse today.'

The Inspector gave a stare of disapproval.

'It seems,' he said, 'that you're making little effort at all to help yourself find work.'

'Fair comment,' said Pross. 'I'd stop my dole if I were in your shoes.'

But Booth seemed angered by Pross's arrogant honesty. 'Tell me what efforts you've been making to find employment,' he sharply said.

'None at all,' answered Pross.

'Why not?'

'Pointless. I wouldn't last ten minutes.'

Booth drew an elaborate deep breath and held it for longer than was strictly physiologically necessary. 'What sort of job would you like?'

With a finger pressed to his lips, Pross mused for a few moments. 'I'd like a job working with old people,' he finally decided. 'I'd like to make things out of old people: baskets and furniture, things like that, all made out of old people.' He brought his hands up to the desktop and worked and formed imaginary things with them to demonstrate his keenness and ability to make things out of geriatrics.

Booth began smouldering. 'Don't you realise,' he said, his glasses slipping down his nose, 'that if you can't convince me of your willingness to work you'll have your benefit withheld?'

'Of course I realise. I've already advised you to withhold it.'

'Then why are you being so defiant?'

'Defiant?' echoed Pross, then, losing patience, said tersely, 'Look, just go ahead and do whatever your job requires you to do, or even whatever you personally want to do, just don't expect me to show an interest, that's all.'

Booth pushed his glasses back and threw Pross a reproachful look. 'You're your own worst enemy!' he exclaimed with a sudden eruption, snatching up the paperweight bearing his name. 'How do you expect to get a job with that stupid name of yours?'

'I told you, the name's Melanie's fault,' said Pross at the moment Booth slammed the paperweight down, generating a loud crack that he seemed surprised to find he'd caused. 'Wow,' said Pross. 'Spectacular stuff. Are you allowed to hit me as well?'

Ignoring that remark, Booth composed himself, then returned to procedure. 'Are there any questions you wish to ask?'

'Yes,' responded Pross with a serious look. 'Yes, there is one important thing I'd like to ask.' He paused there for dramatic effect, and, leaning towards Booth slightly, said: 'Who stole the dope plant from my garden?'

Booth was silent for a few seconds before saying, 'I have to inform you that from this day forth your benefit is suspended. You may appeal to an independent tribunal if you wish. Do you wish to appeal?'

'No.'

'Then the interview is at a close. Good day, sir.'

Booth collected his papers, slipped them into his briefcase and stood up.

Pross also stood up. 'Actually, there is one thing about my claim I'd like to know,' he said.

'What's that?'

'Am I entitled to redundancy money? I must be, I've been coming here for six years.'

Booth made a show of ignoring the question. He walked past Pross to get to the door, a little apprehensively because experience had taught him that occasionally some disinherited Durham doleys suddenly became raging psychos.

Booth opened the door and hurried out.

With a minor sense of piety now rising within him, Pross left the building, sort of pleased with himself for not having lied to protect his claim as he had done on similar occasions.

Coming out on to the street, he strongly felt that he would not be visiting that building again so long as he lived. That chapter was over.

Pross couldn't imagine ever going back there. He couldn't imagine joining that miserable queue once more, though he'd never really felt part of it, even when he was in its midst. He knew that he was far from being a typical claimant. That surely wasn't what his life was about. He'd always had a powerful feeling that he was merely biding his time. Whatever he was biding his time *for* he had no idea, but he certainly was biding it.

And if the worst came to the worst, he thought, he could always make a start on a proper novel. Maybe that would pay the rent?

But apart from that, something was bound to turn up. Something *had* to turn up, because he just couldn't imagine ever going back to that office again and dealing with Richardson or Booth, or seeing the sad, embarrassed, bitter people in the queue.

Fuck her, he thought; fuck him, fuck them all. He'd had quite enough of signing on. He didn't think he should have to do it. What he should be able to do was sign on the sick. People who are physically disabled receive acknowledgement of their plight and receive a state allowance — was *he* not also disabled? According to his friends, he certainly was: he needed his head examining, did he not? According to himself, he was simply mentally incompatible with society, and this meant that he would never be able to do a day of work to the satisfaction of an employer. He liked to think also that it meant he would never shoot a bent and toothless grandmother in the belly because a superior officer had told him to do it.

He might do it for his own reasons, but never because he'd been ordered.

A true welfare state would recognise this condition and make provision for people like him for whom life was a struggle against seriousness, herd instincts and getting up early to arrive at work on time — especially the getting up early. A *true* welfare state would provide a generous *poet benefit*, payable to all sensitive souls.

Poet benefit didn't exist, but maybe he actually *could* sign on the sick? Signing on the sick wasn't much of a career, but he wasn't really after much. Signing on the sick might do him just fine. It had all the security and promotional opportunities that he wanted from a career, and it paid enough for his basic needs too. So fuck them again with wire wool, he thought, and headed home.

Over a cup of tea back home, Pross decided that things really were going to have to change because his life was a mess: his dole money had been suspended and he was in love with a girl who didn't know he existed.

Two big problems.

He just had to get some money from somewhere because the only money he had was three pounds fifty that a particularly desperate search of Ron's bedroom that morning had uncovered.

Things really were going to have to change.

In a flash of self-belief and confidence, he resolved to begin a new life. A life of achievement. A life of productivity. He would be tenacious and conquering. He would be calculating and successful. He would be realistic and sensible.

He resolved to solve the two big problems in his life without delay. 'Procrastination is the thief of time,' he informed the cat, which was curled up on a chair.

About the problem of Jennifer, there were two options: he could wait for Sarah-Jane to return from her holiday with Ron and hope that one day she would bring Jennifer to see him, or he could send Jennifer a revealing, confessional love letter.

Prospero Pi-Meson thought about the problem realistically and sensibly.

He decided to send Jennifer a revealing, confessional love letter.

Jennifer became the second person to receive his current favourite love letter. And just in case *she* also freaked and sent the police around to get him — he was beginning to learn his lesson — he decided to omit his address.

Anyway, he suspected that a bit of mystery would not go amiss in romance.

> DYSTOPIA (Ghetto End)
> TARTARUS.

My Dearest Jennifer,

Must the death-moth be my mournful Psyche? Must I twist wolfs-bane for its poisonous vine? Suffer my forehead to be kissed by nightshade?...

Etc.

He went out to post the letter.

And when he got back home, he turned his attention to the other big issue affecting his life: money.

About the money problem, he saw three options open to him: he could try to suppress his personality, get a job and possibly make it to the top; he could lie and grovel to the independent tribunal and continue signing on; or he could get himself declared mentally ill and claim invalidity benefit for the rest of his life.

Prospero Pi-Meson thought about the problem realistically and sensibly... and decided to get himself declared mentally ill. Melanie's husband was crucial to the plan. Tony was a hospital psychiatrist with the power to declare him unfit for work.

Tony held a clinic at the local health centre on Tuesday mornings, Pross knew. That was tomorrow. Tomorrow morning he would see Tony and get official, hopefully profitable, recognition of the state of his mind.

This was radical stuff: he hadn't got up on two consecutive mornings since the third form at school. This was the stuff of success, he sensed. It was a sure thing, he felt, that he would qualify for mental money if he just put his mind to it. He could fake schizophrenia, or something like that. Tony wouldn't know the difference.

After making this decision, he went out to a shop and bought, with the little money he'd found in Ron's room, a bag of potatoes, a can of beans, some sausages and some milk to sustain him until his mental money came through.

Then he went back home to spend the remainder of the day resting before the big push tomorrow.

And at three in the morning he wrote a message in big, vibrant letters on a large sheet of paper:

> **GET UP, YOU LAZY BASTARD**

This sign he stuck on the ceiling above his bed to encourage him to rise early in the morning, then he snuggled under the duvet.

1.10
Jennifer

John was lying drowsily in Jennifer's bed when a letter from someone called Prospero Pi-Meson arrived.

John had ambivalent feelings about Jennifer, like always wanting to be with her, but often not wanting her with him.

Jennifer was a feather in John's cap. He felt proud when she joined him and his friends in the local bars, even though she didn't like any of his friends and often told him so. But, with typical ambivalence, he often wished she'd stay at home because she humiliated him with her growing moodiness, no longer smiling dutifully and compliantly at his jokes.

Jennifer was often at a loss now to understand what she'd ever seen in John and why she continued seeing him when he was home on leave, although when she thought honestly about it, she knew exactly why — habit.

Jennifer's boyfriend had hair the colour of dry clay and eyes that could only see what they looked at. He liked to watch football matches with a couple of cans of lager beside him, and could actually become happier if one side won rather than the other.

John had been one of the first to ask Jennifer out. The boys in her school had been too fatuous for her to bother with at the time: he had appeared so mature and exciting by comparison. That had been when her sister was in the final year of her music degree, three months before her parents had died. Her parents had tacitly disapproved of John, but when she moved in with her aunt, John was smiled upon because he seemed polite and steady and because he came from a good family. Since then, no one else acceptable had had the temerity to approach Jennifer.

Without knowing it, Jennifer engendered feelings of inadequacy in sensitive people. They couldn't believe that she could ever be interested in them, and never dared to think that they could ever get off with her. Not only that, but some kind of spooky instinct for emotional survival seemed to be at play, creating a fear of ever being her lover. Instincts told that just one week spent with her; a week of her honey smiles; a week of holding her hand; a week of her lush kisses; seven nights of her soft body, might be all that it would take for peace of mind to be lost forever should caprice take her to someone else's loving.

Jennifer's boyfriend was now threatening to beat up Prospero Pi-Meson, whoever he was, for "trying it on with his girl", and was accusing *her* of some kind of complicity and despicable unfaithfulness.

'You must know who sent it,' John insisted, fury rising, intercepting her as she headed for the front door to go to work.

'For the fiftieth time, I don't,' she declared, turning up the collar of her shiny black raincoat and checking herself in the mirror by the door. 'I haven't a clue.'

He didn't believe her.

'That can't be his name,' he decided, 'no one has a name like that. Bet it's that sod you work with.'

Jennifer dismissed the possibility with an exasperated sigh. 'It wouldn't be him.' She pulled the coat's belt tight around her waist. 'Anyway, it's got a Durham postmark. And I don't work with him, he's the vet's son. And he hardly ever comes near me.'

'Your sister's in Durham,' John remarked with overtones.

'No she's not,' Jennifer said to him in the mirror, 'she's in Iceland with some bloke called Ron. She left a message with Elaine yesterday. And why should she want to send it?'

John had to admit that Sarah would have no reason.

'I'll cripple the git when I catch him,' he said, tearing the letter up, 'whoever it was.'

'Don't rip it!' she said, turning to face him.

'Why not?' he questioned, throwing the pieces at her. 'You don't want to keep it, do you?'

'Because it's not yours to rip up, that's why.' She rescued the pieces from the floor. 'Anyway, I don't know why you're getting so bloody riled, it's just a silly letter.'

'Silly. Bloody crazy, you mean. Looks like something a lunatic would write. All that stuff about death.'

Huffishly, she responded, 'Oh, they're just metaphors.'

'You what?' said John, suddenly kicking the skirting board in frustration. His trousers were the very latest in regional fashion. So was his cropped hair, shaved at the back and sides and flat on top. 'The bastard.'

'Be quiet,' ordered Jennifer testily. 'Elaine's just gone to bed. She's on nights this week, as if you didn't know.'

Elaine was the girl Jennifer shared the flat with. She was two years older than Jennifer, not very bright, plain bordering on attractive, with a full figure, and she worked as a Quality Control Inspector at a clothing factory.

Elaine didn't really like Jennifer much, although Jennifer never suspected it because relations between them were always cordial and because she'd never given Elaine a single reason *to* dislike her.

Elaine, to use her own vernacular, thought that Jennifer was snobby and full of herself. A lot of this was simply because Jennifer kept very much to herself, mostly preferring the quiet of her own room to Elaine's indifferent company, and because she didn't "mix" with Elaine's friends when they came around.

John was still fuming.

'Look,' said Jennifer, 'I really don't know why you're getting so upset.'

'He's a bloody weirdo, that's why. What kind of headcase does something like that?'

Jennifer turned petulantly to face him. 'The kind of headcase called Prospero,' she answered.

'So you *do* know him,' accused John.

'I don't!'

'Then how do you know he's the kind of person to do it?'

'John,' said Jennifer coldly, 'I'm going to work.'

She opened the door and left. John slammed it angrily behind her and went back to bed.

Pross awoke abruptly and actually got up on time to begin the first day of his new life: today was the day he would convince the medical profession, represented by Tony, that he was insane.

He put his clothes on and opened his bedroom door to let the cat in.

'Hello, Mr Spock,' he said. 'Allow me to introduce myself. I am Pross, your new master. Your old master, Pross, is gone. Old Pross moped too much and didn't get things done. He has been replaced.'

Spock rubbed up against his leg like an old friend.

The high pressure that four days earlier had brought the season's first frost had now moved back inland, returning bright, clear weather to the north of England.

Outside the health centre, he contemplated taking all his clothes off for Tony's benefit, but thought better of it. He didn't want to overdo things. Tony might have him locked up in a loony bin — he could be a bit prudish at times. Mental, but not too mental, he figured. Nothing too outrageous.

A young nurse with long, straight, flaxen hair and rampaging sky-blue eye-shadow was on duty at the reception. Her face was small and consequently her eyes seemed to bulge out, like a frog's. Despite this, or maybe even because of it, she had a definite physical appeal. She smiled at Pross as he approached, and he nearly fell in love, but the uniform turned him off. 'I have to see Dr Trotter at once,' he informed her.

'Do you have an appointment?'

'No, but he'll see me. I know him, and he said if I ever want help, mentality wise, he'll look at me.'

'Are you registered here?'

'Yes. Long time ago.'

'What name?'

'Prospero Pi-Meson.'

Her small red mouth dropped open ever so slightly so that it formed an almost perfect O.

'Prospero Pi-Meson's your name?'

'Yes. It excites you tremendously, doesn't it?'

Her mouth made another O.

'Your name excites me?'

'No, my haircut. My haircut excites you, doesn't it?'

'Er, yes. It's very nice,' she said, cautiously.

The nurse returned to procedure, warily instructing him to take a seat while she spoke to the doctor.

'I don't want a seat,' he said, 'I've got plenty at home.'

'Pross, hello,' said Tony, with a mixture of compassion and suspicion, coming out into the waiting room to usher Pross through a door and into a consulting room imbued with the smell of surgical spirits. 'You're here to see me in my professional capacity?'

'Hello, Tony,' said Pross in a low voice, sitting down in the seat proffered to him. 'Yes, it's professional. It's the voices. The voices are worrying me.'

Tony, a medium-sized man in his early-thirties with a receding hairline, pale complexion and a wispy, blondish-gingery beard, raised his eyebrows and looked at his patient. 'Voices?' he repeated quietly to himself as he sat down, Pross's medical card in front of him, kneading his cheeks slowly and thoughtfully between the fingers and thumb of his left hand. 'Well, er, Pross, what can I do for you?'

Pross got straight down to business. 'Help me,' he said plainly.

Tony lowered his hand to the table. 'If I can,' he said. 'What's the problem?'

'It's terrible, Tony,' said Pross, 'I think I'm going mad, going out of my mind. Going into it, even, which is a lot worse when you have a mind like mine.'

'I see,' said Tony, kneading his cheeks again. 'And why do you think you're going mad?'

Pross paused, tightened his face into an expression of anxiety, and tensely said, 'Because sometimes I don't hear voices.'

Tony returned his hand to the table, wondering if he'd heard Pross right. 'You *don't* hear voices?'

'That's right,' Pross confirmed, 'sometimes I don't hear voices, and it worries me. I've gone into my mind, right into it, and I need help.'

'You *don't* hear voices?' repeated Tony. 'What sort of voices don't you hear?'

The patient had his routine worked out. 'Nasty cruel voices saying objectionable things about me.'

The oscillating hand went back to work on the doctor's jowls. 'Hmmm. Can you explain in more detail?'

Pross was obliging. 'Certainly,' he said. 'I used to hear people saying objectionable things about me all the time. Things like "Pross, you're a bastard," and "Pross, are you ever going to give me that fiver back?" and "Pross, you're a fool," and "Pross, you're your own worst enemy," and "Pross, you've got your head in the clouds." But now when people say cruel things to me, sometimes I just don't hear them. I can hear the birds singing in the trees above them, I can hear music coming from the radio beside them, I can hear children playing in the street, but I don't hear the disparaging voices...'

Somewhat struck and taken, for the first time, with the allegorical profundity of these rehearsed lines, Pross tailed off and pondered his own words.

'I see,' said the doctor. 'And how long has this been going on?'

Forgetting his own words, he considered the doctor's question a short while. 'Years, now that I think of it.'

The doctor's hand remained around his cheeks. 'I don't believe you,' he said simply. 'You're lying.'

Pross cupped a hand behind his ear. 'Pardon? I can't hear your voice. You'll have to write it down.'

'Pross,' said Tony, beginning to crack a reluctant smile, 'get out and stop wasting my time. I'm not going to sign you on the sick, so don't even try to persuade me.'

Pross was crestfallen. 'Shit,' he moaned. 'Wait a minute, how did you know I want sick pay?'

'Guessed. What were you trying for, anyway? Paranoid schizophrenia?'

'Yeah, something like that. Didn't want to lay it on too heavy in case I was put in a loony bin.'

'Well, I suppose it's the risk you take,' said Tony. 'If you want to malinger, you should try for something less chancy.'

'Like what?' inquired Pross keenly.

'Like backache. You could fool us for years with backache.'

An expression of pain suddenly showed itself on Pross's face. 'Actually,' he said, 'I do have a problem with my back.'

Reluctantly, Tony laughed, but genially indicated with a flutter of his hand that it was time for Pross to leave. 'Pross, as I've said before, you've got a mind as cunning as most any ever devised by nature — use it for work instead of play and you'll go far.'

'I've already gone further than I'd ever planned,' said Pross as he left.

Damn, damn, damn, he cursed to himself on the way home. He was being tormented by growing feelings of inadequacy and ineffectuality. Even though, just like normal people, he'd got up disgustingly early, his new life had come to nought. He still had no income, and Jennifer, as far as he was aware, was still being debauched by someone else.

Damn, damn, damn.

Wrapping her fingers around a mug of hot chocolate during her morning break from assisting the vet, Jennifer had cause to curse herself. Encircling one of those fingers, as heavy as a millstone, as constricting as a noose, was the engagement ring she'd accepted from John the week before.

Why had she said yes? she asked herself again and again. She didn't rightly know why, but it had seemed easier than saying no. When accepting the ring, she'd asked John to keep it secret for the present; but when asked why, she was not able to think of a convincing reason to give him. She just said that she'd prefer it that way for a while.

But John didn't want it that way, and he began to spread the news.

Though John told everyone he met, Jennifer had not yet been able to bring herself to tell anyone about it. Not her aunt, who would have been pleased for her, and certainly not Sarah, who would have hit the roof.

Alone in a room that smelled strongly of surgical spirits, a room where they had put three animals to sleep already that day, she took another sip of her drink.

Finished cursing, Pross now turned his mind to the problems looming over him. How was he going to live? *Could* he get a job? Was stock-market speculation *that* anathema to him? What was he going to eat? What did cat taste like? How many friends did he have who would give him food? How long would they stay his friends? Who would pay the rent? Could he write a best seller before Ron sold the computer? Was there still gold to be viably panned for in the Welsh mountains? How much could he sell one of his kidneys for? Just exactly how many millions of pounds worth of space-race hardware was sitting on the moon waiting to be salvaged by the first person enterprising enough to get there with a wheelbarrow?

Once back in his flat, he went directly to his bed, upon which he lay in sullen contemplation.

He seriously contemplated his future, which was a rare thing for him to do indeed.

After a few minutes, he felt something positive stirring inside his head. This was it, he resolved, this was bloody it: he was going to make a start on proper book. Writing was the only thing he could possibly do for profit.

Yes, he was going to make a real start on a real book.

This was it: a new life. A life of work. A life of success. A life of industry. A life of enterprise.

This really was bloody it, he decided: no more wasting time.

This really was bloody it, he decided: there was no more time left *to* waste.

He craned his neck upward and supported his head with a folded pillow so that his gaze was directed at his potentially word processing computer. He felt that if he could only make his way across the room and switch the machine on, then the battle against his own laziness would be won, and the rest of the course would be plain sailing.

He needed another plot, a plot that would *sell*.

Yes, he was being serious about his writing for once. He had to aim at a *market*. Surely the only market he was qualified to hit was the science fiction one?

A science fiction novel it would be.

The two things he'd written so far were not accessible enough for the typical science fiction reader, he reckoned. Not enough aliens and space travel.

With uncharacteristic dedication and application, he thought and thought... then came up with something.

This is what his idea was all about:

Cosmologists profess that the universe began from a single point in a nothingness vacuum. Well, not quite nothingness, for, they also profess, in the quantum world, vacuums are teeming with fleeting *somethingnesses*. In the quantum world, there are *real* particles, electrons and such, that exist indefinitely, and there are also *virtual* particles, particles which spring into existence on *borrowed* energy. From where is this energy borrowed? From nowhere, that's where. Something from nothing.

These ghost particles constantly spring from nowhere, then fade back into oblivion, owing their brief existence to that phenomenon of uncertainty first uncovered by the physicist, Hiesenberg. They are the products of random statistical fluctuations in energy levels. Over a period of time, just the merest, shortest of time, these fluctuations, these expected statistical quirks, balance out: for every plus, there's a minus, so to speak. It's like rolling a die: do it ten billion times and gross statistical anomalies become statistically unlikely — *but not impossible*.

Once, just once that we know of, the borrowed energy was not immediately paid back. The virtual entity defied the persuasion of statistics, inflated... and lo! the universe was born.

Something from nothing.

Thus the universe is but a gross statistical anomaly.

And every point in space has the frightening potential to spawn a freak universe of its own — honest.

And, in a way, although the universe seems to us to be a whole lot of something, it is still nothing, for when the energies of the whole system are considered, they are found to cancel wonderfully, leaving nothing.

Thus we, the human race, are perhaps no more than opportunists in a cosmic hiccup.

Pross's idea for a story had to do with exploiting the potential of the quantum vacuum for unlimited energy production. He imagined a race of advanced creatures who had just discovered how to engineer somethings from nothings if it pleased them to do so. They were now Lords of Mathematics. They had learned how to load the dice of uncertainty whichever way they chose.

Now, at last, they could really do great things.

So one day a group of the most brilliant creature scientists got together to see if they could apply their new mathematical powers to some practical problems. First of all, they designed and built a bomb which would create a staggeringly big bang — the *ultimate* big bang — whenever detonated. Of course no one intended to use this ultimate bomb because it would destroy everything, but they built it all the same. Their planet's army loved the bomb, stored it, and soon even asked for more like it. Further ultimate bombs were duly supplied. This made a lot of the planet's creatures very uneasy, but their leaders assured them that the bombs would never be used, which, it transpired, was right.

Then the scientists looked at their noble civilisation's energy production methods, and they perceived that there was much room for improvement.

Their planet's existing power stations were scientifically simple but technologically sound fusion reactors. At one end they took in hydrogen — the most abundant element in the universe — and out of the other end was excreted harmless helium and all the energy these creatures needed to live blissfully comfortable lives. These old fashioned reactors were so reliable that not one had failed, caused an injury or polluted their beautiful planet for nearly a thousand years.

They announced that they would replace the hundreds of small fusion reactors scattered higgledy-piggledy about their planet with one enormous centralised Quantum Vacuum Exploiter.

So, with befitting excitement, they hastily designed a new type of power station, one which created a mini-universe in its reactor, sucked out of that universe whatever energy it could get — which was an awful lot — then snuffed that universe out before it ran out of control and inflated at close to the speed of light. It snuffed out the created universe by buggering about with its mathematics so that it merely faded away without so much as a fizz. A dampening equation was injected.

Then it promptly created another universe.

This cycle was repeated once every millionth of a second.

These creatures really were terribly good with numbers and symbols. And they had great confidence in their machines.

The reactor worked admirably. It gave just as much energy to the creatures of the planet as they had enjoyed before, and it could give a lot more if they needed it, which they never did. It worked admirably, that is, until the day when some of the custom mathematics leaked out because an engineer called Upal had neglected to program one of the three hundred computers on the site properly. Upal's beloved creature friend had left him for another creature, and he was very unhappy. Consequently, he was not able to concentrate to his normally high standard.

The actual computer itself suspected a mistake had been made and had tried to alert Upal to query the dubious instructions it had been given. It tried very hard, for a short while, to get its programming corroborated.

But Upal had earlier turned down all the warning systems because the occasional bleeps they made when everything was hunky-dory had begun to irritate him that day.

Like everyone else, he believed that the new reactor was as safe as houses.

The computer, with computer quickness, decided that it must have been given the right instructions after all, and it followed them to the letter, number and symbol.

The computer didn't know about creature love and how it can befuddle organic brains.

The computer in question had a crucial role to play in the functioning of the power station. Its job was to govern the dimensional shielding that kept new universe and old universe apart. It achieved this by maintaining a ten dimensional sphere around the created universe. This sphere was forever twisting in on itself like a revolving spiral. It was forever going into its own centre. Forever evaginating.

Eventually satisfied that it had been given the right instructions by engineer Upal, the computer swung into action, and because of its remiss programming, it allowed a tiny wisp of custom mathematics to leak out of the reactor core. This wisp of poisonous mathematics proceeded to corrupt and contaminate the real universe in all directions at the speed of light.

The speed of light.

No one could see this tidal wave of dangerous mathematics coming. No one would be ready to try to counter and cure it with inverse mathematics. No one would be ready with the anti-equation.

And once the wave of corruption had arrived, it was too late.

The expanding wave of custom mathematics made that thing which is perceived as the electromagnetic force ten trillion, trillion times stronger in the real universe than it should be, and all atoms the wave swept over collapsed into neutrons.

All life consequently ended.

Watch what you're doing with those dodgy reactors was to be the moral to this parable of Pross's.

Well, there it was, an acceptable plot for a science fiction novel. And he'd better bloody-well start writing it now, because time had well and truly run out for him: not only was Ron going to sell his computer, he now had *no* income whatsoever.

Right: action.

Seriously deciding what needed to be done, and when to do it, felt like half the work was done already. In fact, he was so pleased with this fraction of accomplishment, he decided to reward himself for his efforts: he would give himself the day off, starting with a little nap.

And so he shed his clothes and slipped into bed.

But, lying on his back, he glanced upward and beheld the notice he'd taped to the ceiling the night before.

He closed his eyes and tried to ignore it.

He quickly succeeded in ignoring it.

He felt uncomfortable about ignoring it. He was supposed to be a cunning genius, after all: he should be working.

He tried to ignore the uncomfortable feeling that came from successfully ignoring the message and his genius.

He couldn't.

He opened his eyes and stared with deep loathing at the sign.

Aw, fuck it, he thought ruefully, I'm too intelligent to sleep.

1.11
Money For Free

Burdened by what he had so often been told was genius, Pross felt compelled to get back out of bed, and he almost began writing his proper science fiction book there and then.

Almost.

He did actually switch the word processor on. And he did actually head an electronic page CHAPTER ONE. And he did actually plan on the first chapter being as long as the *whole* of his last novel.

But that's as far as it got.

He sat with the keyboard on his lap and waited for the words to flow out.

Waited for it all to start happening.

Sat there...

And waited...

For a book to flow out.

Quarter of an hour later, still with the keyboard on his lap, he hadn't thought of a suitable sentence with which to begin his career as a proper novelist.

He was beginning to get a little anxious.

He was beginning to wonder if he could pull it off.

Luckily, he was spared further creative agony by the arrival of Lilith.

Lilith was having a day off work, and she'd called in on Pross to say hello and see if he wanted to accompany her on a shopping trip to Newcastle.

'I can't,' he bemoaned, now lying on the sofa in his living room, 'I'm too talented to shop.'

'What do you mean?' she asked. Her voice was pretty weird too, sounding like a half-stirred blend of Droopy and Mickey Mouse.

Pross, wearing a burdened look, explained that his genius demanded he stay at home until a proper book was written. He said it was the only way that the rent would get paid, the only way that he could ever hope to earn money to feed himself. He said that he was going to make a start on the book that very day.

'I thought the dole paid your rent?'

Pross told her what had happened to him on the fiscal side since they'd last met.

Lilith was concerned, and promised to bring him some money to tide him over until Ron returned from Iceland.

'I'll come down to see you later on tonight, after I've been to the bank and done some shopping,' she said. 'I'm virtually skint myself, and I don't want to go overdrawn, but I should be able to spare about twenty pounds.'

'Is that all?' he complained. 'It's big money I want. Big. Huge.'

She smiled a peculiar smile. 'Don't kick a gift horse in the mouth. Twenty should keep you in food until the weekend. I get paid on Friday, so if you need some more, to pay the rent or something before Ron gets back, don't be afraid to ask.'

The offers of money were readily accepted by Pross, though he did say this: 'You realise that I won't be able to pay you back, at least for a long time?'

'Doesn't matter,' she replied, 'it's not much.' She laughed a mocking little laugh that showed her askew teeth and added, 'Pay me back if your book's published.'

'When,' corrected Pross.

'If,' she repeated.

'*When*,' he insisted. 'In fact I'll pay you back threefold. In fact I'll give you an IOU for the money right now.'

'Don't be daft,' said Lilith, but it was too late, daft was what Pross was already being. He'd just figured out how he was going to raise money during the period when his book would be under construction: he would sell shares in himself. What a spanker of a good idea, he thought, and went to his bedroom.

Ignoring Lilith's persistent demands for an explanation of his behaviour, Pross set about constructing, on his computer, the layout for the shares in himself that he intended to sell. Five minutes later, he printed the first one:

GENIUS BOND
PURCHASE PRICE £20

I, Pross Pi-Meson, being apparently a genius with a mind as cunning as most any ever devised by nature, promise to pay the bearer of this bond three times its purchase price upon the publication of my first proper novel.

Signed....................

The bond, duly signed, was handed over to Lilith, who condescended to fold it and put it into her pocket.

'Right,' he said, 'you now owe me twenty pounds. Bring it around tonight or you'll be in big trouble with my lawyers.'

This seemed like magic to Pross. He felt as if he'd just printed money. In fact he was so enraptured by the concept of selling shares in himself, he immediately set about reeling off dozens of the things in various denominations. Some for one pound; a lot for five; a lot for ten; some for twenty; four for fifty; and, because it felt so delicious, one for five hundred.

All he had to do now was persuade his various friends to purchase them, though the impossibility of this crucial element of the scheme didn't bother him too much.

Lilith had soon given up on the prospect of Pross accompanying her on a shopping trip, so she had set off on her own just after he'd set about printing his bonds.

It took just under half an hour for Pross to become bored with bonds, a span of time that produced bonds to the value of £956. Only half an hour earlier he had been penniless, but now he was worth nearly a thousand pounds — on paper, at least.

Surely, he thought, such productive activity necessitated a long rest? It bloody well did, he decided, taking to his bed again, not glancing up even once to the vibrant sign on the ceiling.

And he drifted off to sleep.

Amy was her name.

Today there was no school, it being half-term break, and Amy was in her bedroom above the family shop, amusing herself doing what she did every week — checking through the lottery playslips discarded downstairs for winners.

It was her hobby.

The two hundred or so that she'd checked already this week had so far produced only three ten pound winners.

One month before she'd found a five number match, netting the entrant, according to her father, nearly two thousand pounds, whoever it had been.

The expression of concentration on her face was the one shared by all children engrossed in a mentally demanding task of their own choice: a smile with a frown with a tongue-tip occasionally protruding.

Suddenly, the expression changed to astonishment and delight: a six number match.

1.12
The Fucking Idiot

It was not even noon, yet some sadistic bastard was banging on the outer door of Press's house.

He ignored it.

The banging continued, so he shouted, 'It's open!'

Still it continued.

Better get out of bed and answer it, he thought, it might be Rolf.

It wasn't Rolf. It was someone Press felt he ought to know, and he had a young girl with him.

'Corner shop man?' ventured Press.

'Aye, that's me, lad. Does Ron Cantillon live here?'

Press nodded, a bit suspicious of the man's motives.

'Does he know he's won a third share in this week's seven million pound lottery jackpot?'

'No he doesn't, because he hasn't. He saw the draw on telly. Remembered his numbers.'

'He has won,' said the shopkeeper. 'Little angel here checked his playslip. I know it's his because he did some sums on it after I processed it.'

With a smile, little angel waved the playslip.

Press was bemused. 'He didn't win. He watched...'

Then he realised.

'It must have been my cat,' he murmured.

Then he realised more.

'Oh bugger. Oh deep bugger.'

He slumped down, then looked up.

'The playslip on its own doesn't count, does it?'

'No, mate. You've got to have the printed receipt... don't tell me you haven't...'

Jennifer was sitting alone in a cafeteria near to where she worked, eating her lunch and reading. She was on the final chapter of *Great Expectations*. Sarah-Jane had given her the book a few weeks earlier.

This was only the fourth book she had read since her parents' death.

When she'd been younger, intense emotion had affected Jennifer whenever she had come to the end of a book. Even the very first book she had read as a small child had rendered her so. In the closing paragraphs of a novel, even those with "happy" endings, she had always found herself overcome with a powerful sense of what she had eventually recognised as grief, grief that brought choking lumps to her throat.

That was it, she had eventually comprehended: grief. Grief for an experience that's passed away, and a story that's reached the end of its road.

But that vulnerability had left her some vague time ago, she realised.

The last page of *Great Expectations* was being absorbed: Pip had rediscovered Estella, and he could foresee no shadow of another parting.

Jennifer choked up, and actually began to cry a little. This surprised her. She thought she had outgrown the condition. In fact, she couldn't remember the last time she had physically cried about anything. She had not turned out to be a tearful person. Unlike Sarah, she had not even cried when her parents had died.

Sitting at her table in the corner, with tears suffusing her eyes, the picture that Jennifer presented to the world was one of fragile beauty. To a romantic viewer, she might have appeared like a frosted rose whose frozen petals might so easily be shattered and snapped by a clumsy hand.

Jennifer had changed somewhat since the photograph now in Pross's possession had been taken. Now her hair fell not in loose curls, but rather it was straight, bobbed delicately at the shoulders. Her face was different too, it seemed; slightly thinner, maybe, and her eyes seemed larger and wider, though this could be a consequent illusion of the greater expertise in the application of make-up she had developed.

Jennifer's cry was a restrained, silent affair. She put the book into her bag, and after a minute or two she was feeling considerably less sad.

Over her coffee, Jennifer thought about her sister and what she might be doing now in Iceland. She felt that she'd been a bit of a burden to Sarah, and she didn't like to bother her with her troubles now. Sarah-Jane had her music doctorate to pursue, and Jennifer tried not to hamper her, trying rather to present a picture of contentment to her sister.

She wondered who Ron was. Wondered what he was like.

She took out from her pocket the pieces of Pross's letter, which she arranged on the table.

She wondered, as she had done all day, just who Prospero Pi-Meson was, if he was anyone at all. She thought about the name. Prospero, she knew, was a character in some Shakespeare play, but which one she didn't know. And Pi-Meson she vaguely guessed to be something to do with science.

It was too much of a coincidence, she figured, the letter bearing a Durham postmark for it not to be connected in some way with her sister. Maybe Prospero was the chap called Ron? Maybe they were just having a joke with her?

She also wondered what Dystopia and Tartarus meant. She hadn't had time to look in a dictionary that morning.

Once more, Pross was reduced to the necessity of slumping down. They'd searched for an hour, but had found it not. Up and down the road for quarter of a mile on both sides they'd been.

Amy, put on the case by her father, who'd had to get back to his shop, was exasperated.

Pross was sitting on the roadside with his head in his hands.

'You fucking idiot,' said Amy.

'Swear at me again and I'll tell your dad.'

'Are you sure this is where you puked?'

'Positive. Right opposite that gate. Look, there's still some left. This stain is *my* puke, here.' He heaved a sigh. 'It's no use looking any more. That rain could have swept it down miles of sewers by now.' He heaved another sigh. 'The cat'll never forgive me. I know what it's like. Really vindictive.'

But then he saw it. He saw it right where he'd looked first, on the pavement near the road's edge. He hadn't seen it before because it had almost been dissolved, *dissolved by the puke.*

That's where it had landed — in his own puke.

Only a hint of colour in the remaining stain of puke gave it away. It was little more than torn pulp pressed into the pavement, with just a hint of faded pink to differentiate it from the puke-stained concrete slap it was mashed on to. Whatever damage the puke would have done had no doubt been made worse by rain and tramping feet. No writing was visible. It looked like tissue paper that's been through a machine wash in a trouser pocket, then a mangle.

But it was definitely the ticket, that much he could tell.

They both stared at it.

'You fucking idiot,' said Amy, as Pross began delicately lifting it off the pavement, using the edge of a ringpull as a scraper.

'I'm sorry, Spock,' said Pross, kneeling beside the cat. 'I'm really sorry. Honest. Look, you can have all the money I've got left in the world.'

Spock ignored the coins that Pross was tipping out of his pocket on to the living room floor.

Stood beside him, Amy felt opinion welling up inside her again. 'You really are a fucking idiot, aren't you?'

Pross looked up at her, attempting a forbidding glare.

'How old are you?' she asked. 'You act like a little kid.'
'Don't push it, titless.'
'I'll have tits soon, but you'll always be an idiot.'
That reply was so clever, Pross felt like hitting her. 'Why don't you go back to the shop?' he said instead of punching her.
'Dad said I have to stay with you until he comes to fetch me. He worries.'
'Yeah, poor paraphiliacs,' muttered Pross.

On his table, he had reconstituted the lottery ticket as best he could. His best wasn't even worth sending in, he reckoned. It could have been Kleenex for all that was left.

The shopkeeper had promised to do all he could to help Pross secure his share of the jackpot, and, to fulfil that promise, while his daughter was helping to look for the ticket, he'd telephoned the lottery's regional office in Newcastle to explain the predicament.

Even though he could vouch that it was Pross's flatmate who had bought the winning ticket, and even though the lottery organisers knew from their computer records that the only unclaimed jackpot share had been purchased at his shop, they could not agree to pay out without the ticket as evidence. George Cook, the regional controller, was immoveable on the issue.

'You have to think of our security measures,' he explained. 'Our system has to be infallible. There's no room for kindness. It just wouldn't do. Look, I'll tell you what. I'll go and see this guy later, Durham's on my way home, explain it all to him personally. That's all I can do. And if there's any developments, get in touch. OK?'

And that was their position.

As the afternoon wore on, Pross gravitated towards his sofa, upon which he lay in dejected silence, staring at the ceiling.

But when he happened to sigh, Amy said, reproachfully, 'Two million quid.'

Pross soon moved to the kitchen, only to be followed by Amy. Sat at the table, he involuntarily sighed.

'Two million quid,' said Amy.

He moved back to the living room, occupying the armchair this time. He sighed again.

Just as Amy opened her mouth, Pross said, 'I'll hit you with a hammer if you say it again.'

'No you won't,' she asserted. Looking at him strangely for a short while, she then asked, accusingly, 'Are you a puff?'

'I'm going to be by the time you're sexually active.'
The doorbell rang.
'Daddy's here!' screeched the child.
A minute later, the shopkeeper was sat on Pross's sofa, his daughter smiling sweetly beside him.
Pross sat in the armchair.
'So you found it then?' said the shopkeeper, wondering why Pross and his daughter were looking so glum.
Pross showed him the remains of the ticket.
'That's it?'
'That's indeed it. Doesn't look good for me, does it?'
'Doesn't look good at all, mate, 'fraid t'say. That could be anything to my eyes.'
They sat in their respective seats again.
'Ah phoned the lottery people,' revealed the shopkeeper in downbeat Geordie tones. 'Spoke with the top guy at their regional headquarters in Newcastle for quite some time. Explained everything, like. Gave him all the details. But they never pay oot withoot a ticket, and of course like it's all cross checked with the computer account that my retail unit automatically sends back every day.'
'So from their records they must know that *someone* from your outlet won the jackpot?'
'Aye, they know that, like,' said the shopkeeper, 'but withoot a ticket, like, y'can't prove it was you.'
'Fuck,' said Pross.
The shopkeeper displayed displeasure at Pross's utterance. 'Howay man, keep y'language doon in front of little angel, won't y'?'
'Fucking won't,' declared Pross.
Thirty seconds later, the shopkeeper was storming out of Pross's flat, pulling Amy along with him.

Over two million pounds was rightfully his, and he felt like he should be doing *something* to secure it.
Big money.
Huge money.
Two million pounds could buy freedom.
Freedom.
Two million pounds could isolate him from the petty squabble of life.
After some more sighing and cursing his very existence, Pross decided to contact Ron with the news. Ron was good at getting things done.

That's what he'd do: he'd get Ron to do the doing.

By first telephoning his British company, Pross acquired the number in Iceland on which Ron could be reached.

'You'll never guess what.'

'You've got a job?' guessed Ron crazily.

'Nah, not as weird as that. It's to do with Heisenberg's somewhat uncertain Uncertainty Principle.'

And Pross explained the awful truth.

And Ron knew he was telling the awful truth because there was no way Pross could have known he'd done sums on the playslip. 'You fucking idiot,' he snarled. 'Two million quid. Are you sure the ticket's unreadable?'

'Believe me, it's unreadable. It's not even recognisable. I only know it's the ticket because I know it's the ticket.'

After an exasperated pause, Ron got thinking seriously. 'Listen. Tell me everything. Every little detail. Don't leave anything out. There has to be a way around this. And don't lose what's left of the ticket. If you won't try to cash it, I bloody will when I get back next week.'

Pross told him every little detail.

Following the call, for the next two hours, as day faded into darkness, Pross sat with his head in his hands. 'You fucking idiot. Two million quid,' was all that he could say to himself.

And he couldn't look the cat in the eye.

At just past seven o'clock, the doorbell rang. Pross managed to scrape together enough enthusiasm for life to answer it, but immediately wished he hadn't.

The caller was a stocky man, about five feet eight inches tall, with a healthy-looking tan. He was clad in a dark suit. A leather attache case was held by his side. Atop, there was impeccably cropped brown hair; below, a pair of slip-on black leather shoes with small gold buckles. From head to toe he screamed Mormon. Mormons never failed to bring out the militancy in Pross's atheism. They never failed to release one of his rants.

Determined to keep the Mormon monster at bay, he only half opened the door and said nothing at all that might encourage him in his demented mission of religious conquest.

'Good morning, sir,' said the man.

Pross considered the Mormon in silence for a few moments. In a languid tone, he said, 'You're wasting your time, I'm a satanist.'

The man in the dark suit understood, and he smiled in appreciation of his own cleverness.

'Don't worry, sir,' he said in a low voice that had an endearing, lighthearted air about it, leaning towards Pross conspiratorially, as if divulging a great secret, 'I'm not a Jehovah's Witness.'

'I know,' returned Pross, 'you're a fucking Mormon.'

The Mormon's face lost its civility for a fleeting moment.

'I'm not a Mormon, either,' he stated.

It was then that Pross noticed that the caller's case had a tiny lottery logo fixed to it.

The caller nodded to confirm what he knew Pross to be thinking.

'Oh, the biggest bugger of all time and space,' groaned Pross as he slumped down.

But as he slumped, he also steeled himself for action. He jumped up and took hold of the caller's wrist and pulled him into his flat.

Pross immediately showed him the ticket.

But the lottery man shook his head and said it was a worthless mess.

Half an hour later, with Pross at one side of his living room table, George Cook, the lottery official at the other, and Spock sat on the table between them, enough had been said to confirm Pross's fears.

'Well, that's it,' concluded Cook. 'You're obviously an intelligent person. You'll realise it's how we have to operate. The system has to be tamper proof, not that I'm suggesting at all that there's any foul play here. It's obvious there isn't, but I can't prove that, and nor, unfortunately, can you. That thing you showed me could be tissue paper for all we know.'

Pross looked broken.

'Look,' said Cook earnestly, 'if there was just some way of convincing us beyond a shadow of a doubt that it was your ticket that won, we'd be delighted to pay out. Heavens, we've had so much bad publicity in the past, with winners getting named against their wishes and such. It would be great if we could give a jackpot share to a cat that had lost its ticket! What a story!'

Pross still looked broken.

1.13
Make A Wish

Her working day over, Jennifer set off on the fifteen minute walk to her flat. Today, her step was weighed-down and slowed with the burden of knowing that John would be there waiting for her.

She wondered if she ought to give her job up. It wasn't exactly a career job, and she didn't really need the money: a small fortune had been placed in a trust fund for her that she could now freely draw upon. The money had come from insurance payments after the death of her parents and the subsequent sale of the family home.

Having now turned eighteen, Jennifer was arbiter in her own half-share of the inheritance.

Although she could have spent more extravagantly if she'd wished, Jennifer had never taken, or asked for, anything more than the one hundred pounds a month she needed to supplement the earnings from her job. On the first day of each month, one hundred pounds would spookily materialise in her bank account. Without this money she could not have afforded to move into a place of her own. She could have drawn more and worked less, but it hadn't seemed right to her.

But now she was contemplating exploiting the legacy.

Jennifer was often urged by her sister to follow an academic path and eventually go to university; but she was not interested in this course, saying that she just couldn't ever be bothered to stick to something that demanded even a modicum of commitment for so long, saying that she'd rather just get a simple job somewhere to occupy her days.

Now she had such a job, but she felt uncomfortable about depriving someone else of it, someone who might genuinely want and need it, and not just as a pastime.

Walking down the street to her flat, she was, though as yet unaware of it, beginning to galvanize herself into bringing about positive change in her life.

Turning the key in the lock and pushing open the door, she glimpsed Elaine, who'd just got out of bed, disappearing into the bathroom they shared.

Elaine flashed a smile at her.

Jennifer gave a strained smile back. Often she wished that she lived alone. She never felt comfortable.

John was sitting in the living room with his feet up, watching television.

He didn't get up to greet her, or even bother to turn his head to look at her.

In a voice as warm as she could muster, Jennifer said hello to him.

In a surly sort of way and without moving in his seat, he returned the hello, and she gathered from this that he was still sore about Prospero Pi-Meson's effrontery.

In the gloomy dimness of the room, the middle-sized north-facing window offering no more light than the television screen in the corner, Jennifer, standing behind John's armchair and pretending not to have noticed his simmering mood, forced a casual sounding inquiry concerning what he'd done that day.

He said, with some cruel satisfaction discernable to Jennifer, that he'd dropped by to see her aunt to give her the marriage news.

Jennifer said nothing, said it with dignity, and left him to his sulking, going to her bedroom to change her clothing.

In her room, still with her black raincoat on, she sat wearily in a chair. In front of her was the white dressing table her mother had given to her only one week before her death.

She brought her arms up and rested her elbows on the table top, depositing her head into her hands, her hair falling over her face.

She lifted her china-blue eyes and regarded herself in the mirror.

Those eyes met their mirrored twins.

With the determination that can be born from confronting one's reflection thus, she resolved to break the engagement. She was only eighteen, she reminded herself — no age at all, they say — and life was sure to offer her more than early marriage to John. In fact she had recently come to consider and realise that she was simply waiting for her life to begin, and because of this she knew it would be madness to let her relationship with John go any further. She was going to tell him, regardless of the scene he would make.

But she soon vacillated.

She was being unfair, she thought. John had been there in the past, at times when she had so needed company. But, she argued internally, she had outgrown him, and now his company was not wanted or appreciated or even tolerable any more.

Outgrown: yes, that was the word. Thinking about it, she realised that she seemed to have outgrown many people, even finding that she now felt awkward in the presence of those few friends she'd retained from her childhood. She just couldn't think of anything to say to them any more, though she tried hard when she was with them; and whatever they had to say to her, she, with self-reproach, found dull and uninteresting. Consequently, her few old friends had now all but drifted away.

Part of her sternly blamed herself for this loss of companionship, and sometimes she felt quite awful about it.

Shaking off this reverie, with a feeling of melancholy lingering inside, she removed her coat, skirt and blouse, hung them in a cupboard and pulled on an old jumper and a pair of faded jeans Sarah had given to her.

She decided that she would have her tea before saying anything to John about how she felt.

Jennifer brought her meal, an omelette filled with cheese, into the living room where John was talking to Elaine in the flickering half-light glow of the television screen about the car he'd almost saved up enough money to buy.

She sat near him on the sofa, the open fire warming her legs. Using her knees as a table, she ate without conversing, glad that Elaine was keeping John occupied.

Before she'd finished her food, the phone rang. Elaine answered it. Phone calls were usually for her.

'For you. Your aunty Jane,' Elaine said, proffering the receiver.

Jennifer blanched but tried not to appear perturbed.

The phone call was of the expected congratulatory nature. Her aunt made the expected noises of delight, said what a lovely couple they'd make, and asked had they set a date.

Her aunt's two doted-on yapping toy poodles could be clearly heard in the background.

Her aunt was already picturing the dress she would wear for the wedding. Pastel lilac: it would be pastel lilac, she decided. And John would wear his smart navy uniform.

And at the reception she would feed her darling little dogs on wedding cake crumbs.

With John listening, Jennifer hadn't the courage to reveal her decision. There was another reason, too, for her reticence: she now felt that she would be letting her aunt down. Although her mother and her aunt — her mother's only close relative — had been like strangers to each other most of their adult lives, her aunt had immediately offered Jennifer a home after the accident. Because of this she felt indebted. Jane had soon come to look upon Jennifer as being the child she and her husband had never had. She loved her and wanted what she thought would be best for her. For a long time she'd been very worried about her niece, but now she seemed to have got herself sorted out.

So, with all this churning in the back of her mind, Jennifer thanked her aunt for the call.

She couldn't do it. When Elaine left for her night shift, Jennifer couldn't bring herself to raise the stormy issue with John.

They were sat watching a film together, until John began slowly to slip his hands up Jennifer's jumper. She, subtly she hoped, deflected his progression by adjusting her position on the sofa.

And soon after she nonchalantly left the room.

In her bedroom, alone, she found some things to do: folding clothes and tidying. Then she remembered her ignorance about Dystopia and Tartarus, consulting a dictionary.

> *Dystopia: Imaginary place where everything is as bad as possible.*
> *Tartarus: Abyss below Hades where the Titans were confined; place of punishment in Hades.*

Sitting on the end of her bed with the pieces of the letter before her, she delved into the top drawer of her dressing table and retrieved a roll of clear tape, using it to bind the bits of paper together. Then she regarded the whole.

What did he look like? Why was he interested in her? *Was* he mad? How did he know about her? Was it Sarah-Jane's doing?

She was still thinking these things when John came into the room. Seeing the reconstructed letter lying on the bed, he crumpled it up in his fist, depositing it in the waste paper bin. Then he knelt beside the bed and again slipped his hands up her jumper before gently but firmly pushing her backwards on to the bed, where she lay supine.

He began to peel off her jeans, to which she only passively consented.

But, seeing the look on her face, he halted.

'Great. My last day of leave. You get colder every time.'

Jennifer said nothing.

He called her frigid and announced that he was going out for a drink and a game of pool.

When he left, Jennifer felt helpless. She felt as if she didn't have the strength to do what had to be done. She switched the room light off and lay in the dark, hating herself for being so weak and feeble, hating herself for just drifting through life.

In darkness, a fermenter of introspection, Jennifer thought long and hard about herself and what was happening to her, what she was *allowing* to happen to her.

She tried to see herself as others might see her, and after some thought and amateur psychology, she reached this conclusion: that the loss of her parents had instilled in her a sense of futility.

If this was true, she thought, then things were going to have to change. And change, she resolved, was just what things *were* going to do. And the thing she wanted to change most was her relationship with John.

This was the last day of John's leave. Early tomorrow he would be off to join his ship again, which was in dock at its base in Portsmouth being refitted before an imminent tour of duty.

Jennifer decided to break the engagement with a letter. It would be so much easier that way.

For the first time in their lives, Ron and Sarah experienced the aurora borealis. They were some ten miles outside Reykjavik, having been taken there in the car of a man whom Ron was working with and with whom he'd quickly struck up a friendship. The man was called Ivor. Ivor worked as the Computer Operations Manager of the fish packaging firm that had purchased equipment from Ron's firm. He was in his mid-fifties, spoke excellent English — a legacy of the eight years he'd worked and studied in London — and he had a contagious passion for stargazing. Jovially, he'd insisted on taking Ron out to see the aurora, if it would show itself that night.

Now far away from any street lighting, the stars seemed so much more vital. It was crisp and cold outside the car, but they had been given ski-jackets to wear by Ivor, who was explaining how sometimes, especially during such periods of high sun-spot activity as they were experiencing now, the whole sky might become a dancing, folding panoply of iridescent light. And as Ron and Sarah stood together, hand in hand, peering northward, a dull glow began to illuminate the horizon, becoming brighter before sweeping up into an arc of light which almost reached the zenith, throwing out vividly coloured streamers that twisted back to the horizon. Then the arc itself began breaking up into disarray, sending out in all directions folding, rippling curtains of light that finally, but for a dim afterglow, dissipated the display.

Sarah was wonder-struck. She'd hadn't imagined that it would be so impressive. It was the scale of it, she decided, that left one gasping. Out here, the sky seemed very big and she felt very, very small.

Out here, she felt, a person could easily be persuaded to believe in a god. She thought also that that person should be even more easily persuaded to believe in the total insignificance of the human species in that god's great scheme. 'We're just specks, aren't we?' she murmured, squeezing Ron's hand.

'The fucking idiot,' groaned Ron. 'Two million quid.'

Sarah hushed Ron. She wanted to make love in the crisp air under the starlight, but Ivor's presence precluded such a pagan celebration of nature.

What they had seen, Ivor informed them, was a better than average display: 'Right time in the eleven-year sun-spot cycle,' he explained with a broad smile. 'The more sun spots, the greater the solar wind. The greater the solar wind, the better the aurora.'

Ivor seemed to be a truly happy man.

And then a thread of light streaked across a constellation. Sarah-Jane excitedly pointed to where it had fulminated.

'A meteor,' said Ivor, then with a chuckle said, 'Make a wish.'

Sarah closed her eyes tightly and made her wish.

They resumed their appreciation of the northern sky, observing that the aurora on the horizon seemed to be intensifying again.

Ivor pointed out a satellite slowly traversing the heavens. Sarah and Ron had never noticed such a thing before. Ivor observed that it was going directly from north to south. 'Probably a spy satellite,' he said, explaining that such an orbit was an expensive thing to attain, and that only the military were ever that wasteful. 'Maybe it's a scientific research satellite,' he conceded with a grin.

'It's a pity Pross isn't here,' said Sarah quietly to Ron, 'he would have loved it.'

'I wish he was here,' menaced Ron, 'the fucking idiot. Two million quid.'

Sarah hushed Ron again. 'I wonder what he's doing now?' she said. 'You don't think he'll try anything silly, do you?'

'Never known him try anything sensible.'

Sarah was genuinely concerned. 'No, really, do you think he's all right?'

'Course he is,' said Ron grudgingly. 'He's probably out somewhere trying to cadge a drink.'

After their sightseeing they drove back into town, where Ivor dropped Sarah off at the hotel.

He and Ron had a little more work to do.

When, at their first encounter, Pross had insisted to Sarah-Jane that her true identity was Tess, she'd had no trouble completing the name: Tess of the d'Urbervilles. This was despite the fact that she had never read the book herself.

She hadn't read the book before, but, because of Pross's conviction that she was none other than the heroine of that very novel, Sarah had chosen it for her holiday reading material. And during her brief stay in Iceland, in the hours when Ron was away at his place of work and she wasn't solo-sightseeing, Sarah had become absorbed in the sad, turbulent life of Tess, vainly identifying more and more with the tragic heroine.

Soon after saying goodbye to Ivor, she was lying on her front on the large bed in the room she and Ron were sharing, her back arched upwards, lifted by her elbows. Her book was open before her. 'I am, I'm Tess,' she whispered to herself after an hour or so, just as Ron walked in. 'He was right,' she further said. What struck her most about it, though, was not her physical likeness to the character, which was real, but Pross's astuteness in having recognised it in an instant.

'Who was right?' inquired Ron, putting down his briefcase. He took off his jacket and began massaging her shoulders while she continued with the book. His own shoulders were nearly twice the width of hers.

After a few seconds, she answered, 'Pross.'

'About what?'

'About me being Tess.'

Ron reached over and snatched the book away from her. 'Not you as well?' he complained when he saw the irritating title. With the book in his hands, he wandered over to the window and looked out to the streets of Reykjavik. He flicked through the pages of the novel. 'After Pross read this bloody book, I never heard anything but Tess for days. The stupid sod even drew pictures of her and stuck them up around the flat, and when he ran out of paper, he just drew straight on to the walls. Every time he falls in love I have to redecorate.' Ron irreverently tossed the book back to Sarah and went into the small bathroom attached to their room.

'Two million quid!' shouted Ron repeatedly. 'The fucking idiot.'

Ron continued to gripe. Tess wasn't listening; she had just learned that a position existed for her to work as a simple Victorian dairymaid at *Talbothays Farm*. Ron, having received no replies, walked back to his lady friend, curiously regarding the distant look on her face.

'Ron,' Sarah said in a preparatory way, without taking her eyes from the page she was reading.

'What?'

'I want you to call me Tess from now on.'

He threw up his arms in despair. 'That bloody idiot!'

'Be quiet!' chastened Tess. 'I'm trying to read my biography. And don't try to talk to me about stupid computers because I'm not interested.'

Ron took a bath.

Fifteen minutes later, Tess came to the end of *Phase the Second* of her story. At this juncture she put the book down and rolled over to the other side of the bed, lying on her back.

The suggestive effect of the book began to wear off, and Tess became Sarah-Jane again. She started to think of things like packing her belongings away, for she was due to board a plane destined for Newcastle at ten o'clock that very night.

But Sarah couldn't be bothered to start sorting her things out. As an excuse not to start packing, she chose this moment to call her aunt to say hello, a chore she'd neglected to do for weeks now. By deliberate choice, Sarah saw little of her aunt. Since the death of her parents she'd resided almost permanently in Durham, living for the most part in the council flat she'd been illegally given the rent card for, and remaining in the city between scholastic terms. The money bequeathed to her had allowed this independence.

Compared to what Pross now had, the Lucas legacy was small change, but to most other people it was a large, reassuring sum to have in the bank.

To a background of poodles yapping viciously, Sarah-Jane and her mother's sister exchanged a few platitudes:

The weather —

The hotel —

The food —

Sarah was about to mention her new friend's lottery fiasco when the conversation was turned to something else entirely. 'I've got some news for you,' said Sarah's aunt.

'Really? What?' asked Sarah cheerfully.

'It's about Jennifer.' There was an air of restrained exultation in her delivery.

Although she correctly picked up on the happy tone of her aunt, Sarah still worried about the nature of the news concerning her sister. 'What about her?'

A pregnant pause from England... 'She's engaged to be married!'

'Who to?' asked Sarah quietly, hoping that she might have met someone new.

'Why, John, of course!' said her aunt.

'Oh,' said Sarah. She then said that she had to go, quickly putting the phone down.

Sarah-Jane wept.

1.14
Totally Pissed

'Buy me another drink and I'll let you touch my hair again,' said Pross.

Sat alone with Lilith, at a table in the Arts Centre, which tonight was only sparsely peopled, he tried one more time to convince her that Spock had won a staggering amount on the lottery but payment was not to be forthcoming.

Understandably, Lilith refused to believe him.

'Honest, it's true,' he said with lashings of indignation.

She looked at him.

He looked at her.

'Bollocks,' said Lilith, picking up his empty glass and going to the bar.

Pross decided to give up trying to convince Lilith, and instead produced, from inside his jacket, the photo of Jennifer.

For much of the next hour he sighed and drank.

And while he was sighing and drinking, Lilith suffered his ridiculous adoration of Jennifer's image without saying a word.

Soon he was drunk. His head felt suspiciously like it had acquired extra weight and inertia, like it was pulling ten g's in all directions at once. His elbows became slippery and mischievous, belligerently refusing to tow the line and obey the laws of friction when he tried to use them to lean upon the table with. So did his hands when he tried to support his whirling head. Every time he closed his eyes he would immediately wish he hadn't bothered and quickly open them again, then would promptly shut them again just to confirm that it really had felt that bad.

But he was past the point of no return. This binge was going to go the whole way.

As was his lover's lament.

'Oooooh,' he moaned, dropping his intoxicated head into his hands. 'Where is she now?' Who is she with?'

Lilith forced herself to question Pross about his latest obsession. 'So how long have you been in love with her?' she asked.

'Two days,' he murmured, sensing that the room was spinning erratically in a beery maelstrom. 'Two empty, eternal days.' His head began to gravitate slowly towards the table top. Six inches from its surface, he suddenly slumped down, causing Lilith to desperately grab wobbling glasses.

'Careful!'

'Leave me alone,' he groaned, lying with his left cheek on the table top and his eyes staring with death-like intensity into some forsaken world beyond the confines of the room. 'Can't you see that I'm lovelorn?'

'You're not lovelorn,' grumbled Lilith in return.

'Bloody am,' he asserted, still staring without facial animation into his own private hell. 'Cursed with poetic sensitivity too.'

Lilith tried to steer the conversation away from Jennifer. 'You'll spoil your hair if you keep lying on it.'

'Don't care,' muttered Pross. 'What's the point of having it if Jennifer's not here to see it?' Realising his glass was nearly empty, he sighed again and moaned, 'I'm a poet in love, you have to buy me another drink.'

'I've already bought you five.'

'Where's Ron? He'll buy me one.'

'He's in Iceland knobbing Jennifer's sister,' said Lilith.

Badly, is how much that vulgar jibe hurt Pross, and his face showed it. 'I need another drink,' he quietly said, like he meant it this time. 'It's all been loss. Always loss. Loss and muddle. Muddle and loss.'

'You'll only be sick all day tomorrow. You know what you're like.'

Pross reacted by loudly moaning, 'I'm a poet in love. Someone buy me a drink. Anyone.'

Lilith decided he'd had enough already, and was saying as much when Pross's face lit up. 'Listen,' he said to Lilith, 'you've got a car. Give me a lift to Richmond so I can find her. Then I'll woo her knickers off with my huge, throbbing I.Q. She's waiting for me, you see. Me. Me. Me.'

'You need your head examining,' said Lilith, casting him a look. She then began an eloquent oration that was coloured with an almost accusational tone. 'Tony says you constantly fall in hopeless love because you lost that Susan Murray girl when you were younger...'

'What in the hell does Tony know about *my* mind?'

'He should know something, he's a psychiatrist. Anyway, it imprinted within you the futility of love, and ever since then you've been reliving the same pattern of hopelessness; the same life script. You've been chasing the unattainable ever since. And on the rare occasions when you can actually get what you want badly, you lose interest and go off on another futile chase. You used to be potty over Melanie until she started liking you back. There has to be an insatiable longing in your life, otherwise you're lost, doesn't there? It's the chase, not the consummation that obsesses you, isn't it? And you have to fail as well, don't you?'

Pross would not accept such an explanation. 'I've never been able to get what I wanted,' he stated. 'Anyway, Tony's full of crap.'

Lilith continued, 'And he says that this deep-rooted sense of futility spills over into the rest of your life, and that's why you never do anything to help yourself: get a job, or even get out of bed some days.'

Pross would not tolerate such slander. 'Some *years*,' he corrected, 'some *years*.'

'And it's why you wish your life away so often.'

This, too, needed correction. 'It's not only my own life I wish away,' he stated proudly. 'Anyway, Tony really is full of textbook theory crap.'

'Then why *do* you fall in love so often?' said a voice behind Pross.

Lilith laughed as Pross turned nervously around.

'Oh, hello, Tony. Just talking about you. Hello, Melanie.'

'I know,' said Tony. 'I know. So why do you fall in love so often?'

'Because it keeps me busy and out of trouble,' answered Pross simply.

Then something magical happened: a drink was mysteriously placed in front of Pross.

Pross looked up and saw a man with a dark complexion and unkempt, longish hair.

He looked very sad.

Then he walked away without speaking, going towards the door.

'Thanks,' called out Pross after him, although too late: he had already exited. Sitting up straight, Pross said, 'Who was that?'

'No idea,' said Lilith.

Melanie and Tony were equally clueless. 'Never seen him before, Pross,' said Melanie. 'But he looked even more depressed than you.'

That was fighting talk.

'No fucking way, matey,' snapped Pross in response. 'I'm the saddest person in Durham. Me, not him.'

Tony chipped in on his wife's side. 'No, she's right. He was sadder. Trust me. I'm a psychiatrist. He'd been crying too. Did you notice that?'

Lilith alone said she'd noticed just as Pross turned to her for reassurance. 'Lil. Sweet Lil. Tell me I look more depressed. This is important to me. I'm the most depressed person in Durham. Me, not that bastard.'

But Lilith, too, judged Pross to be second. 'You'll have to kill him,' she advised, still in a mood.

And Pross thought about it.

'You're thinking about it, aren't you?' said Melanie.

'I am,' said Pross. 'I am.'

As the evening progressed, Pross became less and less capable of sustained articulation. His head was now pulling at least twenty multi-directional g's, and he had long ago rejected all prudent self-injunctions on his alcohol intake. He was speeding recklessly down the road to the squalid ghetto of Inebriation, wheels skidding. Moderation had been thrown out of the window, and it lay broken miles back down the road, next to the Point of No Return, beside the one-way bridge over the Rubicon.

The time to depart had now arrived. The booze rapidly introduced into Pross's system was beginning to fully assert itself. He was slouched over the table, being discussed by the bar's manager, who knew him, and had seen him in such a state before.

Through half-opened eyes he half-noticed that Lilith, Tony and Melanie all seemed to be engaged in the putting on of their coats. He half-intuited that it might be leaving time. This inkling was soon confirmed when they took hold of him under the arms, persuaded him to rise to his feet and guided him towards the door. He had no idea why they were doing this. He felt sure he could have walked on his own if they'd just had the imagination to suggest it to him.

Actually, it *had* been suggested to him, at least six times.

'The photograph. The photograph,' he mumbled anxiously. 'Where's the photograph?'

'I've got it,' said Lilith.

They were still doing his walking for him. He began to suspect that they might actually know what they were up to and that he might be very drunk.

'I'm totally pissed, aren't I?' he asked in a voice bloated with self-reproach.

'Yes, you are,' said Lilith with a tolerant smile.

They had reached the car park. Lilith humoured him while the three of them tried to shove him into the back of her car.

'Aw, I'm completely pissed,' he lamented with shame. 'It's disgusting. I'm setting a bad example. You'll be doing this yourself tomorrow.'

'No I won't,' she said softly.

Pross now slowly slumped forward, coincidentally in the direction they were trying to push him. Melanie got in beside him, Tony sat up front, and they were ready to take him home.

He wasn't exactly unconscious when they got him home, but he wasn't exactly alert and attentive, either, and he just didn't want to get up off that car seat at all. 'Just leave me here,' he mumbled. 'I'm all right. Just leave me here.'

Before he knew it, he was being weirdly transported to his doorstep, face down, at a confusing height of six inches above the ground.

Melanie and Lilith had an arm each, while Tony took the legs.

His head felt like there was a massive spinning gyroscope clamped inside it, a gyroscope that fought against every turn and movement it was required to make.

They carried him into the entrance hall. Harry was sat on the bottom step, a place where he often rested before attempting the two flights of stairs leading to his attic den. He was sucking the last drops out of a whisky bottle. Another full bottle was on the floor between his legs. The key on the cord around his neck jangled against this full bottle. Three *Players* cigarette stubs adorned the drooping corner of his mouth. Each was unlit. Each was a different length.

Harry watched the assisted arrival of Pross with no curiosity at all in his old eyes. Had he been a witty person, upon seeing the young pretender so bad with beer he might have made this sardonic remark: *Bloody amateurs*.

But he wasn't, and he didn't.

And this was to be Harry's last night alive.

Pross was dropped at the foot of his own door. 'Just leave me here,' he moaned. 'I'm all right.'

Lilith searched his pockets for the required key.

Soon he was lying face down on his sofa, the photo of Jennifer placed on his back.

'Don't just leave me here,' he complained after what seemed only a few seconds, 'carry me to the toilet. I'm desperate.'

But they'd already gone.

Few forces on Earth are more motivating than the need to piss somewhere other than on one's own sofa. Compelled by this need, Pross eventually found himself woozily crawling to the toilet on what he was convinced was a rubber floor, with what he was sure was a spinning gyroscope in his head, and with what he suspected were two wobbling, shifting sacks of coal pressing down on his back.

Between that and coming to his senses some two hours later, hunched and shivering in the bath, all was an enigmatic blank. But the fact that the plug was out and both taps were running, and the fact that there was a lot of dark brown puke all about, surely held the solution to the puzzle.

Appalled by his condition, he managed, without once getting up off his knees, to divest himself of his clothes and even wash himself under the shower, which still wasn't broken.

Moments later he was hugging the toilet bowl, vomiting again. 'Please don't peak. Not now,' he groaned, adding, 'Two million quid.'

Later, he made his way unsteadily to his bed, a bucket placed near should vomiting return.

But, upstairs, Harry was having an even rougher night.

1.15
Dear John

It was done. Jennifer had posted the letter to John, addressed to him at the naval base at Portsea, Portsmouth.

That morning, John had left early to join his ship, and his departure had been difficult for Jennifer. When he had returned from the pub the night before, in a better humour than when he'd gone, Jennifer had already retired to bed. When he came into the bedroom, she had pretended to be asleep. John had known that she wasn't, but hadn't attempted to wake her from fake slumber. He had simply climbed into bed beside her, and very soon both of them were asleep for real.

Jennifer had woken naturally half an hour before the time for which John had set the alarm. She'd got up, slipped into a dressing gown and, unusually, prepared him some breakfast. She'd brought it to him in bed, knowing, or at least hoping, that this was probably the last time she'd ever see him.

A few minutes later, while he was in the bathroom, without him knowing, she'd removed her door key from the bunch in his coat pocket.

After they had both eaten, Jennifer had felt compelled, for reasons not clear to her, to initiate lovemaking. She had grown lately to consider sex with John as burdensome, even odious, but certain within herself that that was to be their final union she had responded with emotion and even passion to his physical intimacy.

And so, on the doorstep, with the sun still unrisen, they had said their goodbyes. Towards the eastern horizon, the sky was a most beautiful blue colour; deep and moving, vibrant and promising. Venus, in the ascendent, had sparkled piercing white in this eastern azure; but westward, all had remained inky black. Nearby, a bird had broken into morning song.

Jennifer had held John tightly, bringing her lips to his. Minutes elapsed before John, a bulging service duffle bag slung across his back, broke away from her lips, squeezed her hand gently, then turned to go. Had he been a more discerning creature he might have suspected from the unusual passion and intensity of that goodbye kiss, delivered with her bare, ivory feet melting the early-morning frost on the doorstep, that it had not been just another goodbye, but a final goodbye. But he hadn't. He'd just thought that she was sorry to see him leaving. Walking away, military adventure ahead of him, a spring had showed in his stride.

A little way down the street, he'd slowed and looked back over his shoulder, but the door had been closed and Jennifer had no longer been in sight.

With a sense of urgency she hadn't understood, at once Jennifer had set about writing the letter to put her asunder from the boyfriend who had known her first, known her without ever really knowing her.

John would be gutted by the letter, she knew that. It was not a long one; just a page of her small, neat writing on blue vellum, explaining in no real depth that she no longer wanted him as a lover and that she felt it would be better if they never saw each other again, at least for a very long while. She'd also included the ring, wrapped in a piece of black silk torn from an old slip of hers. It was not a long letter, even so it had taken her two hours and six attempts before she'd felt she'd got it right. And when it was completed, she'd found herself with no time for her usual morning shower. She'd put on some clean underwear, dressed in a hurry and rushed to work, for which she was a little late, dropping the letter into a postbox on the way.

Letter posted, she'd felt like she was in charge of her life again. She had freed herself from the shackles of John, and that day she was going to tell her employer that she wished to leave his service as soon as possible.

This she had done, receiving permission to quit the job as early as the next day if she pleased, and not being compelled to work out the statutory period of notice to which her contract could bind her.

Free from obligation, she had resolved to make the next day, Thursday, her last as a Veterinary Assistant.

And she had begun amalgamating some vague notions about moving away somewhere — anywhere.

But when Jennifer returned from her penultimate day of work she felt peculiarly reluctant to catch up on the missed shower. Instead, she spent the evening sadly reflecting on the better times she and John had shared together, times when she'd been younger and less discriminating, less critical, and when he'd been enough for her.

She worried that the letter might have sounded too harsh.

And not once in that whole day did she wonder about Prospero Pi-Meson.

1.16
A New Pace

'Loss and muddle. Muddle and loss. Even uncertainty's uncertain in my life. Sorry Spock.'

The cat wasn't listening to Pross's mumblings. It just wished he'd get out of bed and into the kitchen to feed it.

Half an hour later, he did feed it, but he had to take much of the bed with him.

Huddled under the duvet, head throbbing, he yet again mumbled for the cat's forgiveness as it ate. 'I'm sorry, Spock. I'm so sorry. I really am sorry. You were brilliant and I fucked it. Sorry. It'll be OK though. Lend me some of that money I gave you yesterday and we'll enter again this week. I'll draw another pentangle and everything.'

The telephone rang, and Pross began a slow haul into the living room to answer it.

'Hope it's Peg from *Married with Children*,' he strained to say to himself.

It wasn't Peg. It was Ron.

'Pross, what took you so long?'

'Ugh.'

It required no mental effort from Ron for him to figure out the situation. 'Have you been drinking again?'

'Ugh, yeah. I'm a fucking idiot, me.'

Ron had no mind for pleasantries this day. 'Listen, idiot,' he said, 'I've had an idea. There's still a chance, but you have to listen carefully. Right, I used to work with a bloke who now writes software for the lottery sales, and he's told me that the central computer receives sequential ticket information from retail units at the end of each day. By a bloody stroke of good luck, I was the last person to buy a ticket from that retail unit on Friday. The shop closed up right after I left, so the records should show that the winning ticket was the last processed on Friday. Are you with me?'

'Ugh. Slower. Much slower. Scientist experiencing alcohol induced psycho-motor retardation this morning.'

Ron slowly explained things again, and the significance of his discovery eventually hit Pross: they had a piece of restricted information regarding the winning ticket that they could not possibly have known if they had not bought the ticket themselves.

That might do.

It did do.

By relaying it all to George Cook, who in turn put it to his bosses, who checked it out and discovered it to be accurate, Pross was told, not one hour after Ron's call, that payment might well be granted under such exceptional circumstances.

George Cook was going to visit in the afternoon to give the final verdict.

Instead of whooping with joy, Pross just lay sickly under the duvet on the living room floor.

He'd better tell Ron, he supposed in a little while, and drew the telephone nearer to him again by pulling on its cord.

But the Icelandic person who answered the phone on the number Ron had given spoke little English, and Pross was unable to get him to understand anything.

So he gave up.

For the next hour, he lay curled up until all that remained of his hangover was a muddy feeling inside his skull which was then largely dispersed by a cup of tea.

But in that hour, the enormity of his possible new wealth began to sink in.

His life was probably set to change.

A new pace would be introduced.

Now he could *live*.

After his cup of tea, in the time before Cook was due to arrive, Pross wallowed in the bath tub for half an hour. Spending only half an hour in the water indicated to him that his life was already changing. Usually a bath, with plenty of bubbles, a radio for company and the water periodically topped up with hot, was a way to absorb at least two hours of a day.

Ron often called him *Aquaboy*.

But lying in the bath for two hours this day just simply couldn't be done. Things were becoming different now in his mental approach.

He could really *do* things with two million. It could buy freedom. It could buy privacy. It could buy isolation. And isolation was something that Pross was beginning to wish for. He wanted to live somewhere separate. Yes, he decided, he was going to move out of the town and into the country as soon as possible.

Buy a house, that's what he'd do first.

Buying a house was as far as Pross got in planning what he was going to do with the money. Things like holidays and Italian suits never so much as entered his mind. Neither did providing for his family because he was as good as alone in the world.

George Cook arrived shortly after two o'clock, and this time Pross let him straight in.

Cook shook Pross's hand and congratulated him on his definite win. 'It's been confirmed,' said he.

That was it. Pross was definitely due to receive payment.

'My congratulations again,' Cook said as he stepped into the flat.

Pross led him into the living room.

After the civility of a cup of tea, Cook began to offer a short lecture on money management, which was part of his job description. Sat at the table, he produced chart after chart of Unit Trust performance figures and example after example of investment plans, ream after ream of financial information and scheme after scheme of pension policies. 'Of course,' he concluded, 'this advice is just to give you a broad education in money management. We actually recommend that you to entrust your money to specialist accountants who will manage it for you.'

Then he raised another subject, to which Pross in turn raised immediate objections.

'Oh, don't worry, Mr Pi-Meson, travel, accommodation, everything will be arranged and provided for you. I realise it's short notice, sorry about that, but tomorrow's when it's all arranged for. There's two other people sharing the jackpot, don't forget — and they both kept their tickets.'

'I'm not worrying, I just don't want to do it. I really don't want to do it.'

Cook pursed his lips slightly and turned to the window, looking pensively out into the street for a few seconds. He turned to face Pross again. 'Come on, you're not really entitled to the money, after all. We've stretched things for you, do something for us, won't you? This will be excellent for us. Great story, cat picking the numbers.'

This produced an unconvinced look from Pross.

'Look,' said Cook, 'a small cash advance on your winnings could even be arranged so you'll have spending money in London.'

Cash!

Pross ceased being reluctant and began being conniving. 'How large a small cash advance?'

'Say two, or even three hundred, this afternoon?'

There was enough vagueness in Cook's reply for Pross to venture pitching much higher.

'Make it two, or even three thousand.'

Pondering for a while, Cook pushed his hands into his jacket pockets. 'It's a lot,' he said. 'I'll have to get authority for that much. But I don't see why we can't. It's early enough to get clearance pushed through before the banks close.' Brightening, he concluded, 'Yes, should be able to do it in time.'

A pause.

'Just one more thing, though.'

'What's that?'

'We'd like you to bring the cat along for the media.'

'No problem.'

Every issue having been covered, the man from the national lottery shook the winner's hand again before setting off to get the money and to arrange Pross's trip to London, saying that he would be back as soon as it was all accomplished.

One quick meal and one long wait later, Cook returned. Once inside the flat, he handed Pross a first class return train ticket to King's Cross and a piece of paper bearing the name and address of the hotel he'd been booked into (where the presentation was also to take place) and a time to arrive by.

Sticking out of Cook's jacket pocket was a promising looking manilla envelope, which he passed over to Pross. In the envelope was three thousand pounds in tens, twenties and fifties, to be deducted from his winnings. Cook then explained that his part in Pross's affairs was now at an end. He said a final goodbye, said that it had been *interesting* for him, at least. He shook hands for some considerable time and with some considerable vigour before striding out through the door, as if his powers were urgently needed elsewhere in the world.

It was time to spend some.

A car hire company was telephoned. A model with a cd player and a top speed of 150mph was on offer. 'That'll do,' said Pross, and they said they'd deliver shortly.

While waiting for the car, Pross searched his bedroom for his driving licence, only ever required when Ron was too stoned to drive himself home. His eyes fell on the picture of Jennifer, lying on the floor where he'd discarded it the night before.

He felt another letter to her coming on.

He switched on his computer and printed a short note for her. Not one of his stored love letters. Just a silly little something he thought up there and then, a little something to keep her interested and curious.

The car arrived.

A week's hire was purchased for five hundred pounds.

Pross was left with two thousand, five hundred pounds to play with. A whole year's dole. For the first time ever, he had more money than sense.

He began to get suitably excited and childish about the money.

He threw it up in the air and watched it flutter to the floor.

He fanned it out in his hands.

He crumpled it up and had money-ball fights with the cat.

Collecting the notes, most crumpled, some torn, he spread them out flat on the tabletop next to the window. The table became completely covered with earnest promises to pay the bearer.

And Pross worked out that he had enough promises coming to him to cover nine hundred and thirty such tables.

1.17
A Home In The Country

And now he was going house hunting.

House hunting, he figured, was something best done at an estate agents, and since Lilith worked at one such agency in town, then that is where he headed.

The cash he had earlier spread over the table was gathered together and stuffed into his jacket pockets, except for a fifty pound note, which was slipped in with the letter to Jennifer.

He sorted out a selection of cd's from Ron's collection, then went out to the hired car, which was sleek and red.

First port of call was the postbox at the bottom of his street, into which he dropped his second letter to Jennifer.

Second port of call was the estate agents where Lilith worked.

He parked directly outside.

Through the window, Lilith viewed him emerging from the eyecatcher.

As soon as he entered the office, Lilith pointed to where he had come from. Almost telling him off, she said, 'Pross, what is that thing?'

'A Vauxhall *Fastasfuck*,' replied Pross, sitting on her desk.

'And whose is it?' said Lilith, continuing her interrogation.

'Mine, for a week. Five hundred.'

'And where did *you* get five hundred?'

Pross dug into his pocket and pulled out his wad. 'From here.'

Amazement began to show on Lilith's face.

'And who gave you that lot?'

'My cat,' said Pross, matter-of-factly, as he wandered over to look at the photos on display. 'Got any decent houses for sale? Any haunted ones?'

Beginning to realise the truth, for a while all she could find to say was 'You jammy bastard!' which she repeated until it lost all its dramatic impact.

When Lilith happened to fall silent for a moment, Pross explained that he was there to consider the purchase of a property: 'Money no object,' he added, which pricked up the ears of the office manager who was in a back room. Coming out into the front, he stuck his oar into the affair, but Pross made it clear that he wanted to deal with Lilith, and Lilith only. The manager complied with the wish, returning to the back room and leaving Lilith to deal with the business.

Lilith began supplying Pross with details of numerous properties, which he read through. But nothing he was being shown really took his fancy. Most of the bigger houses were located in villages: he wanted to be further away from people than that. He wanted something far away from settlements.

'Well, I suppose the only really isolated places will be up on the moors,' said Lilith, beginning to get a little fed up with producing details of properties only to have Pross turn his nose up at them.

The moors! Pross's beloved moors! Many a weekend he'd spent walking the moors with anyone who'd take him there. Life could be *felt* out there, out there with only bleak hills, sky and wind.

'The moors,' he said with quiet satisfaction, 'that's where I'll live.'

Lilith searched through a number of filing cabinets but found nothing suitable. 'Nothing,' she said, 'nothing at all. Sorry.'

'Not even a little cottage somewhere?'

'No, nothing. Oh, except that thing on the wall display over there. It'll be no good to you. Needs renovation.'

'Which one?' asked Pross, going over to look.

Lilith closed the cabinets, having exhausted all possible properties she felt he might be interested in. Moving over to where Pross was, she stood next to him, touching shoulders, and pointed at the property to which she'd referred. 'This one,' she said. 'We're pushing it as a potential hotel catering for people going grouse shooting, but no one's interested. It's been empty and leaking for years, if I remember rightly. Far too pricy for you as well.

How much did you say you'd won? Two million?'

Pross made no reply. He was silent because he'd just fallen in love. 'A castle. A bloody castle,' he said in hushed delight, 'a real bloody castle. Just look at it.'

'I've seen it,' Lilith informed him in unexcited tones. 'I stuck it up there. And it's not a real castle. It's a nineteenth century mock Gothic castle, built by some eccentric industrialist or other.' She walked back to her desk and sat behind it. 'And even with two million in the bank, it's still too pricy.'

'But just look at it,' he said. 'A bloody castle.'

Prospero Pi-Meson was in love. He was in love with the absurd idea of buying and living in a castle, even if it was mock. And if by purchasing it he deprived grouse killers of a convenient place to stay the night after indulging in their gratuitous carnage, then that made the proposition even more attractive.

'It's bloody enormous,' he said. 'Five acres of wooded grounds too.'

'It's also enormously costly,' said Lilith.

No answer came from Pross. He just stared adoringly at the picture on the wall. 'I could live there,' he murmured. 'I mean I could really *live* there.'

'And you could go bankrupt there as well,' pointed out Lilith.

'Happily, though.'

Lilith huffed, then asked, 'Are you serious about it?'

'More serious than dandruff,' replied Pross quietly.

Lilith sat upright and did something an Estate Agent rarely, if ever, does: she tried to put him off purchasing a property. 'Pross,' she said sincerely, 'it's a huge dilapidated mansion. It's no place to live. A place like that needs to earn its keep.'

'I bet it's bloody haunted though,' he said, infuriating her with his frivolity.

'Pross!' cried Lilith, 'haven't you seen the price of it?' She stomped over to the display and thrust an infuriated, tiny finger towards the pertinent numerical figure. She read slowly and loudly and, she hoped, with a sobering pointedness, 'Five hundred and forty thousand pounds.' She looked at Pross intently, hoping that the invocation of that huge sum might have worked some magic. 'And it might cost another five hundred thousand to convert it into the kind of place you think it is.'

'Chickenfeed,' responded Pross.

Lilith was well acquainted with his capacity for belligerence, and she gave up on her open opposition, knowing that resistance would just make him all the more resolute. 'All right, you win. You want it, I'll sell it to you.' She petulantly got him more details. 'Here,' she said in a huffish way, thrusting a small folder towards him.

Pross took the folder from her and smiled, for he'd just thought of something amusing. 'I know what I'm going to call it,' he informed her.

'Call what?'

'My castle, that's what.'

'It's not a castle, and I'm not interested,' said Lilith.

Thirty seconds of stubborn silence passed, after which Lilith huffed and put her hands on her hips. 'All right, what *are* you going to call it?'

'I'm going to call it Castle Prospero.'

'It's not a castle,' said Lilith.

The folder in Pross's hands contained all the information he needed to confirm his latest love. The property, it advised, was suitable for conversion to a spacious twenty-room hotel with stables, all subject to planning approval. It explained that the building had been closed up and uninhabited for five years while the will of the previous owner had been contested in court by relatives. A gatehouse in the grounds was occupied by the former gatekeeper and groundsman, who had been allowed to stay on rent-free in exchange for watching over the larger property, which was a little dilapidated and mid-nineteenth century in origin, a mile from a small hamlet and a little further from several others. It was set in over five acres of land with woods and a stream.

'Five hundred and forty thousand pounds, Pross,' Lilith pointed out firmly, revitalising her opposition, 'is a bloody lot of money for a mock castle in the middle of nowhere that you mightn't be able to sell again. I mean, it's been on the market for two years now. The fact that we've had to advertise it in all our branches, and not just the specialist property brochures, shows how hard we're finding it to shift.'

Pross ignored her. 'Come on,' he said, 'let's go see this Gothic heap.'

This was official business for Lilith. It was, she informed him, what is known in the trade as an "accompanied viewing". She collected the keys to the mock castle, which were in the hands of the agency, and followed Pross out through the door.

The sedate, unhurried cruise from Durham to the Weardale village of Rookhope, the closest settlement to the mock castle, took them thirty minutes. In those thirty minutes the views changed from the urban residential compactness of Durham City to the ploughed arable fields of the undulating Pennine foothills, then to bland commercial conifer forestation, and, finally, to the bleak, windswept moors of the higher valley.

In Rookhope, they asked an old, hardy-looking man for directions. He sent them back down the tiny road they'd just come up, telling them to look out for a small stone cottage amid a copse on the left, which was the occupied gatehouse.

They drove back along the way they'd come, a road which closely followed the relatively flat course of a small beck running between two impressive folds of moorland. The road was often so narrow that two cars could only just squeeze past each other, so narrow that an oncoming tractor might be a major inconvenience. On both sides of the road ran a continuous drystone wall to keep adventurous sheep at bay. The land lying immediately beyond these walls was partitioned into large, grassed fields, but these climbed only a limited way up the hills before giving way to open moorland.

Above the moors brooded the biggest sky imaginable.

They soon found the tiny cottage, peeping out from a nest of trees. Just beyond the gatehouse were actual gates, large and formed from wrought iron. They were chained and secured with a lock for which Lilith had no key.

Pross pulled up the car outside the gatehouse.

'Toot the horn,' said Lilith, 'see if there's anyone in.'

He tooted.

Dirty net curtains twitched in one of the tiny upstairs windows. An impassive face briefly looked outwards. Half a minute later, the flaking green door of the gatehouse slowly opened and a tall, gaunt, old, bearded, incurious man in an old brown duffle coat appeared. His cheeks were sunken and his eyes watery. Lilith got out to explain who they were and what they wanted.

Stood on his doorstep, the craggy man with watery eyes looked at Lilith's credentials, listened in silence to her discourse and nodded once when she'd finished. He smelt like old twigs. For an unnerving time he said nothing to Lilith, then, with long, shaky strides, walked slowly over to the car. He stooped to peer at Pross through the open side-window, saying, with discernable disapproval, 'Pop star, eh?'

'Poet,' returned Pross. It sounded so much better than jammy lottery winner.

'Humph,' muttered the man, straightening up, what little curiosity he had about Pross now satisfied. He strode back over to Lilith, walked straight past her and into his house. A few seconds later he came back, handed her a padlock key and pointed at the gates to indicate its area of usefulness.

She took it from him.

Considering the openness of the country thereabouts, Pross's castle was remarkably well secluded, not being at all visible from the road or even the gates, which explained why they had missed it coming up. For as well as being guarded by woods, that would have appeared to the imaginative eye from far above as an arboreal oasis amid a desert of moorland dunes, the castle and most of the grounds were set in a shallow, natural depression, so that, from eye-level, the surrounding landscape was hardly interrupted.

A minute of slow driving along a narrow, winding road lined by trees gave them their first good view of the property.

'Well, there it is,' said Lilith in a deliberatively unappreciative way as they came to a halt, 'Castle Prospero.'

'What a house,' he breathed, twisting about in his seat, being able to see the extent of the grounds for the first time. 'Look at all this land. What a garden.'

They drove a little closer and halted again, considering the building as it appeared from a modest distance. It certainly *looked* impressive, even Lilith could not now deny that.

They drove all the way up to the building, parking on a gravel-strewn forecourt. Clambering out of the car, they then walked slowly around the property, viewing it from all sides. As dilapidated mock castles go, seen from the outside this was not an overly moribund one. True, it had seen very much better days, but that was part of its charm. Sadly, it wasn't quite as Gothic in appearance as Pross had hoped for — too plain; not enough gargoyles (it wasn't even very castlely) — but he liked the look of it nevertheless. The main building was about forty paces in length and about twenty-five in width; at least two storeys high, maybe attic rooms as well. Its roof was moderately castellated, with the odd small tower rising here and there. On its southern facing wall, autumn ivy abounded, creeping tendrils almost completely overrunning some of the narrow, arched windows. In the centre of this southern wall an entrance porch with mock fortifications opened up like the black mouth of a cave, leading to a large, solid wooden door with a heavy iron knocker.

Lilith handed Pross the key to the door.

Pross unlocked the door and pushed it open. It was dingy inside. To an easily spooked person, the darkness poised soon to descend upon the land outside might have been thought to be lurking here in malevolent wait.

They hunted for a light switch, which they found.

It didn't work.

The electricity was unlikely to be on, Lilith explained. But enough natural light was available for them to see that a little behind the large main door was a second set of more conventional doors. They opened these and wandered inside, into the even dimmer light of the large, bare reception room.

Soon their eyes adapted enough for exploration.

Beyond this first room lay a spacious area from which a wide staircase curved upwards. It was romantic stuff. Its suggestive effects were not wasted on Lilith, either, who was fast weakening in her opposition to his spending a small fortune on the purchase of a mock castle with a leaky roof. She gave up resistance, partly because she knew that any opposition would be futile, even counter-productive, and partly because she could see that having a friend with such a property could well be a major source of fun. It was certainly a sensational place to hold a party. And, after soon abandoning exploration in the face of overwhelming darkness, when they came out of the house into the late autumn evening, she was almost as taken with the place as Pross himself.

After locking up and handing the keys back to Lilith, Pross ambled several paces forward then turned to appreciate his castle, now silhouetted black against the brooding sky, sombre and dominant, like something rising out of history.

Lilith stood beside him.

'Beautiful,' he said.

'It is,' agreed Lilith. 'Evocative.'

Pross draped his arm over Lilith and began walking her to the car. Mocking the style of the tycoon, he said, 'I want it. Attend to it for me first thing tomorrow.'

1.18
Stoned Again

It had been decreed: tonight, at Pross's flat, there was to be a celebration. Selected friends were invited.

After dropping off Lilith, asking her to contact certain friends of his with the news, Pross set about organizing his party. This simply involved him doing an amount of grocery shopping at a late store, buying expensive comestibles with an offhand casualness which came unsettlingly natural to him. His purchases included a supply of booze, which he swore to himself he wouldn't get drunk on, it being designated for his friends.

He also treated himself to a food binge, courtesy of an Indian take-away.

And Spock had half a ton of delicacies.

After the sumptuous meal, a long lie down in front of the telly seemed appropriate.

At a few minutes after eight, the bright headlights of a vehicle pulling up outside his flat shone into the room. He turned his head away from the television and looked through the window, whereupon, in the orange illumination cast by the street lamp above, he observed a mini-cab speeding off and Suzie, Pete's energetic girlfriend, fumbling with his gate. Suzie, kicking the gate shut behind her, peered into Pross's living room. In the blended light of the street lamp and the television screen, she discerned the lottery winner lying stretched out on the sofa that Ron's mother had donated to her son after it had become unfashionable, Spock soon further devaluing it with its claws.

Suzie waved to Pross. He waved back, beckoning her inside with a lazy gesture so that she'd know he'd left the inner door unlocked, saving himself the trouble of getting up to let people in.

Presently she came into the room. 'Hiya Pross,' she called from near the door as she slipped out of her coat. 'Lilith told me all about it, you jammy thing!'

'Hiya Su,' returned Pross wearily. 'Scuse me if I don't get up, but I'm conserving my fatigue.'

Suzie was forgiving. 'I understand,' she lilted.

'A good fatigue's worth its weight in gold these go-getting days,' he explained, 'and I'm sure you don't want me to squander it on some petty activity.'

'Not at all,' she said. Suzie had a voice and a way of speaking that Pross found beguiling. Hers was a musical voice.

She smiled, and with a coquettish yet innocent manner about the action, quickly kissed the tip of the middle finger of her right hand, applying it to his lips as he lay on his back on the sofa. Then she gambolled over to the curtains and, after a noisy and somewhat petulant struggle, succeeded in drawing them. This achieved, she turned and gambolled into the kitchen to pour herself something to drink, having just been informed that it was brimming with booze and comestibles.

Other people began to arrive, and from each newcomer Pross had to suffer congratulatory squeaks and squawks. So tedious did these reactions become, he announced a total ban on all references to his cat's lottery fortune effective from five minutes after the arrival of the last of his invited friends. The last to arrive, at just after ten o'clock, was Tony, who wasted none of his five available minutes in persuading Pross that he should offer financial compensation to all his friends for having had to suffer his company for so many years.

Listening in and agreeing with Tony, his friends quickly began to resemble an ugly mob.

Although he argued against Tony's suggestion, it was actually his secret intention to shower his worthy friends with gifts galore, but for the meantime all he gave was a shrug. 'Well, I'll see what I can do.'

This seemed to pacify the mob. A celebratory pipe was offered by Pete, and Pross quickly succumbed. It was one of the most serene stones of his life so far. Hardly a single anxious feeling did he experience.

Things felt great with him.

Things *were* great with him.

He lay down and listened to beautiful music. Every instrument could be clearly heard. Every rhythm and every sub-rhythm could be grooved to. Every harmony and every counterpoint could be appreciated. With eyes closed, he let it all drift blissfully into him... until Pete began to get vociferously stroppy about something.

'I can't help it,' claimed Pross in reluctant response, opening his eyes. 'How was I to know what fucking car they'd bring me?'

'You could have pulled it off, or painted over it at the very least,' Pete pointed out, accusing Pross of being normal, thereby also accusing him of being subnormal. That is, accusing him of being stupid.

'I bloody will then,' declared Pross, already on his feet and lifting up a rug beside the door to reveal the cellar trapdoor. He disappeared downwards. One minute later, he emerged with an old pot of black paint and a half-bald brush.

'I'll do it now,' he announced.

He strode out of the flat and over to the car he'd hired, followed closely by Pete and then by Tony, who, for the trip outside, had donned his pair of round multi-coloured reflective sunglasses.

The general suspicion was that Tony believed his sunglasses made him look cool.

The night was cold and damp, a little misty.

Pross looked critically at the piece of embellishment Pete had drawn his attention to. 'Ugh,' he loudly said when the full mass of its tastelessness collided head-on his with his sense of aesthetics. 'Ugh,' he said again, even louder this time. With inadequate stealth, some of the neighbours peeped from behind their curtains.

'I told you,' said Pete.

'It's awful, isn't it?' admitted Pross cheerlessly, paint pot in hand.

'Yep,' said Pete; 'that's one of the prattiest go-faster stripes I've ever seen.'

Tony took off his sunglasses and looked at the stripe, soon to raise dissention. 'I quite like it,' he said. 'Looks smart.'

After curtly dismissing Tony from their company, Pete and Pross again regarded the stripe.

'It's got to go,' said Pross earnestly.

'It has,' agreed Pete, borrowing Pross's tone.

'It won't do,' said Pross.

'It won't do at all,' said Pete.

With a sudden initiation of activity, Pross feverishly over-painted the stripes on both sides of the car with a thick, dripping, wobbly black band.

'That's a lot better,' announced Pete when the job was completed.

'It is,' agreed Pross, proud of his artwork. 'One more thing, though.'

'What?'

'This...'

Pross painted a large, irregular shape on the shiny bonnet. Next to it, he wrote in big letters: GO-SLOWER SPLODGE.

'Oh yes,' said Pete, 'that's just what it needed. Where's Ron's car? Let's paint that as well.'

'I don't know,' lamented Pross. 'Probably at the airport or something. Maybe he left it at his mother's place. I don't know.'

'Shame,' said Pete.

Pross brightened. 'Let's find it and sand all the paint and chrome off and throw buckets of salted water over it. It'd just be a crappy pile of rust when he got back. Then we could hide in Mexico for a few years until he began to see the funny side of it.'

'He'd never find us there,' predicted Pete.

'Not without a car,' reckoned Pross.

But they soon forgot about this fanciful plan to break Ron's heart once back indoors.

The night air induced a strong desire for food in Pross. He had what all dope smokers know as the *munchies*, and it was while lazily chewing on his second *Mars Bar* that he began dreamily making shapes on the ceiling, courtesy of the dope. If he let it happen, a dark smudge above the fire might transmogrify into a Red Indian squaw with a papoose strapped to her back. Almost as soon as this image became real and analysable, it would dissolve and become a smudge again, though once it clearly became a wild horse running across expansive grasslands.

He could get off on dope more than anyone he'd ever heard of, just like he could be sick on booze more than anyone else.

'I hear you're buying a mock castle,' said Pete after an uncharacteristic silence.

Pross was still watching the elusive squaw, or at least catching fugacious glimpses of her. 'It's a real castle,' he answered after a few seconds. 'Castle Prospero.'

'Whatever,' said Pete, and that was that.

Twenty quiet minutes later, Pross announced that he was going to bed.

'Bed?' exclaimed Melanie. 'It's only quarter past eleven. You've never gone to bed this early before in your whole wasted life.'

'It's been a long day,' he explained, 'and I'm getting up early tomorrow to go to London to collect my cheque. So everybody fuck off home.'

1.19
Lilith's First Kiss

The others went directly to their homes, but Lilith, alone, did not.

She did try, but two streets away she turned her car around and headed back towards Devon Road, parking outside Pross's flat. Sitting in the vehicle, she tried to figure out just what in the hell she thought she was up to. If she went to Pross now and told him how she really felt about him, he would probably just turn her away; or worse, maybe, be her reluctant lover for a single night.

She was being crazy, she told herself. There was absolutely no way he could be interested in her as a lover. If she looked like Jennifer, or even Melanie, or even just bits of Melanie, then it might be a different story. She could make a play for him then.

Sat in the darkness, Lilith lamented everything about herself; from her uneven, saggy breasts, to her large, flabby bum; from her missing first chin, to her weirdly present and sagging second one. Christ, she couldn't even walk like a normal person. And was it not Pross himself who'd first joked that she moved with all the grace of a reluctant bag of putty? It was — yet how she still wanted him.

Head getting the better of heart, she started the engine and put the car into gear.

But with an impulsive, jerky motion she pulled out the ignition key, killing the engine. 'Oh what the hell,' she said, getting out of the car, ready to take a chance. After all, she did feel that she shared something special with Pross, something to do with mutual understanding. Maybe that's what he really needs in a relationship, she thought: implicit understanding. Maybe that's why his few previous relationships hadn't lasted?

Having reached the gate, she paused.

Five seconds of deliberation passed.

'Oh, what the hell,' she said again, proceeding.

Soon she was tapping gently on Pross's window, and he opened the door for her.

'Forgotten something?' he asked, standing aside so that she could enter.

Lilith nodded slightly and walked inside, going over to the gas fire and sitting down in front of it. She had resolved to risk all, not least her pride, and fling herself amorously in Pross's direction. Maybe just one night of passion was actually better than none at all? For all she knew, she might hardly ever see him again now that he'd become so wealthy.

She was trembling ever so slightly as he came over and sat beside her, unromantically shoving Ritz Crackers into his mouth.

'Well?' he mumbled, mouth full. 'What have you forgotten?'

Lilith feared she was about to cry. 'There's something I have to tell you,' she said without tears.

'Yeah?' he said, stuffing even more crackers into his mouth.

'Yeah,' she echoed falteringly, her intense gaze directed at the fire.

Her revelation was not forthcoming.

Pross noisily swallowed his mouthful of crackers. 'About the castle?' he wondered. 'I still want to buy it, so don't bother trying to put me off.'

Lilith said nothing. Her heart was telling her to grab the person she wanted, but she had no idea how to actually go about making a pass at someone. Her female instincts told her that she should take it slow, sly and gentle, but her intellect told her to be sudden and brazen about it, in case her victim cottoned on to what she was up to and slipped away to the bathroom to be sick — that's the kind of opinion of herself Lilith's intellect could sometimes have. 'About the castle,' she said at last, her voice a little croaky and tight. 'It's all right. It'll wait till you get back from London.'

'What about it?' Pross wanted to know.

'Nothing. It'll wait.'

'No, tell me. You've got me all curious now.'

Lilith tried to think of something to say about it, wishing that she'd gone straight home instead of weakening and turning back. She was being a fool, she told herself.

'Er,' she faltered, 'I just thought I'd point out to you it'll be quite a while before you'll be able call the house your own. You'll have to get a survey done, and...'

'Survey? What the fuck for?'

'To make sure it's a sound building. You can't get a mortgage or insurance unless you've had a survey done. And then there's the Local Authority Search to be done, to make sure no motorway or something's planned to cut through it.'

'Sod mortgages,' said Pross, swilling down another mouthful of crackers with a swig of milk, 'I'm paying cash. Sod insurance as well. And motorways.'

Lilith said nothing for a short while, then uttered, 'It'll still take about four weeks for the solicitors to deal with the change of ownership.'

'Four weeks,' moaned Pross. A month was far too long. 'What if we pay the solicitors extra?'

Lilith shrugged. 'I suppose it might work. I'll talk with them tomorrow morning.' She was now very close to some sort of emotional display. It was stupid of her to believe, she told herself, that she could ever have the sort of romances her friends enjoyed. It would never happen. She had nothing to offer. She was ugly and peculiar.

Lilith rose to her feet and walked quickly to the door, keeping her back to Pross, knowing that she really was going to burst into unseemly tears this time but hoping she could control her emotions until she was alone in her car.

Pross twisted around, wondering what was up with her.

Subject to another impulse, she halted, turned around, retraced her steps, then blurted out her desire: 'I want you, Pross, I really do want you. I've wanted you for months.'

Then she ardently launched herself at him, lips frantically puckered. But in an automatic self-defence reaction, he quickly raised the Ritz Crackers box to protect his face from assault. Lilith's lips met with cardboard, and her desire slipped out of reach, quickly getting to his feet. Wounded by the cruel rejection, crushed by the failure, she burst into sobs, rolling into a ball on the floor.

It was a few seconds before Pross actually worked out what had happened. She'd made a clumsy pass at him, he came to understand, and he'd humiliated her with a cardboard box.

'Aw, I'm sorry,' he sheepishly said, wondering what to do.

The sobbing stopped.

Kneeling down beside her, he laid a hand on her back, speaking softly. 'You took me by surprise, that's all.'

Lilith stood up, wiped the vestiges of tears away and simply said, 'I'm sorry too. It won't happen again. I promise.'

Pross also rose to his feet, feeling compassion and sympathy. Lilith turned to leave, but then had a change of mind. Steeling herself, she faced Pross again.

Slowly, tentatively, she encircled him with her arms.

Her head rested upon his shoulder.

They stood together, motionless, for many seconds, and she murmured, 'I want you, Pross. I really do want you.'

'Of course you do. It's my hair.'

She gave him a little thump on the back.

'And I want you too,' he diplomatically added.

She lifted her head up and looked into his eyes. She knew that he was being moved by pity for her, and he knew that she knew, but she slowly brought her lips to his.

Her first ever kiss.

Pross began a muted panic. What could he do now? Reject her by asking her to leave? The last thing he could imagine was taking her to bed.

They continued to embrace and kiss. Something had to happen soon, either an escalation of the passion or a cooling of it.

He held her head gently between his hands and drew back from her lips, looking into her eyes: he'd reached a decision, and he knew she could read it in his eyes.

But the screams forced his attention away.

The screams also grabbed hold of Lilith's attention.

With her hand in his, he hurried over to switch on the room's main light, listening intently.

More screams.

Pross moved to the inner door, bringing Lilith with him. The screams, definitely female, were reverberating chillingly around the house's entrance hall. Lilith clung tightly to his arm, her face showing anxiety. He opened the door to the cacophonous hall, wishing he wasn't stoned. Taking a small, reluctant step outwards, he flicked on the light switch near his door.

Lilith still clung to him.

No one was there.

More screams ricocheted around the walls, and panicky feet shuffled down the stairs.

It was Mrs Brown, making her way as fast as she could to the outer door, looking all the while behind her, as if she feared someone might be following. Catching sight of Pross and Lilith, she screamed again. 'Legs! Legs! His legs!'

Pross blanched, saying to himself, with real concern, 'No, not now. Not when I'm stoned.'

'Legs! Legs! His legs!' repeated Mrs Brown.

Pross looked down at his legs.

Lilith looked down at Pross's legs.

Pross greatly wished he wasn't stoned. 'Did she say legs?' he asked.

'I think so,' returned his nervous, clinging friend.

Mrs Brown slowly collapsed into a bony heap. 'Legs,' she wailed, pointing up the stairs.

'Go and help her,' said Lilith, giving Pross a little push, 'she's *your* neighbour.'

Pross resisted the push, so Lilith pushed harder, which resulted in him forcefully defying her. 'No, please. I can't. Not when I'm stoned. You go, please. You go.'

Realising the disturbing effect that Mrs Brown was having on her friend, Lilith asked, 'What is it? Why are you so scared?'

'You can't understand. She's just like my own mother. Wasted bones and no life. A ghost. A fucking tortured ghost.'

'I've never heard you mention her before. Where is she?'

'Not sure,' confessed Pross. 'In an institution somewhere.'

'Don't you ever see her?'

'Can't even contemplate it.'

Looking sympathetically at him, Lilith said, 'It's all right, Pross.'

Squeezing his hand first, she tentatively approached the bony heap on the floor and tried to offer it comfort.

'Legs,' the pale, angular heap said again.

Lilith knelt down and held on to one of Mrs Brown's bony hands.

The hand was lifeless and unresponsive.

'Legs,' trembled the heap.

Pross looked bewilderedly at Lilith.

Lilith returned the bewildered look to Pross.

Pross gave the unwanted look back to Lilith, wishing very, very much that he wasn't stoned.

'Legs,' cried Mrs Brown.

'Legs,' echoed Lilith, gazing at Pross with the same kind of expectant look that was hanging on the face of Mrs Brown.

'Don't you start as well,' said Pross to Lilith.

'Upstairs,' said the heap of bones. 'Legs.'

'Upstairs,' said Lilith. 'Legs.'

'Stop it,' said Pross, 'this is getting weird.'

Pross moved slowly towards the heap of bones and odd clothes that even at the best of times gave him the heebie-jeebies.

'Legs,' it said to him.

'Legs' echoed Pross hypnotically.

'Upstairs.'

Lilith put forward a suggestion: 'Go upstairs and look around.'

'What?' said Pross. 'In my state?'

'Go on,' she urged, 'I'll wait here with her.'

'Legs,' interposed Mrs Brown, again pointing up the stairs. 'Harry's legs.'

Lilith and Pross looked at each other, both silently mouthing the words, "Harry's legs".

Harry's legs held no fear for him, so Pross approached the stairs.

The first flight of steps brought him on to the small landing in front of Mrs Brown's door. Harry was nowhere to be seen. Pross wondered what to do now. The second, narrower flight of stairs leading to the attic flat occupied by Harry began at the other end of the landing, so he decided to investigate in that direction.

At the bottom of this second flight of stairs, there was a strong smell of whisky. These stairs were steeper than the first flight, and Pross wondered how many times Harry must have fallen victim to them. A dim light seeped down the staircase from above. He peered upwards. A pair of legs could be seen lying twisted and motionless over the top steps.

Pross crept upwards, going slowly and apprehensively, his back to the wall. Each step ascended brought more of Harry into view. He realised that Harry was not lying, but was *hanging*, his bottom suspended inches off the floor, while his feet protruded over the top steps.

The smell of whisky intensified.

The smell of Harry's unwashed clothes mingled and competed with the whisky smell.

Halfway up the stairs, he began to see Harry's motionless torso. Another tentative step revealed a contorted face; and he immediately figured how the alcoholic had met his undignified end.

One more step brought Harry into full view. An open whisky bottle lay on its side, the contents having spilled out over the wooden floor and evaporated, leaving a large stain. Harry's face was fixed into a gruesome expression of pain and surprise, eyes bulging out, mouth twisted. This was Pross's first corpse. The sight held him mesmerised.

Three cigarette stubs remained wedged in the corner of Harry's blue mouth.

Gradually becoming aware that Lilith was calling his name from below, he turned and walked down, wishing sorely that he hadn't got so stoned this night. Lilith, who had climbed halfway up the first flight of stairs, called, 'Are you all right? Pross? Where are you?'

Pross came into her view. 'It's Harry,' he said, 'he's hung himself trying to open his door.'

'What?' puzzled Lilith. 'Hung himself trying to open his door?'

Pross sat on the bottom step, pausing to gather his wits. 'Hung himself,' he confirmed, 'with that cord he uses to keep his key on. The key's in the keyhole, and he's hanging from it. He must have fallen over last night and strangled himself, too drunk to get to his feet.'

'Dead?' murmured the heap of bones, reaching out to Pross with her eyes. 'Harry's dead?'

'Dead,' confirmed Pross in a low voice, terrified that she would move towards him.

'My husband,' said Mrs Brown, uttering her desolate words quietly, 'my husband, dead.'

Lilith turned to Pross and whispered, 'I didn't know they were married.'

Taking some time to answer, he said, 'Neither did I.'

'But they don't even live in the same flat,' remarked Lilith incredulously.

Mrs Brown's eyes met Pross's. She mouthed some words, but he couldn't make them out. 'What's that you're saying,' he awkwardly asked. But she did not respond. She was now beyond his inquiry. She was beyond his inquiry and possibly beyond recall, beyond recall from down a terrible road along which marriage to witless Harry may have driven her.

The police were called. Within five minutes a car arrived, followed, at short intervals, by a further four cars, then a forensic team, then an ambulance.

The forensic team took measurements and photographs.

The ambulance team took one look at Mrs Brown and decided that she was in even worse shape than her husband, and then took her to a hospital.

Pross and Lilith spent much of the night giving statements about Harry, and how they'd discovered the body.

In the small hours, the landlord appeared in the entrance hall. He'd obviously dressed in a hurry; no socks on, no shirt under his jacket. Strands of his dark hair, long at the fringe but usually neatly combed back, were falling over his eyes. His face was like stone. Not even glancing at Pross, who was giving a statement to an officer, he walked up and cut into the conversation, coldly asking for the facts; a mechanical inquiry into the circumstances of his tenant's death.

'And who are you?' asked the officer.

'Son of the deceased,' said the landlord.

That came as a thorough surprise to Pross; but when he thought about it, it all made sense. It certainly explained why he'd never gone up the stairs to collect rent. And if Harry was his father, and Mrs Brown his mother, then that was surely reason enough for him never having gone up the stairs at all.

The facts are what Harry's son duly received.

'How do you feel?' asked Lilith gently, observing that Pross, now standing near his own door, was still looking distressed.

'All right,' he lied.

Lilith naturally found herself moving to hold his hand. At first he did not respond, but then returned the supportive clasp.

'I had to be stoned tonight, didn't I?' he murmured.

'When I held her hand,' said Lilith, 'there was no response at all. It felt like a bird's talon.'

'No, please, don't tell me. Not when I'm stoned. That's when they can really trouble me.'

'What can?'

Pross let his eyes close for a moment. Upon their opening again, they weren't looking at Lilith, just into the foggy distance. 'Memories, Lilith. Memories. Sometimes it feels like I get pretty close to losing it.'

'I had no idea,' said his friend. 'I never guessed. You always seem so level. So unruffable.' She paused a while. 'You turn it all into a big joke, don't you? You treat everything as a joke. Maybe too many things.' And after a moment's deliberation, Lilith gently kissed him on the cheek. 'It's time you stopped joking about some of the important things with someone,' she murmured.

But Pross seemed hardly aware she'd kissed him, and seconds later he extricated his hand from hers, commenting, 'It never feels like time, Lilith. Never met anyone I could get serious about.' But he immediately realised he'd said something hugely insensitive. He hadn't really been listening to her, but now he realised Lilith had been offering herself to him as one person he could trust and confide in, drop the joke with, and he'd seemingly discounted her qualifications.

Smiling bravely, Lilith said, 'I'll have to be going soon. I'm at work in five hours.' She hesitated. 'Unless you want me to stay with you longer, that is.' She hesitated again. 'Do you want me to stay?'

An exchange of looks occurred between Lilith and Pross. 'No, it's all right. The dope's wearing off now. I'll be OK soon.'

Smiling painfully, she said, 'Sorry about pouncing on you earlier. Must have smoked too much. See you whenever.'

She turned and left.

He showed no emotion, the landlord. When he'd heard all there was to hear, he looked set to leave, but was thwarted by the occurrence of the bringing down of the body. Ambulance men bearing a corpse-laden stretcher came between him and the door.

Turning away from the sight, he moved over to near where Pross was standing, now alone, in wait to complete his interrupted statement.

Pross watched as the body was carried away, sombre thoughts about the mutability, futility and stupidity of life weighing heavy on his mind.

It wasn't at all meant to be a wisecrack this time, or a deliberate irritation, it was meant to be an ironic comment on the night's events, but it was taken wholly wrong: 'And there's still the shower to get broken,' Pross muttered to Harry's son.

Perhaps something inside Harry's son snapped at that moment; just for that moment. He turned round and gave Pross a fierce look of unmitigated hatred. So laced with danger was this look, that for the first time in his life, Pross was glad to be surrounded by police officers. The furious look soon subsided, and the son spoke slowly and forcefully. 'It's about time I had a word with you about something. Follow me.' Not asking permission to enter, the landlord walked into Pross's flat, going straight into the living room. Pross followed, more than a little cautiously, wishing he could learn to keep his mouth shut. In the living room, the son looked about himself, taking undue interest in the ashtrays scattered about. One ashtray he picked up, finding in it the remains of several joints left there by Pross's friends.

'Interesting smoking habits you have,' said the landlord distastefully, looking Pross directly in the eyes for once, putting the evidence into his coat pocket. 'Interesting gardening habits you have as well.'

Pross didn't answer; though if he had, it's a toss-up whether it would have been something like "I'm very sorry for having upset you just now," or something like "fuck you."

The son walked to the door, where he halted and addressed Pross, again in threatening tones. 'I want you out by the weekend,' he said. 'And if you're not, I'll give the police what I've got in my pocket, *and* I'll tell them what kind of plant I pulled up from the garden recently. You've got until six o'clock on Friday evening to get your stuff out.'

He left the house.

Pross sat down. Aw, fuck him, he soon thought, dismissing the unhappy misapprehension. 'Well,' he said to Spock, 'at least I've found out what happened to Ron's dope plant.' He settled back and smiled at the thought of the landlord's attempt to force him out of the house. So what? he thought, I'm a millionaire with a pad in the country.

At about six a.m., the show was over. The last policeman left the house, saying that it was pretty obvious to them what had happened and that there were no suspicious circumstances.

Pross was very tired, this being the third consecutive night of truncated sleep for him. However, he knew that if he went to bed now, he would not bother to drag himself up in time to catch the train — which left Durham station at 10.30am — even for two million pounds.

He'd have to stay awake.

To kill some hours, he watched breakfast tv for the first time in his life.

By half-past nine, he was washed, shaved, dressed and fed.

Eventually the time for departure arrived. With the cat struggling in his arms, he went out to his car, which was easy to find, being the only one in the street with a messy go-slower splodge.

On the way to the station, he bought a cat basket.

1.20
Mad Mick

Wretched tears had wet her pillow for much of the remainder of the night. She couldn't even give herself away — she was that unattractive. She should never have tried. Those things weren't meant for her.

After leaving Pross's flat, alone in her sleepless bed, Lilith's stoicism had failed, and she had wept pitiably. But come the morning, her tears had strangely dried. And upon the very moment her alarm clock sounded, as she lifted the cover and almost mechanically set about doing what she had to do, anyone seeing her then would have observed an almost fearful resolve in her face.

From the bed, she moved over to sit at her ragged beechwood art deco dressing table. Make up and perfume items were scattered before her. A sneering smile surfaced fleetingly as she regarded these incongruous accoutrements. Falling over her face, her hair felt unnaturally cold. Fingering it, she realised it was still wet with her own tears. She looked at herself in the mirror, holding her tearful hair to her cheek, the only truly feminine thing nature had given her, she often thought.

But it didn't matter any more. Nothing mattered any more. She knew she would never have to cry again. It was all over for her.

Picking up a large, sharp pair of scissors, she looked hard and hatefully at herself in the mirror.

Then she did it.

The new morning found Jennifer much brightened. At this same time one day earlier, she had been sitting tearfully at the end of her bed composing her sundering letter to John, but today something told her that life was on the up for her. And so it was to the accompaniment of subdued but cheerful singing that she showered away the dirt of the previous day prior to setting off for her last day of work at the veterinary surgery.

And after she showered, she dressed. And after she dressed, she sat at the dressing table in her bedroom to put on the small amount of make-up she deemed fit for work. While carefully applying a pale pink lipstick, she heard the sound of Elaine's key sliding into the front door lock. Elaine was returning from her night shift, all yawns and shivers as she closed the door behind herself and picked up the morning post. There were three letters: one for her and two for Jennifer.

Elaine tapped on Jennifer's door before slipping the two letters under it. Then she went straight to bed, exhausted after her ten hour stint of checking garments for unacceptable flaws.

In the dressing table mirror, Jennifer's eye, drawn by the sound of the tapping, caught sight of the envelopes as they appeared on the polished oak floorboards below her bedroom door. The reflected image of one of these letters she regarded with particular curiosity. In the mirror, she glanced at it often while carefully removing a small smear of lipstick from below the corner of her mouth.

Regarding them in the mirror, Jennifer saw that one of the envelopes was of the same style as the one Prospero Pi-Meson had sent her the day before. Her mouth perfected, she picked this envelope up and read the postmark. It was from Durham, and the hand that the address was written in was reminiscent of the hand of yesterday. She felt curiously apprehensive about opening it, preferring to slip it into her coat pocket to save for reading during her lunch break.

It was the first time Pross had ever been to London. He'd never had the money or the reason to make the trip before.

Pross was now in the back of a black taxi heading towards the hotel where he'd been assured a room was booked for the night under his name. He had a small suitcase belonging to Ron on his left, a pocket full of cash, and an incessantly miaowing cat in a special basket on his right.

The sleepless night he'd just had, and the two preceding nights of interrupted sleep, were beginning to catch up with the boredom he now felt. The boredom and the sleeplessness, with their combined strengths, pulled down on his eyelids and occasionally construed to make his head to loll backwards.

Every so often he lost awareness for a second or two.

He looked with tired eyes out of the side window. The time was only a little past noon, yet the light was dim and dreary. The wind was picking up, and drops of rain were beginning to smear the glass. The traffic was dense and impatient as they negotiated a large roundabout. Here, Pross found himself leaning forward slightly and asking the driver, through the half-open glass partition, if it was Buckingham Palace to the right of them.

The taxi driver, a seedy-looking chap with dirty fingernails and short, wiry hair immediately replied, 'Course it is, guv.'

'Thought so,' said Pross, sitting back again, his eyelids getting heavier.

Unfortunately the driver considered the question to have been a dialogue initiator, and he pressed unwanted conversation on to his paying passenger.

'New to the smoke then are ya, guv?'

'That's right,' Pross wearily said, his tired eyes again gazing out of the side window. With a sigh, he slumped further down into the seat. 'If a poet can ever be said to be new to anything unpleasant. We confront and become familiar with so many horrors in our imaginations.'

This unusual comment pricked up the driver's ears and aroused his interest, but for the meantime he simply stuck to the casual conversation that got him through the working day.

But he stole frequent looks at Pross in the rear-view mirror.

Some time later, he asked, 'What'ya carting that cat around for?'

'Because I'm a poet,' answered Pross.

A poet!

The seedy-looking taxi driver also liked to think of himself as something of a poet, and he'd even once, at the age of sixteen, had both a story and a sonnet printed in his school's magazine. This literary triumph he would allude to and proudly elaborate on whenever he could manage to work it into a conversation, glibly reeling off the cherished verses at the slightest hint of an invitation to do so.

He was of course careful not to let slip that the publication which had accepted his poem was nothing but a mere school magazine.

The cab halted behind a long line of stationary vehicles. Large drops of rain impacted against the roof with a fury that seemed malicious. The driver turned to look at Pross again. 'You a poet then?' he asked, a little tentatively, his expression revealing deep interest.

Pross closed his eyes, weariness accelerating. A reply was found for the driver's question: 'A professional melancholic.'

It was the word "professional" that did it. That word impressed the driver greatly. He glanced forward to check that the traffic was still jammed. Seeing that is was and that it looked like it might remain so for several minutes, he turned his full attention to his poetical passenger. 'What, you've 'ad stuff published and that?'

'Loads,' lied Pross with his eyes still closed, hoping that the driver would take the hint and leave him alone. It *was* a lie. He'd never had anything published. He'd never even so much as submitted a work for consideration. In fact he'd only ever written one complete poem, and that was crap, and he knew it, although he'd never admit it, especially to a girl.

'What sort of stuff?' asked the poet-driver.

Pross opened his eyes. 'The sort of stuff I specialise in,' he said, hoping this to be enough to deflect any further conversation.

The driver glanced to the fore again: the traffic was still stationary. He turned back to Pross. 'What sort of stuff's that?'

Pross said, 'Auto-epitaphs.'

Two seconds thinking time.

'Oh those,' said the driver, though he didn't really have a clue what an epitaph was.

He said that he, too, was something of a poet. He waited for some suitably impressed response from Pross.

It was not forthcoming.

'Yeah, I'm a bit of a poet,' he was forced to repeat. 'Sonnets are what I do. Even 'ad one printed in a magazine.'

He was sure that this would elicit an inquiry allowing him an opportunity to recite his triumphant verse.

It didn't.

But he recited the poem anyway...

It was awful. Fourteen lines of pure shit. Pross would be the first to admit, if cornered, that his own poem was rubbish, but compared to this driver's effort he was a gifted genius. For something that attempted to be a traditional-style sonnet, its lines showed a disquieting tendency to have at some times a great clamouring quantity of syllables, and at other times to be sorely lacking in them. It was an attempt to describe in rhyme his eternal love for some freakish lady named Aileen, who, according to the unequal lines, was a peerless beauty of a virgin endowed with a heart at least as true as Sir Galahad's and an intellect to rival Isaac Newton's. Pross closed his eyes again, wishing devoutly that he hadn't asked about that bloody palace.

A car's horn sounded aggressively from behind. 'Oh Christ,' muttered the driver, quickly setting his cab into jerky motion.

The journey was stop-start all the way. The driver filled the starts with curses to the traffic, and the stops with desultory burbling to his passenger. During one of the painful stops, Pross ascertained that the man fervently believed the meaning of life to be accessible in the lyrics of Led Zeppelin songs, if only the searcher has the necessary insight. It was at this juncture that Pross realised with absolute certainty that the incredibly bad poet driving him to his hotel was stark raving mad. Consequently, he began to find the specimen psychologically interesting. He leaned forward to converse with the madman who was steering him through traffic. 'Any Led Zeppelin songs in particular?' he inquired.

'Stairway to 'eaven,' came the immediate reply, 'it's all in there, if y'can understand it.'

'Do you understand it?'

'Not all of it,' said the driver, with a look of the esoteric about him.

Pross sat back again and marvelled, almost resentfully, at how often his path was crossed by utter weirdos. It was still less than twelve hours since he'd had to deal with Mrs Brown's hysteria and Harry's dead legs, and now he was at the mercy of an insane cabby who'd begun reciting the lyric of the song in which he was adamant the meaning of life could be found.

Presently, they were in a line of traffic moving parallel to the Thames. Pross looked at a riverboat passing beside them.

'That's Tower Bridge over there,' said the driver, 'and that's the Tower of London.'

A motorcycle despatch rider overtook them on the left. The worst poet in the cab became agitated and angry. 'Wanka!' he shouted to the distant rider, showing a clenched fist. The driver then turned to look at his passenger again. 'That 'otel y'going to,' he said, 'it's a real posh un. You staying there?'

'Is it?' replied Pross, wishing that the driver would keep his eyes on the road.

The driver turned to the fore again.

'You got big money then?'

'Enormous money,' said Pross, wondering why he was in such a stand-offish mood. Maybe it was just because he was tired, or maybe it was because he was annoyed with himself for having sold out in agreeing to a public presentation.

Eventually the cab came to a halt beside what was obviously the hotel.

'This is it. Six paarnds eighty pence, please.'

Pross put his hand into his pocket and pulled out his money. The journey had been so bad and unprofessional he'd decided to give the mad driver a big tip.

1.21
A Follower

With the back of his hand, the hand in which he was holding the wad of money, he wiped some of the condensation from the window next to him. Through the smeared pane he viewed the hotel's facade.

He wanted to play truant.

He wanted to go on a shopping spree.

And he would have done both if there hadn't been such an enticingly large cheque awaiting him.

The driver again said, 'Six paarnds eighty pence, please.'

Pross leaned forward. 'How much do you think I should tip you?' he asked.

Spock began to wail again.

'Dunno, guv. A paarnd?' He twisted round in his seat to face Pross, his gaze at once alighting upon the bundle of notes.

Pross fanned out his money. 'I liked your sonnet,' he lied. 'You've got talent. Don't you think you're worth more than a pound? A lot more?'

The driver was now at a loss for words. Pross just hadn't turned out to be a normal kind of passenger. Something unusual was happening and he didn't know what to say or do.

He just looked fraught and perplexed.

In fact he looked so fraught and perplexed that Pross almost felt sorry for him. 'Listen,' said Pross, feeling a little compunctious, 'I liked your sonnet a lot, and I'll give you, let's say four hundred pounds, if you'll be my driver for the day. I want to get around and do some shopping. You can take me to the best places.'

The driver looked at the money. Then he looked at Pross. Then he looked back at the money. He found his voice. 'Yeah, aw'right,' he said quietly, his instincts telling him that it was some kind of trick.

'Then here you are. Park this thing somewhere and meet me in the lobby.'

Apprehensively taking the money being offered, the mad driver shook his head in disbelief: a proper poet had given him over a week's takings for only a six pound eighty fare. For the first time in his whole life, wonderful things were happening to him.

The driver seemed to be in some kind of reverie, so Pross reiterated his instructions: 'Meet me in the lobby after you've parked.'

'You mean inside the 'otel?' asked the mad driver, whose face faithfully reflected each change in mood and mental state he swiftly passed through. It was a face incapable of guile. It was a face that would be a tremendous liability in a poker game. Everything he felt, his mobile face showed.

'Yeah, inside.'

'But I've never been inside an 'otel before.'

'That's all right,' said Pross, clambering out of the cab, 'neither have I.'

Just inside the glass doors, a loosely-associated group of six or seven sheepish-looking adolescent girls watched the lottery winner closely as he walked past them.

The lobby was exactly as he had expected it to be: subdued lighting; carpeting that struck a compromise between the functional and the lush; decorations and adornments that balanced the desire for economy with the necessary appearance of opulence; ferns; red crushed velvet upholstery; ostentatious chandeliers.

Pross rang a small hand bell placed on the large reception desk. A moderately made-up woman of about thirty-five immediately appeared. She was wearing a grey skirt and a white blouse. Her short, porcine legs tapered into black stilettos upon which she teetered perilously. She smiled a practised smile and cast a slightly disapproving eye over the basket containing the mewing cat. 'Can I help you?' she asked in the trained nasal voice she would use to its full effect when on the telephone.

'No one can help me,' said Pross, 'I'm beyond redemption.'

Her smile slipped slightly.

She looked at him.

He looked back at her.

In a moment, the practised smile returned. 'Can I help you?' she asked again.

Pross resisted repeating his initial answer, giving his name instead and explaining that he believed a reservation had been made for him.

She asked him to repeat his name.

He repeated it.

She asked him to spell it.

He spelt it.

'Ah, here we are. Mr, er, Pi-Meson. Are you with the lottery people? You're a winner?'

Pross nodded, realising he was embarrassed to admit it.

'You're booked into room 637 for the night, and there's a message here for you.'

With another throwaway smile, she handed Pross the key to his room and a sealed white envelope containing the message. He took both from her. She gestured to a hovering elderly porter, who took charge of the item of luggage and the item of livestock. The porter then guided Pross to his room, which was on the sixth floor.

The porter panned his eyes down Pross, from his haircut to his leather jacket and down on to his faded jeans. He understandably assumed that Pross was part of the pop group staying at the hotel between appearances at one of the capital's music venues.

In the lift, he sociably asked how the concerts were going.

Even though Pross didn't know exactly what the porter was referring to, he guessed enough and eventually said that the concerts were going fine, but they were running out of sacrificial cats for the stage act. 'This is the last one. I caught it myself this morning.'

The porter conducted the rest of his duties without speaking.

In his room, Pross tipped the porter a tenner for his troubles, which was accepted with indifferent courtesy.

Room 637 was reasonably spacious and adequately appointed, boasting a king-size bed, a colour television with closed-circuit films available, a telephone, a comfortable armchair, lots of built-in cupboards, a small bathroom with a shower, and a dressing table.

The cat was let out into the room.

It explored its new surroundings nervously.

The bed looked too inviting. He fell back on to it and let his eyelids close. So tired was he, a dream-like image immediately seized his mind. What he saw was Harry, hanging gruesomely, and, turning away from the mental sight, his own mother in the guise of Mrs Brown loomed into view. Clutching unnaturally large Rosary Beads, a priest looking on in the background, Mrs Brown moved forward in a desperate attempt to hold him.

He opened his eyes sharply, dispelling the image. Sitting up, he remembered he'd told the driver to meet him in the lobby. Had he tried to find the reason why he'd taken a driver who was bad at driving but good at being crazy into his employment, he would have drawn a blank. He had simply done it.

He went back down to the lobby to meet his chauffeur, whom he hoped had done a runner with the four hundred pounds. He was a little disappointed to spy him sitting awkwardly in wait beneath the boughs of an immense tropical plant.

The sheepish-looking girls who'd watched him enter were still there. Pross glanced at them and guessed that they were groupies, or, more probably, autograph hunters and *would-be* groupies of whichever band the porter had assumed him a member of.

The weary, sad-looking, bored young girls gazed with listless curiosity at Pross as he sauntered up to the poet-driver.

Pross noticed they were looking at him.

When he saw his new employer approaching, the bad poet gave a nervous smile, standing up to deliver it. Pross could tell already that the driver was a very much diminished and unsure person when he wasn't in the familiar environment of his cab. He smiled back at the driver, not wondering at all why he'd paid a nutcase to hang around with him but mildly wishing he hadn't. He was bored with him already.

And Pross realised with dismay that, underneath his jacket, the driver was wearing a *Morris Cerrullo World Evangelism* T-shirt. 'Sure you're free for the rest of the day?' Pross asked.

The driver said this to Pross: 'Yes, sir, I'm free. I can give my society meeting a miss.'

'Society meeting?' asked Pross disinterestedly.

'Aetherius society,' answered the bad driver.

This name rang a tiny, vague bell in Pross's memory. 'What's the Aetherius Society?' he asked, trying to figure where he'd heard it before.

This is what the poet-driver's jumbled answer amounted to: the Aetherius Society believes that Jesus is a Cosmic Master living on Venus, sending messages through their leader.

!!

For some reason at first unknown to him, a cold shiver ran through Pross's body. He was very tired, and things consequently had an "unreal" tinge to them. The driver's words had evoked a powerful sensation of *deja vu* in him. He shrank back slightly from his companion, but not so much that it would have been noticeable. He felt that there was something going on which he couldn't quite understand. Then he remembered where he'd heard about the Aetherius Society before: it was that television programme he'd watched on Saturday evening. Only a few days earlier he'd marvelled at the idea that some people were actually dumb enough to believe that aliens were in contact with selected earthlings, and now he'd met one of those people. It was so improbable.

And if this bloke didn't deserve to have the piss taken out of him, then no one did, was Pross's way of thinking. 'Come up to my room,' he said, walking to the lifts.

Pross pressed a button to summon a lift, stifling a yawn. 'How long have you been in the Aetherius Society?'

The poet-driver was free with his personal information. 'I joined this Monday. Used to follow Morris Cerullo, but I saw this programme about the Aetherius Society on telly, so I joined them.'

'So why are you still wearing his T-shirt?'

Looking down at the garment, the poet-driver explained that it had been the only clean thing he'd had available to put on that morning.

The lift arrived. Pross stepped into it, followed by the bad driver, who insisted on pressing the floor button, seeming to think that his chauffeuring duties extended to vertical travel.

In the intimacy of the smooth, slow lift, with piped music softly playing, Pross again praised the driver-poet's sonnet. 'Recite it again for me,' he requested.

The driver-poet readily obliged.

It sounded even worse second time around.

'It's very good,' praised Pross, 'you're obviously a very talented man.'

'I try my best.'

'How old are you?' asked Pross.

'Twenty-six,' he answered.

He looked ten years older to Pross.

'The name's Mick James, sir,' he said, proffering a tentative hand.

Pross shook that hand firmly, looked into Mick's eyes and said, 'My name's Prospero Pi-Meson, prophet of Godfrey the Creator of the Universe. You are the first person to be told this.'

You could have cut the atmosphere with a knife.

The lift doors swished open, and as Pross and his bewildered driver stepped out into the long corridor, an American tourist laden with guide books stepped in to replace them.

It was Thursday afternoon. Covent Garden had been designated for Thursday afternoon.

Pross walked a deliberate pace ahead of Mick. Unlocking and opening the door of his room, he ushered Mick into it. 'In here,' he said, immediately locking the door behind them, as if secrecy was an important consideration. With a tilt of his head he indicated that he wanted Mick to sit in the armchair by the window. Pross's tone was as earnest and as serious as he could manage. 'I have something very important to tell you about the origin of life and the universe.'

Mick sat apprehensively in the chair, a small blue bag filled with coins, some of the fruits of his day's labour, clutched protectively to his lap.

Pross had cruelly thrown poor Mick James into profound mental turmoil, and Mick's face certainly showed it.

Pross stood in silence by the window for a number of seconds, gazing out to the street below rather than at his guest. His hands were in the pockets of his jacket.

Mick sat nervously in his chair, his legs crossed tightly, almost knotted. He was wearing a skimpy blue jumper, threadbare in many places, and jeans that seemed not to have seen the inside of a washing machine for months. His shoes were made from brown suede. His body was thin and angular, and his arms, whether he was sitting or walking, were always held bent, making his bony elbows stick far out at his sides.

Although Mick's face, in its expressions, faithfully reflected every mood he passed through, an underlying expression seemed always to pervade. The underlying expression was one of a frown coupled with a tenseness. It persisted even when he laughed. It was as if all the other facial expressions he produced were merely painted over this permanent undercoat in translucent colours that could wash away in an instant.

And when he did laugh, he looked like an agitated chimpanzee making a screeching snarl, teeth bared.

Pross turned around. 'Who created the universe?' he wanted to be told.

Mick muttered something, became aware of the unseemly knot his legs were forming, uncrossed them, forgot himself and crossed them the other way, finally saying, with brave conviction, 'God did.'

'Wrong,' said Pross firmly. 'Not God, but Godfrey.'

Silence.

'Godfrey?' said the worst poet eventually.

Spock came out from hiding under the dressing table and rubbed up against Pross's legs.

Mick stared in tense disbelief at the animal. A cat in these surroundings seemed so incongruous. Then he remembered that it had come with Pross in the taxi (though why someone should bring a cat to a hotel room was beyond his imagination). He uncrossed his legs again, leant forward and forced his hands under his thighs, palms down. He began to rock slightly, then asked tentatively, 'Who's Godfrey?'

Pross told him about Godfrey by recounting his creation short story.

'I've chosen you,' said Pross to Mick, 'to be the first to receive the Truth.'

The bad poet was unable to respond, his mind struggling to comprehend the revelation just delivered directly to him. With growing consternation and bewilderment, Mick shook his head. All that he believed in, and had believed in staunchly for days now — prayer batteries, visiting aliens, Jesus living on Venus — was being called into question by a young man from whom words flowed like warm honey.

'Why me?' Mick desperately wanted to know. 'Why you telling me?'

'Because,' explained Pross, 'you have a quick mind and a pure heart. Your poem proved that to me.'

Spock jumped on to the bed. Mick continued to fight with his former beliefs. 'But what about the Aetherius Society?' he asked, his eyes turned helplessly to Pross.

'I only know about Godfrey.'

Just five minutes later, Mick was an ardent believer in Godfrey the Creator of the Universe, and in Pross, his prophet. It made marginally more sense than Jesus living on Venus, or the existence of a devil with horns and eternal freehold on subterranean fiery dominions.

Contemptuously persuading Mick to believe in pure nonsense felt to Pross like another one of his blows against world insanity. Another, even more satisfying blow, would be dealt soon, when he would reveal to Mick what a fool he had been to have believed in Godfrey.

1.22
Cutting Cords

The box was beautiful; black, lined with red satin. It contained the first dress Jennifer had ever bought for herself. Often she'd glanced at it in the window of the little shop she passed each weekday on her way to and from the cafe where she lunched; but today she'd bought it. The dress itself was black, and of a fabric which looked like a hybrid of taffeta and stiff cotton. It was tight around the waist and bare above the bust. Below the waist, it became a knee-length swirl, embroidered sparsely with gold and silver spiders' webs.

Today Jennifer's hair was drawn into a small, tight ponytail. A pert fringe sprung out over her forehead. While sipping her coffee, lightly she rubbed the fabric of the dress between the fingers of her right hand, until noticing that two men were watching her from another table.

'Got a new dress then have you, love?' said one of them when Jennifer happened to look up. He was tanned, fair-haired and in his mid-twenties. 'Bet you'd look lovely in it.' She didn't answer, but closed the box firmly and put it back into the carrier bag they'd given her at the shop, turning her face to the cafeteria window.

The men muttered something unkind about her between themselves but ignored her afterwards, except for stolen glances.

After gazing out of the window for a minute or two, her unopened letter was remembered. She retrieved the envelope from her pocket, sliding the nail of her forefinger under the flap to slit it open with a sawing motion. Another sip of coffee was taken. With much curiosity, she pulled out the piece of paper therein.

It bore this message:

Here I am.

My Dearest Jennifer,

For the days together we've never had... please accept the enclosed as token compensation for your loss.

Prospero Pi-Meson.

Enclosed with the letter was a fifty pound note, which was one penny more than the dress had cost.

This Prospero Pi-Meson, she thought — if Prospero Pi-Meson was his real name, which she doubted — was either in love with her, insane or playing an expensive prank. She suspected the latter. But why her? she thought. Why her?

She lingered over the written words. *Here I am.* That was nice. Poetic, she thought.

She tried to find some explanation for the sudden appearance of a mystery correspondent in her life, racking her brains in an attempt to remember if she'd recently met anyone who might be the perpetrator.

She drew a blank.

And still the only clue she had was that the letters were both postmarked *Durham*.

She folded the message up with the money and slipped them into the carrier bag, deciding not to trouble herself any more with futile questions about the real identity and the real intent of the sender. Those issues would either resolve themselves or they wouldn't. There was nothing she could do to find out, at least not until her sister returned from Iceland.

This afternoon, Jennifer was leaving work, her employer having given her permission to finish at short notice. His son could cover for Jennifer until another assistant was found. And tomorrow Jennifer was going to see her aunt to tell her that she'd broken her engagement to John and that she was going to go away somewhere soon, somewhere as yet undecided, although London seemed attractive.

Jennifer finished her coffee and walked back to work, for what she had decided would be the last time.

1.23
Playing Nazis For Laughs

Descending in a crowded lift, the self-declared prophet of Godfrey could hardly believe the delicious absurdity of it: Mick had actually fallen for his made-up tales.

Profound elevator-silence was strictly observed by all during the descent.

And when the doors hummed open on the ground floor, the sleepy prophet strolled across the busy lobby and over to the reception desk, the girls near the door keeping him under scrutiny.

He asked if the hotel had a bar.

It did.

The bar room, he soon discovered, was sizable, and large mirrors set upon the walls added further to the sense of space. At the far end, seated on stools, drinking gin and tonics, were two blonde women in their twenties whose roots were showing through. Pross fell slightly in lust with one of them, and he gave the other one the benefit of the doubt.

A pint of beer purchased, he sat down in a dark corner. Two men, both equally overweight and equally unshaven, entered the bar room and joined the women.

Both men were wearing *Pandemonium On Tour* T-shirts.

They looked like roadies.

Pandemonium, a soft metal band from Manchester, had recently been hyped big in America, and they had an album in the British top fifty.

Before they were Pandemonium, they were an unknown heavy metal band called Osmium. Osmium, someone had told them to their liking, is the heaviest metal known. Even heavier than gold, the person had said.

Before they were an unknown heavy metal band, they were an unknown heavy rock band called Fortissimo. Fortissimo, someone had told them to their liking, is a musical term meaning *very loud*.

While they were Fortissimo, they were also apprentice fitters at a cigarette factory.

By the exaggeratedly effusive and affectionate way the ladies greeted and put their arms around the roadies, it was obvious they were drunk.

And perhaps the roadies were a means to an end, thought Pross.

Before he'd left his room, Pross had called room service, requesting them to bring something for the cat to eat. Roast chicken and milk is what Spock received. It ate nervously, then slinked off to a corner to guiltily defecate.

Mick cleaned up the mess.

A prophet had spoken to *him*.

The history of the universe according to the words of the prophet made perfect sense to Mick. He didn't know anything about physics, but it all sounded wonderfully simple yet wonderfully deep. It all seemed so plausible: the mind of Godfrey had created this universe, and Mick was going to tell everyone he knew about it just as soon as Godfrey's prophet gave him permission to leave the hotel room.

The beer was cold; too cold to be gulped. Pross took frequent small sips. The memory of having been given an envelope by the receptionist made itself known. He took it from his pocket and opened it.

It contained instructions and information from the lottery company:

They gave their congratulations —

He was expected in the *Rhodes* function room —

He was to arrive there by three o'clock —

The presentation would be at four —

They gave their congratulations again.

A clock positioned between the spirit dispensers told that it was now quarter past three. Only quarter of an hour late: plenty of time yet, he thought, settling back into the lushly padded chair, feeling tiredness asserting itself again. Out of academic interest, he worked out how many hours sleep he'd had over the last four nights. Three hours on Sunday night. Six hours on Monday. Six or seven fitful, vomit-punctuated hours on Tuesday. None at all last night. Altogether, only seventeen or so hours over four nights.

And soon he would have to face the boredom and idiocy of the presentation ceremony. People would want to ask him questions, already knowing what kind of answers they wanted to hear.

What a drag.

Again he felt like playing truant. He felt like going up to his warm room, chasing Mick away into the street, then sleeping until the next day. What would the lottery company do if he let them down? Nothing, he guessed. He supposed they'd still pay up.

Bed would be oh so nice now.

But then again, two million pounds was too great a sum to play dice with.

Pross resisted consummating the bed wish, deciding that for once he was going to try to play something the way he was expected to play it — two million pounds was surely worth one afternoon of pain. Quickly finishing his drink, he went to the reception desk to ask for directions to the designated room.

He received them.

Looking around, he saw that most of the would-be young groupies had drifted away.

Or maybe they had been chased away by the hotel management.

Or maybe they were in some room upstairs being debauched by apprentice fitters.

Two remained. They studied Pross.

Presently Pross wandered into the Rhodes room, which was about eighty feet in length. Running along the back wall there were tables laden with simple refreshments for the expected press and tv people. At the other end was a small dais, about ten paces wide and four deep, presenting various razamataz neon displays. Some video lights were clustered at one side of this platform, not yet switched on.

There were lots of lottery company advertisements.

There was also a silver-haired middle-aged man in a dark suit. He was sitting on a desk writing something in a notebook. The desk was at the back of the dais, against the wall.

As well as the middle-aged man, there were two younger men in similar dark suits. They were sprawled over chairs, away from the silver-haired man and not on the platform.

Three attractive young women in dark-blue skirts and matching jackets beamed smiles around the room. They all wore the same shade of red lipstick.

They were from a promotions agency.

The person who saw Pross first, one of the two young men, went over and offered his hand. 'Ah, you must be the lucky winner,' he said. 'You're here at last. We heard you'd arrived at the hotel. You certainly look just like the description Mr Cook gave us over the phone.'

Pross shook the proffered hand.

The silver-haired man came over.

Pross shook the silver-haired man's hand.

Then he shook everybody else's hand.

Then he said how happy the win had made him, but that it wouldn't change his life; and they said how pleased the Company was that someone young had won for a change.

Pross said he was pleased that they were pleased.

They asked him about the cat and laughed.

He laughed with them.

They wanted to know where it was.

He said it was in his room being looked after by someone who would bring it down when necessary.

That was good, they said. It was a bloody good piece of publicity, they said.

Then the most senior of the men led Pross to a trio of chairs on the stage, beckoning two older men over as well.

He said his name was Colin.

He had a moribund Scottish accent.

He invited Pross and the two older men to take a seat.

They did.

He formally introduced Pross to the older men, who were named Gordon and Roy. Gordon was perhaps in his fifties, and Roy looked to be approaching his pension. They were happy and excited and nervous.

Colin told Pross that Gordon and Roy were the other two winners who would be sharing the seven million pound jackpot.

Pross nodded to them.

One of the younger workers handed Colin three small gold envelopes.

Colin turned to the seated winners and spoke quietly through a freshly generated smile. 'These envelopes contain the *real* cheques. The big cheques you'll each be presented with later are just for show. These envelopes each contain a cheque for two million, three hundred and twenty-six thousand, eight hundred and forty-two pounds, thirty-four pence. Except for Mr Pi-Meson's, that is, whose cheque is for three thousand pounds less, that being the amount he was advanced yesterday. Congratulations.'

The senior man with the dying accent handed out the gold envelopes. 'Keep them out of sight in your pockets — we don't want a bit of reality spoiling the show, do we?'

Gordon and Roy laughed.

Colin then explained to the winners how they could expect a torrent of questions from the press. Prospero, in particular, could expect a barrage about his name, his cat, how his cat had come to select the numbers, and what he was going to do with all the money. 'Let's face it, it's really an unusual name you've got,' remarked Colin.

'It is,' said Pross. 'It's medieval.'

The real cheque in the back pocket of his jeans, Pross almost got up and left there and then. The money was his now. But he decided to go through with the game. After all, he'd made a promise to George Cook.

He decided he would try to grin and try to bear it.

'Who's the celebrity?' he asked, vainly hoping that it would be the woman from the *Scottish Widows* television advert.

Colin smiled. 'I think we'll leave that as a little surprise for you all.'

Gordon and Roy laughed.

Fucking stupid bastard, thought Pross. He could feel himself becoming increasingly contemptuous of everyone around him. He wanted to go back home to his friends.

One of the red-lipped women came over and offered the winners refreshments. Pross asked for tea.

As he sipped his tea, he closed his eyes, half asleep, half awake. Colin looked at him and worried slightly: he'd never had a winner nod off on him before.

Off the stage, by the door at the other end of the room, the two younger men were trying to get the other two women to think of them as interesting people and desirable sex partners.

The first of the press people began to drift in, and the extra voices roused Pross from his near-sleep. He gazed blankly around the hall, not thinking of anything at all, except about how bored he was.

The red-lipped women by the door handed out information sheets to the newcomers.

The newcomers went straight to the food.

Among other things, the information sheets bore Pross's name, the amount he had won, and the fact that his cat had won it for him.

It was all marvellously wacky, the sheet said.

Amid no interest whatsoever from the reporters present, a male celebrity made an entrance: a television sit-com celebrity. He was led by Colin on to the stage and ebulliently introduced first to Gordon, who stood up to speak with him. 'Love your show, mate. Wife loves it too.'

'Thanks,' said the celeb, all smiles and bridgework. 'Fantastic win you've had. I enter every week.'

After showing his face to Roy, who seemed confused, Colin then moved the celeb on to Pross, who remained seated. 'And this sleepy young man is the lucky owner of a winning cat. He goes under the rather strange name of Prospero Pi-Meson!'

The celebrity proffered his hand, which Pross shook. 'Winning cat indeed!' said the sit-com star. 'It's an unusual name you've got.'

'It's Antarctican,' said Pross.

'Er, yes,' faltered the star.

For conversation, the sit-com celebrity asked Pross if he liked his show on television. Pross said that he'd never heard of him or his show, which was perfectly true.

The put-out celebrity said that he played a Nazi officer in a popular comedy series: 'A *very* popular series,' he said.

'We can all play Nazis if we want to,' returned Pross with annoying cleverness, 'it's one of life's easiest roles.'

The sit-com star moved away from the aggressive young man, going over to chat to the press instead.

A bearded man with a medium-format camera, a photographer especially commissioned by the lottery company, stepped on to the dais and spoke jointly to the winners. 'I'd like to take some shots of you now, group and individual, if that's OK,' he said, 'before it gets too hectic in here.'

Pross really was feeling quite dissonant with everyone around him. 'It's not OK by me,' he returned, leaning forward with his head in his hands, wishing he hadn't had that drink. He was getting a headache to add to his sleepiness and boredom.

Colin glowered politely at Pross for refusing to pose for the publicity photographs. He stooped to speak into Pross's ear. 'Get the cat,' he said, handing him a telephone, making it sound like an order, 'it's nearly four o'clock. Dial nine for the switchboard.'

Pross took the phone and asked the hotel telephonist to connect him with room 637. She obliged. It rang for several seconds before Mick plucked up the nerve to answer it.

Mick was instructed to bring the cat to the Rhodes Room.

A two-man film crew from a news agency appeared. One man climbed on to the stage and began arranging the lights. The other fiddled with a video camera.

The lights were switched on and pointed at Pross, the glare proving painful to his tired eyes.

Anxiously, Colin looked at his watch. It was now two minutes to four. Upon his signal, the neon displays behind him lit up and triumphant music played. He smiled a smile that remained fixed, tapped Pross on the shoulder to get him to stand up, and announced to the audience of press people that here were the lucky winners.

Gordon and Roy stood, but Pross remained seated.

Press photographers began snapping him as he sat and squinted into the light, his eyes taking a while to grow accustomed to the brightness.

With his smile still fixed, Colin worried deeply. He wanted this presentation to go as smoothly as all the others he'd presided over during his year with the company.

Disinterested reporters drifted over to the stage to ask this week's winners questions.

'Hi,' said a dark-haired young lady to the fore of the bored group of journos, directing her attention particularly at Pross.

Pross's eyes were now coping with the glare. He directed his gaze at the speaker... and what a vision he beheld! At first he was amazed. The lady speaking to him seemed to be none other than Tess. Tess, his most yearned-for literary babe: he'd found her at last. But, he quickly realised with melancholic disappointment, the creature before him was not actually Tess. She didn't quite match up to the Tess that he knew and yearned for. Sarah-Jane was a much more convincing candidate for that honourable incarnation. The lady before him couldn't be Tess because she was, to mention one thing, slightly overweight. To mention another, she had a quite un-Tess-like cold sore violating her otherwise lush upper lip. To mention a third, she had a rich suntan, suggesting, to her discredit, that she had not spent the autumn months as a simple Victorian milkmaid, but more likely as a hedonistic holiday-maker in some place like the Canary Islands.

No, she was not Tess; but nevertheless she *was* beautiful, almost as beautiful as Sarah-Jane, with whom (overlooking the additional weight and the festering lip) she bore a striking resemblance. Despite her not being Tess, Pross felt his heart melt. 'I'll never stop loving you,' he informed her.

'Er, thank you,' faltered the lady reporter who wasn't Tess. She was part flattered, part embarrassed and part irritated. She was a newly-appointed junior reporter and this was only her second unaccompanied assignment. She wanted to handle it, and wanted to be seen to handle it, professionally, and Pross wasn't making it easy for her. Like a professional, she got down to business, formally introducing herself. 'Sophie Hamilton from the Sun,' she said.

'I've stopped loving you,' declared Pross immediately.

This withdrawal of adoration was of little concern to Sophie. 'Really?' she said with haughty indifference.

'Truly,' said Pross. 'Call me Proteus.'

She refrained from calling him Proteus, and continued with the business that had brought her there. 'It's an unusual name you have,' she remarked, inviting a reply.

'Piss off,' said Pross.

He didn't approve of the Sun.

1.24
Front Page News

Sophie Hamilton, the newly-appointed junior reporter who fell a little short of being Tess, was now thrilled. She figured that she had got her first sensational front page headline: LOTTERY MILLIONAIRE SAYS P*SS OFF.

Other reporters excitedly threw questions at Pross.

Cameras flashed.

Gordon and Roy were bewildered.

Colin leapt into the fray, determined to take charge of the growing fiasco. 'Mr Pi-Meson will answer your questions after the cheque presentation. Please retain them until then. Thank you.' He turned on his heel, rounding on Pross in barely restrained hisses. 'Just what in the hell do you think you're doing?'

Pross had had enough. 'Aw shut the fuck up,' he said. He had the real cheque safely in his pocket, so he got up and walked off the stage.

The awkward lottery winner swept past the irate Master of Ceremonies. The latter was shaking with anger, his silver hair trembling with the frequency of his body's pent-up rage. Colin wanted to hit Pross: never before in his year of giving away money had such a calamity arose.

At the same time as Pross stepped off the dais, Mick stepped into the room, trepidation writ large on his face. He was carrying Spock in the cat basket. Immediately he was handed an information sheet by a woman with red lips.

He looked around bemusedly.

Glancing at the sheet, he saw that the prophet of Godfrey's cat had won over two million pounds.

Pross scuttled over to Mick, took him firmly by the arm and ran him straight back out of the room.

Reporters harangued them. Photographers clicked them.

Sophie Hamilton began to chase. So did some other reporters, pursuing a sensational story on the brand-new multi-millionaire who had said piss off.

Other reporters resumed their assault on the free food and refreshments — they'd make a story up later for their editors.

Gordon and Roy were ignored.

Pross and Mick were now in the long corridor leading to the lobby. Mick looked back as Pross guided him swiftly along, swerving past porters and guests.

They were still being followed.

'What's going on?' asked Mick, struggling with the cat basket.

Spock was having a rough day.

'Enemies,' said Pross. 'Enemies of Godfrey.' He released his grip on Mick's arm. Mick continued to scurry along beside him.

They pushed through some swing doors and came into the spacious lobby. Near the reception desk another small but noisy group of journalists and photographers was gathered around a flamboyantly dressed, bearded man. The man was the road manager of Pandemonium. The band had just held a press conference, during which a tabloid reporter had asked about their alleged sacrificing of cats.

The band had thought he was joking and had played along.

Now their road manager was strongly denying that the band actually sacrificed live cats as part of their stage act, and demanded to be told where the sick rumour had originated. One of these journalists spotted Pross and Mick running through the lobby — and they had a cat with them! A cat that seemed to be getting a rough deal.

Consequently, this second group of journalists also pursued Pross.

And beyond the reception desk, just inside the main doors, the two remaining would-be groupies looked on in conjecturing wonder.

Unaware that a second band of journos was now on his trail, Pross trotted over to the lifts. Before he reached them, two swished open simultaneously, and out poured clusters of French-speaking people. He stepped into one of the now vacant lifts and pressed the button for the sixth floor.

And where Pross went, Mick went also.

Mick gazed at Pross in awe: this was the most exciting day of his life.

Mick put the awkward basket down on to the floor of the lift and caught his breath.

The clusters of French people coalesced in front of the doors.

The small band of pursuing journalists barged their clumsy way through indignant French people, and were all set to corner Pross in the lift and assail him with rabid questions. Sophie Hamilton was at the vanguard, no more than a step away.

Their eyes met.

This was the first good look at her face Pross had got. She was oh so beautiful. Never in his life had he felt so attracted to a cold sore.

The journos were about to advance into the lift, but, adrenalin pulling his strings, Mick suddenly leapt in their way, preventing them from entering. 'Leave him alone!' he ordered.

Pross said nothing. The doors of the lift closed shut with an immaculate motion, excluding his pursuers, but also leaving Mick stranded amid them. He slipped a hand into his back pocket: the cheque was still there.

The lift jerked ever so slightly and began to ascend. A Chopin nocturne was playing through concealed speakers.

The long curving corridor leading to room 637 was bereft of people. Although Pross considered his room to be well appointed, it was actually one of the cheapest the hotel offered. Nevertheless, the carpeting under his feet as he walked the length of this "economy" floor was lush, being a deep burgundy in colour along the corridor and a lighter shade in the rooms. Dipping his hand into various pockets to try to find the room key, he remembered that the door would be unlocked, keyless Mick having been the last occupant. As he turned the brass handle, the telephone within the room warbled softly. Tired and more than a little moody, he locked the door behind him, put the cat basket down and fell back on to the bed to the accompaniment of a loud groan of displeasure.

He looked at the ceiling.

The telephone continued to warble, and due to a sort of automatic curiosity, he rolled over and picked up the receiver.

He listened.

It was Colin. Colin cursed him in dying Scottish. He used a lot of taboo words he considered to be obscene and invidious. He said he'd make sure Pross would regret having done what he had just done. He used more swear words.

Pross listened until he said, 'Call me Ishmael,' and replaced the receiver.

He looked at the ceiling again.

But then there was a pounding on the room door, a pounding accompanied by the stifled cries of Mick.

Pross reluctantly rolled off the bed and opened the door.

Mick smiled tensely. 'There's dozens of them reporters looking for you!' he said, and began to take a step into the room, but Pross barred his way.

'Go tell them I'm in room 520,' instructed Pross, and Mick obliged without question.

When doing Pross's bidding, Mick seemed to find a confidence he otherwise lacked outside his cab.

Pross closed the door and locked it. Dejectedly, he fell back on to the bed, already lamenting his loss of Sophie Hamilton, the young lady with the cold sore he'd told to piss off — they could have been so happy together.

His eyelids began to fall again. Desperately he wanted to sleep, but knew that with reporters, Colin and Mick he'd get no peace in this room. On an impulse, he decided to go back home, home to his friends and his new life in the country. He could get some sleep on the train.

And so he collected his belongings together, picked up the cat basket and opened his room door, making his way to the reception desk to check out.

And it was still less than two hours since he'd checked in.

In the lobby, he noticed Colin. Colin was grumbling to the two young men. Pross deliberately sauntered past the three of them.

Colin saw Pross.

Pross winked at his new enemy. 'Thanks for the cash,' he said with a sleepy smirk.

And in one of the phone booths, with her back to the room, there was Sophie. She was giving her paper the story of the brand-new millionaire who had said piss off.

Mick wasn't anywhere to be seen, and Pross didn't really care. He could go on believing in Godfrey for the rest of his mad life as far as he was concerned at this moment.

The two remaining would-be groupies lingered on in forlorn hope of meeting their soft metal idols.

At the reception desk, Pross said that he was leaving, and he handed over his key, refusing to put his signature to the signing-out book simply because he didn't feel like doing it. He didn't have to do anything he didn't particularly feel like doing now.

The woman at the desk was annoyed that he was not following procedure.

Before he had time to pick up the cat and case again, another hovering porter took charge of the two items and asked him where he wanted them taking. Pross said that he was about to look for a taxi. The porter quickly carried them out through the large glass doors, hailing the taxi at the head of a rank nearby.

Sophie put her phone down. Turning around, she saw Pross standing beside the desk. She started walking towards him, but he shook his head to let her know that she would be wasting her time.

A few other reporters spotted him and ran over, attempting to extract comments. But Pross said nothing as he walked out of the hotel.

The furore surrounding the young man with the pop star appearance had the would-be groupies fascinated, and the young man knew it as he proceeded to his taxi, followed by Sophie, who was staying close on the heels of her first big story. On the street outside, he put a tenner into the hand of the porter and slid into the cab, relieved to see that it was not Mick at the wheel. From inside the cab, he looked at Sophie through the window.

She looked at him.

The taxi set off.

1.25
Back Home

The car was not where he'd left it that morning. Where it should have been, in a long-stay parking place within the grounds of the railway station, there was a blue Range Rover.

The night was chilly, and he closed up his jacket.

Putting down his case and cat basket, hands slipping into pockets, he looked around for the car.

He soon concluded that it must have been pinched.

And then he calculated that the check in his pocket could by him another hundred such cars.

Knowing there to be a mini-cab office at the far side of the station, he headed for it.

The queue for mini-cabs was fifteen or so in number. Five of these people had been on the train from London, but the rest were typical local youths on their way home from a nearby nightclub. The youths were all drunk and aggressive. The neuro-toxin they'd paid money for was inhibiting the flow of electro-chemical signals in their frontal cortexes. They were running on primitive brain stem power.

Pross could sense the possibility of violence flaring, and it worried him.

The noisy yobs began chanting something that Pross found unintelligible. Their voices were as gruff as they could manage to make them. Their brain stems wanted them to sound terrifying.

Fearing that he might this night be robbed of the right to take his own life, he nevertheless took a place in the queue of brain-stemmers. He knew that any eye contact between himself and one of those brain-stemmers, however accidental or fleeting, would more than likely lead to a brawl. He was glad that he'd closed his jacket up because even the unusual flamboyance of his birthday present shirt could initiate trouble. And he hoped that the cat wouldn't start mewing, for even *that* could trigger aggression.

This was, after all, the Northeast.

And it dawned on him that a brawl might lose him the two million pound cheque in his pocket.

He looked at the ground and wished his car hadn't been stolen.

Mini-cabs were arriving all the time, taking away the brain-stemmers, and it was not long before Pross himself was being whisked homeward.

Once inside his flat, he freed Spock from imprisonment. The animal needed to be coaxed out of the basket. But once it had explored the room a little to convince itself that it really was back home, a purring contentment overcame it.

The rooms were cold. The gas fire was brought to life, and Pross, a cup of tea by his side, drew his armchair up to the incandescence. Soon he fell into a kind of mental quiescence. Despite having snatched a couple of hours sleep on the train, he was dead beat. But going to bed seemed to present too much of a task at the moment. In fact sleeping itself now seemed to require an effort for which he was not a match. Too tired to go to bed, he passed a full thirty minutes in front of the fire, sometimes thinking, sometimes not, and sometimes trying hard to move himself towards his bedroom.

And he might have sat there all night long had the telephone not startled him back into awareness.

He had a feeling it was going to be someone from the lottery company, or a journalist, so he pulled the telephone's wire out of the socket.

The caller had been Ron.

And so it was that he managed to shake off the inactivity. He took off his clothes, made a feeble attempt at washing then slipped under the duvet.

Thursday, October 2Oth, turned out to be an exceptionally slack day for tabloid news. No ladies had been brutally raped and beaten: the public couldn't be titillated that way, realised the unhappy editors. No children had allegedly been ritually abused by satanists: the public couldn't be titillated that way today, either, grumbled the disappointed editors. No beautiful young models had fucked with ugly old company chairmen: poor public. No vicars had had anal sex with boy scouts: the editors were close to tears and absolutely all the way to visions of financial ruin.

They were hoping for a last-minute sex killing to sell to their readers.

Just in time to save them from a drop in sales, they heard that a lottery winner with a peculiar name had said p*ss off.

That would do nicely.

So, on the day after his visit to London, five tabloid papers reported on their front pages how a lottery jackpot sharer had said p*ss off and been sensationally stroppy. Each printed a different picture of him looking moody. But the headlines were all similar, along the lines of UNGRATEFUL MILLIONAIRE SAYS P*SS OFF, or GRUMPY LOTTERY WINNER FLEES PRESS, or CAT WINS LOTTERY, OWNER SAYS P*SS OFF.

So, overnight, while he slept, Prospero Pi-Meson became a nationwide minor *cause celebre*.

1.26
Celebrity

It was a night of deep, unbroken slumber, and when he awoke and rolled out of bed at just before two in the afternoon, he felt much rejuvenated.

It was persistent ringing of his doorbell that had roused him.

Opening the door, he recognised the man responsible for having woken him as being the same one who'd brought him the hire car days earlier. 'Morning,' said the sandy-haired man in blue overalls reservedly, a clipboard tucked under his arm.

'Likewise,' returned Pross, indicating to the man that he should come inside.

Pross walked into the living room, the man a pace behind. The curtains were closed. 'It's about the car you hired from us,' said the man grimly once they were both in the room.

'What about it?' asked Pross, going straight over to the fire and putting it on full. He sat in front of it, trying to organise his minimal thoughts, to decide what he had to do that day. Go to a bank to deposit the cheque, that's what he'd do first. Then he'd get things sorted regarding his country property.

The man remained standing in the middle of the room. 'Well, do you know where the car is?' he asked.

'Haven't the foggiest,' answered Pross, warming his hands, his back to his visitor. 'I left it parked yesterday morning, and when I went back later it was gone.' He shrugged his shoulders. 'Stolen, I suppose.'

'We've got it,' revealed the man. 'Someone vandalised it. The police found it at the train station. We picked it up and drove it back to our depot. We've been trying to phone you since.' The man thought for a second, then asked with a tone of suspicion, 'If you'd thought it had been stolen, why didn't you inform the authorities?'

Pross shrugged again. 'I wasn't really bothered at the time. I would have let you know today.'

The man couldn't believe what he was hearing. 'You weren't bothered?' he exclaimed, his feet shuffling in some kind of agitation.

'No. I got a taxi home. Who vandalised it?'

The man calmed down a bit. 'We don't know. They daubed the bodywork. Luckily it was only emulsion paint, but it'll still take a lot of work to clean it up.'

Pross turned around. 'That was me. I did that.'

'You did it?' blurted the man. 'You did it? This is going to cost you. That was criminal damage.'

'No it wasn't, it was art,' said Pross, facing the fire again. 'Anyway, it was only emulsion. How much do you want as compensation?'

Instead of answering the straightforward question, the man uttered several noises of incredulity. Not wanting to have this affair drag out any longer than strictly necessary, Pross stood up and said, rather pointedly to get the man's immediate attention, 'Will five hundred do?'

'What?'

'I said will five hundred do?'

'Five hundred? It might. When?'

'Now.'

'Five hundred? Now? You'll have to talk with management.'

'I don't want to talk with management,' said Pross, picking up his jacket, which was lying across a chair, retrieving from it the cash he still had left. He climbed up on to the table, which trembled dangerously under his shifting weight, and tackled the job of opening the curtains. The task done, he jumped down and counted out five hundred pounds. 'Here,' he said. 'If it costs more, let me know.' The man, persuaded to take the money, gave an *ad hoc* receipt and left the flat.

Alone again, Pross immediately set about doing all those things necessary before he could go out: that is he washed, shaved, and saw to his hair.

Afterwards, he allowed himself another little sit in front of the fire.

But eventually he turned the fire off and donned his jacket. Walking out into the street, he noticed how delightful the weather was. Hardly a cloud was in the sky, and the air, though a little chilly, was without movement. Indeed, such was the quiet beauty of the day, it seemed at once to imbue him and foster a sense of sympathetic serenity. Things were going great, he told himself.

Opening his gate, he gazed down the street, which was well endowed with trees. In the sunlight, the rich shades of the autumn leaves were as if afire. A young girl of about fourteen summers, the bolder of two who were loitering nearby, interrupted his appreciation of what might prove the last pleasantly mild day before winter. 'Have you won the lottery?' she asked.

Pross vaguely recognised her as being one of his neighbours. He didn't say anything at first. This blunt question, especially from one so young, seemed so intrusive. And he realised, with some horror, that it would surely prove to be the first of many such similar inquiries. 'How did you know?' he asked, already jaded with having to face this mundane inquiry.

'Me dad told me. It's in the paper we got this morning.'

Pross groaned, deeply wishing he'd never agreed to a public presentation. It had been a big mistake. He'd never get any peace now. And although he didn't know it, he was, at this very moment, being watched very closely from across the road by two people in a car.

'Me dad said you've won over two million,' pursued the girl.

How undignified, thought Pross, that it should become common knowledge he'd acquired his fortune by way of a vulgar lottery win and not by piracy or a Herbal Abortion Kit scam or something else equally glamorous. He groaned again. Things weren't going as great as he'd just thought.

The girl tittered over some whispered suggestion made to her by her shy friend. 'Give uz some money,' she asked, giggling.

He groaned for a third time.

'What's your name?' he asked.

'Clare,' she said in a drawn-out, flat, drab tone.

'Well, Clare,' he said, 'shouldn't you, at this time of the day, be tramping a scholastic path rather than seeking to part a fool and his money?'

This sentence, hypocritical coming from an erstwhile compulsive truant, went a little over her none-to-luminous head.

'What?' she asked in the manner typical of the region's less bright children, a manner beginning with a flat sound and rising through three or four semitones. A sort of mooing sandwiched between consonants.

Pross put the question more plainly. 'Why aren't you at school?'

'It's spud picking week,' she informed him drably. Then she added — indeed, almost demanded — 'Are you gonna give uz some money?'

'Money? All right,' said the fool, 'if you'll do something for me.'

'What?' she mooed, this time with a downwards inflection. This downwards inflection on the vowel sound was born of suspicion. For four years this street had rang with echoing gossip about the strange young bloke from number seventeen, and what he got up to, and what the conjecturing mongers of such gossip declared with spurious certainty he *wanted* to get up to. According to different reports that had filtered back to him, local gossip regarded him as being everything from a virgin to a sex maniac, a wimp to a psychopath, a homosexual to a womaniser, and all manner of other, more extreme things. Sometimes, to relieve boredom, he numbered the people he knew he could successfully sue for slander should he ever be inclined that way, which he never was.

'Get the paper for me,' explained Pross, 'and I'll give you a hundred pounds.'

Clare didn't need to be asked twice. She darted into her house, got the paper, and Pross paid her the agreed sum.

Commerce.

He sat on his gate, back to the road, to read about himself. Clare and her friend hung around while he unfolded the paper. It was the Daily Star. The front page's lesser headline read: SWEARING YOB SCOOPS LOTTERY — turn to page two for story. He groaned yet again, and turned to page two.

Clare, with a disregard for Pross's reputation, leant on the gate beside him. 'Me dad says you're mad,' she said with the frankness of youth.

'He's right,' said Pross, reading the short article about himself. The article merely gave his name, the town and street where he lived, how much he had won, the fact that his cat had picked the numbers, and that he had sworn at reporters. There was also a quote from Colin, who said that the winner had shown "amazing ingratitude", and that "the company deeply regretted having shown such leniency in making payment on a technically illegitimate claim."

Clare's friend kept her distance.

'Is Harry dead?' Clare asked.

'Uh huh,' nodded Pross, still reading about himself.

'How?'

'I strangled him.'

'You murdered him!' she exclaimed before concern took hold of her. Young Clare sidled away nervously, surreptitiously beckoning her friend to follow.

The two people in the car chose this as their moment to strike. So while Clare was sidling nervously and Pross was engaged in reading the paper, Sophie Hamilton, Sun reporter in search of a scoop follow-up story on the lottery winner who had said p*ss off, was sidling boldly. So was the cameraman with her.

The camera clicked.

'Mr Pi-Meson, a word with you if I may?'

Pross looked up from the newspaper and saw a beautiful face, and he almost let out a little whine of heartache.

The camera clicked again, but from behind, diesel knock alerted Pross to a vehicle's approach. He turned to look. It was a black cab, and inside the cab was a driver he recognised and a passenger he didn't. He moved towards the vehicle, opened the door and slid inside.

'Wait!' called Sophie, tapping frantically on the window and trying to open the door.

The camera whirred on motor-drive.

'Keep going,' said Pross, 'there's somewhere important I have to go.'

He turned to look at the reporter he had stopped loving yesterday.

Mick drove on.

And behind them, Sophie Hamilton was wasting no time in seeking out Clare's whereabouts to ask probing questions about her relationship with Pross and the nature of the transaction she'd witnessed from her car.

And Clare would say that Pross had murdered Harry.

And Sophie would investigate that alleged killing.

1.27
Old Habits

Jennifer's first day of unemployment was mostly spent trying to be quiet. Elaine was in bed, sleeping off the last night-shift in her three-week work pattern, and Jennifer didn't want to disturb her. Yesterday, her new life had seemed so full of possibilities, but today it just seemed like her old one, except she no longer had a job to absorb the hours.

The solemnly quiet flat seemed as empty as her life.

The vague plans she'd had about going away somewhere, London, maybe, seemed so much less compelling than they had the day before. And what could she do in London? She had no skills, hardly any qualifications and not enough money from the Lucas legacy to keep her comfortably for more than perhaps three or four years in the capital city. Modelling: that's what people had often urged her to do. But modelling had no appeal for her whatsoever.

Jennifer was bored with her new leisure already. Last night, she'd stayed back at work to organise the surgery, labelling boxes and generally putting the place in order so that her successor could find things easily; and so late was it when she'd arrived home that, after eating, she'd gone straight to bed, too tired to even try on her new dress first. Today she was not tired. Today she was bored. The afternoon matinee on television gave no relief. Anyway, with consideration for Elaine, the sound was turned so far down she could hardly hear what was being said.

So, at just past three o'clock, Jennifer found herself telephoning her ex-employer to ask for her job back, the request being granted after some grumbling. More annoyed than pleased to be going back to her old job, she shovelled some coal on to the fire and some pity on to herself. An armchair was drawn up to the warmth. After ten minutes of staring into the flames, the telephone rang and brought her out of her reverie. She picked up the phone and knew straightaway it was her aunt on the line — she could hear the poodles going crazy in the background.

'Jennifer?' asked her aunt.

'Yes, it's me.'

'I tried to phone you at work, but they said you'd left?'

'I did. I got fed up, but I'm going back again.'

Her aunt sensed that things weren't well with her.

'Is everything all right?'

'Everything's all right. I'll be back at work on Monday.'

'Sarah phoned. I told her about your engagement.'

'Oh.'

'She should be back from Iceland today. She's playing that concert in Durham's Arts Centre tonight. Remember her telling us about it last time she was home?' A pause. 'Are you sure everything's all right?'

'Everything's all right.'

'Have you decided on the wedding date yet? I'd like to know as early as possible. There's a lot of planning to be done.'

Jennifer didn't want to say that she'd called things off. She just couldn't face talking about it right now. Maybe she'd tell her aunt tomorrow. 'Not yet,' she said. 'I'll let you know.'

After a few minutes, minutes filled with her aunt describing the lilac dress she'd ordered for herself to wear at the wedding, and Jennifer politely reciprocating with a description of the dress she'd bought the day before, Jennifer drew the conversation to a close. After putting the phone down, she resumed staring into the fire, forcing herself to think about what she was allowing to happen. There was no reason why she shouldn't have told her aunt the truth about the wedding. And if leaving her job had been such a good idea the day before, it should still hold water today. She realised, with a sense of submissive resignation, that she was doing it again: running away from her life by remaining in the same place. And, unaccountably, another thing occurred to her, something so fundamental she was surprised she had not dwelt upon it before: she couldn't remember the last time she'd laughed. The more she thought about it, the more significant the absence of laughter in her life seemed. But was it a symptom or a cause of her malaise?

She didn't know.

Her thoughts turned to Prospero Pi-Meson. She wondered again who he was. She wondered why he hadn't put his address on the envelopes. That was the most suspicious, unnerving thing.

Presently, Jennifer found herself in her bedroom, retrieving the letter from the carrier bag. The dress she'd bought the day before she also took out. She sat down on the side of the bed to read the letter again, finally placing it on the dressing table. The fifty pound note she put in her purse, although she had no intention of spending it. Getting money in the post from a stranger made her a little uneasy, even though she was pretty sure that it was a prank. She wanted to be able to produce the money in case he really was mad and called to claim it or something, although she was certain the money was legally hers now.

Soon Jennifer put Prospero Pi-Meson out of her mind, giving her attention over to the dress she'd not yet tried on. She laid it out on the bed, regarding it from a position near the dressing table. There was something about new clothes. They were full of promise and possibility. The baggy woollen jumper she was wearing was pulled over her head and discarded, along with her jeans. She rummaged in a drawer for a strapless bra.

Bored Jennifer was going to dress up.

And Jennifer hadn't stopped at dressing up. She'd made-up too, with the vague notion of possibly going out somewhere with Elaine that evening, who now often went to nightclubs in the surrounding towns. The idea remained attractive even after she recalled how little she'd enjoyed herself the only previous time she'd been out with Elaine, a night last year when together they'd gone to a disco held in the back room of a nearby pub.

Jennifer had almost immediately left for home.

She and John never went anywhere other than pubs and the town's one cinema.

Having made-up, Jennifer's eyes were now deep pools of blue; her lips passionate red.

From across the room, she studied her image in the mirror. She liked the dress very much, a perfect fit. She began trying out various accessories that might match. Silver and gold jewellery seemed right. Black stockings were chosen to clad her legs. The right shoes were put on. The coat her aunt had given her for her birthday was taken out of the wardrobe. She hadn't worn this coat yet, but she slipped it over her bare shoulders now. It was long, black like the dress, with wide, padded shoulders, and the feel of the cool satin lining against her bare shoulders was sensual. Dipping her hands into the large pockets, she drew the coat up tight around herself. She'd gone this far, so, she thought, she might as well do her nails to match the lipstick.

With her fingers spread out on the top of the dressing table, lightly she blew over them to hasten the drying of the nail polish. To finish off, she gave one extra-hard blow, which sent Pross's letter sailing away. She caught it before it landed. At that moment, with the letter still in her hand, a trenchant knock sounded on the door. With no reason to suspect it, immediately it occurred to her that this might actually be her mysterious admirer come to call. This thought was alarming, made her heart beat faster, but was soon rejected as unlikely.

She dropped the letter on to the bed and went to answer the knock. As the door swung open, a grim-looking John was revealed.

1.28
Another Follower

'... and when He became lonely, He simply made some friends.'

'Amazing,' breathed Simon, who had come all the way from London with Mick to visit the prophet. Simon, it soon transpired, was taking a correspondence course in how to become a spiritualist, as well as being a prominent member of the Aetherius Society. Simon also believed in ghosts, ectoplasm, time mirages, telepathy, telekinesis and premonitions.

Astrology and tarot cards were big hits with him too.

So were crystals.

'Is that all of it?' asked Simon as the cab headed towards the centre of Durham.

'The rest is history,' said Pross, who had just told Simon's tape recorder all about Godfrey the Creator of the Universe.

Pross found Simon to be just as easy to impress and fool as Mick, and he was certainly in a mood for pissing people around.

'I woke up in the middle of the night last week and felt strangely compelled to get out of bed and turn on my word processor,' he said with an air of the mystic. 'The story just came out. I didn't have to think about it at all. It was weird. It was like someone was dictating to my mind. And another funny thing is that I should have got a word processor in the first place. I felt kind of compelled then as well.'

'It was the Cosmic Masters using you,' declared Simon. 'You must be on the right wavelength. Your house is probably on a ley line too. A ley line's a line of psychic energy that triggers supernatural phenomena.'

Pross had heard about ley lines before and understood them to be complete nonsense. 'It is. Somebody told me last year,' he lied.

It was his intention to lead Simon and Mick up ten dozen garden paths before confronting them with their own stupidity.

Unlike Mick, Simon was deceptive. The deception was that he seemed bright enough to know better, but didn't. Simon was sickly and anaemic in appearance, and this, together with his thick-rimmed glasses, conferred a swotty look. He struck Pross as being the kind of person who'd built a lot of model airplanes as a boy and had never once skipped doing homework. His hair was ginger in colour, thinning already even though he looked still to be in his twenties. Sparse ginger stubble on his chin and upper lip caught the light and glistened like tiny glass splinters.

Pross said, 'And when I'd finished writing, a message flashed into my head: *You are to be Godfrey's prophet* was the message.'

'Astonishing,' breathed Simon in a voice as thin as his hair, looking at Pross in awe.

'I'm just a tool,' said Pross modestly. 'Maybe that's how I came to win the lottery: Godfrey thinks I'll need the money.'

'Really amazing.'

'Told ya it was incredible,' blurted Mick.

It was to open an account in which to deposit his lottery cheque that Pross had told Mick to drive into the centre of Durham, calling directions through the glass panel. It was well past four o'clock now, and that gave little time before the banks closed for the weekend, although he actually had no idea that banks closed so early, never having had call to enter one before. 'Turn right here and we can park near the cathedral,' he said above the noise of the cab. After climbing a narrow road that wound between steep rows of shops and business premises, passing Lilith's estate agency along the way, they were suddenly on a level with the eleventh century edifice. Durham cathedral: sited within a tight loop of the river Wear atop a hill; a majestic, impressive building, dominating the landscape for miles around.

The cathedral was not wasted on Simon. 'Amazing,' he breathed, peering at it through the window.

Mick, in some kind of automatic cab drivers' response, switched the radio on once stationary. The news had just ended, and a severe weather warning was being given. High winds expected across the north of the country later that evening.

Soon they climbed out of the cab, squinting in the light of the low sun.

'Amazing,' breathed Simon again as he viewed the cathedral from the car park.

'I get a spooky feeling every time I come here,' said Pross.

'It's probably a local convergence point for ley lines,' suggested Simon rapidly. 'That's why the ancients built here. You're probably particularly sensitive to ley lines.'

Pross looked intently at him. 'Do you think so?'

'Could well be.'

Pross put his hands into his pockets and regarded the cathedral some more. 'My flatmate saw a UFO above here a few nights back. It hummed and throbbed with light.'

That did it: Simon was now convinced he was on to something big. 'A UFO!' he said. 'It's all falling into place! Don't you see?'

'Not really,' said Pross, 'but tell me about it later. I have to get to a bank. I'll meet you back here.'

He walked off.

The fleeting expression of surprise and anxiety passed from Jennifer's face, leaving a look of numb resignation. Before she asked the obvious question, John grimly said, 'AWOL, that's how. And sorry I had to knock,' he sarcastically added, 'but the pixies took my key.'

She opened the door fully. 'You'd better come in, I suppose.'

He walked straight into the living room, silently followed by Jennifer, who stood near the fire. She didn't know what to say or do. Something inside her was telling her to hold him close and say sorry. It would certainly be easier that way.

John took from his back pocket the sundering letter she'd sent him two days earlier, tossing it contemptuously her way. It landed at her feet. 'Thanks for the letter,' he sneered. In his hand he was conspicuously holding the engagement ring she'd returned to him. He looked drawn and tired. In shame and embarrassment, Jennifer dropped her gaze to the letter on the floor.

John came close to her. She looked into his eyes, saw the hurt there, the pain she'd inflicted. 'You'll be in big trouble for going AWOL,' she said with sympathy.

'Doesn't matter,' he replied. 'They can do what they want to me. If I get back before my ship's due to leave it won't be too bad.'

Jennifer made a slight move to take his hand in hers, but he stepped back and drew open her coat to look at the dress. 'What are you all done up for? Going out with someone tonight?'

'No,' she answered truthfully, moving a little away from him. 'I was just trying some new things on.'

'Like new lipstick and nail polish.' She made no reply to the satiric observation. He stared at her venomously. She'd never seen him look so angry. 'Who is it?' he demanded.

'Who is what?'

'Who is it you're seeing?'

'No one, John. There's been no one but you.' She looked down at her clothes. 'I'll take this stuff off now.'

In her room, she slipped out of the coat, laying it over the bed. The dress, also, she was about to remove, but she hesitated when John appeared at the door. 'Go on,' he said in a surly way, 'don't mind me.' Jennifer reached a hand behind her back and unzipped the dress down to her waist. John lay on the bed, watching her. He was fingering the engagement ring, occasionally tossing it from hand to hand, all done to draw Jennifer's guilty attention to it. She was about to peel down the top of the dress when John missed catching the ring. It bounced off his hand, settling next to a piece of paper on the bed, which he began to examine.

Jennifer leaned over and took the paper from John, casually and innocently she hoped, desperately not wanting to arouse his suspicion, but he had glimpsed enough of it to know who it was from. 'Him again?' he said with anger. 'Is he the one? He is, isn't he?'

Jennifer did not continue undressing. It somehow seemed important to her now that she should not take off the new dress. Instead, she dragged a chair over to the side of the bed, falling down wearily on to its seat. Behind her was a large plain drape hiding a recurrent mould patch on the wall. With her legs to the side, she turned to look at John over the back of the chair, her elbows placed on the curve of black wood which formed its backrest. Her head fell between her hands. Drawing tense fingers through her fringe, lifting it clear from her eyes, she looked at John and found strength. 'It's over between us, John. I don't want to see you again. And you'd better go back to your ship before you get into even more trouble.'

'Who is it?' he demanded, leaping up and grabbing her by the arms. 'Is it him?'

'There's no one,' she answered with quiet desperation. 'Even if I was seeing someone, it would have nothing to do with you. It's over between us. You should have known that months ago.'

John's temper got the better of him. In a burst of anger he threw her off the chair. She yelped in surprise before knocking her head against the floor. 'Tart!' shouted John. Slowly Jennifer picked herself up. Elaine, in a nightdress, appeared at the door of the bedroom.

'What's going on?' Elaine asked apprehensively. 'What's all the commotion? John, what are you doing here?'

The presence of Elaine moderated John's behaviour. He sat on the edge of the bed, his breathing heavy and noisy, his face contorting to hold back unmanly tears.

'It's all right,' said Jennifer with dignity. 'John's back, but he's leaving again soon.' She zipped her dress and picked up her coat, slipping into it. 'I'm going out,' she said firmly. 'I'll be back in one hour. If you're still here, I'll telephone the police and tell them you're a deserter and where you are.'

Jennifer walked past Elaine. John reached for her. 'I'm sorry,' he pleaded, falling to the ground, sobbing. 'I didn't mean to hurt you.' He reached for her legs, but she would not be hindered.

'It's all over, John.'

She walked out of the door. John was too overcome to even stand up. Through tear-blurred eyes, he watched a watery image of Jennifer leaving his life.

He began as seventh and last in the queue, looking at his shoes. By the time he was fifth in the queue he'd begun looking forward, noticing that the cashier was quite promising in a nymph sense of things, although he hadn't yet got a full view of her. By the time he was third in the queue he was catching fuller glimpses of her feminine shoulders and her long hair, although she annoyingly insisted on keeping her head tilted down to attend to her work. And by the time he was first in the queue he was quite taken with her, also realising that she looked a bit like Lisa, the girl who'd got the police on to him, whom he'd almost entirely forgotten about.

Momentarily before looking up from her writing, the cashier asked through the security glass, 'Can I help you?' Then, adopting a smile, she lifted her head to view her next customer.

Her smile immediately fell away.

It *was* Lisa.

Love was rekindled.

Pross gazed at her, thinking about and trying to come to terms with how he'd probably have to spend the rest of his life without her. In his mind's eye he saw it all before him: the barren desolation of his life without his favourite cashier to have and to hold for evermore. It was a life not worth living.

Nervous and annoyed, she again asked, 'Can I help you?'

'Help me? Lisa, you could save my life,' he informed her, his voice quiet and soulful. He decided to send her another love letter, and scribbled one out on the back of a handy slip of paper, passing it to her under the glass screen.

THIS IS A STICK-UP — GIVE ME ALL THE LOVE YOU'VE GOT.

She read it, darted an anxious look at its writer, darted another one at the cashier behind the counter next to her, then pressed a hidden security alarm button. Not a noisy, bells-clanging security alarm button, rather a silent, insidious button. Then, walking away, she asked him to wait, saying she'd be back in a moment.

Bumping her head in the fall had made her feel a little nauseous, but that's all; no cuts, no bruising. And after half an hour's walking, Jennifer felt perfectly well again. The sky was clear but darkening as she wandered down to the river, intending to sit near the wide waterfalls close to the market town's compact centre. She was almost alone by the water, save for some squabbling boys with jam jars. Barbel swam in this river: John had told her that on the few occasions she'd accompanied him on his angling expeditions, back in the early days of their association, watching, bored, as he pretended to be some kind of wise and manly hunter possessed of arcane knowledge of nature's ways. Her distaste of the pastime had soon become apparent to him, and for the last year he'd fished alone, no longer bothering to ask her along with him because she'd begun to complain so much about things, things like the nylon line he unavoidably left behind.

Jennifer left the river and strolled up a steep lane, bringing her to the town's cobbled market square. She was thirsty, and so entered a newsagents to buy something to drink.

'These things never go to the right people, do they?' complained the elderly male newsagent as Jennifer handed over some money.

'Pardon?' she said, wondering why newsagents so often wore maroon nylon coats.

The newsagent nodded to a small stack of papers on his counter. 'Forty years I've ran this shop, getting up at four o'clock every day, and I can only just about afford to retire now. But him, well, he'll never have to lift a finger again. There's no justice, ay?'

Jennifer realised that she'd been looking vaguely in the direction of the stack of papers he'd nodded to and figured that the newsagent had supposed her to have been reading the front page. To help her understand what he was talking about she absorbed the headline of the paper on the top of the pile, learning that a swearing yob had scooped the lottery.

'No, they never do,' she said, accepting some change into her hand and hoping for no further conversation.

But the newsagent wasn't going to let her go.

'And what a name!' he said, taking the copy from the top of the stack and reading slowly, 'Pross-perro Pi-Mess-on.'

She bought a copy of every paper in the shop.

'It was only a bloody joke!' he protested to the three overbearing male bank employees who had approached him from behind, asking him to explain his unusual action. He just couldn't understand how anyone could take such a thing seriously. 'Do you think that I was going to stuff all the love she's got into a bag and run off with it? Where's your sense?' Lisa had now positioned herself back behind the counter, and Pross cast her a spiteful glance. He really was getting sick of humourless people. He'd had his complete fill of them this week. 'How was I to know she was gormless?' Lisa took this insult to heart. She had that *I'm not going to stand for this* look about her, a look which Pross wasn't going to let go unchallenged. 'Of course you're gormless,' he pointedly informed her when it looked as if she was about to say something, 'you've got less gorm than anyone I've ever seen.' But his mood immediately softened. He shook his head with philosophic disappointment. 'We could have been so happy together, Lisa. Country walks. Children one day. Embezzlement.'

Turning on his heel, he said to the men, 'Stuff you lot. I'll take my two million pound lottery cheque to another bank.'

They did some thinking.

'I saw him in the papers!' he heard one say as he walked out of the door.

'Wait!' called the men.

'Fuck off,' said Pross.

The cathedral bells were striking the half-hour as he came out into the street, and by the time he'd walked to another bank, it had closed its doors for the weekend, much to his surprise and dismay. With a cheque for over two million pounds in their possession, anyone else would have employed security men with big sticks and big dogs with big teeth to guard it until it could be banked, but Pross just left it in his pocket. He wandered back up the street, realising that sometimes people would stop and look at him. 'Give uz a smile, Grumpy,' joked one man as he passed by. Such fame was not what Pross wanted. The associations with grumpiness he didn't mind, but the lottery winner stigma he did. It was so without dignity. It was like he was pulling a trailer full of dole giros behind him, and most everyone in the country knew. He wished he'd never gone to that idiotic presentation ceremony. In fact, it seemed to him that he'd been in a mood ever since. Since then he'd been contentious with the people from the lottery company; the journalists; the hotel receptionist; the car hire man; Lisa; and the bank men. But it had always been like this, he knew; the only difference now was that because of his fortune he was meeting so many more people. Nothing had changed. The problem was the same old one: he simply didn't get along with most people. When he was kidding, they took him seriously; when he was being serious, they laughed in his face; when he was being clever, they thought him a fool; when he was acting the fool, they thought they were clever. Were it not for the easy-going relationships he had with his few friends, he'd find it impossible to go on desperately comforting himself with the saving thought that he was an island of sanity in a great ocean of craziness.

1.29
Sisyphus

Deep regret was fermenting within John. Bitter regret. He'd gone AWOL to try to patch things up between himself and Jennifer, but had lost his temper and behaved like a barbarian. He hadn't meant it to be like that. By going AWOL he'd hoped to impress her with his devotion, risking all just to be with her. But it had gone sour. Very sour. He had blown it.

Until she'd walked out of the door, he had not accepted, or even believed, that things were really over between them. Although the letter from her had been considered something that had to be acted quickly upon, it was not foreseen as the end. But the sight of her walking away drove home the finality. Something inside him died at that moment. Never had he imagined that there could be so much pain inside a person. He had lost it all without ever really knowing he'd had it until now. His tears flowed, his face burned and his body convulsed.

After nearly an hour of tears, John resolved to go back to his ship. It troubled him, however, that the last image he had of Jennifer was such a painful one. He was scared that the memory of her leaving, with him sobbing on the floor, his eyes stinging and his throat feeling like it was in a noose, would be the one to dominate for evermore. He was frightened that he would not be able to live with such a sorrow. It would have been so much better had he just accepted the letter and stayed with his ship. There were so many distractions to keep him occupied there. If he'd just accepted the letter, then his last memory of Jennifer would have been one of her warmly kissing him goodbye on a frosty morning.

But now he was going to use his head. She wanted to be free, and he would submit to that want. He was strong, after all. He could take the torture. He was going to be generous and thoughtful; and it would be so much better for him if he returned to his ship of his own volition than if Jennifer called the police and informed on him, which she had threatened to do. Jennifer just hadn't been the same in the days since that letter had come for her. In his bitter mind, John partly blamed the mystery sender for his troubles.

With a feeling of emptiness in his chest and a tightness in his throat, he picked up the letter Jennifer had sent him. He also took the engagement ring. These things he would show to his Commanding Officer to explain his reasons for going AWOL. Closing the door of her flat behind him, he headed for the bus station, determined to put her out of his mind, no matter how long it might take. He realised now that he had not understood his own feelings until this hour. He'd get a bus to Darlington, a train to London, then another train to Portsmouth.

Jennifer took her pile of papers and left the shop. Walking down the street, a few times she bumped into people, her attention given to reading the articles about the abusive millionaire lottery winner with a weird name from Durham who had said p*ss off. It had to be him. There couldn't be two people in the whole world with a name like that, let alone two in one town. She scanned the front pages. GRUMPY MILLIONAIRE FLEES PRESS, read one headline. CAT WINS LOTTERY, OWNER SAYS P*SS OFF, read another. Critical statements from the lottery company abounded, complaining that their generosity in making an unnecessary payment had been thrown back in their face. And there were pictures of him too. Dozens of them; some in colour. Dozens of pictures of him looking moody and, to her eyes, not bad looking at all. But a wind was picking up, putting mischief into the pages. Rolling them into a thick tube, she shielded her newspapers under her coat.

Strongly suspecting that her sister knew something about this Prospero character, Jennifer decided to telephone her, knowing that by now she should be back from holiday in order to play her part in a music production in Durham's Arts Centre... but then, with annoyance, she realised she'd come out without her address book.

The telephone had never been Jennifer's preferred method of communication with her sister — she'd always preferred to write — and that is why she found herself unable to remember Sarah's number, although her address was recollectable.

Directory Enquiries proved useless.

What could she do now? She couldn't go back to her flat because she thought it almost certain that John would still be there, waiting. No, better not risk going back to her flat. She could go to her aunt's, but John might even appear there. She didn't even want to phone her aunt at the moment.

A decision was reached. She was all dressed up, so she'd go to Durham to escape John and find her sister, maybe also finding out something about Prospero Pi-Meson, multi-millionaire lottery winner. A jauntiness that attracted the attention of many passers-by was now in her stride.

The Darlington bus had stopped to pick up more passengers. Slumped across the back seat, propped up against the window, John gazed down the aisle towards the new passengers boarding. He was scared that he would begin crying again; scared that what he felt inside would show outside. The painful vacuum in his chest and the tightness in his throat came back with renewed vigour when he realised that mixed in with the new passengers was Jennifer.

She was carrying an extraordinary number of newspapers.

John furtively concealed himself behind the person sitting in front of him. Jennifer had not seen him, he knew, and he also knew that she would sit near the front of the bus, like she always did. There were no tears coming to his eyes now. He was certain she was going out to meet some new boyfriend, that being the reason why she'd dressed up so much. She had lied to him. Anger was returning. He decided to follow her; find out the truth about why she was ditching him. He had to know. Had to. And throughout the journey she did nothing but read her newspapers, which raised many questions in him.

On his way past, Pross peered into the estate agency where Lilith worked. At first he thought it was someone new at her desk, then he realised it was indeed his friend. 'What has she done?' he murmured.

Upon his entering the agency, Lilith looked up from her work, reacting with a quick smile, then continuing writing.

'Pretty radical haircut, Lil,' said he, referring to her almost shaven head.

'Been meaning to cut it for months,' she said briskly. 'It just got in the way of things.' With one hand, she pushed some newspapers his way while continuing with her work. 'Quite a time you had in London,' she said, pointing at the papers. 'The lottery company certainly seem to hate your guts, judging by what they've said about you. You must have been particularly obnoxious.'

Pross began reading about himself. 'It's all exaggeration,' he said. 'I just got sick of the people there and left.' He leafed through some more papers. A Sun mini-headline made him smile: LIVE CATS SACRIFICED IN ROCK STAGE ACT. He showed it to Lilith. 'I started that rumour,' he proudly said.

Lilith, seeming to be somehow annoyed, said, 'What are you doing here, Pross? I've got work to do.'

Pross, appearing to be absorbed in the newspapers, muttered something about his house. Soon after, having seen all the sensationalism he could stomach, he pushed them to one side. Looking at Lilith, it was now certain in his mind that she was making a show of continuing with her work. It was all to do with what had happened between them two nights ago, he supposed. It was something he'd almost forgotten about himself until just now. It seemed like years ago. But Lilith's attitude now made him feel awkward.

After discussing the business of Harry's death, he tried, for a brief while, to introduce the subject of their brief intimacy, but his courage failed.

Lilith walked over to the window, turning her back to Pross and looking out to the street. 'Are you trying to say something about my stupid pass at you?' she said.

Pross did not answer.

'I was stoned, you were stoned, things got a bit heavy in my head for a while. You weren't too normal, either.' Suddenly, she asked, 'Do you want a coffee?' thereby closing the issue of their brief affair. Pross said he did, and she went into the back office to pour him one.

Returning with two mugs, Pross began sipping his drink slowly, cradling it thoughtfully in his hands.

'You seem to be a bit down,' she remarked dispassionately, going over to a filing cabinet.

'I think you're right,' he said, gazing into his coffee. He did feel down, and he wasn't sure why. 'It's nothing new though, I was depressed long before it was fashionable.'

Lilith sat on the edge of her desk. 'It is quite fashionable, isn't it?' she said, pulling out the contents of a folder, almost like she was humouring, or even just tolerating, him.

Pross didn't answer. He cradled his cup between his hands again and, staring at it, said, mostly for his own ears, 'I'm the most depressed person in Durham.'

'No you're not,' contended Lilith, with a trace of contempt, 'that bloke in the Arts Centre looked more depressed than you've ever been.'

'Appearance can be deceptive,' returned Pross.

'Well, he'd appeared to have been crying. I've never seen you cry. I don't think you could. Not genuinely. Anyway,' she continued, bluntly, 'I don't see why you should be depressed, you're stinking rich now.'

Pross leant back in his chair to sulk. He *was* stinking rich now, and he had no reason, or even right, to feel down. 'Maybe Albert Camus really knew a thing or two,' he wondered out loud. 'Maybe the essence of life is in the struggle. That's what the *Myth of Sisyphus* postulates.'

'The what?'

'The *Myth of Sisyphus*. It's a sod of a philosophy book I tried to read once. Maybe having all this money's taken the struggle away from me, and without the struggle there's no living. I already feel like I've stopped being me. I feel changed.'

Lilith made a derisive sounding laugh, then at once launched into a business conversation. 'I've spoken to the solicitors on your behalf, and they've agreed to give your transaction priority if you're prepared to grease their palms a little.'

Taking a little time to absorb the change in the conversation's direction, Pross said, 'I'll grease.'

She disapproved. 'You will. I see. Well, the first thing you ought to know is that it's customary and good sense to first put an offer in for a property, rather than simply dishing out the asking price straightaway. Do a bit of negotiating.'

Pross said he'd dish out the asking price for the sake of expediency. 'And I don't want to have to talk to anyone but you in this affair,' he said. 'You bring me the forms, and I'll sign them. I'm sick of people.'

Lilith agreed to these terms with dispassionate disapproval in her voice. 'I'm expecting some forms to be faxed from the solicitors today. Where will you be later on this evening?'

'The Arts Centre again. I'm meeting Ron's girlfriend.'

'I'll meet you there then,' said Lilith, almost cutting off Pross's own sentence, 'and we can have things moving by tomorrow.'

Pross felt obliged to leave once the business had been attended to.

Stepping out into the street, the wind had already risen high enough to do what it would with his hair.

The bus passed the ugly modern town hall and turned left into Darlington station. It was quarter to five, and the dirty station was crowded with people on their way home from work. Jennifer alighted and looked about herself, trying not to breathe in the acrid engine fumes but soon submitting through necessity. A frantic trapped sparrow flew to and fro between the small, dim skylight windows of the covered station. It was trying to find a way out, and Jennifer felt for it. John remained on the bus to elude detection, watching Jennifer as she studied a timetable before moving to another platform. She stood at the back of a long queue, having qualms already about what she was doing. Above her was a destination sign. It told John that his ex-fiance was waiting for a bus that passed through Durham. He stepped down off his own bus and slinked out of the station. Outside, he beckoned a waiting mini-cab and asked to be driven to Durham bus station, where he would wait for her, certain that that was her destination.

Not once did he question the reasonableness of what he was doing.

1.30
Moaning Joe

I swear I'll kill him the next time I hear him say absolutely when he means yes, thought Pross as Simon talked excitedly about his theory, saying absolutely instead of yes every twenty seconds. Simon had it all worked out, and Pross listened to the insanity with blatant disinterest.

Mick let his companion do the talking. Pross could tell that Simon was some kind of hero to Mick.

'Don't you see what it all means?' Simon asked passionately, his pale face turned to Pross.

'I think so,' said Pross. 'The universe exists in the great mind of Godfrey and I'm his prophet.'

'But there's more to it. It's all linked with the Aetherius Society.'

'It is?'

'Absolutely. That UFO your flatmate saw over the cathedral was there because of you.'

'It was?'

'Absolutely.' He paused there, before saying in an earnest voice, 'They're talking through you, Prospero Pi-Meson. You've been chosen as the mouthpiece of the Cosmic Masters to reveal the full Truth.'

'Absolutely,' chimed Mick, negotiating the light traffic deceptively well. Maybe he's on Valium today, thought Pross, also thinking about having a warning sign placed on the back of the cab: *TAKE CARE — DRIVER UNDER SEDATION*.

The fire of Godfrey was coursing through the veins of Simon as he passionately explained to a mentally distant prophet his theory. Pross had a lot of things on his mind, all of them good, yet he still unaccountably felt low. It couldn't be because he was still annoyed about that presentation ceremony. He never stayed annoyed over anything long. This wasn't annoyance or irritation he realised: it was sorrow. Differentiating what he now felt from what he'd felt the day before helped him to understand what was troubling him. It was the change happening in his life that was making him feel blue, he came to realise. He'd gained so much, yet still there was a sense of loss.

Simon continued. The Earth wasn't the only planet Godfrey had made friends on once he'd become lonely, he said. Cosmic Master emissaries from these planets, planets more advanced than ours, were now letting us know the full truth about the Universe, spreading the word of Godfrey.

'Absolutely,' said Pross as the cab pulled up outside his home.

John was in position across the road from the pedestrian exit of Durham bus station. He hugged himself to keep warm. It would be a while yet before the bus arrived, he knew. He wasn't planning to do anything to whoever it was Jennifer was coming to see, he just *had* to know what was going on, that's all. Turning up out of the blue and catching her with her lover would give him some sort of satisfaction. It would help put him back on top; give him some dignity. He would turn up, condemn her, show her that he hadn't been fooled, then leave.

His mouth was dry and his stomach empty. The lights of a newsagents beckoned from across the road. After looking both ways to make sure no bus was arriving, he ran into the shop to quickly buy something to eat and drink. In the shop the racks of newspapers reminded him of how Jennifer had been fascinated with the papers she'd brought on to the bus with her. He flicked through a couple and saw that they had headlines on the same theme: a lottery winner.

Prospero P-Meson was the name he read.

Devon Road was the address given.

In Devon Road, there was no sign of Sophie Hamilton or anyone else. Pross, the brand-new millionaire, had been fearing his arrival to excite a crowd; kids, journalists and weird beggars. There was no one. He was almost disappointed.

It was slowly occurring to him that Mick and Simon might be as good as slaves to him. After all, they'd driven all the way up from London to speak with him, and they *did* believe him to be a real prophet. Shit, they did! A prophet! They actually believed him to be a prophet! The implications were at last sinking in. Surely prophets should have it easy? With this delicious thought in mind, he asked Mick to drive on to the nearby kebab shop, which Mick did. Once there, Mick immediately volunteered to buy Pross his meal, and he was in the take-away in no time. This is the life, thought Pross, not listening to a word Simon was saying, but wondering if it might not be such a good idea after all to reveal himself as a charlatan. Ridiculous visions of himself living a life of luxury in his castle came to his mind, with Mick and Simon living as adoring slaves in the stables, on call to tend to his every need. All he'd have to do to keep them hanging around would be to occasionally pretend to have received a message from Godfrey or from aliens or from whoever it was Simon had said was talking through him: after all, that's just what the leader of the Aetherius Society did, Pross remembered from the documentary he'd seen. Yes, he could well imagine something like that, and the mischief of it filled him with amusement. He wondered if he could bite his tongue for long enough to bring such a thing into being, imagining the fun it would give.

While waiting for Mick to return with the food, Pross noticed that every few minutes Simon would crane his neck to look through the windows at the sky. Searches for flying saucers, he presumed.

Soon Pross was back in his flat, eating his kebab while watching the six o'clock news. Mick and Simon also ate. The subdued mood he'd been in since the day before was lifting. He was coming out of the blues. 'Come on,' he told them when his meal was gone, 'let's go for a drink.'

What he really wanted to do was show off his new slaves to his friends. What a laugh. He left a note on the inside of his window for his friend's eyes should they come looking for him. *Gone to the Arts Centre bar*, it read.

On the way, the wind was strong enough to occasionally make the cab veer off course, which seemed to particularly perturb Mick. 'Never been anywhere so fackin' windy,' he declared.

'This stop for the Arts Centre,' the bus driver told Jennifer. 'It's that building there.'

'Thanks,' she replied, apprehension in her voice. Folded up in her pocket was a collection of torn-out newspaper articles about Prospero Pi-Meson.

Jennifer had asked the driver to show her the most favourable stop at which to get off, and the place where she alighted was over half a mile from the bus station and John. It was dark and past six o'clock, very windy. Holding her coat to stop it blowing up around her waist, she hesitated a moment before entering the Arts Centre. Passing through some glass doors and a small entrance porch brought her into a large open-plan room. To her right was a dining area, unlit and closed-off for the evening. In front of her was a reception desk attended by a relaxed, smiling lady. To her left was a large bar room with dozens of tables. There was hardly anyone present. Standing at the bar itself, at the very far left of the open-plan room, two middle-aged men were drinking, talking quietly. In an alcove, a younger, glum-looking man was staring into his beer. Proceeding to the reception desk, she was told that the musical production her sister was performing in was for guests only, not open to the public. She was told, also, that it did not begin for another two hours.

Jennifer didn't want to wait inside the Arts Centre. She was too nervous and agitated. Having only just turned eighteen, she had never before been in a bar on her own. No, she would not wait here, even though this place was not really like a bar. Sarah was not due to perform for another two hours, and so she might still be at her home. Jennifer decided to find a taxi to take to her sister's flat, hoping to catch her before she set off. And if Sarah wasn't in, then she would simply come back here to wait for her. At least that way she would have killed some time. She stepped out into the evening, figuring that she would have to walk towards the city centre to find a taxi. To her delight, a London-style cab came up the driveway of the Arts Centre. She wondered whether to try her luck with it or not. There were people in the back, she could just about make out. Instead of simply letting the passengers out, the driver slowly moved into a vacant space behind the waist-high wall separating the car park from the road beyond, and turned the engine off. The vehicle was not for hire, she understood, and walked onward, fighting against the wind. Shame, she wistfully thought, she'd never been in a black cab.

He opened the door, but a sudden gust caught it, pushing it closed. He didn't try again. Niggling away in his mind was reluctance. He was doing a stupid thing: this was the earliest he'd been to a bar for months, not daring to on account of his track record for speedy over-indulgence. He knew he should go back home for a few more hours. He never wanted to suffer one of his hangovers or throw up again so long as he lived.

But Mick was soon holding the cab's back door open for him.

'I shouldn't be doing this,' moaned Pross, 'it's too early. I'll end up drunk.' Looking at Simon, he said, 'Don't let me drink more than two pints. Hit me if you have to.'

'Hit you?'

'Whack me.'

Apprehensively, Simon agreed. He also said he'd never been drunk himself once in his life and didn't enjoy being in bars. Surprisingly, Mick confessed that he used to be a heavy drinker, but religion had saved him so that now he drank nothing stronger than tea.

Going against his better judgement, Pross clambered out of the cab. Unbending his knees, holding his wind-lashed hair away from his eyes and looking about himself, he noticed the dim figure of a girl in a long black coat slipping away into the night. Over towards the Arts Centre, a man was standing in the doorway.

This was the glum-looking man Jennifer had seen inside.

Between Pross and the Arts Centre entrance lay thirty yards of forecourt which served as a car park for the establishment. In the centre of this dimly floodlit facility was a small, grassed traffic island, and in the middle of that grew a large, old tree, its limbs now swaying wildly in the wind, its branches and twigs clattering against themselves.

Lagging a little behind Mick and Simon, they all three began to stroll towards the entrance.

The man in the doorway commenced walking too.

Cutting across the small traffic island, still lagging a little behind Mick and Simon, still holding his hair back, Pross was suddenly alarmed by a loud crack issuing from the tree above him. He instinctively lurched heedlessly forward, out of danger, passing, mere inches away, as he heedlessly lurched *into* danger, the man who'd been in the doorway.

Their respective, diametrically opposed, lurches resulted in them both stumbling to the ground. Pross, panicking, desperately scrambled up and out of harm's way, but the man desperately scrambled right under the tree, where he fully prostrated himself. 'Come, friendly tree, fall on Sorrow,' he shouted.

But the tree did not fall, nor any branch or even twig.

Pross realised it was the same man who'd bought him a drink. The same man his friends said was more depressed than he.

The man then got up to begin madly kicking the tree and trying to shake its sturdy trunk.

Finally defeated, he slumped down.

Pross looked disbelievingly at the scene until Mick and Simon came up to him, pulling him away. 'He's mad,' said Simon in worried, hushed tones. 'Let's go.'

Dazed and astonished, Pross allowed himself to be led into the Arts Centre, looking over his shoulder at the man all the while.

'Fall, tree,' he heard the man cry. 'Fall!'

Kim, the woman behind the reception desk, smiled at Pross. 'Had quite a bit of luck on the lottery, word has it!'

Still fazed, Pross mumbled, 'A lot of luck. Everything's going just wonderfully.'

Through the glass doors, he could see that the man was still under the tree. 'Who's that lying under the tree,' he asked of Kim, pointing outside.

Kim's face dropped when she saw who it was. 'Moaning Joe,' she said. 'God, he's weird. Scares me, he does.'

'What's scary about him?'

'Everything,' insisted Kim. 'He just sits by himself and cries. He was going on to Debbie about the Antichrist the other night. Don't they have homes for his kind?'

Viewing Joe under the tree, Pross began to suspect that he really was only second best, at least on appearances.

Remembering that he owed Moaning Joe a drink, Pross sent Mick up to the bar to get a round in.

Mick went.

Soon, after telling Mick and Simon to wait inside for him, Pross, drinks in hand, went back outside to talk with Joe, to see if there was any *depth* to the man, any substance behind the appearance of misery.

The bus from Darlington pulled into the station. From across the road, John was grimly vigilant, furtively positioned so that he could see the passengers alighting without being seen himself. Jennifer was not among them. Distraught, he ran up to the bus and peered through the windows. She was not on board. He cursed out loud and hit the side of the bus; cursed himself for confidently anticipating where she would disembark instead of asking his taxi driver to follow the bus. But he had not yet failed. He knew that she'd received communications from Prospero Pi-Meson, and he also knew that she'd been voraciously reading about him on the bus. Therefore, it was not at all unreasonable to assume that she had actually been on her way to meet him. And although she had already got off the bus, that did not matter because, thanks to the newspapers, he knew what street Prospero Pi-Meson lived in.

And Devon Road was the destination he gave to a smoking mini-cab driver a few minutes later.

'Hello there, how's it going?' shouted Pross above the noise of the wind to Moaning Joe, who was now sitting on the ground, head fallen.

Pross was standing a little away from Joe, nervously looking up to the clattering tree for signs of impending catastrophe.

Without lifting his head, Moaning Joe shouted, 'Slowly.'

'Remember me? You bought me a drink on Tuesday, so I've bought you one back.'

A twig collided with Joe's head. Hopeful, he looked up and opened his arms receptively.

Pross was nothing less than awed. 'I've never met anyone who looks more depressed than me,' he shouted.

Still gazing upward with arms open, Joe shouted, 'I'm worse than depressed. I'm bound to agony with seven-fold chains of frosted iron.' Looking at Pross, he enigmatically added, 'We could have splashed in puddles together.'

'Who's we?'

His ocular attention now returned to the tree above him, Moaning Joe answered, 'Me and the daughter of the Antichrist.'

His arms were still held high and wide, like he was expecting holy salvation.

A mighty gust of wind pushed Pross closer to the tree than he wanted to be. Beer spilled and became driving rain. 'Let's go back inside,' he shouted with feebly disguised worry.

But Joe was not of the same mind. 'I'm not leaving here. It's going to fall soon.'

'It's not,' countered Pross. 'It's been here hundreds of years. It's not likely to fall just when you want it too, is it?'

'It is. It has to.'

There came a sudden lull in the wind which caused Joe to now regard the tree with annoyance and disappointment.

His arms were lowered.

'Come inside,' said Pross, 'it definitely won't fall now.'

Like nothing particular had happened, Moaning Joe picked himself up, took a pint from Pross, then strode back into the Arts Centre, ahead of his companion.

Pross followed until they were both sat at a table. Immediately, Mick and Simon came up to him, but Pross banished them to another table until he had time for them.

Frustrated, to another table they went.

Pross offered Moaning Joe his hand for shaking. 'Prospero Pi-Meson.'

The shake was accepted. 'That's a good name. Mine's Joe King. They call me Moaning Joe King these days. Moans for short, if you like.'

Pross needed his curiosity satisfied. 'Who's the Antichrist?'

A tenseness seemed to overcome Moaning Joe. Dropping the register of his voice, he answered disdainfully, 'Not a who, a what. Something only thinly disguised as human.'

'Doesn't she have a conventional name?'

'She does,' said Moaning Joe, 'but I've vowed never to utter it. It's too evil for Durham.'

After but only a few minutes conversation with Moaning Joe, Pross realised he was in the presence of an awesome master. But a master of what, he did not know. A master comic? A master actor? A master fool? A master melancholic? A master of lovesickness? Maybe none of those; maybe all of them. Pross didn't know what Moans was, but he was fucking jealous already.

Moans bore a limited resemblance to Pross. He had a similar leather jacket on, and his hair was cut the same, except Joe's was black and more unkempt. His face was different, though, and his eyes were swamped beneath heavy eyebrows which gave him something of a sinister look. He hadn't shaved today. Pross figured that Joe was about the same height as him, but his build was different. Joe was larger boned and more angular.

Joe hadn't finished with the Antichrist. Without need for prompting, he told more, speaking darkly yet volubly, as if he'd said the words a hundred times before.

'The Antichrist was the one who coaxed me from my safe little island with the shedding of a thousand tears. The one whose tears seemed so honest and true. The one who spun a tangled web of deceit around me.' Abruptly, he changed not only the subject, but the tone. 'You were in the paper this morning, weren't you?'

'That's right. Won the lottery. Over two million.'

'Two million, that's not bad, if material things are what you want. I remembered reading your name. You live in Devon Road, don't you? That's what it said, didn't it?'

Pross confirmed his street of residence.

'I knew someone who lived there once,' said Joe. 'Happy-go-lucky kind of chap, he was. Haven't seen him for a long time.'

A reverie now seemed to be enveloping Joe, but Pross sent it packing by asking, 'Are you the father of the Antichrist's daughter?'

It was time for Joe to speak darkly yet volubly again.

'Our little daughter. Our child. The child she plotted to conceive. The agony of my separation from my child grows a little more each day. She's never even publicly acknowledged that I'm the father.'

'Why not?'

Moaning Joe continued with his autobiography.

'Oh, she thinks she has her reasons all right. All of them pathetic and selfish and weird — *so* weird. I found it all out later, you see. What she did and what she planned. She hates me for that. Hates me for knowing her truly.'

And after a quick sip of beer, there was more — a *lot* more.

'She was going out with someone else, you see, someone she told me a hundred times she didn't love any more. Said she hated him, even. Couldn't bear him touching her. Always she was on the brink of leaving him, which eventually she did, or at least she told me she had. Well, one day she said she'd finally told him all about me, and that they were finished for good. But it was not quite how she'd said it was, I found out later. I found out so much about her later. Nothing had been quite like she'd managed to convince me it was. Nothing. So many lies, lies I think she even grew to believe herself. And looking back, Lord how that girl enjoyed lying. The lies brought such smiles to her face. And I found she'd as soon lie *about* me as to me. She could find enough colours on my palette to paint any fantasy she liked, just to make her life sound exciting and dangerous. And how she'd searched for those colours! You know, one day I remember her looking at me and saying, with an expression of disappointment, that I was just a normal person really. If only I'd taken more heed of that utterance. If only. But I suspected nothing amiss at the time; was too innocent to look. I didn't know what private flight of fantasy she was on.'

He's like a dog with a fucking bone, thought Pross.

'Transpired she'd actually never admitted anything to him about me, but he'd become suspicious through a mutual friend. He was gutted, of course. I guess she enjoyed that — Lord, she'd done enough to bring it about. But now, to keep him, which is what she really wanted, she stopped toying with me, and when I went round to see her the next day she cut my heart out and left me for dead, just as you see me now, twelve months later. Her being pregnant with our little child is what made it hurt so much. After weeks of lovingly uttering sweet nonsense about how it was part of me and part of her, and delightful rubbish about how it was bound to be beautiful and gifted because I was the father, that evening she just matter-of-factly said that she couldn't ever possibly tell her folks that she'd been involved with me. Apparently, they considered me to be wholly reprobate, even though I'd never exchanged more than a dozen words with them in all the years I'd known her casually and even though for months she'd been leading me to believe that they knew what the real score was between us. Can you imagine how confused I was that a person well into her twenties should come out with something like that? And how hurt? And how humiliated?' Joe paused. 'Well, at least I'm not confused any more. I did some investigating and I understand all her reasons now, but they're all pathetic and selfish and weird. I found it all out, and that's something she can't bare — someone knowing her truly. She hates me for that.'

'You've already said that bit,' Pross pointed out, 'word for word.'

'Have I?' queried Moans without embarrassment. 'Anyway, from that evening on...'

Holy fuck, not more, thought Pross.

'... she began doing her best to persuade the other chap that the child would be his, which was the only escape route open to her once she realised what a petty pickle she was in. She was too spineless to tell the truth to her weird folks, even though it was soon clear to me that she'd wanted to become pregnant by me. Covering that up was her biggest lie of all. You know, she even berated me for not losing my temper with her when she told me she was going to continue the pregnancy because *he'd* lost his temper with her.'

'Maybe he is the father, anyway?' suggested Pross.

'He's not. He and I talked it over once it was all out in the open, and there was no chance of it being him. She wanted my child, and my child is what she got.'

'So you *know* this other bloke?' remarked Pross with surprise.

'A close friend,' confessed Joe with shame and sadness. 'You know how it goes.'

'Not really,' answered Pross.

'Well, don't be in a hurry to find out. It's awful.'

All at once, Joe lost his equanimity and became tearful. 'The agony of my separation from that child grows greater each day.'

'You've said that bit before too.'

'My prerogative, pal,' said Moans plainly as his equanimity returned. 'She couldn't have done me more harm even if she'd sat down with a pen and paper for a month to plan it all. And there's a lot I haven't told you about. I uncovered an awful lot about her afterwards. An awful lot. I could tell you how from that evening on she revelled in the sadism of power, laughing with giddy delight whenever she'd managed to hurt me, which wasn't hard for her to do considering she was carrying our child. And she would hurt me simply because of the few people she could hurt in some way, I was the only one she ever *dared* hurt. I could tell you how I was just a convenient subject for her to exercise her weird ego on. I could tell you how she never truly wanted me, just wanted me to want *her*. I could tell you about the lies she's *still* telling about me. I could tell you some of the lies about *other* people she told me, lies verging on the truly wicked. And I could tell you about the weird stuff, the really weird stuff.' Joe tailed off, staring with harrowing desolation into his drink. 'I could tell you so many crazy things about that crazy person, the craziest thing, though, is that I still feel tenderness towards her.'

'Crazy,' murmured Pross.

Joe became tearful again.

Well, there was no doubt about it, realised Pross with painful humility: not only did he look it, Moaning Joe *was* more depressed than he. Joe's story certainly knocked spots off his own Susan Murray tale, which he now knew he'd never be able to recite again, it being so feeble a heartbreak by comparison. In fact, observing Joe in his tearful state, Pross knew that he'd never really been heartbroken himself at all.

Joe's mood now seemed to be swinging from forlorn incomprehension of all that had happened to him to extreme bitterness. Gripping his glass, he hissed, 'Scheming, plotting, lying, cunning bitch.'

Pross shook his head, sympathetically echoing Joe's words. 'Yeah, scheming, plotting, er...' He pretended not to remember the rest of the sentence and dried up.

'Lying, cunning bitch,' added Joe helpfully.

'Yeah. What a scheming, plotting, lying, cunning bitch.'

Joe suddenly fixed Pross with a threatening glare. 'Don't you call the Antichrist a scheming, plotting, er...' This time it was *he* who seemed to be having trouble remembering the descriptive sentence.

'Lying, cunning bitch,' added Pross helpfully.

'That's right — lying, cunning bitch,' said Joe. 'Don't call her that.'

'Sorry, Antichrist,' said Pross.

Numerous people were drifting into the bar now, but no one came anywhere near Pross and Joe. Their alcove was empty.

Joe soon became morosely reflective once more. 'Never let yourself get involved, Prospero Pi-Meson. Never let yourself get involved. Never anything more than a stolen glance across a crowded room.' Then he took his drink into his disproportionately large hand and leant back in his chair, saying nothing and not looking as if he was about to — ever again.

Feeling moved, Pross brightly offered some inane words of support, giving Joe an encouraging little punch on the arm. 'Never mind, Moans, you'll find someone else one day, someone with substance. You just had terrible luck with the Antichrist, that's all. There can't be many others as spineless and immature as her about. At least I hope not.'

'I know that,' said Joe. 'And don't patronize me. I put up with enough of that from her. I played the fool and clown for that girl's amusement a bit *too* well.' He slumped over the table, beating his fists down. 'Idiot!' he cried. 'I should have known better than to have believed in someone who'd shoplifted from Oxfam.'

'Well, that had to be a mistake. What's she up to now, anyway?'

Joe was still slumped, looking a thousand times more miserable than Pross had ever managed to. 'I don't know, and I don't want to know. I keep well out of her way because she can't resist the temptation to play out pathetic fantasies to get off on her weird ego trips. Her old boyfriend soon left *her* for good, though, once he knew the real score. The last I heard was that she was running around with a bunch of morons. House-breakers and jailbirds some of them, I happen to know. Kidding herself she's living it up. I know she's still telling her folks that the child is his, telling them that I'm crazy to believe it's mine, even telling people that I refuse to take blood tests when it's actually the other way around. But I know that wherever she is, and whoever she's with, she'll be making a great show of appearing to be the very essence of sweet reasonableness. That's her speciality deception.' Joe straightened up, a bitter grimness sweeping over his countenance. 'But my eyes eventually saw beyond the facade. Her web of lies grew so tangled it caught the wind and blew clean away, and she was revealed behind it, a scheming spider.'

'Nowt but a scheming spider,' echoed Pross sympathetically.

But Joe immediately fixed him with another glare. 'Don't you call the Antichrist a scheming spider,' he ordered.

'Sorry, the Antichrist,' said Pross.

Joe began to look tearful again, so Pross began saying, 'She sounds to me like...'

Joe cut in, 'Don't you call the Antichrist an evil-minded, cheating, malicious, pathetic, spineless piece of shit,' he ordered. 'Only I can attack her with an unsullied conscience. Only I know what really happened.'

'I wasn't going to,' protested Pross.

'Oh, sorry, mate,' said Moaning Joe immediately.

'I was going to say that she sounds so mixed up she could benefit from a trip or two to an analyst.'

Moans nodded, and then he was off again. 'Too right. Maybe one day she'll get herself sorted out. But then again, she'd never admit to having done the things she did, not even to a doctor. She sticks to her stories with pathological tenacity. She's the kind of person who'll tell a dozen lies to avoid telling a single truth; and even if she *has* to admit to having told a lie, she'll blurt a dozen carefully rehearsed specious excuses for the untruth. And I was the victim of all her lies and duplicity each time.' He paused briefly. 'Duplicity: she's the queen of that. All I want from her is some honesty and straightforwardness. It's what I've got a right to because of the little one. I've pleaded with her for honesty, even begged for it, but I think maybe it's time for me to wrest some honesty from her, even if I have to do it in some ugly way.' He looked Pross in the eye. 'I could give you so many examples of her continuing duplicity. Do you want to hear it *all?* All the different stories she invents for the different people she deals with, stories that try to make herself look wronged and innocent in the eyes of others?'

Pross shook his head. 'I've already heard more about her than I care to. I really think you ought to find someone else, it can only help.'

'There'll never be anyone else. I could never trust again, especially in my own judgement. Losing my child like that broke me completely.' A reflective pause. 'Never get involved, Prospero Pi-Meson. Choose isolation every time, never intimacy. Don't take the risk, she might be like *her*.'

'I won't,' said Pross.

'Do you know,' continued Moans, 'that girl's so calculating, she even told me she'll get back together with me one day, after she's played the field a bit. Or maybe she's really waiting for her folks to all die off so that she needn't go on living a lie.'

'You mean you'd have her back? Where's your pride?'

Joe clenched his large hand into a fist and brought it up to his chest, saying firmly, 'I'd never have anything to do with her again. I'll never again expose myself to her machinations, not even to get access to my child. It's over. I'll never have anything to do with...' Joe's discourse abruptly ended. A vision had thrown him out of miserable equilibrium. 'My God, it's her,' he murmured, looking over Pross's shoulder.

'Who?' asked Pross, turning around in his seat.

'Her,' said Moaning Joe.

'Who?'

'The Antichrist. It's the Antichrist. She's come looking for me. All her neurotic, dimshit folks must have died and I'll be able to see my child. They're all dead — what fabulous luck!'

'Where? Where?'

'There,' pointed Joe, squinting myopically. 'There.'

But Pross knew better as Joe began to rise from his seat to go over to the Antichrist. Staying him with an outstretched arm, Pross said, 'Joe, it's not the Antichrist.'

'It is,' insisted Joe, 'it's the Antichrist. She's come looking for me.'

'No it's not,' said Pross. 'It's Sarah-Jane Lucas.'

Joe remained in his half-seated, half-standing position. 'Are you sure?'

Pross was sympathetic. 'Sorry, but I'm positive. I know her.'

Joe slumped down into his seat. 'I really thought it was the Antichrist. She has her hair.'

'Believe me,' said Pross, 'that's all they have in common.'

'That's the third time this week alone I thought I'd seen her. Mind you, I'm crap without my glasses.'

Debbie, the small barmaid with a scandalous way of talking, came over to clean their table. She cranked her face up into a smile to perfunctorily speak to Moans, who was still slumped, addressing him in the same tone of voice that nurses use for elderly, difficult, stupid patients. 'Hello, Joe. How are you today?'

'Sunk in deep resentment,' was the reply.

Debbie scurried off as soon as she reasonably could.

'I just want some honesty and straightforwardness,' moaned Joe to himself. 'Just some honesty. She could end so much of my torment with just five minutes of honesty. What will I have to do to get it? I've tried so hard. Is it selfish of me to want it so badly?'

'You've just been too soft all along,' judged Pross. 'If you want to take your own kid for a walk in the park, instead of wandering around crying all day long, just go round and do it whenever you feel like it. And if the silly bitch demurs at all, or plays any of those pathetic games you've hinted at, turn round and slap her one, then drag her to a clinic and force her to get blood tests done so that she can't go on clinging to that story of you not being the father with those idiot folks of hers. And if you've got the time afterwards, go and slap her crap folks around a bit too. Sounds like they've got it coming to them.'

'You're not the first to suggest that,' said Joe.

'So go and do it.'

'It's too late,' said Joe resignedly, 'all the damage has been done. I'm broken. I realised that fully tonight. That's why I threw myself under that tree. I've come to the end. It's closing time for me.' A wry smile came to his lips. 'Vague intentions of suicide had long been my comfort. The proposition makes life bearable, don't you think? But tonight, I just couldn't go on.' The smile faded, overwritten by grimness. 'One day though, I'll bloody do it. The pain only grows. Everyday it grows. I'm laid bare and broken. This agony will never end.'

Staggering, thought Pross. Here was a man so desperately brokenhearted he was wont to throw himself under trees to end it all, and Pross felt truly humble in his company. But instead of wanting to stick by this miserable man to learn everything he knew, Pross was finding himself resentful of him. Joe was belittling him. Joe was standing on his toes. Compared to Joe, Pross looked like just an *amateur* melancholic. Moaning Joe's miserable perfection embarrassed him.

Lilith was right — Pross *would* have to kill him.

Suddenly, all heads in the room reacted as one, turning sharply to the windows as, with a splintering crash, the tree in the car park split in two, dumping tons of wood right where Joe had been lying.

'You bastard,' said Joe to Pross in a low voice, turning from the window. 'You utter bastard. I should have been under that.'

Pross was both aghast and repentant. 'I'm sorry,' he said, 'I'm really sorry. How can I make it up to you?'

'Kill me,' was the immediate reply.

'All right,' agreed Pross. 'Listen, I know the address of a drug addict across town who sells heroin. Agness Old, they call her. Here's a hundred pounds. Go to Agness at once — seventy-six Central Avenue — and tell her that someone called Pete sent you. Buy as much smack as you can. Get a syringe and needle as well; she's an addict, so she's bound to have them. Shoot the lot up. You'll lapse into a coma then die in your sleep. Trust me, I've studied painless ways to die.'

Moaning Joe seemed immediately cheered and touched by the offer. 'You're giving me a hundred pounds to kill myself with?'

'Yes. Here, take it.'

Joe graciously accepted it. 'Thanks,' he said. 'This is the best birthday present anyone's ever given me. I mean it. I'll get that smack. Trees are so unpredictable.'

'Is it your birthday today?'

Joe nodded slightly. 'My twenty-ninth.' Standing up, he said, 'I'm going to go and get that smack. I just can't cope with the pain any longer. It gets so much worse each day. Each day my sorrow grows a little more.' If it was at all possible, Moaning Joe now looked even sadder. 'My little sorrow,' he murmured, before becoming resolute. 'I'm off to buy oblivion.'

'That's the dispirit,' Pross said encouragingly, pleased with his word play. 'Seventy-six Central Avenue. Say that Pete sent you. Say it slowly, she's a bit thick.'

Moaning Joe lived up to his name one more time before taking steps towards the door and, he declared solemnly, seventy-six Central Avenue to buy overdose oblivion.

A few seconds later, there was a tap on the window behind Pross.

It was Joe, set to speak volubly again.

'Never let yourself get involved,' Joe said through the glass, 'it could be with an illusion. She might shine simply with light reflected from the bright people around her. She could merely mimic her way into your affections. Behind smiles can lie sour intentions. Never get involved. Never.'

He faded into the night.

'I won't,' mouthed Pross, seriously thinking that if it could plunge a person so deep into resentment as Moaning Joe had obviously sunk, then he'd be wise to avoid it for as long as he might live.

Moments later, another tap sounded on the window. 'Watch out for spiders' webs,' said Joe.

'Always,' replied Pross.

Joe merged with the night once more.

But then a third tap.

'The bitch!' shouted Joe, before departing for good.

1.31
An Ally's Help

Sarah-Jane's home in Eldon Place was one of eight making up a small block of newly-built council flats. They were vandalised already, and it was with some trepidation that Jennifer pushed open the door of the communal entrance serving the individual dwellings of the block. Wind rushed through broken panes. She praised herself for having had the good sense to ask the taxi driver to wait for her in case her sister might not be in. She remembered her sister having once said that she lived on the first floor, so she ascended the concrete staircase. Litter abounded. The smell of urine was discernable. Fittings were broken. Idiotic graffiti was everywhere: she wondered why it was that the people least able to write were the people most predisposed to do it in large letters on walls. Jennifer had always imagined that Sarah lived somewhere more pleasant — she could certainly afford to. This place scared her. She knew that she would now always be worried for her sister so long as she remained here. Maybe that's why Sarah had never even hinted at the conditions under which she lived. But it must be cheap, she figured, and Sarah was the kind of person to whom a flat was just a place to sleep.

After reading the numbers above the doors, Jennifer rapped the knocker of 284, studying a Neighbourhood Watch sticker on the inside of a narrow wire-mesh glass panel beside the door. No one came to answer. She rapped again, noticing that there was damage to the door. Evidence of some break-in it looked like, but obviously not recent. Coarse, aggressive voices came from within the flat next door. She was frightened. This was such a dismal place. She peered through the glass panel and into Sarah's home, dimly illuminated by the light of a street lamp coming in through a window. It looked comfortable and ordered in there. Once more she rapped, then turned to leave. An old Cliff Richard song began blaring out from a downstairs flat.

It was the night of Sarah's musical presentation, and she was dressed accordingly, exactly as she had been the first time Pross had met her, only one week ago this very night. When in conversation with Moaning Joe, he had seen her from his alcove, but she had not seen him.

Now she was seated alone at a table enjoying a drink and reading a book.

Before going over to her, from his alcove, he gazed appreciatively her way as she read. It was a moment of poetry. A dreamy moment of beauty. A moment contaminated by Mick and Simon coming back over to him.

'Can we talk now?' asked Simon, his face alight with boyish enthusiasm. He struck Pross as being the very kind of person who would buy his quantum vacuum science fiction novel if he ever got around to writing it.

'About what?'

'About you and Godfrey and the Cosmic Masters,' beamed Simon.

'What about me and Godfrey and the Cosmic Masters?'

A smirk overcame Simon's insipid face, a face which looked like it was made from putty splashed with tea. Mick smirked too, as Simon revealed a secret. 'I've got a fully-charged prayer battery in the cab. We can discharge it skyward from near the cathedral. That way the Cosmic Masters will know some people down here are trying to contact them back.'

'We'll do it later. I want to talk with a friend first. Sit down over there again for a while.'

But when he looked her way, she was gone.

'Bugger,' he said.

After asking at a house in Devon Road, John was told the exact whereabouts of Prospero Pi-Meson's abode.

He walked up to it and tapped on the door. A man with combed-back dark hair answered.

'Yes?' said the man curtly.

John, with his hands in his jacket pockets, said, 'I'm looking for someone called Prospero Pi-Meson, does he live here?'

The man looked John over for a few seconds. 'Friend of yours, is he?' he asked with obvious distaste.

John sensed he had an ally here. 'The bastard's no friend of mine,' he said.

The man was tensely quiet; thinking. 'He lives here. I'm his landlord. If you want to catch him, there's a note on the window saying he's at the Arts Centre bar.'

That's just the kind of thing John wanted to hear.

John was running short on cash. All the taxi rides had taken their toll on his wallet. Walking from Devon Road to the Arts Centre — he knew it would not be too far, nothing in Durham was, it was a uniquely compact city — he kept his eyes open for a bank cash point.

Burying his hands deeper into his pockets and pulling his shoulders in, he walked swiftly onwards, defying the wind, determined to find Jennifer this evening. He'd come this far, so he would not turn back, even though he was tired and hungry. He was made of stern stuff, he reminded himself, one of the nation's brave young defenders.

1.32
The Landlord

Giving him a start, a hand fell heavily on to Pross's shoulder. He turned his head around. 'Hello, Pross, famous grump,' smirked Tony from behind round, multi-coloured sunglasses. 'Seen the tree out there?'

Melanie was with him. Her long, brown hair was windswept. She asked, laughing, 'What in the hell did you do to get the lottery people so mad?'

'Nothing much.'

'Have you seen my sister at all lately?'

'Why?' returned Pross, realising the enquiry had made him feel uncomfortable.

'Just wondered where she's been hiding herself these last few days, that's all.'

'Saw her today.'

'We just saw that sad-looking bloke who bought you a drink the other day,' said Tony. 'He was running down Central Avenue.'

Bugger, thought Pross — he never thought Joe would actually *do* it. He thought he'd just pocket the money. Who could still feel suicidal just after being given a hundred pounds for free?

Oh, well, what the hell, he concluded.

Winking, Tony asked, 'Are the drinks on you?'

Keen to show off his slaves, Pross glanced Mick's way and snapped his fingers. Mick came over and took Pross's drinks order.

To the bar he then went.

Pross gave a quick and smug explanation to Melanie.

'They think what?' bellowed Tony.

'Shush,' urged Pross. 'It's true. They think I'm a prophet.'

Tony and Melanie were flabbergasted. 'How?'

'The seedy-looking one's a London cabby,' explained Pross. 'He picked me up yesterday, and I told him my Godfrey story like it was true and he believed every word of it.'

'What about the other one? The pasty-faced one.'

'Him? Oh, he's some sort of official of the Aetherius Society.'

Pross had to explain the Aetherius Society too.

Tony made some noises of incredulity.

'Honest. They think I'm a prophet receiving telepathic messages from alien spaceships spreading the word of Godfrey. It's brilliant. They run errands for me and believe every word I say. Should I tell them that you're from Mars?'

'But it's impossible,' said Tony.

'No it's not. You look like a fucking Martian.'

Melanie smiled crossly and punched Pross's shoulder. 'Leave my bloke alone.' Now it was her turn to make incredulity noises. 'It's insane. No one could believe something like that. They're probably after your money.'

Pross put his finger to his lips, urging her to keep her voice down. 'Shush, they might hear. It's insane, all right, but far from impossible.' He then proceeded to regale man and wife with disdainful examples of ridiculous prophet and Messiah worship from down the ages. 'Prophets and messiahs come and go all the time, and there's always been people ready to believe in them. Some Dutchman declared himself to be God in 1950 and got thousands to follow him. And what about that David Koresh bloke at Waco the other year? There's an unlimited supply of nutters out there just waiting for the right kind of insane idea to latch on to. A lot of stupid folk with superstitious needs. Anyway, it's a good time for prophets — end of the millennium and all that.'

Tony made some more noises of incredulity. 'Jeez, it all happens to you, doesn't it?'

'Twice, sometimes,' complained Pross.

Mick came back with their drinks, deposited them, then rejoined Simon.

Melanie and Tony finally got around to sitting down, both first unburdening themselves of coats. 'We called at your place before coming here,' said Melanie. 'Moving out already, eh? Can't stand another night in Devon Road?'

Pross was puzzled. 'Moving out? Not yet.'

'So why are you having your stuff taken out then?'

'I'm not.'

'Well, it's all piled up in your entrance hall.'

Pross was even more puzzled. He suspected the involvement of burglars until Melanie explained that it was his landlord who was doing the work. Now it was obvious what was happening: the landlord was turfing him out. 'Shit,' he said, smirking as well, 'I forgot. My landlord hates me and said he wanted me out of the flat. He threatened to grass on me to the cops if I didn't leave. He found some joints in the ashtray on Wednesday night and said he'd give them to the police if I wasn't out by the weekend.'

Melanie was outraged. 'But he can't do that. It's blackmail. They weren't even your joints.'

Pross shrugged. 'I don't give a shit. And I don't give a shit if he does go to the police, either. It'll only be a fine at worst. I don't even suppose they'll accept his evidence. It's hardly the proper way to go about things, is it?'

Melanie wanted to know whatever it was Pross had done to annoy the man.

'Nothing. I just try to make conversation with him, that's all.'

She now fully understood.

Pross really didn't give a damn if his landlord went to the police or not, but he was slightly concerned that his personal belongings were being dumped. And what about poor Spock? He would have to go back home to sort things out.

He looked at Mick, clicked his fingers and expected him to come over to receive his latest driving instructions.

Mick did not respond, rather he exchanged some words with Simon.

And it was Simon who came over instead.

'Pross,' he said respectfully, apologetically, 'we really are anxious to discharge the prayer battery, and it would be so much better if you were with us. You're on their wavelength, after all.'

'Later,' said Pross, 'we'll do it later. I promise. But I have to get back home first.'

Less than one minute elapsed between Pross leaving for home to rescue his belongings and Jennifer returning to the Arts Centre. The fallen tree held her gaze for a while. Entering, Sarah-Jane was nowhere to be seen, so she did something uncharacteristically bold. She simply sought out the place where Sarah was due to perform and walked into the hall, discreetly sitting at the back. No one bothered her.

Actually, if she'd simply mentioned to the receptionist that she was the sister of one of the players, then a message would have been relayed, and she would no doubt have been included among the legitimate guests at the unimportant performance. But Jennifer was seldom one to assert herself in any way.

Twenty minutes later, the curtain was raised on a string quartet, with her sister on cello. Sarah was beautiful and dramatic in her period dress. Jennifer felt proud.

Somewhere down that way, remembered John as he walked onwards to the city centre, was Sarah-Jane's flat. Unknown to Jennifer, he'd been there once before. He was wondering now if he should go a little out of his way to call on her, just in case Jennifer had not actually come to Durham to meet Prospero Pi-Meson but to meet her sister. He thought the prospect unlikely, but checking it out would not waste much time. The Arts Centre could wait a little while, he thought, turning off the main road to seek out Eldon Place, asking passers-by for directions.

Simon was a scruffy official of the Aetherius Society. Simon was also a millionaire many times over. Simon had made a huge fortune out of a small fortune left to him by his deceased mother eleven years earlier. The small fortune had been a property. A London property. Simon, eighteen and at polytechnic studying quantity surveying at the time, managing to just scrape through his degree even though he'd burnt enough midnight oil to fill a tanker, had sold the property, and with the proceeds had simply bought another one. Three months later, he sold the new property for a profit, and this time bought two smaller properties. Soon he sold that lot, generating another profit. With odious ease, he continued to convert profits into profit-making property. Every single time he got lucky with the locations of his properties: it seemed that as soon as he bought a property in an area, that area would become yuppified and sought after. Then he met a man with big greedy property speculation ideas who was after capital. Simon became a sleeping partner in a wide-awake business. South-east property prices soared.

Not many people knew about Simon's wealth. Not even the Inland Revenue. Mick, who had only known Simon for a few days, certainly knew nothing of it. Everything about Simon gave the appearance of penury. He lived cheaply in a rented bedsit, searched for bargains when he went shopping for food, never paid a bill until he had to, and was seldom parted from a shabby green anorak. Apart from his associations with various unorthodox religious organisations, he had no friends, and except for visits to such "mystic" places as Glastonbury, he never ventured outside London.

Simon wasn't into property speculation any more. He had pulled his capital out of the business just a month before the collapse of the London property market. He had pulled out on the advice of his partner, who had predicted the bursting of the south-east property bubble. His partner had moved his own operations to the north of the country, where prices had continued to rise for some time; but Simon had decided to remain in London and retire from the game with over seven million pounds sitting in various accounts bearing his name. He didn't want to be away from the Aetherius Society. He was an influential member.

'Later. We'll do it later,' said Pross, half-irritated, half-laughing. 'I'm the bloody prophet here. I'm the one who gets the messages. Just hold on. I have to get back to my flat first.'

Travelling through the streets of Durham, Simon was becoming meekly forceful. He desperately wanted to discharge his prayer battery to lure a flying saucer down, and he was beginning to become a little peeved with Pross for being so dilatory. 'I've got two hundred hours of prayer energy stored up in that battery,' he mumbled, the imagined exigencies of the situation almost pushing him to open insurrection against the prophet of his own beliefs.

Presently they were outside 17 Devon Road. Followed closely by Mick and Simon, Pross walked up to the house he'd lived in for the last four years. Pushing open the outer door, he found the light on and mounds of his personal belongings blocking the way. Many of Ron's belongings were also evident. Clothes had been thrown indiscriminately on to the floor. Although this was exactly how he was wont to treat his clothes anyway, he felt such a liberty by his landlord to be an outrage. His books were heaped up in one corner. In another corner was his record player. More substantial items of furniture were heaped up near the staircase. Even his bed clothes were lying dumped.

On top of the record player lay the photograph of Jennifer. Pross picked it up and removed it from its frame. No doubt Sarah-Jane would want the photo back; after all, it was only on loan to him. He slipped it into his jacket pocket. And there was the T-shirt that Ron had confiscated from him a week ago. That was picked up too.

Mick and Simon were keen to know what was going on.

'I'm being unlawfully evicted,' said Pross, not concerned about having to live somewhere else until the mock castle became his own, but mildly concerned for the security of his personal effects. Some of these things had sentimental value to him, he supposed (but couldn't quite think which things and why). 'But don't worry about me. I've got my eye on a wonderful place in the country near here. There's even a little house in the grounds for you two to live in, if you want. The grounds are big enough to land a whole fleet of flying saucers. I was up there two days ago, and the vibes were incredible. Lots of ley lines. Must be lots of them. Great place to get messages.'

This news excited Mick and Simon considerably.

Spock, hearing its master's voice, came in from the garden, rubbing itself around Pross's legs. He picked it up and cradled it like a baby. At that moment the landlord came into the hall from inside the flat. He was carrying the word processor.

'I suppose you realise what you're doing's illegal?' said Pross, amused by his evictor's grimness. He was a millionaire, and petty things like being chucked out of a dismal flat didn't bother him in the slightest. Soon he was to live a life of peace and luxury in his sprawling country home.

In stern silence, the landlord roughly placed the computer down on to the floor.

'Careful,' said Pross.

The landlord made no reply, but went back into the flat. Pross instructed Mick to take the computer into the safety of his cab. He didn't want to have it stolen since it had all his love letters stored on its hard disk, not to mention the seventeen best suicide letters he'd ever written, and was ever so fond of sending out.

Mick obliged.

Followed by Simon, who was obviously nervous and apprehensive about the heavy scene, Pross went into his flat. It was all a little puzzling. The last time he and the landlord had spoken together, the landlord had only threatened to inform the police about the petty amount of dope if he didn't voluntarily leave the flat by the weekend. So why the eviction? Was it because he'd won the lottery? Was the landlord insanely jealous?

Pross, soon to exercise his talent for appearing to be flippant, caught the landlord in the act of ripping down the Rolf Harris posters from his bedroom walls.

'I've gone off him too,' said the lottery winner, still cradling Spock. 'I'm more of a Des o'Connor man these days.'

The landlord worked on with a fury. There was hardly a vestige of Pross's four-year habitation of this room left.

'Would you like to talk about something?' goaded Pross. 'Got a problem? Jealous because I've won the lottery and you haven't? Pissed off because you were never invited in for a smoke?'

Mick returned. He and Simon breathed various comments on the crime being committed.

The landlord suddenly stopped his obliteration and walked over to Pross. He was seething with real anger. Pross just couldn't understand what he'd done to turn him so ferociously against him. He knew that there'd never be any love lost between them — after all, he'd been goading him about the shower being working and various things like that for years — but even that was surely no reason for this sudden fury.

As the landlord, a taller than average man in his physical prime, leanly muscular, came closer to Pross, the latter's heart suddenly began to beat faster. Even the cat coddled in his arms like a baby seemed to sense trouble.

The landlord stood before Pross. 'Go on, say it,' he hissed.

Mick and Simon took cautious steps backwards.

'Say what?' asked Pross.

'Say one of your wisecracks about that shower.'

This was utterly ridiculous, thought Pross. The man was obviously unhinged. A bit of silly, surreal goading about the shower had turned him into a psychopath. 'Actually,' said Pross in a manner of apparent conciliation and retreat, 'I don't think I'll bother you about the shower still working any more...'

The landlord's temper appeared to diminish slightly.

'... but those windows are still letting in light.'

This was not a wise thing to say under the circumstances.

'Everything's a fucking joke to you, isn't it?' snarled the landlord. 'Why do you make everything into a fucking joke?'

'Because I can, and it is,' returned Pross simply. 'Anyway, what does it matter to you? I pay my rent.'

'Matter to me? Matter to me? It matters a hell of a lot to me when I'm called out of bed in the middle of the night by the police because my father's died and my mother's gone crazy, and when I get here you come out with another one of your fucking stupid wisecracks about that shower.'

'Aw, I hadn't meant it like that,' said Pross. 'It was meant to be ironic. I'm sorry.'

Simon quietly urged Pross to make a departure.

'Sorry?' laughed the landlord bitterly. 'You're sorry? Not as sorry as I was this evening when that bloody reporter girl from the Sun came knocking on my door to ask me about my father's death. She told me you'd boasted you'd killed him to one of the kids in the street, that's what she told me. You won't even let me grieve in peace.' He let out a short, noisy breath and looked around the bedroom, almost tearful. 'I was born in this room, I was. This used to be my grandparents' house.' He turned back to Pross, anger resurgent. 'I want you and your crony out of this house. I'd rather burn this place down than have you living here. Your stuff'll be in the hall till tomorrow evening. If it's still there then, well, I'll just toss the fucking lot out into the street.'

Pross felt as if he'd just stumbled badly into a hole he'd dug earlier simply to pass the time away. 'Aw, how was I to know that stupid kid would believe me? I didn't kill Harry.'

Harry's son was now shooting his sentences off like machine gun fire, his hands darting and pointing. 'I know you didn't kill him,' he raged. 'I know it. I know it. It was one of your stupid jokes. The police said they were sure there was no one else involved. I went to see them because of you.' He stabbed a finger into Pross's shoulder, something not at all appreciated. The cat struggled to be free, but was held tight.

'Calm down, will you,' said Pross, but with not enough sympathy or understanding or contrition in his voice for it to ameliorate the volcanic anger of Harry's son. Pross's words were sounding more antagonistic than soothing. 'Calm down and loosen up. Loosen up before you give yourself a breakdown.' Pross then suddenly thought he realised why Harry and Mrs Brown's son was such a mess: maybe he was carrying around the guilt and shame of not loving his own parents, or even bothering to go up the stairs to see them. 'Listen,' he said with this understanding in mind, beginning to stretch a hand out to touch the landlord reassuringly on the shoulder, 'I'm sure that none of it was your own fault...'

But the instant Pross lifted his arm, the landlord reacted, and it came powering in too fast to be dodged. An explosive right-hander aimed square on to Pross's left eye hit its target, twisted his body round, took his legs away and left him at the mercy of gravity, his bulk crashing heavily towards the edge of the table upon which his computer had once rested.

A short, piercing screech ripped from the tiny cat as it absorbed the fall of Pross's helpless body.

1.33
The Funeral

There was no loss of consciousness. He was back on his feet in what seemed to him to be no time at all, ready to defend himself, determined to defend himself. But when he looked, there was no combatant to be seen. There was only Mick and Simon. In fact there were *two* Micks and *two* Simons.

There was also confusion.

Simon took hold of Pross, assuming him to be woozy.

Pross pushed Simon away. 'Get off me,' he snarled, 'I'm all right. Where's that bastard?'

'He's gone,' panted Simon.

There was a screech of car tires outside. Mick ran to the window. 'That's him leaving now,' he jabbered. 'Jesus! Never seen a Cortina go so fast.'

Simon held on to Pross again, only to be pushed away once more. 'Will you leave me alone? I'm all right.'

But he was not all right, he soon came to realise. The room appeared to be profoundly distorted. Simon, standing no more than a pace away, had a blurred twin hovering in the air by his side. And there were two Micks; one sharp, the other fuzzy. It was hard for Pross to make any sense of what he was seeing. The first thought to flash into his mind was of some kind of brain injury. He put a hand over his left eye, looking with the right: everything appeared normal. Moving his hand over to the right, looking with the left eye only, everything still appeared normal, if a little blurred. But with both eyes seeing together, or rather not together, things were *very* weird.

His second thought was of a detached retina.

His third thought was of the cat, remembering he'd fallen badly on to it.

With Mick jabbering crazily about something, and Simon looking pale and scared and repeatedly saying that they'd better leave in case the landlord came back, Pross bent his head down to look for the cat, assuming it to be hiding or lying injured somewhere.

Pain was making itself felt.

With an intellectual effort, Pross identified two shapes on the floor as being one cat. He bent down to touch it, but missed. Putting a hand over his damaged eye, he repeated the motion, making contact this time. There was no reaction to the touch. Lifting up its tiny, frail head, he saw that it was dead.

John stalked around the block of flats where Sarah-Jane lived. There were no lights on, and the curtains were all open. He would not even waste time knocking on the door. Jennifer was obviously not there. But John was almost certain he knew where to find her. She would be wherever Prospero Pi-Meson was. And he knew for certain where that was: the Arts Centre bar. Thanks to the newspaper he'd seen, he even knew what Prospero Pi-Meson looked like. He walked onwards with no lessening of determination, the wind casting litter and leaves against him.

'Dead,' said Pross, laying Spock's head back down.

'You fell on it,' jabbered Mick. 'It was caught between you and the table.'

'I know,' said Pross, now sitting on the edge of the bed and beginning to feel nauseous. The pain was intensifying. He variously held fingers out in front of his eyes. 'I can't see properly,' he said for his own benefit. 'Everything's double.'

'You ought to go to the police,' said Simon. 'He could go to jail for what he's done to you.'

Only two minutes earlier, when Pross had risen to his feet after being sent spinning, he would have fought his landlord tooth and nail if he'd still been there. Fought him for having landed that damaging blow. But now he was beginning to think straight. He acknowledged that his own part in the affair had been not entirely innocent, for he had been a source of annoyance to a bereaved person. Harry, apparently father to the landlord, had died; and although bereavement was something Pross had no experience of, he was belatedly prepared to accept that it could be a source of deep distress. Far too belatedly.

Pross decided to let this incident drop. He'd brought this down on to his own head.

He moved back over to the cat, examining it to make sure it really was dead. It was. There was nothing to do now but dispose of the body. Toss it into the river from the bridge near the cathedral, that's what he'd do. Just like Melanie had done with her cat when it had died. He'd have a little pagan ceremony. Spock had been a good cat.

Before switching off the last light, Pross examined his eye in the mirror on the wall by the inner door. There was much bruising evident already; and beads of blood, now semi-congealed, had welled-up below his eyelid.

'That's gonna to be a beauty shiner,' said Mick. 'I came off my moped once when I was doing the knowledge and...'

'Knowledge?' interrupted Pross, annoyed to find himself making normal conversation with someone who was stupid enough to believe him to be a prophet.

'Learning the taxi routes for the exams,' explained Mick proudly, and Pross vaguely remembered having heard somewhere that London cabbies had to pass tough tests. 'Anyway, came off my moped, I did; and blow me if the 'andle didn't get me straight in the eye. Bloodied up like yours, it did. Seeing double for days. Doctor said it was normal, 'e did. Something to do with the eye muscles getting bruised. Puked as well, I did.'

Pross had all three of those symptoms. This tale of Mick's put at rest his fear that he might be suffering from a detached retina, and he decided not to present himself to a casualty ward.

Traversing the cluttered hall while carrying Spock's corpse in his arms, wrapped in a pillow case, proved to be a difficult operation for him. It was only by closing his good eye — his bad eye was too painful to close on its own — that he managed to succeed in the venture and join Simon, who was waiting in the back of Mick's cab.

Pross was feeling a renewed contempt for Simon and his half-witted beliefs. His piss-taking acceptance of Simon's ridiculous theories had gone far enough. His principles would not be compromised any longer, even if he would be losing a source of amusement. Once they were all back at the Arts Centre, he would stick the boot into Simon's various fallacies. He would show Simon up in front of everyone. It would be one in the eye for religious idiocy.

The centre of Durham City was buzzing with weekend activity: from puritan students looking for real ale to half-witted local yobs intent on lager revelry. To his fore stood a wide bridge, closed to traffic, and thanks to directions given to him a minute earlier, John knew that the way to the Arts Centre lay across that bridge.

Before reaching the bridge, he came across what he'd been keeping an eye open for: a suitable bank. The gathering in front of it told him that it had a cash point. People were pulling money out to pay for their weekend. John joined the queue: his excursions since going AWOL had cost him dearly. Standing in the long queue, he looked over to his left. Beyond the bridge, a castle loomed high on the hill around which this small city was built. Mists rising from the river imbued an ancient feel to the aspect.

John had no mind for sentimentality.

'There's a space over there,' Simon told Mick.

With the arrival of the cab from London, the car park in front of the cathedral, only an actual stone's throw away from the castle, was now full. This meant that there was probably a service of some kind going on inside.

Pross was holding the dead cat in the pillow case. Simon was holding his prayer battery. Mick was holding open the back door of the cab for his passengers, who climbed out into the night air. 'But you've got to be with us,' pleaded Simon, 'it's you who's on their wavelength.'

'Do it without me,' said Pross, addressing two Simons, eye throbbing, 'I've got a funeral to conduct. I'll be in the Arts Centre later.' He turned and left.

Simon was disheartened. Without the prophet of his beliefs by his side, discharging the prayer battery would surely be a less efficacious business. But there *were* Cosmic Masters out there. He was certain of it. Benevolent beings from other planets keen to pass on the truth about Godfrey. After all, had not the prophet's flatmate seen a UFO hovering over the cathedral only a few days before? If only the prophet would help him to make contact. But there was nothing for it: he would have to do the job alone. Sheltered from the wind beside a war monument in the cathedral grounds, he fixed the prayer battery on top of a tripod and aimed it skyward.

Mick was filled with a sense of mysticism.

The problem of how to walk with distorted vision was soon solved. The knack was to look well ahead and not down at the ground. Kerbs were tricky, though. People seeing him probably thought that he was drunk as he slowed to tackle the four inch impediments. Even so, the bridge was soon reached. It was an old bridge. Sandstone is of what it was made. Standing on a parapet halfway along its span, looking downstream, he held the cat out at arms length, trying to think of some words to say appropriate to the demise of something feline. The banks of the river were wooded on both sides. The smell of decaying vegetation was strong. Gently he took Spock out from the pillow case. 'Well, cat, you were a damned good companion and benefactor to me. I'd like to think I was good to you too. Sorry it had to end so soon. So many mice left unchased. So many trees left unclimbed.' His voice began to choke. 'Sorry. You were a good cat. So sorry.'

A group of people were coming. Being seen tossing a cat into a river could lead to all kinds of trouble. In fact being seen at all could lead to trouble — Pross reminded himself that he was famous now, and he had a two million pound cheque on him to protect.

Hiding the cat with his body, he tried to look casual, gazing down to the dark water below. He still felt nauseous. Even more so. 'Don't do it!' cried one of the people jokingly as they passed. 'You've got everything to live for.' He wondered if this was a reference to his new wealth. No, he was getting paranoid. No one would recognise him. By now people would have forgotten what they'd read in their papers that morning. The group of people — students, judging by their non-local accents — laughed at the joke made by one of their own number and continued onwards. Pross watched them until they were some distance away, then turned to walk over to the other side of the bridge, judging it to offer a more picturesque view. Spock would be committed to the waters under the shadow of an ancient castle.

Two shadows and two castles.

Pounding footsteps were suddenly heard. Someone was running. He didn't turn to look. Just someone in a hurry to get somewhere. But before Pross reached the opposite parapet, he fell victim to a tackle delivered from behind. Spock went dropped, and Pross himself was down on the pavement, pinned under the weight of an assailant. 'Die, you rich bastard,' hissed his combatant, and strong hands began to squeeze his neck.

Less than six hours earlier, Pross had confessed to having strangled Harry, now he was undergoing an identical fate.

His heart was thumping already, his body, for the second time in less than fifteen minutes, having released those hormones which facilitate fight or flight. Flight was impossible. An instant ago he'd been wandering across the bridge, cradling his dead cat, but now he was firmly pinned down under a determined assailant. Wayward locks of his hair were lying over his eyes, obscuring his damaged vision, and the glare of a street lamp above was reducing residual sights to coloured diffraction patterns around the intervening strands. The lamp bestowed inappropriate bright halos around the twin heads of his back-lit, shadowy attacker. Pross was winded, shaken, slightly dazed, very scared and instantly on the defensive. He reached up instinctively for the throat of his assailant, whom he supposed to be his landlord, and began a desperate attempt to counter-strangulate.

'Don't lay a finger on me,' said the attacker threateningly.

Pross kept trying.

'I'm warning you,' said the attacker again, with choking difficulty. 'If you so much as bruise my neck you'll regret it for the rest of *my* life.'

Slowly it dawned on Pross that there was something terribly familiar about this hiss he was hearing. Just as slowly, he slackened his grip, coming to half-realise that it was Ron who was trying to kill him. He dropped his hands, and his assailant's hands also gave mercy.

'Ron?' asked Pross dubiously, brushing hair away from his eyes, closing one eye completely and squinting with the other to identify his back-lit opponent.

It *was* Ron.

Pross was livid at having been so violently assaulted, and with uncanny simultaneity, each of them resumed their strangulation of the other, calling each other a tirade of disparaging names in whatever choking voices they could manage.

This trial of strength continued for a few seconds, until Pross dropped his hands from Ron's neck and began making some particularly disturbing gurgling noises. 'You're killing me!' he just about managed to say.

Ron slackened his grip slightly. 'Five percent of what you've won and I'll let you live.' He pulled his hands away completely to allow Pross to reply unhindered.

This was Pross's reply: 'Fuck off. Fuck off. Fuck...'

Ron set to work again. 'Five percent,' he demanded, squeezing his hands around Pross's neck.

Pross was beaten. Exhausted, dazed, in pain, nauseous, barely able to breathe, he gave up all resistance. 'It's a deal,' he croaked and wheezed.

Ron grabbed a handful of Pross's hair. 'When do I get my money?'

'What money? Leave my hair alone.'

Ron shook Pross's head around, making him feel particularly sick. 'The money you just promised me, that's what money.'

'I've spent it all,' lied Pross hopelessly.

'Like shite have you. Not even a twit like you could blow two million in one day. How much have you got left?'

'How much of what?' laboured Pross.

'Of my lottery money, that's what.'

'*Your* lottery money!' spluttered Pross.

'I went out and bought the coupon, didn't I?' argued Ron. 'How much have you got left?'

'Seven pounds twenty.'

Ron's hands went around Pross's abused neck again. 'How much? How much?'

'Lots and lots — honest,' cried Pross, successfully avoiding getting a further rough handling. 'I haven't even put the cheque into the bank yet. Get off me, I can't breathe.'

'You've still got the cheque? Where is it?'

'In my pocket. Get off me, will you?' With one-handed difficulty, Pross pulled out the folded and somewhat battered cheque. 'Look.'

Ron grabbed the hand holding the cheque, crushing it until it relinquished the treasure.

'Ow,' cried Pross in real pain. 'It's yours. Take it.'

Ron's interest in sitting on Pross was now completely over. He got up, taking the plunder over to the lamppost. Reverently he unfolded the cheque and looked long at the unbelievable figure while Pross recovered from his ordeal. Beholding the mighty cheque, Ron's face now bore the exact same expression that Pross's had the very first time he saw Jennifer's photograph: awe, love, desire, regret, passion, all mixed into one. Sometimes, for a fleeting instance, more of one than the rest, and sometimes other facial nuances as yet unknown to lexicographers, those elusive nuances that throughout history have sent poets running for their quills and painters running to their canvases. To the despair of those same poets and painters, such elusive nuances have always defied perfect artistic crystallisation, soon sending the poets running in frustration to bawdy taverns, and the suffering painters to gunsmiths.

'You bastard,' cursed Pross, rubbing his neck. He picked himself up, brushed himself down and shifted himself along to the parapet he'd failed to reach on his first attempt. Convinced that he was going to throw up, he leant over the side. Being strangled, he decided, was even worse than being punched in the eye. In a flash of uncharacteristic superstition, he reasoned that the fate he'd just undergone was direct karma for having said he'd strangled Harry. Leaning over the bridge, he moaned, 'I swear that's the last time I'll ever confess to killing Harry. I've learnt my lesson.'

Ron was still bound and gagged by the potent numerical spell.

'Oh, Harry's dead, by the way,' groaned Pross.

Ron pulled his mind away from the money. 'What? Harry's dead?'

'Yeah.'

Ron walked over to Pross. 'How?' he asked with shallow curiosity.

'I killed him,' confessed Pross, expecting something awful to happen at once.

But Karma appeared to be biding its time.

'What in the hell are you doing here, anyway?' he asked in a voice loaded with contempt. 'You're not supposed to be back until next week.'

Ron didn't answer. He was looking with amazement at something on the ground. 'Hey, isn't this your cat? Is it dead? What's it doing here?' He picked it up. 'It is. It's dead. Dead.'

A splash was heard below as Ron leant over the bridge beside Pross.

'It floats,' remarked Ron. 'Spock floats.'

1.34
Six Years' Salary

With no sense of ceremony at all, Ron had tossed Pross's cat into the water, and, leaning over the parapet, the only, perhaps the best, comment Pross could make on the audacious effrontery of it was to immediately throw up. A pint of ale and a semi-digested kebab were dramatically liberated.

'You've only gone and spewed right on the cat,' rebuked Ron, looking down to the water below.

'Urrgghh,' groaned Pross, quite unable to see whether or not he had actually puked on to Spock.

He felt awful.

'Been drinking?' surmised Ron. 'Been chasing the flagon?'

Pross couldn't generate an answer.

Somebody was walking by, and as Ron turned to look, Pross retched again, hot, bitter gastric liquids filling his mouth. The person walking past was John, his pocket sixty pounds better off for his ten minute wait in the cash point queue. John glanced at the two people, one leaning over the bridge. 'Can't hold his opium,' said Ron to the passer-by, but the passer-by was not interested in the affair. He hadn't seen enough of Pross to know who he was.

'How did the cat die?' asked Ron, stooping to tie his shoelace.

'It was in a fight,' moaned Pross, distastefully wiping his lips.

In a mood for quiet reflection, Ron leant against the wall of the bridge, gazing upstream through rising mists. Spock's body had long since drifted under the arches. 'Remember when we did this with Melanie's cat? It was a good night, that. You puked that night, didn't you?'

Pross was silent awhile, then he whined, 'I was going to recite a funeral poem for Spock, you bastard.'

'Saved you the bother.'

'Give me my cheque back,' groaned Pross.

Ron handed it over. Pross put it into his pocket while still looking down to the wind-rippled water.

'You don't half puke up a lot, Pross,' remarked Ron casually, jauntily, even, but definitely not sympathetically.

'I know.'

'Puking up as much as you do is suggestive of cosmic intervention.'

'I know.'

'Someone up there's got it in for you.'

'Everyone up there's got it in for me.'

A thoughtful silence from Ron... 'You step in dog shit quite often too, don't you?'

'Seldom out of it.'

Another thoughtful silence... 'Over six years' salary.'

'What?' mumbled Pross.

'Over six years' salary — five percent of my winnings.'

'My winnings, you mean,' Pross corrected.

'I bought the ticket,' stated Ron forcefully.

'I paid for it and my cat picked the numbers,' groaned Pross.

'Out of *my* taxes.'

'Doesn't matter.'

While Pross remained hanging over the bridge, recovering from the second shaking he'd had that evening, Ron explained how he'd managed to find him. 'I'd just got home in my car when I glimpsed you disappearing into that cab, so I followed. Parked up near where you got out and ran like crazy after you.'

Leaning over the bridge, contemplating his vomit, something that had been troubling Pross's conscience for years now was about to get the better of him. A lamb had been slaughtered to make that kebab, and all he'd done with it had been to throw it up. It was so unnecessary. The poignancy of this particular example finally gave him the resolve to do what was unquestionably best.

'From this moment on I'll never eat the flesh of another animal again,' he groaned, 'and I mean it. The little furry bunnies and things will be safe with me.'

Ron was cooly philosophical. 'What about the little fishes? Still going to eat them?'

'Thicky fishes don't matter,' replied Pross, 'they look so bored and stupid.'

'Well you look bored and stupid too,' argued Ron, 'but you can count and spell and do all sorts. You even had a girlfriend once.'

'Twice,' corrected Pross.

After a few minutes rest, Pross began to feel less ill, and even felt able to stand upright, although there was still no coming together of his double vision. He felt drunk; felt as if he might as well be since there'd be nothing to lose — he already had the hangover. 'I thought you weren't coming home until next week,' he said with lashings of disapproval.

'I wasn't,' said Ron. 'But be buggered if was going stay out there all weekend, leaving you back here in charge of a pile of money rightfully mine. I tried phoning but there was never any answer.'

'I disconnected it last night. Forgot to plug it back in.'

'I phoned Melanie eventually, and she told me you'd been in London yesterday picking up the cheque. So they accepted my evidence?'

'Yeah,' groaned Pross. 'That's what did it. The ticket was useless.'

As they walked back to Ron's car, Pross began putting the blame for his eye injury on to his latest assailant. 'Just look what you've done,' he complained when they were inside the vehicle, parked illegally near the cathedral, inspecting his eye in the rear-view mirror.

Ron switched on the interior light.

'Did I really do that?' he asked, half proud, half remorseful. 'All the white bits are turning red.' Something else caught Ron's attention: two men were making strange, ritualistic gesticulations around a metal box on top of a tripod. 'Hey, those two blokes over there — aren't they the ones who got out of that cab with you? What are they doing?'

Pross looked but couldn't see anything. He was feeling too sick to bother holding a hand over his bad eye. Anyway, he knew what the blokes were doing. 'I can't see,' he said. 'Everything's gone double, thanks to you. Got me with your elbow, you did.'

Ron was now completely disinterested in Pross's injury, even though he believed he'd actually inflicted it himself. 'What *are* they doing?' he said again.

'Probably trying to make contact with aliens. Remember me telling you about that program on those nutters who pray into boxes?'

'Uh huh.'

'Well, that's two of them over there. I met one of them in London yesterday and told him my Godfrey story and he believed it. They think I'm a prophet receiving messages from aliens eager to spread the truth about Godfrey having created the universe.'

Ron watched them some more.

Pross said, 'Fuck them, let's get to the Arts Centre. Everybody's waiting for me there.'

The Arts Centre was only a few minutes drive away. Entering the building, Pross saw two floors, twice as many people as normal for a Friday evening, and two reception desks. Closing his good eye, he managed to make it to the gents, where he studied his two reflections. It was very hard to make sense of what he was seeing, but he could tell that both of him were a mess, especially the one in sharp focus (the blurred one could be given the benefit of the doubt). His clothes were dirtied and dishevelled, and his face felt like it ought to be swelling up, but didn't seem to be. He gave his bad eye a thorough examination in the mirror. No white now remained to be seen, it all being startlingly blood-red. Thankfully, his nausea was lessening. The pain, however, was worsening. Around his neck he noticed some bruising.

He rinsed his mouth out several times and brushed the dirt from his clothes.

The string quartet were not the only performers. The night was to be a mixture of music, verse and theatre. After Sarah's performance, a troop in period dress played fifteenth century music on replica fifteenth century instruments. Jennifer was so delighted to have made the effort and come to Durham. It was so long since she'd felt so good. But it was at times like these she especially missed her parents. With Sarah-Jane up on stage, looking so striking and so passionate, she thought how proud and moved her mother would have been if she'd been there to see it.

Presently, more mundane considerations had to be entertained: Jennifer needed the toilet. Some minutes later, when a break came in a recital of verse, leaving her coat behind, she followed signs that led her back out past the main reception, near which were doors marked ladies and gents.

John looked with envy at the immaculate collector's car parked in front of the Arts Centre, but he did not pause to appreciate it. Into the building he went, convinced that he would catch Jennifer in the company of Prospero Pi-Meson, whose picture he had seen in the paper. His thoughts were all of dominance and pride. He wanted — needed — to come out of his affair with Jennifer on top. He had to be the one to do the final leaving. If he and she were there, he would gain satisfaction from having outwitted her by catching her being unfaithful. He would gain satisfaction from watching her lover get scared while he says his final sarcastic, caustic words to Jennifer. In his mind he rehearsed phrases he might have call to say to Prospero Pi-Meson, aggressive phrases like "keep out of this, you," and "just you watch it, wanker, this hasn't got anything to do with you". In his mind's eye, he pictured himself dramatically storming out into the night, leaving Jennifer crying and Prospero Pi-Meson trembling. She would see that Prospero Pi-Meson was not a real man.

Although he walked the length of the bar room twice, looking keenly about him, neither Jennifer or Prospero Pi-Meson did John see. They had not come here, or they had moved on elsewhere. He had wasted his evening and let her slip away. If only he'd followed the bus instead of presuming where she would disembark.

He felt useless and stupid.

John didn't hang around. He had to get back to his ship. Leaving the Arts Centre, he walked back the way he had come. Tears were trying to flow again. He would not let them show.

From the train station across the city centre he would be able to travel direct to London.

Pross gave himself another inspection in the mirror. He looked better now. Felt it too. Felt less like a calamity. Considering the various roughing ups he'd suffered, he considered his hair to be still looking pretty cool, and by tilting the nozzle on the electric hand-dryer he was able to give it a good blowing before joining his friends for a drink.

With hair revived, he went to take hold of the door handle, missed the first time, but quickly made contact. Stepping out unsteadily into the spacious bar room, he was met by two Melanies coming the other way. Behind him, the door to the ladies opened. The Melanies stopped him, then turned him around to face the nearest light, gazing with fascination at the developing shiner. 'Shit! Pross, who did that?' both Melanies asked. Jennifer looked up upon hearing the name. She saw the person on the front pages of all the newspapers she'd bought. The same person who'd sent her a morbid love letter. The same person who'd sent her fifty pounds. The same person who'd just won a fortune. His face was bruised and bloodied.

'Your husband did it,' said Pross with exaggerated grievance to Melanie. 'He hit me because I wouldn't put my hand down his trousers again.' He looked directly at Jennifer, standing in the doorway. Although her heart had suddenly begun thumping, she smiled at the obvious fib she'd just heard, but her gaze quickly dropped to the floor in shyness and embarrassment when he glanced her way. He merely saw two overlapping shapes that did not seem familiar.

Tony appeared.

'Shit! Pross, who did that? Are you all right? Do you want to borrow my shades to cover it up?'

'And look like a pratt?'

This offended Tony, and he skulked off into the toilets, muttering things about his friend's "hostility problem".

Melanie also gave up on him, going into the ladies.

Pross turned around, put a hand over his beaten eye and made sense of the room. Over by the back wall were some of his friends.

Sanity at last.

'It's him,' was a whispered remark made by someone as Pross crossed the room, 'the lottery winner in today's paper.'

It *was* him. He was actually in the same room as her, even though he obviously hadn't recognised her. Maybe he didn't actually know what she looked like? Maybe he'd never even seen her before? Without hardly knowing she was doing it, she drifted along behind him as he made his way over to his friends. And when he sat down with his back to most of the room, she placed herself on a seat near to him, near to the person she wanted to know more about. Hers was not one of the seats belonging to the collection of tables occupied by his friends, but a seat at a table five or six feet to the back and side of him.

She could hear almost every word spoken by him.

Altogether there were now, including Melanie and Tony, six of Pross's friends surrounding him. With so many people, Jennifer felt nervous. If he'd been on his own, she might have simply gone over to him to reveal who she was. But he wasn't; and for all she knew, one of the females in the group might even be his girlfriend. This thought would keep her from approaching him.

Jennifer watched and heard as Pross lowered himself down on to a chair, lowered the side of his head down on to the table, and lowered the tone of his voice. 'O let the day perish in which I was born,' she heard him moan, 'the day my unhappy heart began its joyless labour.' She watched as a muscular, uncommonly tall young man carrying two pints of beer took a seat opposite to him, facing the room.

People wanted to know what had happened to his eye.

He didn't reply. He'd suddenly thought that the sight of a large amount of cash belonging to him might raise his spirits. Systematically, he began withdrawing the assorted contents of his pockets, placing them on the table. Out came a snapshot of Jennifer, a *Prospero's Lass* T-shirt, a folded lottery cheque and, what he was hunting: numerous crumpled banknotes. Counting the money revealed to him that he only had a little over six hundred pounds left from the three thousand he'd originally had. He could hardly believe that he'd spent over two grand in two days, and yet was still sober. Where had it all gone?

The sight of so many unearned banknotes elicited excitement among his friends.

'Here, have it,' he said, smiling and tossing the notes around, 'take a hundred each. Plenty more where this came from. It's not as if I had to work for it, or something. Have a good time on me tonight. I owe most of you, anyway.'

After an initial show of reluctance, his friends accepted the cash gratefully: Pross was disappointed in them.

'A hundred each? How puny your greed,' he said disdainfully. 'It's a pittance. A mere pittance. I'll force a lot more on to you all as soon as I cash this baby!' And he picked up the lottery cheque for all to see.

Ron grabbed the cheque from him. 'Six years' salary worth of this is mine!' he kept on saying to the accompaniment of insane laughter. 'Six years' salary! Six years' salary!'

Looking down, Pross counted out his remaining cash. Thirty-one pounds left: he'd better start getting pissed right away while he could still afford to.

1.35
Comeuppance

John was given his ticket by a clerk with dandruff and a cold who grudgingly told him, when asked, that the next train to London was due in seventy minutes. He put the ticket into his wallet and wandered out of the brightly-lit booking office.

Leaning against a cold iron railing, watching whistling porters loading mailbags on to trolleys, he couldn't ever remember feeling so hopeless and alone. He was nothing. Just a nobody with only a mediocre future to look forward to. He knew he wasn't even officer material. And he didn't even have Jennifer any more. Prospero Pi-Meson, a millionaire, a big somebody now, might well have been the one who'd taken her away from him. Prospero Pi-Meson now had it all, and he now had nothing.

He had been robbed.

The atmosphere of the station seemed to enhance his feelings of despair. Train stations were all about leaving places and moving on. John didn't want to move on. He wanted Jennifer back. And if he couldn't have her back, then he wanted to be leaving with some pride.

Without having taken a conscious decision, he put his hands into his pockets and walked back towards the city centre.

He had seventy minutes to kill, and his Jennifer was somewhere but a few miles away.

'You look as if you could do with someone buying you a drink.' The sudden voice gave Jennifer a slight start. She looked up. 'What'll it be? Let me guess... Gin and tonic?'

Jennifer didn't know what to do. Automatically she chose the smoothest way, 'Er, yes please,' regretting it at once, and it was nothing to do with never having had a gin and tonic before.

Two minutes later, with a drink in her hand, she was politely suffering the indifferent company of someone who'd introduced himself as Terry.

For reasons she was not able to understand, Jennifer led Terry to believe that her name was Elaine. It seemed to be a way of preserving her privacy.

Terry was on the pull. From across the floor he'd watched Jennifer until he'd become convinced she was not with anyone; waiting for someone, maybe, but he'd take the risk. With courage plucked up, over to her he had gone.

Terry, wearing a padded hunting jacket over a grey suit, was in his middle thirties, and it was no time at all before he began boasting about his success in pub quizzes. 'I've won three this week,' he said. 'One on Sunday, one on Wednesday and one yesterday.' He then, from a slow start, broke into a dysfunctional giggle that erratically rose in pitch and tempo.

Jennifer forced an expression of interest. 'Really?'

'Do you like quizzes?'

'Er, I watch Mastermind sometimes.' And always Jennifer's attention kept drifting back over to Pross, ignorant that his attention was now actually given exclusively to her. With his hurting head in his hands, he was looking at overlapping snapshots of her lying on the overlapping tables before him, whining quietly with the sorrow of his passion.

'What's the matter with you now?' complained Ron.

'I'm a poet in love, that's what's the matter.' This was said regardless of Moaning Joe having earlier revealed to him, by comparison, the true shallowness of his feelings. But Joe wasn't here to outdo him, so he could get away with declaring to be lovelorn again.

Ron had had enough of Pross's unsubstantiated claims to poet status. 'Years I've known you now,' he said testily, 'and except for that weird one you did on the toilet door about Melanie's bum, I've never yet known you write a whole poem. What makes you think you're a poet?'

'It isn't necessary to constantly churn out verse to qualify as a poet.'

'So then what *does* make you claim you're a poet?'

'Because,' explained Pross, 'poets suffer bright, painful glimpses of the past...' He stopped, believing for a moment he'd just made that definition up, but then remembered he'd heard it on the radio a few days earlier. This was annoying: he'd liked to have made it up.

'Well?' pursued Ron.

'Well so do I,' stated Pross, thereby justifying his claim to poet status. 'Blindingly bright and unbearably painful ones. Twice a minute, usually.'

'That often?'

'That often. And that's why I still weep for Susan Murray.' He pointed to the photo. 'And that's why this one will haunt me forever.'

He whined again.

Ron wouldn't have any of this poet business. 'Poet? Hah! You're just a miserable bastard. Jesus, you're getting most of my winnings, yet you're still moaning on about things. You must be the most miserable bastard on

Earth.'

Pross, with painful honesty, gave news on that issue.

'I'm not the most miserable bastard on Earth,' he miserably confessed, his ego ruined, his miserable outlook on life blighted by an unacceptable quantity of relative personal happiness. 'I met the most miserable bastard on Earth earlier on today, and I'm nothing compared to him. Just a miserable failure.' He looked defeated for a moment, but then brightened. 'Aw, fuck it, I'm still young. Plenty of time for me to get a lot more miserable yet.'

'For instance,' Pross heard someone behind him saying, 'do you know who invented the telescope?'

Ron suddenly dropped down out of sight.

'Ron, what's up?'

Ron was now horizontal over two chairs, using the table to obscure himself from general view. 'It's Rab C.,' he said, 'don't let him see me. I'm supposed to be in Iceland. Fuck, if he sees me with you he'll blame me for what you did last Friday.'

Pross turned around in his chair and saw two blurred images of the person he had grown to hate even more than Ron did.

'Well?' pursued Scoones, 'the telescope — who invented it?'

Jennifer felt obliged to guess. She was about to say "Galileo", when Pross called out, 'Hans Lippershey.'

'No!' whispered Ron. 'Don't. He might come over.'

So what? thought Pross. Things were very different now. Six years' salary was coming to Ron soon.

Rab C. had heard Pross's answer, and felt deflated. He couldn't now impress Jennifer with the delivery of that particular piece of what he thought to be incredibly recondite information. He turned to see the owner of the voice and was dismayed to find that it was the very same loony who had harassed him the previous week.

Turning back around, he was further dismayed to find his beautiful companion grinning. 'He's right,' he muttered. 'Hans Lippershey.'

Rab C. decided to change the subject of his conversation. Jennifer soon wished he hadn't, for only when he wasn't talking about quizzes was he more boring than when he was talking about quizzes, for when he wasn't talking about quizzes he was talking about his job. As he began regaling her with computer department managerial anecdotes, surreptitiously peering down her cleavage, Lilith arrived in the room and at once presented Pross with forms to read and fill in concerning his intended purchase of the country property.

The arrival of Lilith temporarily distracted Pross from taunting Rab C.

Ron was still hiding.

Her haircut caused quite a fluster.

Pross put his signature to the documents without even reading them. 'There,' he said. 'Sorted.'

Lilith heard a desperate voice come from down below: 'Pross, leave him alone. Please.'

'Why are you hiding, Ron?' asked Lilith.

'Shhh! Don't say my name.'

'Why are you hiding, Sandra?'

'Job security,' explained Ron. 'Pass my drink down, will you?'

Lilith passed it down, then went to sit on the far side of her sister.

Behind Pross, Scoones had come to the end of another computer department manager anecdote. He laughed his complicated laugh, leant back in his chair and said, 'I tell you, Elaine, you've got to have a sense of humour to do my job!'

That did it. That was all Pross could take. 'That wanker's for it,' he said, putting his glass down. Then he stood up, intent on making Rab C. rue the Friday... but Ron lunged for him under the table, grabbing his legs and pulling him back.

'No!' beseeched Ron.

Unbalanced, Pross tried to hold on to a chair to steady himself but aimed at the false image. So he fell over instead, pulling Ron some of the way out with him.

Turning to the tumbling commotion, Rab C. saw Ron on the floor under a table, and his mystery antagonist on the floor nearby.

It was a mystery no more.

Rab C. went over to Ron, who was trying to hide again.

'Ronald Cantillon,' said Scoones, 'come out from under that table.'

Ron popped up, a look of fresh innocence on his face. 'Oh, hello there, Tel.'

'Mr Scoones to you.'

'Wanker to everyone else,' said Pross, sitting up.

'Iceland,' said Rab C., ignoring Pross, 'is where you should be now.'

'Going back tomorrow,' said Ron. 'Had to come back to sort something personal out. Only missed an afternoon's work.'

Pross had now had even more than he could take. 'Fuck off out of my life, Scoones,' he said, picking himself up. 'I hate you even more than Ron does, so fucking watch out.'

Ron dropped his head into his hands.

'You're fired,' said Scoones to Ron.

'You're hired,' said Pross to Ron. 'Six times the salary this twat hired you for.'

Scoones left the scene.

Ron was not pleased... at all.

'Thanks,' he groaned, 'fucking thanks.'

'So what?' said Pross. 'You don't want that job any more, do you?'

'I bloody do. I heard today that Scoones is leaving soon. I'd probably have got his job. I won't even get references now.'

'Oops,' said Pross.

'Oops,' said Ron.

'Aw, fuck it,' said Pross, swilling down the remainder of his pint, 'you don't understand how rich I am now.' He paused. 'Ten years' salary. We'll make it ten years'.'

Ten years' salary quickly brought Ron around to Pross's way of thinking.

Jennifer was perplexed as Scoones returned to her, seething. She began asking what the trouble had been and how he knew those people, but Rab C. refused to discuss it. Immediately picking up her glass, he said he'd get them refills each, and went to the bar, not giving her time to say she'd rather not have another drink.

In a state of elated breathlessness, Mick and Simon arrived, their faces aglow with enthusiasm. Simon was carrying the prayer battery. 'Did you get any messages?' he asked excitedly.

'Lots,' sneered Pross at the overlapping Simons. 'Sit down here and let me tell you all about them. Mick, go and get me a lager.'

Mick went.

The run-in with Scoones had put Pross in the right mood for sorting out Mick and Simon too, and, by extension, every religion on Earth.

Following the invitation, Simon sat at Ron's left, opposite and across from Pross. Carefully he placed the prayer battery on the table. Mick, back with the drink, pulled up a chair and made himself unobtrusive.

'What's this?' asked Ron, feigning ignorance, casting his eyes over the metal box with an aerial.

'It's a prayer battery,' answered Simon. 'It stores the spiritual energy of prayers.'

'What's inside it?'

'It's a secret,' glowed Simon, 'known only to the leader of the Aetherius Society. He was taught how to make them during psychic transmissions from extraterrestrials.'

'Why does it have to be a secret?' Pross wanted to know.

Simon had an immediate answer. 'The Iraqis are heavily into paranormal research, and they'd love to know more about it so they can turn it into a weapon. That's why its workings can't be made public. It's forbidden even for me to look inside.'

Pross could hardly believe the stupidity of what he'd just heard. 'If it's so bloody valuable,' he argued, 'why don't the Iraqis simply get an agent to join your dumb sect and pinch one of the bloody things? Don't you credit them with even that level of competence?'

Simon made no response. Pross's growing scepticism and abrasiveness was a mystery to him.

'Answer me,' pursued Pross.

'Leave him alone,' rebuked Ron, jumping at the opportunity to side with someone opposed to Pross — anyone. 'There's a lot of sense to what he says.' He turned to Simon and said, 'Did you know that the universe was created by a physicist called Godfrey?'

After this, and after Ron said he'd seen a UFO himself last week, he and Simon got on like a house on fire. Both of them agreed that it was Pross the aliens were coming to see, even though he himself was becoming sceptical. Every time Pross tried to interject some sense, Ron flicked his bad his eye. Fed up with being continually hurt, Pross took to studying the documents pertaining to his country house, which included photographs.

'For instance,' said Rab C.'s voice behind him, 'do you know the medical term for the knee-cap?'

'The patella, wanker,' Pross called out.

Rab C. was livid. He took hold of Jennifer's drink and said they should move to a table further away. Jennifer refused, but her muted protestations were overwhelmed when he put his hand on her back and ushered her away.

'She's been looking at you all evening,' said Ron.

'Who?'

'The girl with Rab C. They've moved back a few tables. She's absolutely gorgeous. Far too young for him. She was looking at you long before he turned up. She doesn't seem to like him much.'

'Who would?' said Pross, who had hardly noticed her, and when he had, there'd been two of her, overlapping and weird.

'Go and chat her up,' said Ron. 'It'd really piss Scoones off. He's always trying to chat up the girls at work, but never gets anywhere because he's so ugly and boring.'

'Nah, all love is doomed,' returned Pross, emulating his new hero, Joe, and just managing to overcome his desire to ogle.

'Go on,' urged Ron, 'don't be scared.'

'I'm not scared.'

'You are. Well, don't chat her up if you're too scared, try to get her to wear your T-shirt — you've got enough bail money for once. It'd crush Scoones if she put it on.'

Simon suddenly blurted, 'Is this the house you told me about? The one with the vibes?'

He had got his hands on the property brochure and documents Lilith had brought with her.

Pross reluctantly nodded.

'Amazing,' breathed Simon. 'It's where we should set up the centre for the paranormal.'

Simon then revealed to Ron that it was his dream to establish a centre for the teaching of such beliefs as he held. Beliefs like ley lines, UFOs, visiting aliens and, since this afternoon, the belief that a physicist called Godfrey had conjured up the universe and an enlightened prophet called Prospero Pi-Meson had related the news. People would come from all over the country, the world even, to visit the centre. There'd be lectures and prayer meetings; audiences with the prophet; batteries galore. 'It would be a focus for... the energies,' predicted Simon.

'Good idea,' said Ron, who, to Pross's horror, was trying, with a beer-moistened finger, to rub out the name of the payee on the lottery cheque.

Pross snatched his cheque from Ron's possession. He also took back the property details from Simon. 'Get your demented hands off. I wouldn't let you and your religious insanity anywhere near my house.'

'Religious?' objected Simon. 'What've the things I'm talking about got to do with religion?'

'Everything, you thick bastard, it's just another brand, that's all.'

Simon was startled.

'I mean,' continued Pross, 'just because it's a new idea doesn't mean to say it's not religious in nature. All religions were new once.' He pulled an example out of the air. 'What about the Jehovah's Witnesses? They didn't exist until a lunatic called Charles Russell made an insane interpretation of the Bible in the last century. He said the second coming of Christ would happen in nineteen-fourteen and got thousands to follow him. We got the fucking First World War in nineteen-fourteen! But *millions* now follow his insane interpretation of what was already an insane piece of fiction, fiction mixed in with barbaric episodes from Jewish tribal history. And what about your spiritualism?'

'That's not religious,' cut in Simon.

'Of course it is!' insisted Pross. 'It's just like all religions: comforting nonsense for weak-brained people.' Simon was about to defend spiritualism, but Pross didn't let him get a word in. 'Let me tell you about the history of spiritualism.'

Simon reluctantly held his tongue as Pross gave a dissertation.

'It all started when some dodgy bloke called Andrew Davis wrote a book called *Nature's Divine Revelation*. The book argued that after death, the human spirit lives on, and that there is no reason why a departed spirit shouldn't make itself known to the beings it's left behind.' Simon nodded enthusiastically. 'But,' gloated Pross, 'here's the bit conveniently ignored. In the same year that the book was published, two sisters from New York apparently began acting as unwitting mediums for dead spirits. They were the focus for all manner of bangs and rappings and other phenomena which allegedly defied normal explanation. Well, it wasn't long before the bangs and rappings and such spread all over the world. Now here's the telling bit: the sisters later admitted they'd faked everything, just for laughs.' He threw his hands up into the air. 'Yet here we are, over a century later, and the mediums still play their games of deceit and self-deceit.'

Satisfied he'd done enough to dispel Simon's belief in spiritualism, Pross quietened down and leant back in his chair, closing an eye and reading the figure on the cheque to help give him some enthusiasm for existence in such a crazy world.

Simon was not dispelled, rather he was bewildered. Five hours ago, Pross had been completely on his side, but now it seemed he had completely turned against him. What did it mean? Maybe Pross was just upset and emotional after having been hit by his landlord. He thought he'd try offering a few words of kindness. 'How's your eye?' he asked sympathetically. 'Still seeing double?'

Pross grudgingly nodded.

'I've got some homeopathy cures in my bag in the cab. There might be something for bruises.'

Pross looked hard at Simon, then said, 'Would you agree that homeopathy claims to work by exposing the body to minute traces of chemicals that in larger doses produce the same symptoms as the ones you're trying to cure?'

'That's it,' agreed Simon uneasily. 'It's like inoculation. Not chemicals, though. Substances.'

'What concentrations?' asked Pross.

'Tiny. You dilute, then dilute again.'

'I worked it out once,' said Pross, 'and typical homeopathic concentrations after multiple dilutions were around a few tens of molecules per spoonful. Sea water,' he revealed, 'contains similarly small amounts of every stable molecule in existence. A spoonful of sea water should be able to replace every homeopathy cure going. What do you think of that?'

Simon didn't think anything of it at all. 'It's a miracle you weren't seriously hurt,' he said, regarding Pross's bloodied eye.

'Who created the universe?' asked Pross suddenly.

Simon said, 'Godfrey did.'

'And who created Godfrey?'

Simon was silent.

'I'll tell you,' said Pross with malicious glee, 'I did. I made the story up. Godfrey is fiction. I lied to you. You're a gullible fool. Now let me tell you about astrology...' He didn't get a chance. Ron tapped him on the arm and pointed down to the table. Pross put a hand over his bad eye, looked down and panicked: his lottery cheque was rapidly absorbing a puddle of beer spilled on the table. In the ensuing panic, Simon was forgotten.

'Me cheque,' whined Pross, peeling the soggy thing from the table, 'me poor cheque. All the writing'll bleed.'

Although Pross made light of it, he was becoming acutely aware of the delicacy of his fortune, aware that if the cheque should be ruined he'd be unlikely to get a replacement. Off to the toilets with it he hurried, intending to dry it under the hand blower to arrest any degeneration of the writing. Crossing two inclined floors, he heard Scoones say, 'For instance, do you know which is the only bird in the world to hibernate?'

Walking into the Arts Centre for the second time that evening in his search for Jennifer, John recognised Prospero Pi-Meson in an instant. Although he'd merely glimpsed him disappearing through a door, there was no doubt in John's mind. That was him. That was Prospero Pi-Meson. That was the person on the front pages of the newspapers. That was the person whose interference he considered to be instrumental in the breaking of his engagement. And there was Jennifer too.

All his suspicions had been born out.

Jennifer didn't notice John approach: she'd been looking at Pross.

'The whippoorwill,' said Scoones.

Jennifer turned back to face her unwanted companion, and was deeply startled to see John standing behind him.

'Surprise, surprise,' drawled John dryly. 'Think you could trick me?'

Jennifer flushed cold. Her gaze dropped, fixing on her drink.

Scoones was tapped heavily on the shoulder. He twisted his head around to see who'd done it. 'Scram,' ordered John.

Scoones looked towards Jennifer for some explanation of what was going on. Almost imperceptibly, she hinted with a movement of her eyes that it would be a good idea if he actually did scram. He took another look at John, looming angry and yob-like behind him. Reluctantly, he scrammed, muttering complaints with as much defiance as he dared exhibit, taking hold of his drink and wandering over to the bar to play a quiz machine.

Jennifer didn't know what to say. She didn't want to say anything. She didn't want to *have* to say anything. It was her life, and she owed explanations and excuses to no one. 'Leave me alone, John,' she implored quietly, still looking down to her drink on the table, 'it's over between us.'

'You lied to me.'

She lifted her gaze. 'I didn't lie to you. I've never lied to you.'

John began shaking his head. 'You lied. You said you weren't going out anywhere tonight.'

'I wasn't.'

'So what are you doing here?'

'I only decided to come here after I left the flat.'

'So why were you all dressed up? Do you think I'm stupid?'

'John, please, just go. I'm sorry for everything, but I don't want you any more. It's as simple as that.'

He looked at her coldly, then asked bitterly, 'Where are you sleeping tonight?'

She closed her eyes and heaved a sigh. 'John, it's got nothing to do with you where I stay tonight.' She looked at him again, looked at the only person she'd ever made love to, the only person she'd ever slept with. 'If you must know,' she said, 'I'll be staying at Sarah's.'

'Who was that bastard sitting here?'

She was anxious to exculpate her recent, if unwanted, companion. 'Nobody. Just someone who came over and bought me a drink. I'd never seen him before.'

'So what were you doing here in the first place?' Before Jennifer could explain, John bitterly provided his own answer. 'I'll tell you why. Prospero Pi-Meson, that's why.'

'No, John, no. I came here to see my sister.'

'Sister?' He glanced around the room and satirically said, 'Funny. Don't see her anywhere.' His eyes settled on the door of the gents. 'But maybe she's in there. Maybe I'll go in and have a chat with her.' He walked towards the door.

'No, John,' pleaded Jennifer, rising half out of her seat in an impetuous pursuit. 'Sarah's...'

Too late. John was through the door.

She slumped back down.

A little behind the first door was a second. John pushed this second door open and found Pross apparently drying his hands under a blower, his back to the room. He walked slowly over to near where Pross was and leant against a washbasin, making an acrimonious study of the person he believed had replaced himself as Jennifer's lover.

After losing two pounds in as many minutes on the quiz machine, Scoones decided to go and get drunk somewhere else. This place had turned into a nightmare. Leaving the remainder of his drink on the bar, he zipped up his hunting jacket. Realising he needed to relieve himself, he proceeded to the gents. Upon entering, alarmingly, out of the corner of his eye, he saw the yob who had threatened him, loitering. And there was that weirdo friend of Ron's too. He felt his pulse surge, but walked on up to the wide, stainless steel urinal regardless of the combined threat. To turn around would be to show he was a coward.

He whistled to make a show of nonchalance.

But it seemed like a very long time to him before he managed to begin urinating.

However, neither Pross nor John were looking at him: John was looking only at Prospero Pi-Meson.

Prospero Pi-Meson looked to John like the kind of person he'd always hated.

Prospero Pi-Meson, with his long hair, ridiculous shirt and almost effeminate stance did not measure up as a man by any of the yardsticks John used. Yet here he was, doing great and taking his girlfriend away from him.

As before, it was still not John's intention to do any harm to Pross. He did know Jennifer well enough to know that that would not help to get her back. But as he watched him from behind, thoughts of how easily he believed he could score a violent victory were in his mind. Prospero Pi-Meson was a little taller than he was, fit and athletic-looking to boot, but did he have the guts to go with it? John liked to think that *he* had guts. He was one of the nations brave young defenders: a trained warrior.

After many seconds of anxious deliberation, Jennifer, fearing for Pross's safety, suddenly left her seat and ran over to Ron, who was learning from Simon that a huge gravity vortex was probably responsible for the Bermuda Triangle. She interrupted the conversation, stretching over the table to speak. 'I think your friend might be in trouble in the toilets,' she said pressingly.

'What?' said Ron, looking bewilderedly at Jennifer. 'Trouble? What kind of trouble?'

'Help him, please,' begged Jennifer before turning away and making for the corridor which would lead her back to the auditorium, anxious not to be present when John came out of the gents.

With a second press of the button, Pross switched off the blower. Satisfied that the lottery cheque was dry, he slowly turned around. Holding his left hand over his bad eye, he examined the piece of paper that would surely change his life. It was staggering. In his hands he had a cheque for two million, three hundred and twenty-three thousand, eight hundred and forty-two pounds, thirty-four pence. Never mind the economics, the mathematics alone were staggering. And all of it mine, he silently gloated, dimly aware of a presence other than that of some man whistling at the toilet. Pross's hand dropped from his eye, and he began fumbling with the zipper of his inside jacket pocket. From now on he was going to treat the cheque with a bit more care. It would be kept in his securest pocket until he was in a bank.

But before he could slip the cheque away to safety, it was swiftly removed from his hand. Snatched away. Looking up, he saw overlapping images of an unfamiliar person. The person glanced down at the cheque, screwed it up tightly in his fist and threw it to one side. It bounced off the corner of a condom dispenser and unluckily fell into the gutter of the urinal, a couple of feet from the three-inch wide drain tube.

Scoones' heart raced as he continued his business: *they were throwing rolled up paper at him.*

Pross was bewildered. He quickly raised a hand to his bad eye. The person lost his hovering twin and snapped into sharp focus. It was a person he couldn't recall ever having seen before. It was a person who seemed to be more than a little angry about something. Ignoring the unfamiliar, angry person for a second, he quickly turned his head left to look for his cheque, unsure where it had landed.

Scoones, a short, overweight man, knew he had to continue his show of nonchalance. If he showed any fear now, he would be lost. His management training would save him. This was all about attitude. This was all about standing up for himself and assertiveness.

So he did something to show his supreme confidence, show that he hadn't been worried by the paper assault.

Feeling adrenalin course through his body for the third time that evening, Pross turned to face the person again, trying to understand what was going on. The person released a low but malicious laugh, taking a few steps backwards to lean up against a wall, obviously enjoying something that was happening. 'That's both of us losers tonight,' he sneered.

Pross, mindful of the mystery person's words, immediately looked for his cheque again — in the right place this time. In a scene that nearly stopped his heart beating, he saw where it had landed. And with a stream of piss, a whistling fat man was absently hosing the two million pound ball of paper along towards the uncovered drain tube, as if it were no more valuable than the cigarette butts floating along with it. Worse still, that fat man was bastard Rab C. Scoones. It was now only inches away from being consigned to a sewer. Instantly, Pross dived across the floor towards the feet of Rab C., but a spurt of Scoones piss pushed his hopes and dreams over the edge of the drain tube just a fraction of a second before his hand slammed down to create a barrier.

Scoones, his legs suddenly bowled away from under him, tumbled backwards over Pross. Ron came rushing through the door. What he saw was his friend stretched out on the ground with his hand in the urinal, beneath a frantic Scoones who was clutching his dribbling willy and twisting about in a fit of panic and surprise.

In the confusion, John, fearful of the large newcomer who had burst in on them, the same person who'd spoken to him on the bridge, slipped out of the toilets, well satisfied with the chaos he'd unwittingly caused but not about to hang around now that he was so heavily out-gunned. To the train station he headed.

1.36
Union

'What the fuck are you doing to my friend, Scoones, you dirty pervert?' menaced Ron, taking him by the legs and pulling him violently off Pross, dragging him over to the door. 'And as for you,' he said to Pross, 'I've told you before, don't scrounge for cigarette ends in the toilet.'

Grabbing hold of Pross's legs for the second time that evening, Ron began hauling him away from the urinal as well, intending to drag him to a neutral corner.

'Get off me!' shouted Pross, determinedly clinging on to the edge of the gutter in opposition to Ron's efforts. 'Get off me!'

Ron knew Pross well, and he knew from the tone of his voice now that something important was happening. He dropped his friend's legs.

Pross pulled himself up to the drain tube, peering down it with his good eye, much to Ron's astonishment. All he saw was blackness.

Scoones, positive that he was being assailed, or sexually assaulted, or something even worse, staggered to his feet, only to stumble backwards, coming to a much needed rest against the washbasins. He was breathing heavily, and his willy was still hanging out and dribbling.

'I've lost the cheque!' cried Pross, attempting to squeeze his hand down the drain tube. It was far too tight. 'Lilith!' he shouted to Ron. 'Get Lilith. She's got small hands. Hurry!'

Ron didn't hurry. 'You stupid git,' he said despairingly, standing over Pross, observing his frantic retrieval efforts. 'Is it down the drain? How'd it end up there?'

'Get Lilith!' shouted Pross again, still peering down the tube. Ron just tutted, and it struck Pross that his friend probably didn't understand the full tragedy of the situation. He looked up at Ron and said, desperately, 'They won't give me a replacement, you know.'

'Of course you'll get a replacement,' contradicted Ron. 'Cheques aren't like money.'

'I *won't* get a replacement,' Pross blurted out. 'I was lucky to get away with this one. You know the lottery people didn't have to cough up in the first place, and now that they hate me I don't...'

'Hate you?'

'Hate me,' repeated Pross pressingly. 'They corporately hate my guts. Wrote nasty things in the newspapers about me, they did.'

Upon hearing those sobering words, Ron said and did nothing at first, thinking for a few seconds. Hate him: that was something Ron could well imagine. Suddenly he fully understood the situation: ten years' worth of his salary had literally gone down the drain. He bolted out of the toilets, raced over to Lilith, hauled her out of her seat, took her by the arm and ran her up to the door of the gents. She shrieked and squawked all along the way, horribly conscious of being the centre of attention of many people in the room. When she realised that she was expected to enter the gents she defiantly grabbed hold of the back of an occupied chair, refusing to budge. Rather than waste a second of time explaining the exigencies of the situation to her, Ron used as much force as was necessary to yank her grip away from the chair and throw her over his shoulder.

Into the gents, Lilith unwillingly went.

And in the gents, Scoones, regaining his composure, was coming to realise that he'd merely been peripheral to the violent activity. Something had been lost down the drain tube, he surmised. A cheque, he'd heard them say. Come to think of it, the ball of paper they'd thrown at him had been about the size of a cheque. Lottery people, did they also not say? Come to think of it, his secretary had mentioned something about a local lottery winner that morning. Oh dear, he nervously thought, I've pissed Ron's friend's fortune away. An immediate retreat from the building was called for in case some *real* violence came his way. So, while Pross's attention was given to peering down the tube, Scoones, forgetfully still with his gear hanging out, edged his way along the wall and to the door, anxious to be gone before the big bugger returned. Too late: the door flew open and the big bugger breezed past him, carrying a wriggling female over his shoulder. Tragically, this was Lilith's first glimpse of a willy. Her fixed gaze and disappointed expression alerted Scoones to his state of indecent exposure. He tucked himself away and proceeded with controlled haste to his car.

He was too scared to go back to his own house, and spent the night at his mother's.

'Get your jacket off and roll your sleeve up,' barked Pross to Lilith as Ron tipped her off his shoulder, 'my cheque's down there.'

'What!' cried Lilith. 'You want me to put my arm down *that!*'

She began backing away.

Ron grabbed her, tying to pull her jacket off. Pross got up off the floor and helped. Lilith screeched, 'No. No. No.'

But soon Lilith's jacket was off, and the sleeve of her blouse was forced up to her shoulder. For months she'd fantasised about being ravaged by Pross, but the way, the reason why, and the place where he'd practically stripped her tonight was a long way from any of her dreams. Held horizontal by Ron and Pross, she was lowered down towards the filthy drain hole.

Sent by Melanie to rescue Lilith, Tony appeared. Ordered by Ron, he quickly became part of the team determined to insert bits of his sister-in-law down a toilet drain. With special responsibility for her defiant arm, he gripped his own hands around her one, positioned it over the drain hole and forced it down as Ron and Pross steadily lowered her. The subsequent scream of disgust and abhorrence was ear-piercing; but once her arm was actually fully down the drain, Lilith's spirit broke, and she became resignedly compliant.

'Can you feel anything? Can you feel anything?' Pross desperately wanted to know.

'Slime,' whimpered Lilith, on the verge of tears.

'Can you feel the surface of the water?'

'Surface of the piss,' corrected Ron.

'Shhh,' urged Pross, 'she'll get rebellious again.'

'No,' she whined, her unfortunate face showing every aspect and iota of the revulsion she was feeling, 'just slime around the sides. I'm in as far as I can go.'

They hauled her out. She was rigid with horror, staring in total mental recoil at her arm, which was smeared with stinking black and green slime all the way up to her shoulder.

Waving a hand before her eyes and snapping his fingers, all to no avail, Pross observed, 'She's gone fucking cataplectic.' Handing her over to Tony, he said, 'Here, psychoanalyse her. The cause of this one even you might get to the bottom of.'

Cruelly joining in on the joke, Tony gingerly (in case he should get himself dirtied) led Lilith over to near the washbasins. She passively allowed herself to be leant up against a wall, whereupon he began his work. 'Is there anything you'd like to talk about?'

His patient suddenly shrieked and ran over to the soap dispenser.

Pross and Ron, in the meantime, were still frantically trying to retrieve the cheque. They'd had the idea of holding a flaring match over the drain to see what they could, which turned out to be nothing very encouraging. The vertical drainpipe seemed to meet with a wider horizontal pipe a little more than an arm's length down.

The doors to the toilet opened. In came two men.

'Use the cubicles,' shouted Pross irritably. 'We've lost something down here.'

The men, shocked to see a girl present, did as was suggested, each going into one of the many cubicles.

'It can't have got far,' said Pross, peering down the hole. 'We could get some pick axes and rip the pipes up, or we could find out where the sewer manholes outside are and use a net to catch it.'

Desperate measures, agreed Ron and Tony, but perhaps worth a try.

Lilith was vigorously washing her arm in a basin of soapy water.

As Pross held another match over the tube, the sound of a cistern flushing came from one of the cubicles. Alarmingly, from down the tube the babbling sound of running water could be heard. He threw a match down the hole and realised that the horizontal pipe the vertical pipe met with was also connected to the outflow from the cubicles. The second cubicle flushed. More water swept along the horizontal pipe. All was lost. The cheque would be on its way to a main sewer by now.

'It has to be gone,' said Pross in a low voice. 'It's too late now.'

Seemingly to confirm the worst, the periodic automatic flush of the urinal itself chose this moment to spring into action, issuing gallons of water that poured down the drain hole. Pross's last hope was that the cheque might float up on a column of water.

It didn't.

'Fancy bringing the bloody thing out in the first place,' said Tony at the autopsy, conducted around their drinks at their table. Morale had severely slumped. No one felt good. 'You're your own worst enemy, you are. Are you sure they won't give you another one? You'll at least try, I hope. It's worth losing a bit of pride over.'

'You bloody well will try,' said Ron. 'You've lost me my job.'

Pross was lying with his cheek on the table top, groaning, staring across and beyond the overlapping images of the room. His eye throbbed, he couldn't see properly, he had a headache, he still felt nauseous, he'd lost over two million pounds, his cat was dead, he'd been evicted from his home, he'd been thrown off the dole, he'd got Ron sacked, and he'd met someone even better at being miserable than himself. 'I didn't ask you to come back from Iceland,' he said for Ron's ears.

Ron wasn't listening. He was in his own little world of hate. 'Bastard Scoones,' he said, 'Bastard, bastard Scoones.'

'You should have hidden it somewhere safe,' implored someone else. 'Who in the hell was it who tossed it away?'

Another quiet moan from Pross. 'Told you already, I don't know. Never seen him before. He just walked up to me, snatched the cheque away, screwed it up and tossed it away before I knew what was going on. I didn't see where it had gone until it was too late.'

'You don't suppose he was in with Scoones?' suggested Ron.

'Don't think so,' answered Pross.

'Bastard Scoones. Bastard, bastard Scoones.'

Pross was too full of self-pity to blame others. 'My life's a great river of woe,' he said in a morose voice.

Ron, his head now in his hands, testily added something to that metaphor. 'Your life's a great river of woe that forever breaks its banks and floods over on to me.'

'Aw, fuck off,' groaned Pross, still slumped over the table. 'Everybody fuck off. Everybody's a bastard except me.'

'Hi!' said Sarah-Jane brightly, suddenly appearing. Her role in the presentation was over, and although the finale was still being performed on

stage, she had left by a backstage door to join her new friends in the bar.
'Ron! What are you doing here?'

Ron gave her only the most downbeat of return hellos.

She turned to Pross, then saw that he was in an even sorrier mood than Ron. Pulling a face, she asked, 'And what's up with you?'

'I'm sunk in deep resentment. Bound to agony with seven-fold chains of frosted iron.'

Sarah addressed Ron instead. 'What's up with him?'

'He's having one of those lives,' explained Ron to Sarah as she remained standing. 'Come sit next to me,' he requested, but Sarah couldn't because Simon occupied that position. Ron realised her trivial dilemma, and nudged Simon. 'Fuck off, Simon. We're sick of you.'

'Yeah, fuck off, Simon,' said Pross. 'I've just had another message from Godfrey. He says you're a thick bastard with a crap anorak.'

'Don't be cruel,' said Sarah, bewildered, but readily taking the seat Simon was compliantly vacating.

Mick followed his leader in leaving the company. 'Godfrey loves you,' he said to Pross.

'Godfrey forgive you,' added Simon, and they left.

A loud groan issued from Pross. He'd started a religion. Pross, the militant atheist, had started a religion. He began exclaiming bitterly. 'Godfrey! He still believes in Godfrey! He's going to tell other cranks — maybe soon there'll be hundreds of loonies praying into batteries and looking for spaceships over Durham cathedral. In a thousand years time there might be enough of them to fight a war.'

'Shut up, Pross,' said Ron in a low voice.

It had not escaped Sarah's attention that a pall of despondency was hanging over her new friends. No one was chatting. No one was smiling. She was confused and uneasy. Looking towards Pross, from whom the endemic despair seemed to be emanating, she asked, 'Whatever happened to your eye?'

Pross didn't answer. He was staring down at the table top. After a few seconds, without raising his head, he spoke quietly, but it was not to Sarah. 'Will someone go to the bar and get me a drink?' Melanie obliged. Pross began absently flicking around the photo of Jennifer, thinking dark thoughts about how twenty-four-and-a-bit times around the sun were quite enough for him.

Sarah pursued her inquiry, touching his wrist. 'What happened to your eye? Pross, tell me.'

Saying nothing, he stopped flicking the photo around and looked at it instead.

Sarah remembered how mopy he'd been over Jennifer the previous Sunday, and she naturally wondered if this was the reason for his current blue mood. Humouring him, she asked, 'Do you still love my sister then?'

There was no answer.

'Speak to me, someone,' she pleaded. 'What's the matter with everyone?'

Pross handed the photo back to Sarah. 'I never really loved her. How could I? Never even met her. I was just in love with the idea of love.'

Putting the photo away into her bag, Sarah said, 'It's a good job for you, because she got engaged this week.' She linked her arm around Ron's, and asked him quietly, 'What's up?'

Ron told her.

'Aw, you poor thing,' said Sarah with deep sympathy to Pross. 'Are you sure they won't give you another cheque?'

'Maybe, if I crawl. Maybe not. They're not obliged. And I could hardly embarrass them into giving me a replacement cheque since the press and the public are all against me.'

Sarah now fell into the deep blue overwhelming the rest of the group. No one spoke for many minutes, until Pross said, 'Can anyone give me back some of that money I gave you? About a hundred will do.'

'Why?' asked Melanie.

'To get some smack from Agness Old.'

'Smack?' said Tony.

'Smack,' confirmed Pross. 'I seek oblivion.'

A general reluctance to part with cash was exhibited.

'Come on,' he urged, 'it's my money. I gave it to you.'

Cash was not forthcoming.

Pross's head lolled backwards to the accompaniment of a deep sigh. 'Too poor to die,' he moaned, sinking a little deeper into resentment. Absolutely everything that could have gone wrong had. This was it: he resolved to die, the only way he could afford. Pushing his chair back, he stood up, saying in a measured voice, 'I am just going outside, and may be some time.'

Sarah reached over and held his jacket sleeve between her fingertips. With concern evident in her tone, she asked, 'Where are you going?'

'Outside to throw myself under a fucking tree.'

'Bye now,' said Ron.

To her absolute astonishment, Sarah thought she could see her sister standing beside the reception desk. Her fingers involuntarily relaxed and let Pross slip away. He began walking slowly towards the door, disappointed and hurt that no one was trying to hinder him.

'Pross, stop,' called Ron.

Pross turned around. 'Yeah?'

'Your hair's peaking.'

'But it's too late. I'm a beat poet.

He continued walking.

Ron let him go. He had his own life, less ten years' salary and a job, to get on with.

Now outside, too poor to die with certainty, Pross sat on the fallen half of the tree on the grassed traffic island. 'Come, Death, effect life's biggest favour,' he implored, looking up at the standing remainder.

But the wind had abated considerably now.

So he waited, hoping for a gust.

No merciful meterological occurrences occurred.

After a minute, he began to get impatient. After five minutes, he began to get cold. After ten minutes, he began to lose hope. It seemed he was doomed to live. All was lost. And what a miserable life it was he was doomed to live. A life with no money and no money coming in, not even dole. It looked as if he might actually have to start writing his proper novel if the wind wouldn't hurry up and oblige.

To increase his despair, he now remembered that his word processor was in Mick's cab.

And Mick had been viciously sent away.

That was it. That was the final straw. It couldn't get any worse. He'd had it all, but it had all been lost in one horrible evening.

He closed his eyes and dropped his head.

'Your hair is peaking, isn't it?' said a voice.

He opened his eyes. Before him were blurred images of the girl who'd been with Scoones. He closed his bad eye and she became an angel, an angel in a fluttering black dress. Everything about the moment conspired with her beauty to make him fall so much deeper in love than he'd ever really fallen in love before: the dark of the night, the radiant play of the floodlight upon her hair; his forsaken mood, her redemptive interest in him.

Pross could find no words to say.

From a shoulder bag, the vision kindly offered him something. 'Here, you can have this back. I think you'll be needing it more than me.'

The scene's moments each seemed to last forever; enchanted moments crystallised in time.

Pross slowly took it from her for examination: it was a fifty pound note. It now dawned on him who she was.

'Jennifer?'

She smiled a little, then asked, 'What are you doing sitting out here all alone in the cold?' she asked.

Time was still hanging motionless for Pross. 'Waiting,' he eventually replied.

'What for?'

Looking soulfully at her, he said, 'For the wind to pick up again so the rest of this here Tree of Death will fall on me.'

But there was now only a gusty breeze, which played with Jennifer's hair. She smiled gently. Pross opened his bad eye, and she gained a twin. Her smile remained. 'You look funny sat there. Just like a cartoon castaway on a desert island.'

'And I'm staying on this cartoon island till this tree does me a favour.'

'Mind if I share your little island in the meantime?' And before Pross could answer, she'd sat down beside him, not caring if she might soil her clothes. 'It's cold out here,' she remarked.

'I'm used to it now.'

'Can't I coax you back into the warmth?'

Pross was overwhelmed by her.

'If you can't, no one can.'

'Don't sit on your island waiting for the Tree of Death to fall,' she said, 'grow older with me.'

Everything in the way Jennifer looked and acted and spoke enchanted Pross. 'A voice like the gentle cooing of the very Dove of Peace itself,' he said to her dreamily, and she smiled.

Could it be? Could it be that ever so slowly she was moving her lips to his?

But the everlasting enchantment was broken for Pross by the sight of Lilith rushing over to her car.

She was upset, he could see that. Maybe she'd come out to see if he was all right, not knowing that Jennifer was with him. He called Lilith's name, but she did not acknowledge him.

Away she drove.

Returning his gaze to Jennifer, he saw that silver spiders' webs were woven into her dress. These brought to mind the experiences of Moaning Joe, who'd said he'd had a web of deceit spun around him.

'I want you to tell me something,' he asked.

'What's that?' wondered Jennifer, beginning to shiver in the night air.

Before putting his question to her, he began taking his jacket off, offering it to Jennifer. She refused it. 'It's all right, your friend just gave me this to

wear.' And from her shoulder bag she produced the *Prospero's Lass* T-shirt.
 She put it on.
 'It's funny,' said she, and smiled.
 'That's all it was ever meant to be,' said he.
 'The question?' she inquired of him.
 'Oh, the question. Have you ever shoplifted from Oxfam?'
 She looked at him. 'Oxfam? Why ever should you ask something like that?'
 'Have you?'
 With an air of bewilderment, she answered, 'No, of course not.'
 'Sure?'
 'Sure.'
 'You need your head examining,' she said, but soon her hand slipped into his, and he held her close.

Part Two

Beyond the Joke

2.1
Separation

He was tediously alone in an elevator. Unexpectedly, the doors opened, and he made to step out, but was arrested by the reflected image in a mirror across the corridor, which showed the doors to have stayed closed. Overpowered by this evidence, he remained confined within. Thus had gone the dream that had taken him to noon.

It was meant to have been a *fait accompli*, but, in keeping with the course of his life, he'd slept for longer than was wise, and now she was already back from assisting the vet at the Saturday morning surgery.

She'd had no clue this was about to happen.

Despite her expressed anguish, Pross continued to collect the few belongings, clothes mainly, he had brought with him, placing them in his borrowed suitcase. His other possessions, including all his books, he had abandoned.

'You don't talk about how you really feel,' continued Jennifer, sat on the edge of her bed, feebly holding the spray of flowers she'd bought that morning, their heads inclined helplessly to the floor. 'You hold everything back. You've been through hell lately, but you never even mention it.' A second later she added, 'except as a joke.'

Still collecting his belongings, he answered her in a level voice. 'I'm not holding anything back. I've told you how I feel, and I feel I want to go. Apart from that, I don't feel anything, except very sad.'

His possessions accumulated, Pross looked at Jennifer, indulging in the desolate thought that it was likely to be for the last time. She was a rare creature. Rare in that her face seemed to be incapable of ever looking unattractive. There was no angle from which it could be viewed unfavourably; no expression it could muster that would detract. And Pross had quickly learned that the rarity also extended to her nature.

Tears were beginning to wet her eyes, and Pross felt for her, but at the same time it seemed ridiculous to him that anyone should feel such emotion over his departure.

'I'm sorry,' he said, finding himself moving to embrace her; she, with frail, hesitant limbs, standing to return the clasp she knew was to put them asunder, the spray of flowers held against his back. 'Don't cry. Please don't cry. Not for me. Never for me. I'm not worth it.'

Jennifer wanted him to stay so much it surprised her, considering she'd only known him for two weeks. She wondered if it was just the being left that was hurting, not really to do with the person leaving.

As they continued to hold each other, Jennifer's eyes dried. He was relieved: he didn't want to walk away if she was weeping.

'Where will you go?' she asked, concerned. 'You've got nowhere to live.'

'I'll find somewhere.'

'You haven't even got any money.'

'I've got my bus fare back to Durham.'

Another concern crossed Jennifer's mind, which she softly expressed. 'Sarah called me at work this morning. Ron's having a bonfire party tonight. I told her we'd be there. She's coming to collect us.'

'Then go without me,' he almost tersely returned.

Confused and saddened, Jennifer said nothing awhile, then, almost as a mark of resignation, she allowed her eyes to fall closed. Soon she was lost in the gently swaying, sacred embrace of their soft-dying romance. With nothing for her senses to fix upon, she found herself recalling the melancholic ambience of a walk in a wood on a still, misty autumn eve. Her head soft-fallen against his shoulder, the scent of the flowers rising to her, time passed too easily before she sensed his preparation to move. With eyes now opened to the floor, she said, 'Would it change things if I told you I think I'm growing to love you?'

Without even considering the proposition, Pross answered, 'Don't love me. I'll be bad for you.'

Jennifer became annoyed, and stepped back. 'Pross, why have you started saying things like that?' she asked, looking intently at him. 'Why?'

'Because I've never been any good for anyone. Maybe that's why I stay alone.'

'Don't be so bloody ridiculous,' she scolded, 'you've been good for me. You've given me two of the funniest weeks of my life.'

Five hundred times is how much easier it was for him to walk away when she was arguing and criticising than when she was tearful.

Pross turned for the door, saying, with a little bitterness, 'Yeah, I'm good at making people laugh. Bye.'

Once outside, a powerful sense of escape being felt, he found himself imagining the scene within. Would she have thrown herself distraught on to the bed? That prospect, he was ashamed to discover, gave him a perverted sense of satisfaction.

But he refused to dwell upon it further. Instead, he momentarily reflected upon how strong his character was: there were few people who could resist such a temptation as Jennifer.

Where, exactly, he was now going, he knew not. The flat he'd shared with Ron had been determinedly, albeit illegally, reclaimed by the Landlord. Moreover, since that evening fifteen days ago when he'd lost his lottery money, flat and Ron's job, Ron had not been his usual self on the two occasions they'd met. It was obvious to Pross that Ron was, at least, trying to distance himself; at most, angry and resentful. Picking up on these vibes, he understood that it was as if Ron had decided that the four years of flat-share silliness and trouble had come to its inevitable sticky end, and now was the time for seriously getting on with his life, and the continued proximity of a Pross was a serious danger to his seriousness.

Things had changed. So many things had ended.

He headed for the bus station.

The electricity supply was now restored. So too was the water. Above, a roofer was emergency roofing. Below, some labourers were labouring, finishing the clearing and cleaning. The van load of junk shop furniture had already been unloaded.

The place was now habitable in Simon's opinion.

Amid the banging and whistling, with late-afternoon sunlight structuring with ethereal beams and shafts, the dusty, airy, resonant room, Simon pressed the play button on the cassette machine.

Another hearing of the Words of Truth.

Once upon a time, commenced Pross's recorded voice, *there was a brilliant physicist called Godfrey who succeeded in producing the Equation of Everything. He was a white-haired, kindly old professor, and, like many of the people working in his field, he had grown old, weary and sad-eyed trying to develop the elusive theory that successfully unifies all the forces of nature into a single one...*

And in the short time until the story ended, Simon was rendered virtually transfixed by the profundity of the Words of Truth as told by Prospero Pi-Meson, the Prophet of Godfrey.

The story told, as his own version of reality began to slowly apprehend him, Simon turned to his companions and said: 'And now let us complete the charging of the battery for the mission to make Prospero believe in himself again.'

And they held hands to form a circle around a prayer battery, chanting low mystical utterances as they shuffled slowly clockwise while Simon earnestly invoked all the powers that be.

2.2
The Vision Thing

When he'd said "piss off" to a Sun reporter at the cheque presentation, he'd unwittingly staked his claim to overnight tabloid sensationalist stardom: LOTTERY MILLIONAIRE SAYS P*SS OFF! being the Sun headline. And it hadn't taken long for the papers to learn that Prospero Pi-Meson, whose cat had won a lottery fortune for him, had subsequently lost the cheque down a toilet.

AND OFF WITH P*SS TO YOU! had been the headline two days later.

The various reportings of Pross's huge loss generally took the view that this whole affair was very much in the line of "serving him right" since he'd caused such a controversy and had been so vulgar and ungrateful when the cheque had been presented to him in an act of virtual charity.

Fortunately for Pross, the young woman who'd exclusively won the next week's ten million pound jackpot was soon revealed to be a former prostitute. This had swung tabloid attention perfectly away from him: he was only a third sharer in a lower than average jackpot, after all.

And as for the money, the various reported murmurings from the lottery company concerning how they'd never been obliged to pay out in the first place since no ticket existed, and how they had no plans to issue a replacement cheque, all added to Pross's singular resolve to make not even a phone call to them regarding the loss, much to Ron's, and everyone else he knew's, displeasure and complete incomprehension. To get his cheque replaced, if at all possible, would involve, as he saw it, grovelling and apologising for something over which he had no regret. In his heart of hearts, he'd rather be seen in the papers begging for his dinner than begging for a fortune. Dinner begging had integrity, begging for a fortune was *truly* vulgar.

'Any food going?' he asked morosely as Melanie opened the door.

For some reason he could never quite fathom, whenever he knocked upon Melanie's door she always smiled and let him in, even though he picked on her husband and would never openly and honestly admit to adoring her. For to ever honestly and genuinely say he loved, or even liked her, would be like losing the life-long battle with her that she herself had started: he was too competitive.

Smiling and letting him in was what Melanie began doing.

'Just cooking some pasta, actually.'

But then she saw the suitcase.

'No! No! No!' she shrieked, quickly pushing him back and closing the door.

'Aw, Melanie, let me in, please,' he said to the closed door.

'You're not moving in, no way,' replied Melanie from the other side. 'Get on to the lottery people and get your cheque replaced then buy a mansion.'

'Please, just for a week or two.'

'Go and live with Ron.'

'I can't. He's moved back in with his parents and his mother hates me. Come on, Mel, let me in. I beg you.'

'Go and beg his mother.'

'I did,' he lied, 'but she told me to fuck off. No *vision thing*, you see. Not like you, you've got puddles of vision.'

'You're not coming in. You'll get ensconced.'

'I won't get ensconced,' he promised, suspecting he was still lying. 'I just want to talk to you for a few hours, like we used to in happier times.'

'What about?' asked Melanie with deep suspicion.

Pross opened the letter box and spoke through it in a cheerless tone. 'About the decay of hope.'

'Go and talk to Ron about it.'

'I did,' he lied once more through the letter box, 'but he couldn't sweeten the bitterness in my soul. Only you can ever do that. You're special, you are, Mel.'

'Stop being nice to me just because you want to stay in my house. If you're going to be nice, be nice honestly. Tell me honestly you love me and you can come in.'

Pross became stern. 'Let me in, you bitch,' he said, but then immediately became griping. 'Come on, Mel, you owe me — it's your fault I'm burdened with a stupid name, after all.'

'No it's not.'

'Yes it is. If you hadn't teased me so much at school for being poetic and clever and nicknamed me Prospero Pi-Meson, I'd never have formally adopted the idiotic millstone to make you feel guilty once you'd started liking me. It was the only way I could ever punish you for the horrors you visited upon me as a sensitive adolescent.'

'Don't start that again. It's not my fault, it's yours. I didn't force you to do it.'

'You practically did. And you're the reason I played truant so much and left school as soon as I could. I could have been a high-energy physicist if it wasn't for you. Been the first to detect gravity waves. You ruined my education with your cruel torments, Melanie Trotter, so let me in.'

'No. Stop talking bollocks. Tell me honestly you love me or fuck off.'

'It's when my headaches started too.'

'Fuck off.'

'Please, let me in. I'm lonely. If I...'

Pross fell quiet.

Melanie became suspicious.

'What are you doing?' she asked.

'Listening,' said Pross strangely.

'What to?'

'I fancy... I fancy I heard a misty noise — from yon graveyard way.'

Another silent period.

'There, I heard it again. I believe it was a call, Melanie. A far call bidding me journey thither, to the haven of the grave. It must be my time, Melanie, for who would inhabit this bleak world alone? So long, companion of my youth.'

Melanie knelt down to look out through the letter box.

Pross looked in.

Her large brown eyes met his greyish green.

He flattered her with some customised Shelley...

'In those eyes, where whoso gazes
*Faints entangled in their mazes...*bitch.'

And then, with a feeble moan, he fainted.

Despite the "bitch" addition, Melanie was nettled to find herself relenting. 'Oh, come on in then,' she grumbled, opening the door to him.

'A gullible bitch at that,' he remarked plainly, picking himself up. 'Your eyes are crap. Everyone knows that.'

Entering the living room, he encountered Melanie's husband sitting on the sofa.

Tony looked curiously at the suitcase.

'Homeless,' said Pross.

After depositing the suitcase somewhere in the way and insulting Tony just to keep his hand in at it, dinner was presented to the largely uninvited guest.

Over the pasta meal, Melanie tried to get Pross to explain the mystery of why he had left Jennifer.

'Felt like it,' was about the best shrug he could muster.

Melanie gave him a disapproving look, but held her opinion on the matter to herself. Instead, she turned the conversation towards Ron's Guy

Fawkes party that night.

'Don't know much about it,' stated Pross. 'Ron never calls me. Sarah spoke to Jenny about it.'

'He's having it at his folks' place at Croxdale,' said Tony with his mouth full. 'Loads of big fireworks apparently. You coming?'

'Can't,' said Pross, 'not with those folks hating me so much.'

Ron's folk's did hate Pross, and their self-satisfied retirement house in Croxdale, a few miles outside Durham City, was where the hatred was most concentrated. Pross was *persona non grata* at this swirling vortex of hate, mainly on account of Ron's mother being convinced that he had been, and probably always would be, a druggy influence on her son, although the exact opposite was the true case.

Pross, of course, had so often played up to her worst suspicions.

'So you're not going?' asked Melanie.

'Can't, can I?' said Pross, glad that he had a perfect excuse not to: Jennifer was perhaps going to be there, and she was the last person he wished to see.

After the meal, Tony retreated to what he liked to call his study, citing some unfinished work as the pressing reason.

'Some last dots to join?' enquired Pross.

Melanie hit him, then told him to clear the dishes.

He cleared the dishes.

In the kitchen, his gaze fell upon a photograph of Melanie's younger sister, out of date, for Lilith had now hacked off all her hair. Poor Lilith, he thought.

He'd found himself thinking about her quite often these last few days, regretting his attitude to her after she'd confessed a desire for him. But, looking at the photo, he knew why it was so hard to take her desires seriously: she was so unattractive. She had no place in the game — that's the attitude that naturally emerged.

And now that she'd hacked all her hair off, she was even less desirable.

Poor Lilith, he thought again.

2.3
The Sign

She had not thrown herself on to the bed after Pross's departure. Jennifer had been angry, not distraught; disappointed, not brokenhearted. He'd stayed for two weeks and now he was gone, was her adopted attitude. And in the light of a cloudless, early November afternoon, with a week's groceries needing to be bought and videos needing to be returned, she found little time to sigh or cry.

When these tasks had been seen to, with the flowers concealed within a paper bag, she began the ten minute walk to St Andrew's church, warmed by the coat that was the last thing her mother had ever bought for her.

Even now she saw no shadow of what was later to come.

Even when in the churchyard, placing the flowers amid a bed of fallen autumn leaves on to the white marble grave of Rachael Ann and William James Lucas, tragically taken two years ago from the day, the shadow drew no dark forms for her inner eye to see.

St Andrew's lay on the very edge of Richmond. A narrow, tree-lined lane of not too great length brought visitors abruptly from a busy road to a secluded, ancient stone church, whose roof had recently attracted lead thieves. Historically, only the walled grounds to the front of the church had received coffins. Many so curiously weathered as to appear melted during some by-gone swelter, aged headstones existed there that testified to a centuries-old continuity of Christian burial. But newer, neater, white marble and stained-green gravel graves were now being assigned to an acquired field behind the church, till recently a farmer's toil.

In this field, in a corner, under a large tree, could be found the grave of Jennifer's parents, and beside that grave, on a low wooden bench, she sat for some time.

This was her first visit. "It was just a cold stone, not them", had been her expressed attitude. She hadn't even been at the funeral, a sickness having afflicted her that day.

To have been accompanied by Pross had been her wish this morning, but he hadn't even asked why she had bought flowers.

Many thoughts and memories passed through Jennifer's mind as she gave her parents her company on this the second anniversary of their death. But things were becoming different, she realised. The feelings of numb loss she'd carried were changing: something was fading, but another thing was emerging. Before, she had always missed them as a child would. Missing the security; the help; the guidance; the comfort;. feeling lost and unprotected. But now, passing out of childhood, she realised she was regretting that she would never be able to know them as people. She had always been a child, and they had been her parents. But on knowledge of some things she was sure: she had always known they were special. Kinder and more thoughtful than others; gentler and surely wiser. And they had loved each other very much too. Theirs was a lover's story she wished she knew better: their mistakes, their dreams; how they had come to be together, and how they had stayed so.

Jennifer, standing now, quietly told Rachael Ann and William James that she loved them, then left for home as tightness came to her throat.

But that much she had expected.

What she had not expected was that, an hour or so after leaving the grave, when the day's light began to thicken with shadow, she would find herself sitting alone in her unlit room, save for the company of a growing sense of abandonment that was beginning to choke with a grip she feared able to put an end to her.

Jennifer gave enough room to introspection to know that what she was feeling now was the choking hands of the invisible presence that had haunted her for what seemed forever: she always felt alone, even when with people.

Presently, her feelings reminded her of the ambience of a poem she'd read at school, and she sought it out from among her dusty books.

The passage she had in mind, she discovered, went thus:

> *I feel like one*
> *Who treads alone*
> *Some banquet-hall deserted,*
> *Whose lights are fled,*
> *Whose garlands are dead,*
> *And all but she departed.*

That was it. That was how she could often sadly feel put into imagery. The feeling of being estranged from the laughing hubbub of life and youth.

Jennifer knew herself not to be a gregarious person. So easily could she feel awkward when talking to people. And when she felt awkward, which was often, she knew that she was acting like a damper upon whatever occasion it happened to be. And although she might feel on such occasions that she has her fair share of clever or witty remarks to make, her shyness would doubt her own thoughts so much so that she would find herself lacking the courage to utter them. Hence people brought Jennifer little comfort. Even John had never been any real company for her, even though she'd had no reticence when around him due to his long-standing familiarity in her life. He had never been a suitable partner for her, being so dull of mind, and as she'd matured she'd grown to loathe his presence. But Pross had been different: he had sparkled, and she couldn't imagine ever meeting the likes of him again. She missed him and wanted him back, she admitted, especially this night. She really needed him tonight. Never had she taken to anyone as easily as she had to him. She thought that maybe it was because he was so ready to act the foolish child to amuse that she'd never felt any embarrassment when with him: she couldn't inadvertently say or do anything sillier than he was wont to do himself on purpose. He had made her laugh so many times. He was a perfect distraction, and Jennifer wanted him for that, if for nothing else. He was also good looking, and she knew that they had made an attractive pair.

The only thing she didn't know was why he had suddenly left her when it had all seemed to be coming along so good, so good that she'd told him she was growing to love him before he left, and she was not free with her expressions of affection — she had never once told John she loved him, and he had never asked. Pross, however, had made a dozen effusive, silly speeches about her being the misty incarnation of all his ethereal dreams; about her being too sacred to even touch; and when he did touch her, which had been often, about her kisses being like summer rain.

And love had been a word he'd used many times.

But not in the last few days, she realised. In the last few days it had been as if some killing frost had crept over his doting exuberance for her.

Maybe he'd just wanted to satisfy his lust. Men were like that, weren't they?

When informed, Sarah wondered the same thing too. She had just telephoned her sister to confirm her and Pross's attendance at Ron's party that evening, but was told that the relationship was already over. Like Jennifer, it was disappointment, too, that Sarah felt. She was disappointed that someone she had come quickly to promote as an ideal companion for her younger sister had proved to be so fickle. However, her vague instincts spoke differently, and so she persuaded Jennifer to attend Ron's event on her own.

Jennifer demurred at first, but finally agreed.

'I'll set off to pick you up in about half an hour,' said Sarah. 'You can stay overnight if you want. There'll be spare rooms. His family have gone away for the weekend.'

'No, it's all right, I'll make my own way over. Elaine's driving up to Newcastle in a few hours. She can give me a lift. She'll be glad of some petrol money.'

Sarah-Jane suspected her sister might be lying to get out of attending, but hoped she wasn't and gave the address of the house. 'Ten o'clock the fireworks start,' she reminded Jennifer.

When the light began to thicken, Pross, too, began to feel a choking sense of sorrow.

'For fuck's sake, switch the light on before I top myself,' he said to Melanie, who was intently performing step aerobics by a dim window, clad in a hundred pounds worth of lilac Lycra.

She ignored him.

In the sullen light, Pross's gaze fell on to another photograph of Lilith. Thinking about her this time, he began to feel scornful of himself. She was a dear friend who had come to love him, and he had treated her like her desires and needs were insignificant and comical.

He was a brute, he decided.

It was done. In the field by the stream, by the light of a burning torch, the final charging of the prayer battery had been realised. A full two hundred hours of directional prayer energy was now captured, ready to be unleashed on to their faithless, wandering prophet.

And now they ruminated under the stars. Two of this peculiar gathering had never before experienced the night sky away from smothering city lights. Never seen Orion dominate. Never lain on their backs in the dewy grass to ponder the imponderable. Never felt smaller; never felt greater. Never felt more humble; never felt more godlike.

None of them had ever seen a meteor, and a meteor is what convinced Simon that the time was at hand.

'Amazing,' he breathed, peering heavenward. 'It's a sign — Durham's over that way.' He became valiant, and announced: 'We get Prospero tonight.'

2.4
Wounded Hearts

Pross needed his head examining — Melanie had just told him so. In fact, after her aerobics workout, she'd begun badgering him so much about him not trying to reclaim his winnings, and about his leaving Jennifer, he'd eventually been forced to ask her for ten pounds so that he could go to the pub to get some quiet.

Ten pounds. Ten measly pounds. He'd had to ask for ten pounds when fifteen nights ago he'd had a cheque for over two million in his pocket.

Only briefly is how long he dwelt on this irony whilst walking to the Arts Centre bar. He prided himself on his powers of self-denial. He could endure, and turn to comedy, any misfortune.

But by the time he'd reached his destination, he was, for the first time in his life, too sad for comedy. Forsaken is how he felt. Utterly forsaken. Yet he knew — not the least for Melanie having just screamed it at him — that he had no real business with the condition, for that very morning he'd willingly left the manifestation of all he'd ever so publicly ached for.

The absurd thing was that, before he'd set off, he'd found himself taking particular care to get his hair looking sultry in case Mary, the attractive girl who occasionally served at the bar, might be there. He yearned so much for comfort, yet this very morning he'd abandoned the sweetest of affections. The ambiguity was not hidden from him, yet he still cast a hopeful glance towards the bar upon entering the building.

He actually did need his head examining, he decided for the first time ever.

Mary was not there, and his heart sank even further. Yet he knew perfectly that even if she had been there, he would have gone home alone. For although he fell into what he called love ten times a day and found himself longing for the companionship of the various objects of his wandering desire, he was remarkably adept at avoiding even the slightest real involvement. If someone he desired ever returned the sentiment, something compelled him to slip away from them. The few consummated relationships he'd fallen into had actually come about by extreme coaxing or sheer force: prior to Jennifer — who'd done a little gentle coaxing herself — his last girlfriend had actually physically dragged him to bed, with him trying to hold on to furniture. He only wanted when he was not likely to get, and if he did inadvertently get, then he quickly got out. Getting out before he could hurt them with his inevitable abandonment was a prime consideration. He could not ever imagine himself leaving someone who really needed him, someone whom he had grown to feel empathy for, someone he had allowed to make an emotional investment in him: so he stayed alone. He was frightened of committing himself because he was so steadfast in his resolutions.

He held this excuse to be true and often told it to himself.

Jennifer had been different only in that she'd needed to do less coaxing than an angel would have. But he still left her, and now he was feeling so forsaken for having forsaken her.

That's how he often reasoned it, but these reasons felt unsettlingly uncertain today.

He really did need his head examining, he decided.

There was no one he knew in the Arts Centre bar, and if ever he'd needed company, he needed it tonight. Everything had been a joke until now, even misery and love, but the joke seemed to have ended.

After drinking half his beer faster than doctors would recommend and leaving the remainder, he found himself walking out with a sense of urgency, as if he had somewhere better to go.

Outside the building, he closed up his jacket and walked across the car park. Soon he was at the little grassed traffic island where he'd first spoken to Jennifer, only fifteen nights earlier. Here he unconsciously slowed to a halt. The fallen half of the tree had now been removed, and the remaining half was shored up with metal poles.

He sat on the grass where he'd sat before, and felt like crying. Really crying. But he knew he wouldn't, although he had plenty to cry about. His two million pound fortune was gone. His flat was no longer his. His dole had been cancelled. He'd put Ron out of work. His cat had died after he'd fallen in a fight and landed on it. He'd been ridiculed in the newspapers. And to top it all, he'd felt compelled to say goodbye to Jennifer, who'd miraculously materialised in his life like some redemptive angel as he'd sat alone in this very same place fifteen nights earlier, similarly longing for oblivion.

Oblivion: it had never beckoned so persuasively. To exchange a moment's pain for an eternity of merciful nothingness.

He now seemed to be grieving. Yes, the anguish and despair was that extreme. He felt like he was in deep mourning, and realised he was mourning his own dead self. Tonight he knew that it was all in vain. He likened himself to a wraith in a shadowy realm, and even the outstretched arms of an enchantress like Jennifer could not pull him into the light. He would forever be alone in this darkened world, gazing upon the living through tear-dimmed eyes, but never able to reach out his yearning hands, hands bound to his sides with unbreakable chains.

'I was made lone,' he concluded out loud, then dropped his head and expressed a low moan.

> *'As when some great painter dips*
> *his pencil in the gloom of earthquake and eclipse,'*

quoted a male voice mirthfully. 'That's what you look like.'

His careering slide into despair arrested by the sudden voice, Pross slowly looked up.

It was Moaning Joe, except he wasn't moaning, or even looking as if he was capable of such a small business.

'Shouldn't you be dead?' observed Pross baldly. 'I paid good money for it.'

'I came back from the dead,' said Moaning Joe as he stepped closer, his face curiously oozing a beatific smile. 'Lured back by a glimpse of the possible.'

'I wish I could come back from the dead,' said Pross, dropping his head into hands again. 'I'm a ghost, that's what I am. Haunting a dark land.'

There was only silence from Moaning Joe. Eventually, Pross looked up to check that he was still there. He saw that Moaning Joe was holding out his upturned hand, a hand bearing four small capsules.

Pross looked at Joe for some kind of explanation.

'Of ten fruits from the Tree of Life procured, four remain,' said Joe, proffering them to a bemused Pross. 'Go on, take them — you paid good money for them. Anyway,' he added, a lot less pompously, 'I've got more on order.'

Pross cast Joe a quizzical look.

'That woman you sent me to didn't have any smack. All she had was ecstasy, so I spent the hundred pounds on ten tabs. You saved my life trying to kill me, Prospero Pi-Meson. I'd never taken the stuff, but I took one that night...' Joe began to quote again:

> *'So deep the power of these ingredients pierced,*
> *Even to the inmost seat of mental sight*
> *That Adam, now enforced to close his eyes,*
> *Sank down, and all his spirits became entranced*
> *But him the gentle angel by the hand soon raised...'*

Pross had never taken ecstasy, either, and didn't personally know anyone who had. The rave and club culture was not something that had ever encroached on his life, since most of his life was spent in his bedroom. This was the remote Northeast, not London, and he was most certainly not a mover in the circles of youth fashion. And, contrary to a lot of peoples' conjecturing, he was not a heedless drug user. Indeed, within his small circle of friends he was about the least enthusiastic. He'd always refused speed (having observed it to be the morons choice), never smoked cigarettes, only occasionally smoked dope and hadn't done acid for years.

However, Pross was not entirely ignorant about ecstasy. He knew it was usually called E; it was not addictive; and it was supposed to make one happy, but then again, so was whisky. But whatever cynicism he inevitably had about its supposed effects, he was certainly not inclined to be prejudiced against the stuff by what he'd read in popular newspapers about youngsters dancing until they dropped, sometimes dead. From reading *New Scientist*, he *knew* that such deaths were statistically much rarer than swimming accidents, and were for the most part preventable. Those one-in-a-million-trip rarities had usually keeled over from dance-induced heat exhaustion, or dehydration, or from ill-advised overenthusiastic water drinking leading to electrolytes being passed out of the body, leading to coma and death.

'I've never had ecstasy, either,' said Pross, accepting the four capsules into his own hand, studying them. They were gelatin, coloured brown and purple, unmarked.

'Then,' bellowed Joe rapturously, about to quote again, 'I insist:
*that those eat now, who never ate before;
and those who always ate, now eat the more!*'

He then began laughing, laughing at himself. 'Go on, take one. It's the purest stuff that's been around in ages, according to reports.'

'Are you on it now?' asked Pross.

'Good Lord, no. I'd be far more serious about feeling happy if I was. It does that, you see — makes you take happiness seriously. Well, it does with me, at least.'

As far as Pross could make out, Joe was talking nonsense, but he talked it so eloquently as to be convincing.

'Is it anything like acid?' enquired Pross, a little fearfully. His last acid trip, a three-tabber, had been somewhat bad, he guessed, although he'd never really had a good trip to compare it with, he also guessed. Anyway, after the last trip, years before, he'd found himself more than a little reluctant to take the ride again.

'It's a feather bed.'

'Is it anything like being stoned?'

Pross didn't even like getting stoned in public. It rendered him too defenceless. Tied his tongue up. Ron got stoned almost every day, sometimes even going to work in such a condition. Pross couldn't even go to the shop. Beyond his few close friends, everyone else spooked Pross after a smoke.

'It's a blessed balm for wounded hearts.'

Pross popped a pill.

2.5
The Examination

Simon had been one of the three High Priests of the Aetherius Society in London. There, ninety-seven people had taken notice of him every Thursday night. Except for the Thursday before last, that is, when he had presented his discovery of Prospero Pi-Meson's Truth to the meeting, whereupon the other two High Priests encouraged the faithful brethren to chase him out of the building. They would brook nothing of Simon's mad, seditious talk. Talk of the Creator having been a physicist. Talk of a young man, a prophet who had lost faith in himself but who was receiving telepathic messages from extraterrestrials. They would brook absolutely nothing of such nonsense — telepathic messages from extraterrestrials were wholly the privilege of their established leader, and anyone else who said they got them was obviously a liar.

But, encouraged in whispers by Mick, some of the brethren had later sought out Simon to hear more — especially about the multi-million pound fortune Mick had revealed Simon to be in possession of, a fortune about to be set to work on the advancement of the cause of all things paranormal and New Age.

And so, the next night, in his dirty bedsit, Simon elaborated upon his message to Mick and the straying nine.

The Godfrey Society was a natural advancement on the Aetherius Society, said Simon. The Aetherius Society had veered off course, missed the message, got it mixed up with Juda-Christianity which itself was a distortion and a twisting of the Truth as first revealed to Adam. But now a great unfolding in the convolutions of the Universal Truth was surely set to occur, and only they and Prospero Pi-Meson knew about it. Emissaries from other planets, other children of Godfrey, with civilisations, technologies and cultures so much more advanced than ours were now tentatively seeking to pass on their wisdom; their knowledge of the Creator. They were testing the receptivity of the squabbling human race to the Truth, investigating to see if planet Earth's society was ready. And the telepathically communicating aliens who had once sought to use the leader of the Aetherius Society as their instrument had now chosen another voice. 'It's all to do with Prospero, the Prophet, being on the right wavelength,' Simon had said, and there had been no one there to know any better.

Simon had also said that he had that day purchased a large property on the moors of County Durham, a property that the Prophet had revealed to be a cosmic hub. Ley lines galore. This was to be the pulsing heart of the Godfrey Society, and from there they would assail Prospero with their convictions, bringing him back into the fold. Humanity needed him if it were to reach the stars before destroying itself.

These people had taken so much notice of Simon that night that they promised soon to give up their London lives to assist in the establishment and running of the Godfrey Society's headquarters, help make it a paying venture by offering courses in New Age beliefs. Crystals, healing, and the like.

One of them, named Phil, had volunteered to permanently relieve the Aetherius Society of a prayer battery, finding himself unprecedently popular as a result.

And Simon and Mick had themselves travelled north the very next night, joined three days later by Phil, who had ridden up on his old motorbike, the stolen prayer battery strapped to it.

So now Mick was driving Simon and Phil and a fully charged prayer battery from the refuge in the moors down to Durham City, where they assumed Prospero Pi-Meson, Prophet of Godfrey, still to be living. Despite the influence of his cab's lights, it was darker out there than he was confident, and he seemed to take an amount of convincing before he'd accept that the road didn't fall off the edge of the world around each shadowy corner. He wasn't very good on hills, either. And if the corner happened to be on a hill, then his cab was sent into stutters.

It wasn't like Oxford Street at all.

'Ugh!' blurted Pross, 'it tastes fucking awful!'

'You're not supposed to chew it,' said Joe despairingly.

'I was curious,' protested Pross between grimaces. He then remembered that he'd left half a pint of beer inside and loped back in to see if it was still there.

It was, and he sank it to swill away the bitter pill.

He'd expected Joe to follow him in, but Joe was nowhere to be seen, so he went outside to look for him, but Joe was not there, either.

'Man of fucking mystery,' muttered Pross, who immediately began feeling almost as forsaken as when before Joe had distracted him. He was now at a complete loss to know what to do with his evening, let alone his life. He didn't want either of them. Still, he'd taken some new drugs, so that at least might provide a distraction. And even if the trip was to turn out bad, the prospect of a drug-induced psychological nightmare mercifully offered hope of something better than he was feeling right now.

He went back inside and bought another drink, sitting at the bar this time. For a Saturday night there were few people in, and no one he knew. Maybe people were attending firework displays? he reasoned. Over by the quiz machine were four local lads, and Pross couldn't help overhearing their philosophies, presumably culled from some Nazi-type party propaganda.

'And what about the Abo's? They're supposed to be about fifty generations behind us,' said one.

'They should be gassed,' said another.

How any of that throwback foursome could see itself as relatively advanced staggered Pross, and listening to their theories filled him with despair. The existence of those lads and the thousands like them made it all seem so hopeless to him. This was not a sanguine night for Pross, and listening to them made him think that he'd really had enough of life on this planet. Turning to address them, he said, 'And if you do gas them, who in the fuck is there going to be left for you to imagine superiority over?'

'Who in the fuck asked you to open y'poncy gob?' snarled one, once the shock of being challenged had passed.

They were an odious collection, and Pross realised he was actually spoiling for a fight with them. A fight against all that was wrong with the world, as perfectly represented by those four thickhead wastes of DNA, thickheads who for the span of their lives would be using up resources and polluting the planet, giving only their petty crime and aggression in return. But he wasn't really thinking about the justifications. He wasn't thinking at all. He just knew he was going to do something desperate. He'd had enough.

He could have argued eloquently, but he didn't. What he did was to make the pretence of replying, slipping off his seat to step towards them, then crashing his fist on to the bridge of the nose of the biggest one, then immediately hoofing another in the midriff. An attack was the last thing they were expecting. Both went down, the first silently and the second with a guttural utterance. He was being hit, he realised. Turning to his right, he brought a third person to his knees with a heedless attack. Three of the four were now down, and the fourth had disappeared somewhere, run away it seemed.

Less than ten seconds after the first blow, Pross was rushing out of the building.

But he hadn't done or said any of that. There had been no fight. He'd wanted to smash them so badly, imagined the scene, believed he would have emerged victorious, believed the attack would have been adequately brutal, but had done nothing, hadn't even challenged them verbally.

They were still at it, passing the shit around, not knowing how close they'd come to desperate retribution. But Pross's anger was subsiding. What was the point in getting upset about the ruination of the world? What was the point? What was the fucking point? It was all meaningless.

'Hello Pross, thought I'd find you here,' said a subdued female voice, and Pross realised that his heart had raced for a moment, thinking it was Jennifer. Turning around, he saw that it wasn't. It was her sister, and she was looking grave, but her expression seemed to soften a little when she saw that he himself was looking far from carefree. 'You picked a bad day to leave her,' she said, stood beside him in a long, black coat. She had no make-up on, and her hair was drawn into a tight ponytail.

'Why's that,' asked Pross, feeling awkward.

'It was two years ago today our parents died.'

'How was I to know?' he retorted, an unwelcome sense of shame being felt. 'She didn't say anything.'

'She wouldn't. Not her. I don't suppose she's very happy tonight, Pross.'

'Nor am I,' responded Pross, turning back around to face the spirit dispensers.

'She was happy. At least happier than she's been for two years,' said Sarah. 'Just wanted you to know that.'

'Are you thanking me or laying guilt?' he muttered, immediately regretting the crass, evasive, defensive gibe.

'Neither,' stated Sarah stiffly. 'Just wanted you to know she really liked you.'

Pross said nothing, except to suggest that they move to a table, out of earshot from the throwback foursome.

The impending conversation promised to be new ground for Pross. He had never really had to answer to anyone except himself before about true affairs of the heart. He wasn't relishing it.

'So why did you leave?' asked Sarah-Jane bluntly once they were both seated.

'Because I felt I should.'

'That's no answer.'

'Can't give any other one.'

Sarah was in a fearfully serious mood. This was threatening to become a heavy grilling, and Pross wanted out. He felt himself about to walk away, but forced himself to stay out of courtesy. And besides, he couldn't think of anywhere else to go.

'Is there something about her you don't like? Or did you just get bored with screwing her?'

'No. No,' said Pross immediately. 'She's a dream come true.'

'So why are you here and not with her?'

Sighing with exasperation, he realised he'd have to express a plausible answer otherwise he'd get no peace. After a struggle with contemplation, he said, 'Because I don't want to see her wasting her precious days chasing after what she thinks I am.'

'And what do you think she thinks you are?'

'Worth it,' said Pross decisively.

Upon that retort, Sarah cast a disapproving look his way, but then, much to his relief, she seemed about to let the issue slide. But although her stern look subsided, she remained horribly terse. 'Getting Jennifer out of her bedroom and into some company tonight seemed a pretty important thing, so I persuaded her to come this way without you to stay the weekend with me at Ron's mother's house. So if you want to see her, that's where she'll be later. Elaine's giving her a lift down. Ten o'clock the fireworks start.' Then, firmly, she added, 'But don't tell her I came looking for you.'

'Ron's mother hates me,' said Pross. 'She thinks I might corrupt him. Make him take drugs or shoot the queen or something.'

'His family's gone away.'

'I can't come. I really shouldn't see Jennifer,' he reasoned.

'Fine,' said Sarah, rising from her seat, obviously intending expending no more breath on the issue. 'See you around.'

She walked out.

Sitting with his drink, Pross was aware of a certain feeling of satisfaction arising from her departure. He felt in control. He felt solid and self-contained, just like he'd felt that morning when he'd left Jennifer's flat.

'Getting anything yet?' chirped a voice.

Pross looked up to see Joe.

'Where did you mysteriously disappear to?' asked Pross, a little curtly.

'The toilet, and then the bar to get a drink,' said Joe innocently, not understanding how Pross could have imagined he'd vanished.

'Oh,' said Pross, realising it was probably only five minutes since he'd seen him last. 'I looked for you.'

'Should have looked in the middle cubicle,' said Joe, now gazing in the direction Sarah had taken. 'Pity I missed your friend,' he sighed. 'I've seen her here before, haven't I? Who is she?'

'My girlfriend's sister.'

Joe sat down opposite Pross, wanting to know, 'How come you're looking so miserable tonight when you've got a girlfriend who probably looks like her?'

'I left her this morning.'

'So she's your ex-girlfriend,' deduced Joe, then speculating, 'Maybe someone else's girlfriend by now?'

Those two thoughts hurt Pross, and it must have shown.

'Sorry,' said Joe, shrugging his shoulders, 'just stating the obvious.'

It was obvious, but Pross found himself dwelling upon it now like it was suddenly horribly in danger of actually being real.

'Anyway, back to the original question. Are you getting anything yet?'

Pross was momentarily puzzled, but then realised that Joe was referring to what he himself had now forgotten: he'd taken some E.

'No, nothing at all.' He felt a little proud: he was immune to a reputed happiness drug. 'It'd take more than a tablet to affect my mood.'

Joe just gave a little smile.

Pross took a drink.

As did Joe.

'So,' said Joe, placing his palms together and leaning forward a little, 'tell me why you left your girlfriend this morning.'

'Oh for fuck's sake,' protested Pross, throwing his arms up, 'not another one. Why can't people give me a break?'

Joe gave another little smile. 'Just curious, that's all. Curious why you left her when it seems you want her still. At least it seems you don't want anyone else to have her.'

'Leave out the head examination, will you?'

'OK,' smiled Joe, immediately saying, 'So tell me about your childhood.'

Pross sighed with exasperation.

'Well tell me about your adulthood then,' laughed Joe.

Pross threw him a look.

'Well just tell me the bits I haven't read in the papers.'

'What have you read in the papers?'

'That your cat picked the winning lottery numbers, you lost the ticket but somehow proved your entry and got the money, pissed off the lottery people, lost the cheque and aren't getting another because you lost the ticket and pissed off the lottery people.'

'The cat's dead now, and that brings my life and all you need to know about it up to date.'

'OK,' smiled Joe.

Pross took a drink.

As did Joe.

Mere seconds later, Pross began to realise that he was feeling uneasy. Agitated, slightly. Anxious, slightly. Queasy, slightly. It was a very sudden thing, and he felt compelled to get up and use his limbs; walk a little. He told Joe he was going to the gents, a facility which he felt he needed to use anyway.

It was the drug, he realised. He was worried: this seemed like how he remembered coming up on acid. Now that it seemed imminent, he definitely didn't want a drug-induced psychological nightmare this night of all nights.

In the gents, he occupied a cubicle, taking first a tiny, nervous piss, then sitting on the edge of the seat to hopefully compose himself.

He became aware of visual changes. Like on acid, colours were becoming enhanced, but only subtly. His perception of space was becoming distorted too, but again only subtly.

He sat there for what seemed many minutes, waiting. Something big seemed poised to happen. He kept examining things to test for the onset of full-blown acid effects. Looking at the flesh on his hands; the door hinges; the ceiling; the pattern on his shirt. Nothing seemed to be more than subtly altered.

He waited some more.

This was ridiculous, he thought, he'd have to leave soon. He'd been here ages.

People were coming into the toilets. Two, at least. Talking. He recognised the loud idiocies: it was a couple of the throwbacks. Their presence allowed him to perceive that he now felt no anxiety whatsoever. In this town, on acid, or even dope, he would not have felt comfortable exiting the shelter of the cubicle while such unwholesome people were near, but now he felt no concern whatsoever.

Unbolting the door seemed like a symbolic emergence, and he even made a point of strolling to the basin, near to the urinal that the throwbacks were using, to wash his hands.

At the basin, he found himself looking across to the urinal gutter, the site of his cheque tragedy, fifteen nights earlier.

'Are you a fuckin' cock watcher, or what?' bellowed one of the pissers to Pross. His face had the drawn, sunken look shared by many jerky, aggressive males.

'You wish,' answered Pross, and fortunately for him the yobs didn't get the gibe before he added, 'My two million pound cheque's down that hole.'

Understanding came over the pissers.

'Are you the lottery one that lost ahll that fuckin' money?' said one, excited.

'Right where you're pissing,' answered Pross.

'Ah read ahll aboot that, like,' said the other one.

'You two are pissing on my dreams,' he said before leaving.

Coming out of the gents, he was aware that the room seemed more intimate and lively than before, brighter and warmer.

'Was I in there long?' he asked Joe before sitting down.

'Not really.'

'I'm definitely getting something *now*,' he remarked as he retook his seat.

'And how is it?'

He thought for a few seconds, then began to smile. 'I think it's going to be a feather bed.'

Joe smiled back.

Pross was intrigued with the effects. He was sweating slightly, but that was of no consequence. What was really significant was that he began to feel a sense of incredible freedom, like the brakes were being taken off him. Looking around the room, the people all seemed more animated. There was life here, and *he* was alive too. He seemed to be catching peoples' eyes all the time, and they were nice people. Happy, laughing people. And the women all looked radiant.

And the most intriguing thing of all was the dawning awareness of a grin beginning to spread itself across his face.

'So tell me why you left your girlfriend this morning,' said Joe.

The ambience suddenly changed for Pross. He seemed to become intimate with his own thoughts. 'I don't know,' he said quietly. 'I don't know.'

He fell silent.

'So tell me about your childhood, then,' said Joe.

'What do you want to know?' murmured Pross.

'The usual things. Was it happy?'

Pross was well aware that Joe was playing the analyst, but he had no objection to playing along with him since he seemed both able and keen to voice the things that he would simply mutely feel, or avoid feeling, or dismiss as irrelevant, at other times. The drug seemed to be allowing him the novelty of discussion without repression or fear of admission. He wanted to take this ride further, to see what could be seen. For the first time in his life, he knew he would not be throwing an automatic blanket of evasion over awkward questions. 'No, it wasn't happy, I suppose. But there were times when I was happy.'

'And when were they?'

A little reflection provided the answer. 'When I was outside, playing.'

'So you were mostly unhappy at home?'

Pross reflected some more. He was amazed by the clarity of thought encouraged by the drug. And what was important was that he was saying what he felt, not what he'd intellectualised. He'd always known he'd had an unhappy childhood and had been shaped by it, but now he was almost lamenting the discontent and not just cynically dismissing it.

'I was unhappy at home. That's where the unpleasantness was.'

'Abuse?' inquired Joe.

'No, no,' said Pross. 'Well... no sexual abuse, if that's what you mean.'

'There's other kinds of abuse.'

But Pross hardly heard him.

'The existence of sex was something never ever acknowledged in my house,' continued Pross quietly, almost entirely for his own ears. 'Neither was love,' he added. 'Love was a word absolutely never used.'

'That's a shame.'

'There was sporadic physical abuse at the hands of my father, but nothing too serious, although I bear one or two scars to this day.' Pross looked earnestly at his companion. 'But you see, Joe, it was the constant *likelihood* of anger and violence erupting that was most damaging, not the occasional blows themselves.'

'I can imagine.'

Pross began to look sad. 'My older brother and sister copped for much more of the real violence than I did,' he confessed. 'My brother was once strangled into unconsciousness by my father, and he seemed to have a particular dislike of my sister. Being the youngest, I was the most protected by my mother, who would make distraught pleas such as *Don't hit him on the head*, when violence erupted.' He paused there, as if viewing a distant scene, but then returned to Joe with another earnest, almost impassioned, observation. 'It was the absence of the normal love and affection *demonstratively* lavished on a child that was so wrong. I have no recollection of ever, ever, being touched affectionately. My mother, who certainly loved me, was unable to show her love in the normal, ever so important ways. I never even had my hand held.' A look of sad regret overcame him. 'Never even held my own mother's hand, not even when I was crossing the road. It was never offered, you see. And before long even if it had been offered, I would have slapped it down. The only time she ever tried to hug me was the same day she was committed to an institution. I was sixteen at the time, but she'd become convinced I was a little boy again. Wasted from self-inflicted starvation, dripping the Holy Water that foolish church gave her to banish her imagined demon tormentors, desperately clutching her Rosary Beads, she shambled over to me with her arms awkwardly outstretched. I sidestepped her and left the house.' He fell quiet before saying, almost apologetically, 'It's not that my parents were evil or calculating in the things they did, it's just that they were so feckless and ignorant.'

'You seem to have ambivalent feelings about them,' perceived Joe.

'I do. I do,' admitted Pross. 'If they'd been pure bad, it would be easier to live with. But they weren't bad, just inadequate. I don't feel any hatred or resentment for either of them; they did their crap best.' Looking Joe in the eyes, he continued, 'But I never loved them. Never even looked for love from them. I was able to shut them out of my mind. So by the time I was about thirteen, and my mother came shambling up to me to ask, out of the blue, if I'd be better off if she were dead, I said an immediate yes. The next day she overdosed, with my father's knowledge I'm sure. I found her unconscious when I came back from school, but I didn't even interrupt my plans for five minutes. Went out to kick a football around and bully a few kids.'

'But she didn't die?' realised Joe.

'No, she survived. And she kept on surviving. Overdoses; an electric fire in the bath; throwing herself under a bus.'

'Quite a guilt deposit you must have.'

'She never stopped making sacrifices to provide more materially for me,' rambled Pross cheerlessly. 'It was her perverted way of showing her love. She never spent any money on herself. Never. Got her ugly clothes from jumble sales; and hardly ever ate at all. Eating was too good for her, you see. And when she did eat, she did it standing up — sitting down was too good for her as well. Biscuits, fried eggs, stale bread and boiled potatoes constituted her entire diet.'

'You sound resentful,' observed Joe.

That comment seemed to spark Pross. 'Yes, I do feel resentment. I do. I resent that she neglected herself so much. But from a very early age, it was like I built a wall around myself. I saw what was happening, but didn't let it touch me.'

'That was the best way,' said Joe supportively.

'But I never let *anything* touch me,' countered Pross, 'or anybody. I became terribly defiant, rejecting all control and authority over me. And I became something of a loner too. I was hardly ever in the house. I was out on the streets all day long — bullying other kids, more often than not.'

'So how come you're so sweet now?'

Pross smiled. 'I bought a Simon & Garfunkel album when I was fourteen and it made me too maudlin to cause any more trouble.'

Joe laughed, but Pross had already become serious again. 'It was touch and go, Joe. Touch and go. I used to be a bully and a trouble maker, just about as delinquent a young case as you're ever likely to come across. But I guess it was my burgeoning intelligence that saved me. Were it not for me being smarter than most, I'm sure I'd be languishing in a cell right now. My life could have gone either way.' He paused to reflect, then said, 'But don't think I got clean away with it. Definitely not.'

'So what are the hangovers?'

Pross was jumping on the questions now. 'Insecurity. Definitely that. The perpetual feeling of being unwanted and unliked. If we're going to get analytical about it, maybe I was such a bully as a child because I was wanting to give people a decent reason *to* dislike me. A reason acceptable to me. I suppose I still try to make people dislike me in more subtle ways. I'm also a very insular person. I feel a little proud that I can ignore my desires for companionship, comfort and love.'

'That's something you shouldn't be proud of.'

'I know that,' retorted Pross, 'I know that. Anyway, it's a sham. It must be, I fall in love with just about every girl I ever see. You see, Joe, at the same time as rejecting affection, I also seem to desperately crave it.'

Pross knew he was saying things he'd partly said to himself before, and occasionally even to others. He'd even pulled out some of his pre-constructed, pithy sentences. But now it seemed deeper, whereas before it had just been detached reasoning. Now it was emotion. Now it was *him*, and not his intellect.

Joe was analytical in his aspect, pondering Pross's gushed words. 'So tell me, why do you still reject affection? Is it because you've never learned to trust it?'

'Must be,' answered Pross quietly.

'So tell me why you left your girlfriend this morning, even though you still want her.'

Joe's questions had finally brought Pross to the answer he knew he'd been dismissing all his life.

'Because I was scared,' he confessed quietly. 'Scared of ever *really* wanting someone. Ever depending on someone. Ever needing someone. I've got by by never needing or wanting anyone, not even my own mother.'

Speaking sympathetically, Joe said, 'You've kept that defensive wall up around yourself for too long. You're just scared to let anyone at all inside, where they can do you harm.'

'I know.'

'But they can also do you good,' said Joe. 'Maybe it's time you dared to let someone in. After all, you crave affection, you said so yourself.'

'I do. But I've always turned love into a big joke. It's always a joke with me. And every other need in life I might have is laughed at.'

'You're not laughing tonight.'

'No, I'm not.'

'Maybe it really is time you dared.'

'Maybe it is,' agreed Pross. 'It's never felt more fucking right, and if I've ever met someone worth the risk, it's Jennifer.'

'Then take the risk,' said Joe. 'Admit that you've been a coward, then be brave.'

'I admit it,' said Pross, becoming bolstered, 'and I'm going to be brave.'

That discourse had simply been the most profound experience of Pross's life. Never had he really, earnestly confessed his needs and wants and fears before, especially the fears.

'Well you'd better hurry up and find her before the drug wears off,' said Joe pointedly, but also smiling.

'And I tell you what else I'm going to do,' continued Pross, 'I'm going to get that fucking lottery money back.'

'Excellent behaviour,' smiled Joe. 'Hurry. Go and find her. Love her, and let her love you.'

Hurrying was suddenly paramount in Pross's mind. Joe was right, for despite the big, brave talk, when the drug wore off, he might lose his resolve.

He still had five of the ten pounds Melanie had lent him: enough to get a minicab to Ron's mother's house, where Jennifer was headed, on the edge of a village some three miles outside the city. He had to get there right away, especially considering that there was going to be fireworks — he certainly didn't want to miss those while tripping. He stood up, preparing to depart, but at once experienced a most overwhelming sensation, like a wave, or rush, of pure, warm, sweet bliss had passed over him.

'Wow,' he murmured, with a highly appreciative, far-out expression. 'Ecstasy.'

Joe smiled

2.6

The Great Mission

Joe had declined an invitation to go along with Pross, citing other bonfire party commitments for the evening.

Outside, on the steps of the Arts Centre, Pross paused to consider the perfect serenity of the evening. All was well with the world, except that he very soon began to feel cold, surely more cold than he would have normally felt.

'A small price to pay,' he laughed to the beautifully dark sky, and was at once overwhelmed by another wave of sensuous bliss.

Walking across the car park, he felt good — *so* good. Every sorrow he'd ever embraced was erased, every anxiety melted. The unredressed wrongs and unavenged insults of his lifetime were blown away like the insubstantial clouds that they surely were. Everything was beautiful and nothing hurt.

In fact he felt so overwhelmingly good, he was compelled to lie on his back on the little grassed traffic island, simply to enjoy the novel perspective.

A vehicle was nearing, but he paid it no heed. He didn't even look as it stopped right next to him. He just lay there, smiling hugely.

'Prospero?' inquired a nervous male voice from the vehicle.

Pross slowly turned his head to see Simon, formerly of the Aetherius Society, latterly of the Godfrey Society, pointing what he recognised to be a prayer battery at him through the side window of Mick's cab.

'Believe!' implored Simon as he pressed the button. 'Believe in yourself!'

'I do!' laughed Pross, throwing his limbs around excitedly, 'I do! I believe!'

Simon's spirit rose almost as high as Pross's. The prayer zap had worked! It had bloody-well worked! He had brought about a *bone fide* mystical miracle.

Pross jumped to his feet, then into the cab. Then he remembered something: 'Where's my word processor?' he asked of the driver.

Mick looked puzzled. 'Wot, y'mean that computer thing you left in the cab?'

'Yeah. Where is it?'

'Safe,' said Simon in the most convincing and appeasing way he could muster. 'We'll bring it back to you.'

'Excellent behaviour,' grinned Pross. 'Drive,' he called to Mick.

'Where to?'

'Onwards! Forever onwards!'

Throughout the ten minute drive to Croxdale, Pross was in full bullshi mode. 'Waiting,' he explained, squeezed in between Simon and Phil, answering Simon's inquiry as to why he had been lying on his back on the traffic island.

'For what?' Simon respectfully asked.

'That's the weird thing,' said Pross with an air of awed wonder, 'I'd just felt persuaded to remain there. I had this sort of vague feeling that something inescapable was going to happen... and then WHOOSH! You zapped me with belief.'

'Amazing,' breathed Simon. 'It would have been the forces working on you again, keeping you where we could find you.'

Temporarily playing along with Simon's lunacy again was getting him driven to Ron's mother's house for free. Anyway, it was damn good sport, so, shaking his head to show humbled defeat, he said, 'I can't deny it any longer. I've been chosen.'

He was too cramped. He wanted to sprawl, and at once decided that he should be the sole occupant of the cab's rear seat. So, with a foot, he pulled down one of the two spring-loaded, rear-facing cinema type seats and told Simon to sit on it. 'I need to lounge,' he explained. 'That was quite a blast you gave me. I'm winded.'

'Of course,' said Simon sympathetically, moving over.

'You too,' said Pross, addressing a person unknown to him, who also complied. Soon he was reclining across the full width of the cab's seat. It was also wonderfully warm inside the vehicle.

Sorted, he thought.

'I've never met a prophet before,' lisped Phil to Pross, trying his best to make conversation.

If Simon and Mick were weird, then Phil was weirder than the both of them stitched together by their knob ends. Phil was about five-nine, and in his twenties. Thin and feeble was his build, and his hooked nose and pointed features very much resembled those of the puppet, Punch. Punch — yes, that was it, decided Pross, that was who he reminded him of, except Phil lacked the commendable attitude. But he did have an appropriately squeaky voice, which clinched it for Pross.

Phil's voice was an improbable mixture of every mockable impediment available. Phil lisped. Phil spluttered. Phil camped. Phil's voice belonged in a Tex Avery cartoon.

Pross was about to say something in reply to Phil, when his world seemed to pleasantly wobble for a second or two, taking his attention away. It was if his eyes had sort of shuddered, which was closely followed by another wave of bliss. '*Yes*,' he breathed appreciatively.

'What is it?' asked Simon keenly. 'What happened to you? You went into a sort of trance.'

'I got a surge,' said Pross.

'Maybe we crossed a ley line,' suggested Simon keenly. 'You're really sensitive to ley lines, remember. You're on the right wavelength.'

'Yes, I'm on the right wavelength,' agreed Pross.

'Have you had any more extraterrestrial messages?' asked Simon intently.

'I'm getting a powerful one right now,' said Pross, producing the air of mystery that never failed to breeze Simon along with it, 'the strongest ever.'

Simon gawped.

'So that's it,' murmured Pross.

'What? What?'

Pross looked into Simon's bespectacled eyes, and said: 'Our great mission, Simon. Our great mission. The reason we've all been brought together. The greatest mission ever.'

Adrenalin gushed into Simon's bloodstream.

'What mission?'

Pross grasped Simon's shoulders and proclaimed: 'To succeed where Christ failed, Simon.'

The ambience instantly changed for Pross: became chilled. That was an intense thing to have said in his present condition.

'Great!' lisped Phil in his unique cartoon voice, as if a trip to the seaside for donkey rides had just been suggested.

Simon was awe struck.

Pross was somewhat struck, also, and he released his grip on Simon to lean back against the seat. It was the drug, he told himself, that was making things seem *so* profound. But nevertheless, the atmosphere felt so electric he actually began thinking that maybe it was true. Maybe he *was* on a mission? This dangerous thought insisted on surfacing, despite him trying to push it down.

He was inclined to become scared. Scared for his own sanity. This was a most unreal journey.

Aw, fuck it, he thought a second or two later, getting over his drug-induced, if somewhat fleeting, megalomania crisis. He was simply in a cab with two nutters and being driven by a third, having a laugh at their expense. And he was tripping to boot. The day he couldn't handle this sort of thing without thinking he'd been sent by the powers that be, would simply be the day he'd stop doing it.

Possession of his voice was now returned to Simon, who asked, 'What mission? Where did Christ fail?'

'The mission to create peace on Earth,' answered Pross.

'Great!' spluttered Phil, stroking his trimmed beard.

'How?' asked Simon.

'By influencing all minds with mine,' returned Pross, with passion rising, 'You see, Simon, this very night I achieved nirvana.' He held up a clenched fist. 'I am now Buddha. I am now Christ. I am the Saviour. I am Prospero Pi-Meson.'

'Amazing,' breathed Simon.

'Th'what's nirvana?' lisped Phil.

'The serenity in my soul,' answered Pross, relaxing to produce an example.

Then the biggest wave of nirvana yet hit Pross, and he virtually swooned.

'Another ley line?' asked Simon, thrilled.

For a purpose, Pross began chortling to himself.

'What is it?' asked Simon, smiling bewilderedly. 'Why are you laughing?'

'The Cosmic Masters just told me a space joke,' said Pross.

'Tell us it,' begged Phil.

'You wouldn't understand it. It has to be told telepathically.'

And so on for the next two minutes.

Tonight was Guy Fawkes night. Tonight was also a night he had exclusive occupancy of his mother's house with its adjoining paddock on the very edge of a small village. So Ron had brought the two elements together for the advancement of fun.

Ron was a big bloke, and he liked to do things big whenever he could, and he'd decided to do Guy Fawkes big this year. As well as the bonfire he'd amassed, for months he'd been spending too many pounds on display size fireworks bought from a local manufacturer.

He'd not told Pross about his collection because he knew Pross would have wanted to let them off straight away.

Sat in the uncomfortable tidiness of his mother's lounge, with it's unsettling flowery decor, Ron handed some of the bigger ones around for appreciation. 'They look like fucking mortars!' he said, schoolboyishly.

It was now past ten o'clock, and Ron was getting impatient. So, ushered by him, to the paddock the group headed.

It was a good night for fireworks. Dry with little wind, and reasonably mild.

Down the far end of the field, Ron threw a makeshift lighted torch on to the petrol-drenched bonfire, and quickly it was ablaze, churning out rising folds of dense smoke.

A few minutes later, he lit the first firework.

2.7
The Golden Millennium

As the cab came to a stop, Pross clumsily manoeuvred his way out, ending his fantasy conversation with Simon mid-sentence, such was his hurry to see Jennifer.

Approaching the front door of Ron's absent folks' house, passing down the dark drive many parked cars, some, such as Lilith's and Melanie's, he recognised, some he didn't, a loud thud sounded from beyond. Moments later a sphere of light burst high in the sky above his head.

Nearing the door, his presence triggered a security light.

On the edge of the village, well away from the dissecting trunk road, Ron's family home, with its adjoining paddock, was a very private place. Along one side of the one acre paddock ran a disused railway line; the back and other side were bordered by a farmer's field; and the remainder was bordered by the house and its outbuildings.

Ringing the doorbell proved fruitless: everyone was surely in the paddock.

Mick, Simon and Phil were soon stood by Pross's side.

'Whose house is this?' lisped Phil. 'Th'why are we here?'

Pross ignored him, the problem of entry now being the only question needing to be resolved: ecstasy, it seemed, did not confer fantastic multi-tasking capabilities to the brains of its users. Although he had been enthusiastically bullshitting his followers all the way there, he was now annoyed with them pestering him with distracting questions, and wished they'd leave him alone.

Tonight was for Jennifer. Tonight was for love.

'See you around lads,' he said, enjoying the sadism of deflating them. He started towards a short fence fortified with bushes which, if scaled, would put him in the desired field.

Simon was troubled. He seemed to be losing his prophet again. It was just like it had been two weeks ago.

'Th'where are you going?' asked Phil.

'Bugger off. I'm not the Saviour and you can't come with me. I'm staying the rest of the night here, and I'll thump anyone who disturbs me.'

'Th'why?' spluttered Phil.

'Don't question him,' rebuked Simon immediately, sensing that Phil was becoming an irritation to the Saviour.

'Th'sorry,' lisped Phil sheepishly.

Having reached the fence, Pross found that ecstasy wasn't at all good at helping a person climb a two metre impediment.

He stood in front of it and puzzled.

The trio were soon annoyingly by his side.

'What about the mission?' asked Simon. 'When do we start?'

'What mission?' said Pross, preoccupied with figuring out how to climb a small physical impediment. Lifting a foot on to what looked like a suitable step, another rush of hallucinogenic bliss buffeted him, delaying his ascent.

'The mission to create peace on Earth,' pursued Simon.

No answer.

'Can't we th'watch the fireworks th'with you?' asked Phil, who just couldn't seem, for more than two seconds at a time, to grasp the magnitude of the situation: of being in the company of the saviour of mankind.

Simon gave Phil a look that triggered Mick into action. Mick suddenly rounded on Phil, his accent gaining strength for the job, 'Wot's the facking maa'er wiff y'. Can't y'keep it shat?'

The viciousness of Mick's jumpy assault, verbal but almost physical, cowed Phil into silence.

The trio sensed a landing, and realised that their saviour had jumped down to the other side of the fence while they'd been squabbling, putting them asunder.

But Simon was no longer perturbed. He'd just had a revelation of his own: he would simply just have to keep firing prayer energy at Prospero to overcome his sporadic antipathy.

'It's OK,' said Simon to his two disappointed companions. 'I know what to do. We'll go back to the house to put some more charge into the battery, then we'll come back and get Prospero in the morning.' Walking to the cab, he said, 'Come on, back to headquarters.'

Phil was disappointed. 'Are we going already?' he spluttered. 'Can't we ssstand here a bit and th'watch the fireworks?' Then he remembered that he was supposed to be keeping himself quiet and cast a nervous look towards Mick before following his companions to the cab.

During the ride back to the moorland house, Simon fell deep into thought.

Having climbed the fence, Pross could see fewer familiar faces in the firelight than unfamiliar ones — people from Ron's ex-work place and friends of Sarah, he was to learn. But Pete and Suzy were there. So were Nicky and Karl. Melanie, Tony and Lilith were also visible.

Lilith. Poor Lilith. He hadn't seen her since the night he'd lost his lottery cheque. She was laughing now, he could see, but he knew she was about to be hurt seeing him with Jennifer. But that couldn't be helped, he told himself, feeling troubled. Then a smile came to his face when he pictured how over-the-moon Ron would be to learn that he was going to try to get the lottery money.

It was going to be a good night. Everything was going to be beautiful.

The aroma of bonfire and gunpowder reached him.

Another thud: more felt than heard this time. A dimly fizzing projectile coursed skyward. Halting to follow it up, viewing it through hazy smoke as it voyaged awe-inspiringly high to explode into an overwhelming sphere of light that almost spanned his full field of vision, Pross began to fancifully imagine that he was witnessing the very birth of the universe, each point of light on the expanding sphere being an entire galaxy forming out of the primeval dust.

As the last galaxies of the burning sphere surrendered to the night, he proceeded towards the group. He was moments away from real intimacy. Moments away from admitting and explaining that he'd been too blind and proud to see beyond his own defences. Moments away from honestly asking her to accept him back. Moments away from daring to love. Moments away from her summer rain kisses.

She wasn't there.

He stood still, tiny firelights flickering in his eyes.

The gathering noticed him. His friends called his name and beckoned. He did not move. His friends were puzzled. Sarah-Jane, hands dipped into coat pockets, came forward. 'Changed your mind?' she observed approvingly as she neared him.

With understated urgency, he asked, 'Is she here? Where is she?' It had not even occurred to him that she might not be waiting for him. The disappointment was sobering, and his naive, drug-assisted reunion optimism faded like the vividness of a dream upon waking.

Her voice conveying sympathy, Sarah said, 'Sorry. She hasn't turned up. You know what she's like.' Viewing his face by firelight, Sarah could see that he was deeply upset. She just didn't know what to make of him. He was a pendulum and a conundrum.

Murmuring, 'I'll ring her now,' leaving Sarah behind, Pross turned to walk the fifty yards or so over to the house, a dim wedge of light from an open back door being his beacon. At the door, he triggered another security light. The door led into the kitchen, and the kitchen, he observed, had a telephone fixed on the wall. Sitting at a pine table, he dialled Jennifer's number. Scared is what he suddenly felt, waiting for his lover's voice. What was he going to say to her? That everything was going to be different from now on because he'd taken a drug? That wouldn't sound too good.

The dialling tone sounded strangely small and distant: that was the E, he reasoned. He worried that he might not be able to make sense of what would be said to him.

He was almost relieved to hear Jennifer's answering machine activate. But this is what he further heard:

'Sarah, I know you'll phone wondering why I haven't come to Ron's. I've decided to go away somewhere. I'll have left by the time you ring. I know you'll worry about me, but don't, I'll be all right. I can't tell you where I'll be because I don't know myself yet. Anyway, Aunty Jane might come looking for me — you know what she's like with me. Sorry for it all being so sudden, but I had to do it tonight, especially after what happened between me and Pross. If I don't do it I think I'll die tonight. Bye. Don't worry. Love you.'

There was no immediate shock or outcry, or even in-cry. He just listened with unnatural impassivity.

After listening, slowly he let the receiver slip from his fingers on to the table. Just as slowly, his head fell into his hands. But all at once he became egotistically conscious of the drama inherent in the scene, imagining how he must look to a sympathetic observer. Then his earlier quirky preference for a drug-induced psychological nightmare came to mind, and he began indulging in the spooky irony, running away with the notion. This gathered pace until another bomb exploded on high to arrest the intense introspection.

Suddenly there was stark, hollow grief. Lifting his head, then standing, he slowly replaced the receiver, feeling much like he was sprinkling dirt on to a coffin, too numbed to cry.

To her surprise, there had been very little to pack, two manageable suitcases having proved sufficient for her immediate needs, reasoning that anything else required could either be bought or sent for. And, having reached eighteen, with full access to her half of the inheritance established, money would not be tight.

She had no idea at all what she was headed for, and that prospect seemed appropriate: Pross had casually abandoned her, so she would casually abandon herself. A cheque to cover two months rent was left for Elaine; an apologetic message was left on her employer's answering machine; and the outgoing message on her own answering machine was changed so that Sarah or her aunt would discover that she had gone.

At nine o'clock a minicab had been called to take her to Darlington

train station.
And that had been Jennifer's life untied.

It *was* like she was suddenly dead to him, except he knew it was he that was dead, cast into some other world. Walking away from the house and over to his laughing friends in the field felt like leaving her graveside after the funeral. No more balmy waves of druggy bliss were to wash over him. All the drug had for him now was an almost palpable feeling of loss.

Before he was even fully aware of being within the crowd, the crowd had gathered that he was out of his head on something, and not at all happy.

Sarah-Jane wished to know about her sister. Pross lied to her, or at least he concealed the truth. 'She didn't want to come,' he said, feeling guilt for being the agent of her undoing.

'Typical of her,' said Sarah. Noticing how affected he seemed, she asked, 'Are you all right?'

Looking away from Sarah's eyes, he accidentally caught Lilith's. This was the first time he'd seen her since the night he'd lost his cheque. She smiled at him. He couldn't smile back.

'Are you all right?' asked Sarah again.

'I'm tripping,' he returned with a calculated air of weariness, 'I don't really want to talk.' Walking a little away from the festivities, in the shadows he found a log to sit on.

He was tripping, and didn't really want to talk: that is what went around.

Occasionally, amid the laughter, one of the girls, usually Lilith, would remember about him and venture to ask him if he was all right, and he would answer that he was, although having a bit of a bad time. 'It'll pass,' he would shrug his shoulders and say. So, although sometimes viewed with concern, he remained alone on his damp log, face warmed a little by the fire, saying next to nothing for much of the night but dwelling upon his loss in deafening, repercussive silence; the fireworks, laughter and spitting of the barbecue being like distant sea sounds to him.

Ron had not yet acknowledged his presence. Pross wanted to tell him that he'd decided to try to get the lottery money back, but felt somehow inhibited from saying it now.

As the night aged, he became aware, in unexpected increments, of welcome lessenings of the drug's influence upon him, and as he ascended from the numbing, cold deep, like a bubble in oil, he found himself looking Lilith's way more and more often. He felt so for her. She was so worthy of happiness, but would never have what she wanted most in life: him. It was easy for Jennifers, but Liliths had no hope.

The next time Lilith gave him her concerned attention, he almost reached out and took her in his arms, so much did he want to comfort her. It would be like making amends for everything bad he'd ever done in his life, not least hurting Jennifer. He'd sacrifice himself for someone else's happiness. She could have him for the rest of his life. He was strong like that. And who knows, maybe he would grow to worship her? Lilith. Dear Lilith. Maybe she was what he *really* needed in life. Maybe that's why he'd left Jennifer, because deep down he knew he should be with Lilith, whose attractions obviously had no superficial element... or was he just indulging in idiotic guilt and speculation. No, Moaning Joe had shown him why he'd left Jennifer — but that seemed so theoretical now.

Suddenly annoyed with himself, he squeezed his eyes tightly. Fuck it: he wished he could stop his mind. There was turmoil in there now.

He wanted to join his friends closer in by the glowing fire, but could not do it, realising he was particularly reluctant to face Ron. Was Ron really giving him the cold shoulder tonight? Or was he simply imagining it in his drugged condition? He wasn't sure. He had asked to be left alone, after all.

Sometime just before midnight saw the departure of the last stranger to him. Only Ron, Sarah, Melanie, Tony and Lilith remained, sitting on chairs and logs by the dying fire. Finally, he summoned what seemed to be the necessary courage to move into the group, shuffling over to sit beside Lilith.

She turned gently surprised eyes to him, and he noticed how large they appeared without their usual frame of hair. 'You all right now?' she asked.

He managed to quietly say something to make her laugh, then soon became captivated by the whispering flames.

His friends simply continued chatting and dreaming between themselves.

As the drug deserted him more, and the fire's embers became ashen, he began to feel an unbearable emptiness, and was disturbed to find himself picturing, almost hallucinating, Jennifer's face clear in his mind's eye. Hurt and confused, endlessly she was turning away from him.

Unaware he was actually vocalising, he murmured, 'Don't leave me. Please don't leave me.'

'Who?' said Ron, puzzled.

The voice jolted Pross. Without the emotional honesty conferred by the drug, he found himself instinctively searching for cover, feeling reluctant to admit his fear of losing Jennifer. 'The deep-eyed, melancholic Enchantress of the dying fire,' he said with affected sadness. 'She's stealing away now to her woodland grove, leaving my sighing heart longing for her sorrowful beauty.'

'I've shagged her,' boasted Ron, eliciting loud laughs from his stoned friends. Moments later, he rose to his feet, 'Anyone coming inside?' he said, Pross feeling he'd been deliberately excluded from the invitation.

First, Sarah-Jane stirred. Then the others stirred. But as Lilith made to stand up, Pross, sitting next to her, gripped her hand, almost desperately. 'Please,' he whispered, 'stay here with me.'

Lilith hesitated, unsure and a little apprehensive.

As the others moved away, Pross said, 'You can have me, Lilith. I'm yours forever. You deserve me.'

Lilith was silent until, with an almost dismissive air, she said, 'Sorry, Pross. Can't keep you company any longer. Told my boyfriend I'd pick him up from work when his shift finishes. I'm going to be late already.'

'Boyfriend?' murmured Pross unbelievingly. 'You don't have a boyfriend. You've never had a boyfriend.'

Coldly extricating her hand from his, she said, 'Go inside with the others. You'll catch your death out here without the fire.' And then she walked away, leaving him helplessly alone below icy stars and a rising moon. He watched her fade into the night, then let out a resigned breath that seemed to take all his life away with it. Pulling his knees up to his chin, he endured impassive solitude until the fire's last fading glow lay weeping alone amid the ashes of its life, when finally the full crassness and arrogance of his offer to Lilith sunk home, and he groaned his bitter regrets into the night.

And then he could hold back no longer, and sobbed uncontrollably.

In the big room, only candles lit the faces of the three followers of Godfrey, bedecked in their Aetherius Society robes for a special Mass.

Draughts dramatically flickered the flames.

To conduct the ominous meeting, Simon stood on a box to elevate his authority. In his hand he had the book that contained the teachings of the Aetherius Society. He lifted this book high when he spoke. 'Prospero Pi-Meson is not a just a prophet — he is the prophecy. He truly is the Expected One, the one the book foretells. The one who is to prepare Earth for the great millennium of peace. Everything he said confirms it.'

'Great!' spluttered Phil, eliciting embarrassed shuffles from Mick.

Enraptured by his own conclusions, Simon read aloud from the Aetherius book: 'His magic will be greater than any ever seen on Earth. Happiness will abound come the Golden Millennium that is nigh. There will be no more war, or sickness, or old age. All those who do not heed his words will be removed from the Earth, and the good will live without sinners in their midst.'

And Simon was just as convinced of his own role in bringing about the

Golden Millennium: to zap Prospero, the Expected One, whenever his belief in himself weakened, that's what his task on Earth was. That was his hugely important part in the great Cosmic Scheme. Perhaps within Prospero, the great battle between Good and Evil, foretold in the Teachings, was being waged at this very moment, and if won by Good, the Golden Millennium would then dawn.

And with concentrated prayer energy, he could tip the balance in favour of cosmic enlightenment whenever it was necessary.

It was time to begin recharging the battery, declared Simon, pointing dramatically to it in the centre of the bare room, atop its tripod. 'No one sleeps tonight. Every man-minute of prayer will be needed to charm the Expected One back here, where the forces are concentrated. Then the New Age will dawn at last.'

Moments later, now holding hands with Mick and Phil to form a ring, Simon began chanting sacred chants while all together they turned slowly around the instrument that was crucial to world peace.

Om, wallah wallah, om. Om, wallah wallah, om. Om, wallah wallah, om. Om, wallah wallah, om. Om, wallah wallah, om. Om, wallah wallah, om. Om, wallah wallah, om. Om, wallah wallah, om. Om, wallah wallah, om. Om, wallah wallah, om. Om, wallah wallah, om. Om, wallah wallah, om. Om, wallah wallah, om. Om, wallah wallah, om. Om, wallah wallah, om...

But then Phil had an asthma attack and had to drop out, falling asleep on the floor soon after, curled up in a corner.

The two remaining believers steadily circled the battery until break of day.

2.8
The Final Irony

The house lights had long been switched off. For an hour or so after Lilith's departure he'd sat hunched on the log in the dark, crying until it hurt, then crying some more. Then just emptily sitting. But eventually he succumbed to fatigue and made to stand up to walk over to the sleeping house. His legs were stiff and unresponsive: cold through to the bone, he realised.

He also realised that, psychologically at least, the drug had now all but worn off, opinions and abstractions replacing unhampered emotions.

But physically he felt feeble.

The security light blazed into operation, startling him.

Half expecting to find it locked against him, he entered the house by the kitchen door, and once within, he tortured himself in a way he knew he would not be able to resist: he again dialled Jennifer's number to listen to the message. But listening, he found, was different this time, the drug no longer an issue. He was mentally more resilient. His defences were much re-established.

The message played, the receiver replaced, he stared into nothing for some minutes. Eventually, more out of resignation than of generosity, he murmured, 'I wish you every happiness, Jennifer.'

Jennifer was gone who knows where, and it all seemed so ironic. She'd gone off to find a new life, it seemed, and for sure would forget about him soon. He'd come of age just a few hours too late. A few hours earlier and he could have spoken to her before her disappearance.

Irony. His life was full of fucking irony. Always had been.

It now occurred to him, for the first time, that Sarah-Jane would blame him for Jennifer's flight. And Ron, in sympathy with his girlfriend, would also censure him. The way things had gone lately between Ron and him, there might even be a scene, and that was something he couldn't face. He couldn't face any of his friends again. He had hurt so many of them, it seemed.

Alone in the living room was where he spent the rest of the night's dark hours. For some reason, a duvet had been left out on the sofa, and, more for the warmth it promised than for the prospect of sleep, he pulled it over himself.

Not once did he knowingly dip into sleep.

The wide sofa accommodated his restless body until the dawn's first light made nebulous, swaying silhouettes of the bare-boughed trees overhanging the paddock. Lying on his side, gazing one-eyed through the glass patio doors, he began to fancy that the mysterious, mighty trees had converged silently, inexorably, during the night, like some great encircling army of most secret nature and fell power, finally but resolutely moved to vengeful action by some no-longer-to-be-suffered injustice.

Beckoned by the scene, sliding open the cold patio doors, he stepped out into the still, pristine world of the early morning, wandering slowly across the dewy field and over to the log upon which he had sat much of the night.

With great whooshes of its wings, a heron beat its way into the air from the branches of the tree above him.

Soon he found himself reseated on the log, staring emptily at the cold ashes of the bonfire, now grey as the sky above.

A new day was dawning, and for once he was up before the world, but this was another irony, for everything was over for him, he felt. It was closing time for him. He didn't know what to do or what would become of him. He'd never felt so contrary to things, and this time the contrariness had never seemed so malign. It was all futile. Not only was there no place for him in this world, this world seemed to have been subtly devised to slowly break him, maybe eternally break him. Everything that happened to him was part of some punishing design. And whenever he *had* been lifted by hope, it was only to make the inevitable fall harder still. Death by Disappointment.

And now he was becoming superstitious. It was surely the *final* irony.

Finding himself seriously, consciously, entertaining a "singled out for punishment" philosophy scared him a little, more the thinking of it than the thought. His mother used to think that way. Thought her way to mental hospital that way.

Mercifully halting him on his morbid track, his attention was diverted by rustling in the undergrowth nearby, but, turning his head, he could not see the animal culprit.

Looking down again, he noticed the impression of his own shoes in the earth, made the night before. He could scarcely believe that only a few hours earlier he'd been sat in the very same place. It seemed like some distant dream-time.

But last night *had* happened, and an undeniable memory of it remained. He *had* deeply expressed long-dismissed fears and wants to Joe. He *had* determined to re-establish his relationship with Jennifer. He *had* been devastated when he'd failed to find her. He *had* resolved to regain his wealth.

He *had* looked penitently to Lilith for redemption. And although the drug had completely worn off now and the intensity of the experience was much dimmed looking back along from but a short length of Time's misty road, the insights surely held true, and he suspected that if ever he was to be content in this world, he would need to use that precious knowledge.

The ugly dead fire began to revolt him, and he was moved to anger at himself for wasting time looking at it. Passing down to the far end of the field, he leaned up against a post sunk into the earth beneath a dark, looming tree.

Decisions were unexpectedly reached. Powerful decisions. Returning indoors, he set about writing a letter for Sarah-Jane to pass on to her sister. The letter was an explanation and an apology.

It began thus:

Dear Jennifer,

Please excuse me the necessity of writing you this letter, but there's so much I have to say to you before I can rest tonight...

By seven a.m., the letter to Jennifer was complete. It told honestly of many things. It told of the things that had happened to him since seeing her last, the things which had opened his eyes to his own fears. It told of those fears. It told of running away from the terror of being abandoned. It told of his conversation with Moaning Joe. It told of his trip. It told of how he had soared on the expectation of a reunion with her, only to have his world come crashing down. It told how sorry he was. It told of how much he had adored her, and how he knew he would never meet another so irresistibly right for him again. It told of how quickly he had been growing to truly love her, and that was surely why he felt he had to leave.

It wished her every happiness.

This letter he left lying open for Sarah to find whenever she might awake. He also left a separate letter for Ron, expressing remorse for losing him his job and flat, saying that he would make it up to him, maybe try to get his lottery money back for that purpose, even though he didn't rate his chances much and knew the newspapers would find out and ridicule him. The letters placed prominently, he quietly left the house, walking back towards Durham for he knew not what. He certainly wouldn't feel comfortable staying at Melanie's much longer. Anyway, he'd only bring ruin to her — he brought ruin with him everywhere. He was putting himself in isolation from people he cared about from now on. It was the least, and the most, he could do. '*To humbly express a penitential loneliness,*' he muttered deridingly, tramping the lane leading from the house.

He began wondering how much money he had in the world. Exploring his pockets revealed himself to be worth a single five pound note plus a few pence in coppers, and that was borrowed money. But he knew he could never get a job, let alone hold one down, if only because there would always be a Scoones somewhere in the equation, and he couldn't even tolerate a Scoones by proxy, let alone directly.

He also had three tabs of E left, but couldn't imagine ever feeling inclined to take those rides.

Quarter of a mile down the lane, where the cinder of the unclassified road met the dual carriageway to Durham City, upon seeing a simple bench made from an old railway sleeper, it became apparent to him that his limbs needed a little bit of rest before he could proceed with walking.

He was suddenly dead beat.

And so, despite the cold, he lay himself down on the damp bench, eyes soon closing, the passing of vehicles and the occasional cinder-crunching pedestrian sounding strangely remote and lulling.

And what was intended to have been a short rest became a shivery, post-drug-trip drowsy state that was more akin to hypnotic chemical sedation than wholesome sleep, strange, fleeting images coming uninvited into his mind.

Forty minutes later, curled up as best he could manage, he was struggling to comprehend a chanting drone seeping into his consciousness.

Om, wallah wallah, om. Om, wallah wallah, om. Om, wallah wallah, om. Om, wallah wallah, om. Om, wallah wallah, om. Om, wallah wallah, om. Om, wallah wallah, om. Om, wallah wallah, om...

Half-opening his eyes, he encountered an unreal sight: Simon in long, embroidered red religious robes aiming a prayer battery at him. Behind Simon was Mick, in a plainer, white robe. Behind Mick was Mick's cab, its back door open. Inside the cab was Phil, also in a white robe, sat on one of the rear-facing pull-down seats, guiltily gnawing a Mars Bar like he was embarrassed to show his teeth or be seen eating it at all.

'Believe and come with us,' ordered Simon, striking the zap button.

And then he waited.

Pross lifted his head and remembered that he was supposed to be succeeding where Christ had failed, or something like that. He soon lay his head back down again — succeeding where Christ failed strongly seemed to be a kind of afternoon type thing.

Simon began chanting again.

Pross took another look at the cab. In particular, he looked at the comfy seat. Taking a deeper breath, he rolled off the cold bench and crawled, hands and knees, towards it, passing geriatric dog-like under Simon. Once within, he hauled himself horizontal on to the large, wide, warm back seat.

Simon and Mick exchanged looks: not as dramatic a miracle as the previous night, but at least the Expected One was where they wanted him.

After bundling the prayer battery into the cab, Simon pulled down the other rear-facing seat and occupied it.

Mick got into the driver's seat and started the engine.

Lying horizontal, looking with indifferent despair at Simon and Phil, who in turn were looking apprehensively back at him, Pross decided that the best thing he could do in life was to close his eyes and keep them that way for as long as he could.

But at least it was warm in the cab.

Half asleep in her dressing gown, Sarah-Jane shuffled downstairs to make herself coffee. A letter she soon found and read. Despite it revealing that her sister had abruptly left for who knew where, the letter made her cry for Pross; and all the doubts and misgivings about him that had ever surfaced in her mind, she now shamefully regretted.

Even Ron cried a little when he read it.

2.9
Anonymity

The journey through the night had given Jennifer much time to reflect upon what she was doing, and she had come to the opinion that what she was doing was not really important. What *was* important was that she was doing *something*. And the plan for this particular something was that for the first week only she would treat London much like she was on holiday, staying in a hotel, but after that she would try to find work and somewhere to live.

Jennifer knew enough about London to know that King's Cross Station was a haunt of drug addicts and prostitutes. If unsavoury things were indeed inclined to happen there, she found that they were certainly not inclined to happen at seven o'clock in the morning, the time her train arrived in the capital city.

Struggling to pull down her suitcases from the high rack above her seat, a helpful voice sounded behind her.

'Please, allow me.'

'No, it's all right,' she found herself saying, about to continue the struggle.

'It doesn't look all right,' laughed the voice, as an arm came over her shoulder to pull down her suitcases for her.

The cases were deposited at her feet, and Jennifer thanked the young man, the first black person she had ever spoken to in her whole life. This detail she consciously thought as she stepped off the train, following the stream of people.

Once beyond the ticket barriers, she put her cases down and looked about herself.

It seemed a different world.

The man who had helped her with her cases was about to pass by. She felt sure he would try to talk to her, but he walked straight past and went on his way. Everyone was just on their way, and it hit her that for the first time in her life she was completely anonymous. In Richmond, every fifth person who saw her would have known what street she lived in. But not here. A thousand people she reckoned to be in her sight, but not one of them had ever seen her before, or would ever knowingly see her again.

She liked that.

She picked her cases up and walked.

2.10
A Big Move Up

Nervous silence reigned until Pross, unremittingly horizontal, slowly began to realise that they'd been travelling too long to be headed into Durham City.

Opening his eyes and staring nowhere important, too tired and dispirited to care enough to sit up, he quietly uttered, 'I don't want to go this way.'

No one responded.

A few moments later, he turned his lobotomized gaze away from nothing and on to Simon, who became troubled and nervous. 'I said I don't want to go this way.'

More silence.

It dawned on Pross, with merely a sense of impatient exasperation, that he was being kidnapped by inept loonies. So, reaching a hand forward, he gripped Simon's knee, squeezing out the rhythm of his sentence: 'I — said — I — don't — want — to — go — this — way.' Finished squeezing, he held a stare at Simon, who was either mutely defiant though terrified, or just mutely terrified. He couldn't tell which.

Slyly fumbling, Simon pressed the zap button on the prayer battery, hoping that a trickle might remain. As he did this, he miraculously conjured up an excuse for whisking Pross away and found a voice with which to convey it. 'We're going to get your word processor for you first.'

Although not entirely convinced, Pross closed his eyes again, too tired to bother further. Besides, one place was as good as another to him now. In fact, his life had turned so bad that being kidnapped was a big move up — at least he was warm now.

Suddenly Phil lisped something irrelevant. 'Th'we've been up all night!' he said, childlike.

Opening his eyes to look at Phil, Pross noticed for the first time that he had a small piece of pink tissue paper lodged in his trimmed beard.

'Have we crosse'th one yet?' continued Phil's lisp.

'Shhh,' urged Simon in a low voice.

Pross closed his eyes again. 'Crossed one what?' he asked with a mixture of intolerance and weariness.

'A ley line,' explained Phil, oblivious to Simon's wish for him to keep quiet. 'That's th'where we're going now. Back to the house that's got lots of them. A special bedroom's been prepared for you and everything. Th'Simon says we have to get you back there so you can th'start the Golden Millennium.'

Golden Millennium? wondered Pross between wondering why he'd ever been born.

Relieved that the former menacing manner had departed, Simon leaned towards Pross, saying quietly, 'I've bought it, Prospero. I've bought the house with the ley lines.'

A few silent seconds.

'What, the one I was going to buy with my lottery money?'

Simon nodded, although Pross's eyes were still closed. 'It's going to be the Godfrey Society's headquarters.'

More silent seconds.

'Where did you get the money from? It was hundreds of thousands.'

Simon was instinctively subdued, and sat back in his little seat.

'It th'was his own money,' blurted Phil, additionally spluttering, 'He's got millions and millions in the bank.'

Bedroom, thought Pross, I definitely heard him say bedroom.

And he fell asleep.

Ten minutes later, the vehicle rolled to a halt outside the large, rusted wrought iron gates that excluded the world from Simon's new house. 'We're here, Prospero,' said Simon portentously. 'At the focus of the forces.'

Pross came out of his slumber and partially sat up, looking about himself. They were indeed at the place he'd planned to buy himself.

'I need a th'wee,' said Phil suddenly, scrambling out of the cab like he'd left it to the very last second. Round behind some bushes growing wild beside the gates he ran, his robe catching on thorns and ripping a little.

Mick also got out of the cab, his face bearing its customary tense frown as he walked over to work the lock of the gates, his robe dragging a large twig with it.

He looked like some particularly jumpy Ku Klux Klanner.

Soon Phil was scurrying back from behind the bush, anxiously examining his torn robe.

A minute later, gates having been opened, onwards they were soon rolling, rolling slowly along the private autumn-leaved wooded lane of the house and estate where Pross had once envisaged living in secluded contentment.

A tatty black and rusted-chrome motorcycle was parked in front of the house.

Mick drew his cab up beside it.

'That's my motorbike,' said Phil to Pross.

Motion ceased, Simon looked at Pross with grave eagerness. 'When does it all start?' he asked.

'Where's my bedroom?' returned Pross.

'The Golden Millennium — when do we start?' pursued Simon.

'Bedroom,' said Pross, opening the door.

The passengers stepped out into the morning sunshine. It was a beautiful autumn day, still and damp, and the grand house was arrayed in wind-remnant patches of red and gold ivy.

Phil looked at Pross. 'You've got an amazing aura,' he lisped. 'I've never seen such a ssstrong aura on anyone. I can th'sense auras, you know?'

'Bedroom,' said Pross to Simon with increased insistency.

Obliging his wish for rest, straight to his room did Simon take Pross, up the grand, wood-paneled staircase and along the entire length of the dingy west corridor.

Having arrived outside the room, when Simon looked like he was about to say something, Pross opened the door himself, entered, and closed it behind him, excluding his guide.

He could smell fresh paint.

The room was barely larger than the bed it concealed. The walls were a dark, old-blood red. The high ceiling was white. Two small crystal pyramids were set on wrought iron stands at either side of the headboard. Above the headboard was a shelf, groaning with volumes. Reading the spines revealed the works to cover numerology, spiritualism, pyramid power, and magic. But most of the books dealt fancifully with crystals: dowsing with crystals; healing with crystals; the "Universal Energy of Crystals"; aura balancing with crystals; aura cleansing with crystals; releasing one's inner power with crystals; and just about everything else with crystals excepting a genuine usage, like putting some on fish and chips. Badly painted symbols akin to the ones on Simon's robes adorned the walls. Pamphlets about the Aetherius Society lay on the bed. So did a robe similar to Simon's, but in gold, presumedly intended for Pross to wear. Ancient black velvet curtains inadequately hid the window.

Recessed into the side wall nearest the door was a washbasin, and its taps, he discovered, worked.

So did the electricity.

Sense of exploration satisfied for now, he removed his clothes, pulled the robe over himself as a blanket and slept.

He dreamed of Jennifer, distant down a street, back to him, walking on.

Downstairs, Simon once more enroled Phil and Mick to assist in re-energising the prayer battery. Every little drop of prayer energy was welcome.

2.11
Their First Encounter

The hotel Jennifer finally chose from the hundreds listed in the *Yellow Pages* was in Nottingham Street. This, according to the accompanying advert, was near to the famous Baker Street, and it charged sixty pounds a night for a single room. She booked for two nights, paying with her recently acquired credit card. Following signs, she soon found herself outside the train station at a taxi rank where black cabs were arriving continually. Everything was so busy, she observed. It was still only eight o'clock on a Sunday morning, yet this world she was now in was already wide awake.

The journey took her down the even more famous Harley Street, which was every bit as conservative, dignified and moneyed as she would have expected it to be.

The ride to the *Kenton Hotel* was over sooner than she'd have liked. After awkwardly handing the driver the required four pounds eighty for the journey, being not at all sure of the correct paying protocol, she clambered out with her luggage. On the pavement, she looked about herself, observing that Nottingham Street seemed to specialise in hotel accommodation, most every property along its four-storey length being so dedicated.

As her taxi pulled away, only then did she recall that it was customary to tip London taxi drivers, and she worried that her omission may have caused offence.

Viewed from the outside, the *Kenton Hotel* was a little too discreet for Jennifer's liking, and whilst not looking sleazy, it certainly looked shady.

Walking through its doors, she began to feel apprehensive and vulnerable.

After pressing a silent button on the small reception desk, she stood alone in the foyer, not sure whether the bell was of any use.

A middle-eastern man came through a door. He gave her a "yes, what is it you want?" look, and soon Jennifer was asleep in her second-floor room, door reassuringly locked, catching up on her missed night's rest.

When she awoke, in the early afternoon, she did not at all feel like leaving the room, but made an effort and went out.

There was somewhere in particular she wished to visit.

Although money was not an immediate problem for Jennifer, and promised not to be for many years to come, she nevertheless felt ill at ease boarding a cab for the second time that day, asking the driver to take her to

Camden Lock. These two cab journeys, she knew, would together cost as much as she used to earn in a whole morning at work.

But it had felt good, simply putting her arm out to be taken wherever she wanted.

In her memory, it was always winter when, as a small child, she would be questioning her mother while helping her prepare food in the snug kitchen of their Richmond home. Eight or nine, she figured she must have been during that phase of curiosity about what had then seemed to her to be an event remote in history: her parents first meeting. Whatever details those conversations disclosed to her infant ears, few she could recall now, except that a French restaurant in Camden Lock had been the place of first encounter, one rainy autumn afternoon, when both parties had individually sought comfort in a coffee, with fate arranging adjacent tables.

Proceeding down a street named Parkway, the driver turned his head a little to ask, 'Awright if I drop you a'the janction, or d'you wanna go all the way to the Lock?' Faltering a little, Jennifer replied that it would be, not that she really knew one way or other. Travelling further down the street, the junction he was presumedly alluding to came into view, as did crowds of people crossing left and right. Near the traffic lights, the cab swung to the left, stopping. After a half-attempted fumble with the door handle, she sat back in her seat and asked the driver to take her all the way to the Lock.

The cab moved on, turning left.

Across the road, she observed a tube station pouring people out into the street. Most everyone was young. Seeing how they were dressed, she began to feel out of place in her expensive, shiny black raincoat, a recent present from her Aunty. Most everyone she saw was dressed in mismatches of colours and styles. Grungy, she decided.

Shops selling leather-wear and alternative jewellery lined the way, most pitching out into the street at least some of their contents, and competing music thumping out from all. So thick were the crowds down this particular street, the driver more than once had to assert his way forward, albeit slowly, through spillages of people intent on ignoring the usually sacrosanct demarcation between road and pavement.

Not far on, the road rose slightly, and Jennifer realised that they were actually passing over a bridge. Looking to the side, she saw that they were over a canal's lock system, and the hitherto mystery of the area's name was solved for her.

'This do?' asked the driver, and Jennifer said it would. Alighting on to the street, she opted to pay the driver through the side window as she had observed other people doing along the way.

She tipped him a pound for the four pound journey, which he accepted with no special ceremony.

So now she was stood over a canal, beside a busy road, being jostled by passers-by, rain beginning to fall upon her. Looking about, she saw a restaurant nearby called *L'Ecluse*, and fondly believed it to be the very one in which her parents had first met.

She crossed the road to go to it.

2.12
Muddy Pool Molecules

He slowly became aware. Eyes opening to slits, vaguely recalling his dreams, his mind's first task was to speculate how even more grieved he would surely have been if he'd been any *real* length of time with Jennifer before their, or rather his, split. What if it had been two years, not two weeks? What dreams would haunt him nightly then? What tears would stream?

But he knew that was why he'd left her so soon, scared of ever having such pain. Moaning Joe had shown him that. But Moaning Joe had also encouraged him to see how living with such a fear could never really be living at all.

Becoming more mundanely aware, he began to think about where he was and how he'd got there, and quickly decided that it didn't bear thinking about. He'd been sort of kidnapped, and his life had turned so generally bad he was compelled to let people treat him like a Messiah.

He wondered what time it was. Three o'clock, perhaps.

Bugger. He was getting hungry.

He found himself touching the pillow beside him, thinking of how her fragrant presence had occupied this space only the day before, imagining she was with him now. Wishing she was with him.

He began to choke up, but fought it by making a conscious decision not to think about her any more — she and he were surely irrevocably split. There was nothing he could do about her now, except perhaps learn from the loss. But the only thing to be learnt was how not to make the same disaster with the next love, if fate were ever to throw such an irresistible treasure his way again. But that would be so unfair to Jennifer. She had not suffered just so he could perhaps get it right in the next relationship. No, he couldn't do that to her, he felt. He couldn't imagine being so mercenary and opportunist. He was strong like that, even when he knew that he was being foolish to himself and that life was for living and getting on with. But maybe he'd just found another excuse for denying himself the comfort of love? 'Oh bollocks,' he breathed, annoyed to find himself slipping into further introspection and self-doubt.

But one thing he knew for certain was that he could never again become transiently besotted with anyone like he used to. He was cured of nympholepsy, for sure. He couldn't ever imagine falling in what he used to call love at first sight again. Love had become too real for comedy and frivolity.

He wished he could be more like other men. He wished he could iron out the love element from his life, and just shag girls picked up at parties the night before, or whatever most blokes his age did.

But he knew he could never do that, since he'd always feel like he was letting himself down.

'Bollocks,' he breathed again.

Then he had a thought. The thought was this: he would get Jennifer out of his mind by doing what he'd always found to sad to do before.

He would look upon even love from an evolutionary psychologist's viewpoint.

Genes. That's all life was, after all — genes muddling their way through eternity. What he perceived as *self* was just a single, overcomplex link in a chain that stretched all the way back to a freak combination of molecules which had accidentally spawned a *cancerous* molecule in a warm primeval sea, or muddy pool, or cosmic gas cloud some billions of years ago. So what he experienced as love was surely just a genetically selfish desire to mate with, and thus pass on his genes with, what he perceived as being a suitable partner. Jennifer was eminently suitable because, being so intelligent, she could nurture his offspring successfully, equipping them with resources, both physical and social, that would in turn increase *their* chances of passing on the genetic material. And Jennifer's alluring beauty, too, would probably pass on to these offspring, thus further increasing their chances of attracting high-calibre mates. And their probable beauty, if they were female, would make it more likely for the natural fathers to stay with the family, adding to the protection and resources; or, if male, would make them more attractive to other females, thus helping the spread of the muddy pool genetic material.

He decided that, from now on, whenever he found his mind straying to Jennifer, he would conjure up an image of that muddy pool bubbling with slimy unpleasantness.

He sighed, turned his head to the side, and stared blankly at a crystal pyramid, mercifully thinking of nothing for a while, except to note that his hair smelled of bonfire. But then he began thinking of...

Muddy pool. Muddy pool.

It helped. It really helped. Just the comic absurdity alone helped.

Actually, he made himself admit something now — deep down he felt he was going to be with her again. Yes, surely he was. But perhaps that feeling was just an extension of that vague feeling he supposed everyone carried with them at all times — that one day everything would be right. That all lost loves would return. That all that ails one would be cured. That youth and vigour would return.

Pissed off to find himself becoming wistful, he tried to explain that vague, all-things-will-be-perfect feeling from his newly adopted evolutionary psychologist's viewpoint.

That vague feeling was universal, he decided, and it was what kept people going. It was necessary to keep the transient vehicles of DNA rolling for their seventy summers. Having evolved such big brains, brains able, if they dare, to recognise the pointless muddy pool molecule in the baggage hold, mechanisms have also evolved to enable us to beguile ourselves on a grand scale. Mechanisms to make it all seem special. Mechanisms to make it seem mystical and transcendent. That was religion, he realised. That was the explicit comfort of all religions — that one day everything would be right, even if you have to die first. So *that's* what religion was — a glorified manifestation of the innate, universal belief that things will be better. Something that draws on that belief. Anything. Anything that defies the unbelievable, terrifying thought that this is all there is ever going to be in it for *you*, and that even this won't last a blink of an eye in the cosmic scale of things. That belief gone wild.

That was his own particular evolutionary flaw, he decided. That gene wasn't dominant enough in him to make him a successful breeder. He was mentally unbalanced. Too analytical. The genes that had made him thus were a evolutionary dead end. He needed to be just a little bit more beguiled to be happy, and thus wont to get out of bed and shag his muddy pool molecule around. But cheating the muddy pool molecule by denying it continuation gave him a sense of wicked achievement, he realised. It was his self-denial streak, although he couldn't really explain that streak at all from a evolutionary psychologist's point of view.

So he blamed his mother.

He sighed again, turned his head to the other side, and stared blankly at another crystal pyramid.

Muddy pool. Muddy pool.

A quiet tap sounded on the door.

He ignored it.

A second later, in came Simon, robed and carrying the prayer battery. Behind him was Mick and Phil, carrying his computer and printer. Pointing the battery at Pross, Simon was nervous yet resolute. 'Believe!' he said, pressing the zap button. And he looked at Pross, reverently expecting a reaction.

Mick and Phil put the computer down on the floor.

They looked at Pross too.

'Morning nutters,' said Pross dully, regarding them sideways.

'Morning,' they chorused unsurely.

'Now go away again,' said Pross.

Disappointment showed on Simon's face as he went away, taking the battery and his underlings with him.

'No, don't go away,' said Pross urgently as they exited.

Simon returned.

Pross said, 'I'm hungry. Is there any food here?'

Disappointment even more evident on his face, Simon said, 'We're going to the village soon to get provisions.'

And Simon left the room again, his robe swishing and rustling.

He closed the door behind him.

'No meat,' called out Pross. 'And get me some hair shampoo.'

Muddy pool. Muddy pool.

Pross looked at his computer. Would he ever get around to writing that proper novel? He should do it now. He should get out of bed and start right now. He needed to make his contribution to art, otherwise he could never really feel at ease lying in bed all day not contributing to art. But why bother? he decided a moment later from an evolutionary point of view. There was no art, just elaborate courtship displays. If he were to write a *Hamlet*, or devise a Unified Field Theory, it would just be a way of showing females what a clever, and therefore resourceful, father he could be, and what clever, and therefore more likely to survive in the jungle of life and pass on their genetic material, children he could sire. For *Hamlet*, read *Shag Me, I'm Dead Clever*. *Hamlet* was Shakespeare unwittingly displaying his peacock feathers. A peacock has evolved, through runaway sexual selection, huge, showy courtship feathers, and that's what human creativity was, thought Pross: runaway sexual selection. Every time he got depressed and frustrated because he felt his creativity was being wasted or stifled was just because of those pointless muddy pool molecules continuing on inside him. Nothing spiritual or mystical was really being expressed in Beethoven's *Fifth*, just an abstract, runaway mating call. Thinking thus, rock stars became the product of a genetic urge to show the whole world what a great mate they could be. For *Sgt. Pepper's*, again read, *Shag Me*.

Pross reflected some more.

Men were usually the large-scale cultural show-offs in the world of evolutionary psychology. After all, men can sire thousands of children. How many more creatively renowned men have there been compared to women? As well as being culturally repressed, women necessarily invest much of their cleverness and spare hours into nurturing the few offspring they are capable of having, whereas, since men can potentially mate with hundreds of thousands of women in a lifetime, they are therefore more likely to spend their time in garrets writing poems about autumn to broadcast their sexually desirable cleverness to the whole world.

No, he wouldn't bother typing a pathetic courtship display. If his muddy pool molecule was going to use him to make an elaborate courtship display to other muddy pool molecules, it could bloody well pick one that didn't involve so much hard work for him.

It was a pity he couldn't sing, he wistfully thought. And if he hadn't smashed that guitar in an act of frustrated inability the day after he'd bought it when he was fourteen...

He sighed, turned over again and looked again at the first crystal.

Muddy pool. Muddy... Millions in the bank — I definitely heard him say millions in the bank.

Could that be true? Could Simon, the sad nutter who believed him to be some kind of Messiah be a multimillionaire? Well, he'd somehow bought this house — or at least he'd said he'd bought it.

The potential implications were slow to arrest Pross.

He continued to stare at the crystal.

Then he stared at the ceiling.

Epiphany.

Millions in the bank — Simon somehow had millions in the bank. And he was throwing it away on madness! Perhaps he could get a piece of that madness? It was a Godfrey-given golden opportunity to pay Ron back, and he wouldn't have to grovel to the lottery company and be ridiculed even more in the press. And it would be a fuck sight easier than writing a proper novel.

Yes, this was an opportunity all right. The kind of opportunity his show-off muddy pool molecule couldn't resist. And did *his* muddy pool molecule not have at its disposal a mind as cunning as most any ever devised by nature? he reminded himself. This was surely the time to use it with a vengeance instead of regarding it as his worst enemy.

Anyway, he was doing it for Ron, not himself. For Ron.

All of a sudden, he didn't feel anywhere near as suicidal as he'd felt only an hour ago, now that he had an occupation to distract him: creaming Simon. Although it was mad, utterly mad, what was happening to him, it was the best job he could ever have hoped for: he didn't have to get up in the morning, and he could be as silly as he liked — in fact the sillier the better.

Prospero Pi-Meson had found a suitable job.

2.13
A Stranger's Embrace

Seeing that it was not a grand affair, being not much more than the Frenchified equivalent of some of the more exclusive tea shops catering for tourists in her own historic, picturesque home town of Richmond, Jennifer decided to take some refreshment within. So, very conscious that she was perhaps retracing her mother's steps of twenty years past, Jennifer entered the restaurant.

Just inside the door, she was greeted in French by a waitress who only briefly looked at her. Despite the perfunctory nature of the exchange, Jennifer felt her face flush at the embarrassment of the perceived expectation of having to converse in a language she knew not well at all. But before she could muster an answer, the petite waitress, afflicted with an uncommonly narrow, sharply turned-up nose, asked, 'Table for one?'

'Yes, please,' returned Jennifer, soon to be shown to the nearest table, where she sat and examined the menu, relieved to find that it was written in English. Crepes were the speciality, indeed the mainstay, of this restaurant, she quickly ascertained, and decided upon a variation referred to as a *Florentine*.

Her eyes now free to wander, she looked around the room. Red was the colour of most, if not all, the woodwork, but the majority of the vertical surfaces were presented as bare brickwork. Large photographic prints of rustic peasant people adorned these walls, and the stained-black wooden floor supported a few more tables than comfortably possible for the given space. The people eating, she observed, were not particulary representative of the type of people dominant without. There was more of a middle-classness about most of the diners. Even the young woman alone at the table next to her, whose attire and chunky jewellery tended towards grunge, had a certain air of sophistication about her.

Another waitress visited Jennifer and took her order, to which she'd added coffee. Now feeling warm, she stood up to remove her coat. As she sat down again, the young woman at the next table leaned over to her with a nervous, fidgety motion, and spoke. 'Excuse mee,' she said with a French accent, her words as fidgety as her motions, 'Ah told a fwend ah might be ee-er, could you watch for eeem while Ah'm in the ladies?'

Taken aback a little by the unexpected approach, Jennifer reacted only by nodding her agreement.

The woman immediately smiled, smiled like a favoured child just handed a sweet she'd at first been refused. 'Eee's called Robert,' she said, and, touching her own shoulder, added, 'brown 'air theese length.' And then she was off, bracelets and other metallic adornments jangling. Not many tables away, a young man, short with a powerful, purpose built body, eyed her traversing the room with an almost resentful aspect, then turned his attention briefly to Jennifer, holding his gaze when she happened to look his way.

Jennifer turned her head away, pretending not to have noticed his attention.

Jennifer knew she was a looker, and fast was she becoming inured to the percentage of eyes that strayed her way wherever she went. Invasive eyes that two months ago might have rendered her self-conscious, were now inclined to render her indifferent. But those occasional sullen, resentful glares of the kind she suspected she was still receiving from the squat young man would always disturb.

Now looking, with affected casualness, towards the door, Jennifer witnessed a shorter than average man come into the restaurant. He had on a long black coat of expensive design but cheap treatment, tight faded jeans, a paisley shirt and paisley waistcoat, and pointed brown ankle boots with cuban heels. His face was almost comical, with a long, ski-jump nose jutting out from under close-set, indeed off-set, eyes.

He seemed to be in want of a good night's sleep.

These things Jennifer casually noticed about him as he glanced around the room, but then she noticed his hair. 'Robert?' she suddenly found herself uttering, and his subsequent look of mildly bewildered acknowledgement confirmed the accuracy of the presumption. 'A French woman asked me to watch for you. She's in the ladies.'

'Oh, er... er...,' he faltered for a moment, lampooning his own confusion. 'OK,' he said in a more together voice. 'Is this her table?'

Jennifer answered that it was.

While taking the seat where the lady of his acquaintance had been sitting moments earlier, Robert, rather formally, introduced himself to Jennifer, offering his hand for shaking. When the exchange of names was completed, he said, tilting his head a little, 'You're from the North, aren't you? Darlington way?'

His blue eyes held her gaze, like he was deeply interested in hearing her reply.

His apparent ease at locating her home town to within a dozen miles or so impressed Jennifer, particularly in view of her being aware that hers was not a strong northern accent. Indeed, often had she been accused of being "posh" by the rougher element of her school because of her "foreign" tones, tones modulated perhaps by the fact of her having had a southern father as an influence on her infant tongue.

Upon answering that she came from Richmond, North Yorkshire, Robert warmly returned that he himself was from Darlington, surprising Jennifer greatly, for his accent and vocal demeanour hugely indicated otherwise. Accentwise, Robert wouldn't have sounded out of place addressing a Conservative Party conference on business matters.

The French lady returned. Upon seeing Robert, she smiled broadly, opening her arms to him. Robert stood to greet her, saying, in a silly, sugary way, 'Yvette!'

They hugged, with Yvette kissing Robert's stubbly cheeks.

'How are you doing?' asked Robert.

'Great,' returned Yvette.

Jennifer found herself smiling to see the warmth of their friendship.

Yvette was beautiful, and not dissimilar to her own sister, observed Jennifer. More angular in the body than Sarah and a little taller, though, and with facial features more clearly defined. Sarah's was a softer face than Yvette's, but neither could be declared more appealing than the other, particulary with both sharing equally large and deep brown eyes, and both choosing to darkly shadow their eyes with make up.

The coffee arrived for Jennifer. After placing it on her table, the waitress then greeted Robert by name and enquired as to his order. Robert requested a beer, stressing, almost apologetically, that he would be ordering food later.

'Ah'll av a bee-er too,' added Yvette impulsively.

The crepe she had ordered now arrived, and as Jennifer proceeded to eat, she and Yvette accidentally caught each other's eye. Yvette smiled at once, her head making appealing little nervous jerks. Jennifer began to smile back, but Yvette had already returned her attention to Robert, suddenly needing to confer some apparently urgent and important chatter about someone called Peter, for which her voice now became wonderfully serious and low.

Unable not to overhear snippets of her conversation, Jennifer found Yvette's voice an altogether not unpleasant sound. Charmingly French, it also had a childlike quality, like she was talking with a burned tongue-tip. Robert, for his part, responded with the same level of apparent deep interest and involvement he had shown when discussing Jennifer's Richmond roots.

Hearing Robert's voice now, in the light of the information he had given her, Jennifer could discern subtle traces of his declared northern origin. Curious to her ears were the inconsistencies in those traces. When pronouncing the word "so" his tongue was particularly undecided, most times giving it a clipped approach, but sometimes giving it a telltale, stretched, "s-urr" treatment, straight from the council estates of Darlington.

'Jennifer, here, is from near where I come from,' said Robert to Yvette, unexpectedly pulling Jennifer into the conversation.

'Reelee?' said Yvette to Jennifer, expressing delight at the fact. 'Ow long av you leeved in London?'

'This is my first day.'

Both Yvette and Robert responded remarkably upon hearing that fact. Both straightened in their chairs, Robert making a gooey sympathetic and delighted noise, Yvette actually holding her arms out to embrace Jennifer. 'You're going to av a wonderful time,' she said, jewellery jangling.

Jennifer found herself smiling and returning the offered embrace.

'We'll look after you,' said Robert, then accosting the waitress as she walked by, instructing her to put Jennifer's bill on to his, and anything else she might want.

2.14
The Crystal Age

Faintly he heard Mick's cab start up.

He cast the robe-come-blanket aside and began putting his clothes on.

Muddy pool. Muddy pool.

After washing his face, he sat on the bed. Finding the Aetherius pamphlets, which had presumably been left out for him, he began to read. He read about the founder of the Aetherius Society, who claimed to have received the secret design for the prayer batteries in a psychic transmission from Cosmic Masters. He read about how it was forbidden for anyone to look inside a battery, or *spiritual energy radiator*, as they were fancifully called. He read about the Golden Millennium. He read about the Expected One who would lead the way for the arrival of the Cosmic Masters, in their unveiled glory. He read about the predicted end of all monetary systems. He read about the Earth's possible membership of the Interplanetary Parliament. He read particularly about an invisible flying saucer, referred to as the Third Satellite, which often orbits Earth, under the command of The Karmic Lord Mars Sector 6. He read of how the saucer's presence enhances all spiritual actions of a selfless nature by a factor of three thousand. He read that the next predicted date for the saucer's return was a mere three months away.

This, spacecraft, he immediately felt, would be crucial to his own scheme, whatever it would be.

And while he read of these and many other even more absurd things, from the back of his cunning mind, delicious aspects of the required plan for enriching Ron, and maybe himself, began making themselves known.

It was clever. Damned clever.

It excited him.

But then he started feeling guilty. What he was planning was pure deception. But then again, he argued internally, it couldn't be deception because he'd already told Simon he'd simply made Godfrey up. Bugger it, it was Simon's fault for being so dumb.

He heard the cab return.

A few minutes later, after a little tap, Simon again entered Pross's bedroom, this time silently bearing food — cheese sandwiches.

Pross was lying on the bed, staring at the ceiling.

Sitting up to accept the food, Pross regarded Simon for some moments, then quietly, curiously, said, 'Tell me about the Golden Millennium, Simon.'

Unsure at first, Simon sat on the end of Pross's bed. Although initially hesitant, he soon found his pace. His voice becoming portentous, he talked about the period of bliss poised to becalm the world; of the emergence on Earth of the Expected One to lead the way forward, preparing Earth for the arrival of advanced extraterrestrials, openly intervening in human affairs once humans have learnt to control their incessant squabbling; of the subsequent conquest of disease, old age and famine; of the end of monetary systems; the entry of Earth into the Interplanetary Parliament.

Throughout, Pross said nothing, just ate his sandwiches.

Leaning close, Simon said, 'It's you, Prospero Pi-Meson. You're the Expected One, the Earth Master to usher in the Cosmic Masters. Like you told us last night, you're going to create peace on Earth by influencing everyone with your mind.'

'Any chance of a cup of tea?' asked Pross, handing Simon his empty plate.

Mystically deflated, Simon took the plate and muttered that there was indeed some tea available.

And he went to get it.

Once Simon left the room, Pross lay his head down on the pillow and looked at the ceiling again, again pondering his peculiar circumstances: he was in an isolated, dilapidated country house, the object of religious adoration, regarded as the person who was going to change the world with his mind. Just how the fuck had this happened? "Like you told us last night", Simon had said. It was all to do with that, and slowly the details of the previous night's druggy cab ride surfaced in his memory, and he began to more fully recall the "succeeding where Christ had failed" bullshit he'd conjured up for his gullible companions. That bullshit, he realised now, could perhaps work as many wonders in his life as his ill-fated lottery win should have, as *well* as paying Ron back.

When Simon appeared with the tea, about to hand the cup over, his motion was arrested by Pross sitting up a little, adding a kind of spaced-out, cosmic look to himself.

'What is it?' asked Simon, his eyes coming alive, pushing his glasses up. 'The ley lines? Messages?'

'I don't know,' murmured Pross, continuing to exist exotically while Simon gazed on. Then, lying back again, he said, 'It's passing.'

'What was it?'

'Strange feelings, Simon. Powerful feelings. Strange thoughts. Strange ideas. All cramming in at once. Like a million things had all been said to me at once.'

'Transmissions,' said Simon.

'Maybe,' admitted Pross softly before sitting up fully, holding out his hands for the drink. 'I've never experienced anything like it. It was a bit scary.'

'It'll be transmissions,' concluded Simon. 'Has to be. Please listen to them. They're using you.'

'I will Simon, if that's what you advise,' said Pross, acting a little dazed.

Much relieved, Simon handed the tea over to Pross. Then, rucking up his robe, he retrieved a bottle of hair shampoo from an underlying pocket. 'One pound eighty for the shampoo, and one twenty for the sandwiches,' he said plainly. 'No charge for the tea, the workmen left a box of teabags and some UHT.'

And he stood there, waiting for three pounds.

Monster bugger, thought Pross, instantly comprehending the implications of Simon's obvious miserliness: getting a fortune out of him was surely going to be harder than he'd first considered. He was going to have to be *hugely* cunning.

Covering up his amazement and disappointment, he withdrew a five pound note from his pocket — save for a few coppers, the only money he had left in the world. Slowly handing the note over, he said, 'You perplex me, Simon.'

'Why? How?'

Giving him an appraising look, Pross quietly said, 'You purport to wish the Golden Age upon mankind, yet you cling to the old age. Why is that, Simon?'

'I don't!' objected Simon to this unexpected and outrageous suggestion, pushing his glasses up, his tired eyes kindled with passion, eyes which had not closed in rest for over a day now.

'You do, Simon. You cling to your riches. Yet you know that when the Golden Age dawns, your riches will be valueless. Why is that, Simon? Is it because you do not truly believe?'

'I believe. I do. I believe.'

Pross gave him another critically appraising look.

'I believe,' said Simon again.

'Prove it to me, Simon. Destroy that five pound note. Rip it up.'

Mute horror.

A grotesque miserliness existed within Simon. His money had come to him against all odds, and he wasn't ever going to part with it. These things he never consciously realised, but always felt. It couldn't be said that just the thought of spending an unnecessary penny worried him, because he never *spent* unnecessary pennies. And before even necessary pennies were spent, he would fret and weigh-up and consider to a pathological extent. The only extravagance he'd ever shown in his life was to pay for the house. But even that was necessary in his mind, for he had formed business plans.

So now, faced with the loss of five pounds, a shock set in.

It was like asking a mother to kill her child.

'Do it, Simon,' urged Pross, 'I need to know your strength. I need to know you're greater than others.'

Putting his tea aside, standing up, Pross held Simon by the shoulders. 'Do it. Do it.'

Hesitant at first, Simon tore the money into two pieces that fluttered down on to Pross's feet. Mortified, he watched each piece's lurid descent.

The deed done, Pross released Simon, then lay down on the bed again. Taking a sandwich in his hand, he said, 'I like to eat alone.'

For some moments, Simon stared at the fallen pieces. Then he left the room without saying a further word.

Pross got up to collect the pieces. A bit of *sellotape* and he could spend them down the pub later.

Not only had he saved himself three pounds, he knew he had won a major battle against an obvious neurosis. Not only would Simon never consider charging him for future meals — which would be a life-saver — he had been psychologically primed for bigger things.

Parting Simon from his money was now an absorbing mind game to Pross. From his new viewpoint, it was a battle of two muddy pool molecules fighting for resources, and the winner would be in a better position to attract mates. He would go along with it. It's what he was put together out of food to do for that pointless molecule of his. And anyway, he owed it to Ron, although how that self-generated commitment could be explained in evolutionary psychology terms he didn't know until a few seconds later when he decided that giving money and time away charitably was a way of showing potential mates how richly resourceful one is. *Look at this girls, I can afford to give away thousands — worth shagging, am I not?*

While drinking, he flicked through the crazy books on the shelf. And crazy they were. Pseudo-scientific nonsense. It wasn't even clever pseudo-science — that's what annoyed the most. But Simon still fell for it all, unable to spot the glaring holes in the logic and principles.

If anyone could invent better New Age mysticism wrapped up in scientific-sounding theory, Pross felt he could.

And he jolly well would.
Ridiculous ideas began teaming.

Over breakfast, Sarah-Jane had come to realise that she was not overly concerned for Jennifer. In part, she was actually pleased that her sister was doing something impulsive for once, like a normal person might. If Jennifer had been going penniless to the city, that would have been a real worry, but she had more than enough money to buy safety, and Sarah trusted that, although inexperienced, she would soon learn to look after herself well enough.

To her Aunty Jane, however, Sarah knew it would constitute a family crisis, and she resigned herself to the necessity of returning forthwith to Richmond to break the news and spend some regrettable time.

In the early afternoon, just after Sarah left for her Aunty's, Ron re-read Pross's letter to Jennifer, and, to his surprise, he cried again.

Putting the letter away, he decided to ring his friend to offer what solace and support he could. This decision did not come easy, for since he'd never known Pross directly express his true feelings, the likelihood of him doing so now was hugely scary. However, telephoning Melanie revealed that Pross had not returned there, and no one else he rang had seen or heard anything of him since the previous night.

Ron grew concerned, and even fleetingly considered contacting the police.
But he decided to watch a video instead.

Finished drinking and reading, Pross slipped the stiff golden gown, of ecclesiastical cut, over his own clothes... and felt like a pillock.

He started taking it off again.
Muddy pool. Muddy pool.
But then he steeled himself. He was going to give this one a shot — for Ron.

So the scheme continued...

By unravelling some thread from his curtains and tying a few knots here and there, he was able to fashion a harness, a harness in which to suspend from his finger one of the inch-high crystal pyramids on the stands beside his bed.

He put the construction in his pocket under his gown.

Right, this was it: he was ready to take on the mantle of the Expected One and announce the advent of the Golden Millennium.

With not a little trepidation, he left the room to seek out Simon.
The only light in the corridor was that admitted by high, dirty windows

at the far ends. Cold, empty rooms, some considerably larger than his own, lay either side of him as he, almost stealthily, moved on, snooping a little as he went.

Arriving at the top of the curved, wooden staircase, halfway along the corridor, muffled surges of voices could be heard. More praying, he realised.

Then a spooky thing: he began to hear his own voice, and was confused to the point of being truly unnerved until he realised that what he was hearing was the recording of himself reciting his Godfrey story that Simon had made a few weeks earlier.

Nerve restored, down the staircase he slowly moved, trying to bestow upon himself the same unworldly, thoughts-obviously-anchored-beyond-reality appearance adopted by those gowned ladies in old ghost story films — the ones who've just half-seen an image of a deceased lover in an upstairs mirror and have wandered, in a kind of ethereal state, downstairs to faintly inform the rest of the household.

In those films, once seen, they're usually met on the lower steps by some concerned young dandy who dashes to their side.

Seeing Pross, effulgent in gold, Simon, also robed, dashed up to him.

Upon reaching him, on the bottom stair, Simon kneeled, then bowed his head.

Taking a few seconds to gather himself, Pross began his act. 'All is being revealed to me, Simon,' he said in a murmur. 'There is nothing but Godfrey in the cosmos. Godfrey is the essence. Godfrey is the mathematics. Godfrey is the symmetry.'

Simon looked up, deep reverence in his bearing.

'I have much to tell. Much to tell,' continued Pross, gesturing to Simon that he should rise. Rise Simon did, and together they walked on towards the prayer battery, erected atop its tripod in the centre of the bare room, one of them affecting a hallowed state, the other almost moved to tears.

Mick and Phil looked on.

Coming to the battery, Pross gazed at it, as if drawn to do so. 'Everything's become clear to me here,' he said. 'This is the place. It's all crystallised perfectly for me now. I know what I have to do.'

'It's the ley lines,' said Simon. 'They channel the messages.'

'Yes, it's the ley lines,' agreed Pross peacefully, placing his hands on the battery. 'They're the key, Simon. They're the key.'

Awe was bounteous as the three men of Godfrey observed Pross.

Then someone's watch beeped the hour.

Simon and Mick turned disapproving eyes on to Phil.

'Th'sorry,' he lisped.

'What time is it?' asked Pross, far too normally.

Mystically deflated, Simon uttered, 'Two o'clock.'

Two o'clock — that early? thought Pross with surprise, then realised he'd fucked up in asking, so quickly sought to rescue his glorious image.

Turning his back to the battery, he addressed his followers in revelatory tones. 'I am Prospero Pi-Meson, the Expected One, and to recreate Eden with your help is my task.' He paused, then repeated, 'To recreate Eden.'

Simon murmured something, his mouth remaining a little agape.

Mick looked to Simon for his lead.

'The prayer battery's mine!' spouted Phil. 'I ssstole it from the Aetherius Society. Th'Simon told me to.'

Mick raised a fist to Phil, who cringed. 'Shadup, will'ya?' he said, then looked again to Simon, but Simon was in his own dream.

'The Expected One,' proclaimed Simon, kneeling.

Mick then also knelt.

And Phil too.

And Pross continued with his revelation.

'Peace. Love. The Golden Millennium. Earth's readiness for entry into the Interplanetary Parliament. The abolishment of all monetary systems. The end of all want. That is what I, the Expected One, have been instructed to achieve... and it has this afternoon been disclosed to me how.'

'How?' spluttered Phil suddenly, eliciting more disapproving looks.

Pross decisively answered the question. 'By utilising extraterrestrial knowledge to construct a global empathy machine, allowing all minds on Earth to be influenced by mine, bringing peace, harmony and enlightenment to the four corners.'

'Amazing,' breathed Simon.

'I was chosen because I know about science, and last night I learnt about bliss from the Cosmic Masters. They filled me with their bliss. And in the Golden Millennium to come, all will experience my ecstasy.'

'Amazing,' breathed Simon.

'Great,' lisped Phil.

'Ley lines,' said Pross, 'are the key. The ley lines have channelled the messages from the Cosmic Masters to me, and that's what we're going to use to spread my peace: the ley lines. That's why Godfrey put them there so very long ago.' Looking now directly at Simon, he revealed, 'We're going to use the ley lines to transmit my serenity around the globe.'

'Amazing,' breathed Simon.

'Great,' lisped Phil.

Now Pross played his master card. 'And I have been told to have the

Global Empathy Device constructed by midnight, February the first.'

February the first! Simon took only a second to realise the significance of that date. Jumping to his feet, face beaming with boyish enthusiasm, he said to Pross, 'The next Spiritual Push!'

He turned to Mick, who quickly understood, or pretended to.

When Simon looked again at Pross, he saw puzzlement in his eyes.

'The Spiritual Push!' said Simon again, expecting Pross to now show comprehension, which he did not. Pushing his spectacles back, Simon then tried, 'The return of the Third Satellite.'

Pross's confused look remained. 'I know nothing of these things.'

Simon realised he needed to furnish an explanation. 'Spiritual Pushes are times when a spacecraft called the Third Satellite orbits the Earth...'

'It's invisible!' blurted Phil, standing up.

Mick stood up also.

'It's invisible,' conceded Simon, 'and to radar. The Aetherius leader received a psychic transmission telling the dates of its visits. February the first's the next time. Midnight. That's why the machine has to be ready by then. Don't you see?'

Phil could restrain his short tongue no longer. 'Every th'spiritual action is magnified three thousand times by the th'spacecraft!'

'Don't you see?' said Simon to Pross, 'the spacecraft will magnify your serenity transmissions three thousand times. Midnight, February the first is when the Golden Millennium begins.' He turned to the others, pushed his spectacles back again, and in a raised voice said, 'February the first!' and punched the air.

Turning around, he saw that Pross now had a crystal pyramid dangling from his finger, and thus equipped, dowsing Pross went, accompanied by his mystified followers.

To Phil's immediate questions concerning the purpose of Pross's exploration of the ground floor of the house, no answer was given by Pross, and Phil quickly became bored with asking, instead remarking on the size of a particular cobweb in a room corner.

Simon, enthraled, said nothing.

Pross's trek uncovered a number of basically furnished rooms being used as places to sleep by his followers. Also discovered was a bathroom, and a kitchen equipped with a tatty washing machine, a fridge that looked like it had been in a fight, and an oven that looked like it had been in Poland.

All ground floor rooms having been visited, beginning to look troubled, Pross paused for thought. 'It must be in the garden,' he murmured, then followed his finger outside, roaming to and fro, absorbed in his task.

Except for a sprinkling of splutterings from Phil about distant sheep and funny shaped clouds, respectful silence was maintained by the group.

Simon frequently scanned the skies for UFO's.

On the boundary of the wood, many yards from the house, the crystal began circling, insignificantly at first, then in ever larger figures.

'Here,' said Pross, removing the thread bearing the crystal from his finger. 'This is it.'

'This is what?' inquired Simon, speaking for the first time.

'This is the place. This is the pole.'

'What pole?'

'The Earth's ley pole. This is where we'll position the empathy device on February the first. This is the precise point where all the Earth's ley lines originate, shooting off to the four corners.' His voice becoming awed, he added, 'The most dynamic place on Earth, hidden since the dawn of time, now revealed to us for our sacred purpose.'

Simon was overwhelmed once more. 'Amazing,' he breathed, kneeling down to place his hands flat on the earth. 'I can feel it. I can feel the energy.'

He began taking deep, ostentatious breaths.

Looking uncertain, Mick knelt down also, similarly placing his hands flat on the earth, taking similar breaths.

Phil joined in too.

'What's it s'posed to feel like?' he asked. 'Th'Simon, what's it s'posed to feel like? Th'Simon?'

But Simon was oblivious to him. 'Here,' breathed Simon reverentially. 'Here.'

Pross said, 'No other place on Earth will do,' but what he thought while observing Simon pawing the ground was that he'd made a pretty good start. Perhaps all he had to do from now on to secure Ron his compensation was to connive a little, speak in a kind of self-assured, biblical manner, gen up on Aetherius nonsense a bit more, and look a bit serene for a while.

Easy money. He'd put on bigger acts to just to sponge a beer in his time.

Simon had millions, claimed Phil, and Pross had observed Phil to possess a talent for being indelicately frank. At the very least, Simon had the property.

Maintaining a suitable equanimity about himself, he began walking back to the house, now a looming grey form against a darkening sky.

His followers followed.

Breathing a little hard, Simon came up to Pross's side as the latter moved towards the front door, crunching gravel under his feet.

With Simon's arrival, Pross halted, appearing pensive yet tranquil.

'Not long now, Simon,' he said quietly, gazing at the house. 'The Golden

Millennium is almost upon the world.'

'February the first,' said Simon eagerly, pushing his glasses up, then doing a quick UFO scan.

Mick did a quick scan too.

Phil found a funny mushroom and became absorbed with it.

'But it's up to you as much as me, Simon,' said Pross, injecting an air of concern into his delivery, still viewing the house. 'I'll do my part, but will you do yours?'

'Of course I will,' answered Simon, a little offended.

Now looking at Simon, Pross asked, 'Do you know what your part is?' Before Simon could answer, Pross said, 'To support me, Simon. To trust me. To believe me. To give me everything I need to carry this momentous thing off without delay or hinderance. Godfrey wisely arranged things for me — he even tried to give me this special place — but I lost faith and lost his support. But he also wisely brought you in to help me. You've already helped me believe in myself again, but there's more you have to do. You have to provide me with what I need to get the job done this time, now that you've helped me see things clearly.' He returned his gaze to the house, adding soberly, 'It's an elaborate device. And no one else on Earth sees the Truth like you do, so no one else will help.'

Money. Pross was talking money. Simon knew that right enough. 'What do you need?' he asked, bracing himself.

'Crystal pyramids,' answered Pross. 'Thirteen small crystal pyramids.'

Relief became evident on Simon's face.

Continuing, Pross explained, 'The Cosmic Masters transmitted powerful, secret knowledge to me, Simon. Knowledge I must use to start the Golden Millennium. Crystal pyramids are the key to the working of the Empathy Device. It works on the principle of energy resonance. It's like marching soldiers making a bridge collapse. They march in tune with the bridge's resonant frequency. A specific alignment — no, a sacred alignment — of crystal pyramids has been revealed to me that will amplify my serene mind waves to an intensity great enough to be sent around the world along the ley lines, inducing sympathetic bliss in all, allowing the Millennium of peace to begin.' He dangled the quartz pyramid before Simon's eyes. 'Thirteen crystal pyramids — that's all I need from you, Simon. That and a few benchtop engineering tools and some electronic components that'll cost no more than a few hundred pounds. Extraterrestrial science has learned efficiency. It uses the power of nature. It uses zero point energy.'

'Amazing,' breathed Simon. A fantastic energy device comprising of aligned crystal pyramids made wondrous sense to him. Simon was a person who believed that the lost city of Atlantis had been powered by a mountainous crystal pyramid. He believed that because he'd read it in one of his New Age books, and Pross had browsed that very book this afternoon. He'd even heard about zero point energy in a science documentary he'd seen about various inventors claiming to have accidentally, albeit in a minuscule way, tapped the almost unlimited energy of the quantum vacuum. Most of these inventions involved cracking water into its constituent molecules in novel ways, resulting in unfounded claims to excess heat production, the excess speculated as perhaps coming from the zero point source — the energy of the sea of virtual particles constantly being created and destroyed. Watching the documentary, Simon hadn't really grasped the underlying principles, but he *had* embraced the near mystical element of "mysterious" energy sources.

'Do you know what zero point energy is, Simon? There's enough zero point energy in a teaspoon of water to boil all the Earth's oceans. And I now know how to extract it, just like I know how to amplify my spiritual energy. Once the world has been made peaceful, I'll make zero point energy fully available. No more want. No more pollution. And all I need from you first is thirteen crystals.'

'You can have them,' said Simon, smiling with relief and wonder.

'Diamond pyramids,' said Pross. 'I need diamond pyramids. The design calls for *diamond*.'

'Diamonds? Great!' said Phil, thrilled.

Phil might have been thrilled, but an almost funereal look immediately shrouded Simon, and he wandered a little away from Pross, thinking and deliberating, gazing over into the distance where the sun had just sunk below the high moors.

And Pross walked a few yards in the opposite direction, over to a small stone and crumbling mortar wall no higher than a tennis net, which seemed to serve no purpose.

Mick looked confused and perturbed, eventually following Simon.

Pross stood beside the wall, waiting. Phil came over and stood beside him, soon becoming uncomfortable with the silence. 'Th'Simon thinks he might be gay,' he lisped out of the blue, thrilled by the glamour.

'That's all right,' muttered Pross, dropping his serenity act considerably now that Simon was over yonder, 'I'm not homophobic. Some of my best friends don't mind gays.'

Fuck, that was a clever joke, thought Pross, wishing there'd been someone around to appreciate its cleverness.

'I'm not homophobic either,' said Phil. 'I like Th'Simon. He's my best friend.'

As far as Pross was concerned at the moment, the best thing about Simon, and Mick and Phil for that matter, was that he knew he could successfully take them all on in a fight if things got out of hand, like say a tussle over a pile of cash or a diamond.

Simon, tagged by Mick, came over, caution and reluctance written all over his face. Standing near Pross, not looking him in the eyes, he enigmatically said, 'It was an investment, you know.'

Not particularly knowing what he was talking about, Pross made no reply.

'The house,' explained Simon, still reluctant to look Pross in the face. 'It was an investment.'

'A selfless investment the world will celebrate for a thousand years, Simon,' said Pross.

But Simon's ears had become deaf. 'I'm going to have it converted into a centre for New Age studies,' he continued, disregarding Pross's prediction. 'We'll offer courses to paying guests. Mick's going to be the caretaker.'

Mick nodded confirmation of this. 'Sick of cabbying.'

'I'm going to be cook,' said Phil proudly. 'I used to work in a restaurant. I'm cooking th'supper for us all tonight.'

'That's right,' affirmed Simon. 'Anyway, no matter what, this property will hold its value. My old business partner told me. There's a lot of Japanese investment coming to the Northeast. A property like this will be sought after soon.'

'You have to let go, Simon. You even told me yourself that in the Golden Millennium monetary systems will be abolished. People will have what they need then, and no one of worth will want more.'

His lips slightly parted, now looking over to the moors beyond, Simon had the appearance of a person unconvinced and troubled.

Seeing the worry and doubt written on Simon's face, Pross moved a few steps nearer to the house, surveying it. 'This house will become priceless to humanity, Simon. It will be more than you ever imagined. Things are being revealed to me even as we speak.' Pross then went on to explain how here positive energy was maximum, and destructive negative energies were minimum, thus providing the most advantageous surroundings in which to pioneer the New Age of science. This was where New Age science would soon be born. 'A new age for science will dawn with this project. Science for the Golden Millennium. Science that works with and not against the New Age. A laboratory guided by the Aquarian shift in consciousness already overcoming the world, allowing science passage into the Golden Millennium.'

A passion entering his voice, he went on to say, 'Once we've prepared the world with my bliss, here is where the extraterrestrials will come to teach us their great secrets. We'll have all the energy we'll need, and with their guidance, devices to eliminate pain and diseases will be created here. Ageing will be conquered. The environment will be cleansed. Here is where it will all come true.'

Towards the door, Pross walked.

But Simon was still wounded by the thought of having to buy diamonds. He lugubriously scanned the skies for UFO's, then followed his master.

Then Mick and Phil too.

Coming indoors, Simon sat on what looked like an old school chair, a large stone fireplace guarded by two carved griffins haunting the deep shadow behind him.

He brooded.

Pross was sat on the grand staircase, secretly brooding on Simon's broodiness.

'Can we light the candles?' asked Phil, and Simon's muttered consent set him on a round of fire raising.

Mick began lighting some candles too.

Pross began thinking.

What Pross had been thinking two hours earlier was that perhaps all he need do was invent a costly scheme necessary for the emergence of the Golden Millennium, then persuade Simon to provide the funds so that he could make it real — plenty of room for personal enrichment there so long as big money was floating around to buy diamonds with, money which would have ended up in his own pocket. What he was now realising was that it wasn't going to be that easy. Simon, apparently the greatest miser since Scrooge, would never simply hand him a million pounds, or whatever, to develop the Global Empathy Device. He might possibly be persuaded to fund such a thing, but for sure he would scrutinise and question every single invoice, remaining in control of the finances. He'd even charged his own Messiah for sandwiches, after all.

Even more cunning than he'd first envisaged was going to be required.

So Pross thought some more, and then hit on an idea: he would demonstrate his magic to Simon. That way, once convinced, Simon would be considerably more free with his sponsorship.

So he moved nearer to Simon, who was gazing despondently to the floor.

When Pross came beside him, without looking up, Simon dolefully said, 'Diamond?'

'Diamond,' confirmed Pross.

A pause.

'Why diamond?'

'It's the purest, greatest crystal in existence, Simon,' explained Pross in a sympathetic tone. 'That's why Godfrey arranged for me to win the lottery — he knew I'd need a few million pounds to buy them with. Thirteen pure diamond crystals correctly aligned will amplify my mind waves and transmit them at a frequency the ley lines can absorb. Only diamond oscillates at the same frequency as the ley lines. Other crystals could crudely amplify my mind waves if aligned correctly, but only diamond can achieve ultra-high amplification and transmit at the ley line frequency to spread my bliss around the world.'

Simon returned to gloomy silence.

As it emerged from the dark into candlelight, Pross, appearing to be absorbed in arcane thought, approached the prayer battery. Knowing he was being gloomily viewed by Simon, he placed a hand on to it.

'Can we light the fire as th'well?' asked Phil, oblivious to Pross's antics.

Simon nodded his permission while continuing to observe Pross.

As it had already been laid with kindling and logs, Phil soon had the fire smoking and flaming.

Candlelight flickering in his eyes, Pross turned to look at Simon and said, 'I know how I might be able to prove it to you, Simon. I might be able to prove it to you *tonight*.'

'Prove what?'

'Crystal energy resonance — but without the need for diamonds.'

'How?' asked Simon.

Holding out the crystal pyramid he'd dowsed with, Pross said, 'I don't have diamond yet, but quartz might do for three people *within* the resonance pattern.' And then he suddenly hurled the pyramid at the stone wall above the fireplace, where it smashed to pieces.

Phil squealed.

Mick looked uneasy and jumpy, then looked to Simon.

Simon looked aghast — that pyramid had cost him ten pounds.

'Th'what did you do that for?' asked Phil nervously.

Suddenly gripping Simon tightly by the shoulders, looking vigorously into his eyes, Pross said, 'Do you want to sample my serenity tonight, Simon? Be the first to glimpse the New Age? The Golden Millennium? Ahead of all others? This very night, Simon? *This very night?*'

Simon's stupefaction was total. Utterly stupefied. Utterly unable to muster any kind of answer to the momentous question.

So long did Simon remain dumb-struck, it began to get more than a little a awkward for Pross, holding him by the shoulders, needing a reply.

'Can I be the first as th'well?' chimed Phil.

'And me?,' asked Mick after some hesitation.

Thank fuck for that, thought Pross, using the questions as an excuse for releasing Simon from his grip. 'You can all be first,' he said to his followers. 'You three worthy people, ahead of the whole world, shall glimpse the New Age.'

'But how?' lisped Phil in confusion. 'You haven't th'made the thing device th'yet.'

Saying nothing for now, Pross went over to pick up the crystal pieces, his golden robe glittering in the firelight. Six enchanted eyes remained fixed upon him as he collected shattered fragments. Returning to the battery, standing beside it, holding out the crystal fragments, he said, 'By placing these pieces of quartz around the house in a close correlation to the sacred alignment revealed to me, I might be able to directly bathe you all in bliss.'

'Amazing,' breathed Simon before finding some questions. 'Why can't we use quartz in the empathy device?'

'Because quartz doesn't radiate at the right frequency for the ley lines. But that won't matter here because you'll be directly within the energy field. And only diamond can amplify to the level required to energise the whole world. All crystals have the potential to tap zero point energy, but diamond has by far the most, and pyramid shapes enhance that energy trillions of times.'

'Amazing,' breathed Simon.

'Great,' lisped Phil.

Muddy pool. Muddy pool.

Fixing Simon with a preparatory gaze, Pross said, 'Simon, tonight you'll learn the true power of crystals. We've had the stone age, the bronze age, the iron age, the steam age, the nuclear age, the computer age, soon we shall enter the final, purest age of them all, the *Crystal Age*. Do you want to be the first to experience the crystal age?'

Simon breathed, 'Yes.'

2.15
Paul McCartney

They were moving on to Robert's favourite bar.

Jennifer squeezed herself in between her two new friends as they all three clambered into a cab outside the restaurant in which they had only just met some two hours earlier.

'You're quite a shy person, aren't you?' remarked Robert very soon after the cab set off.

Yvette immediately protested in a stereotypically French manner. 'No,' she said, face jumping into an expression of disagreement, touching Jennifer's arm, 'shee ees not shy.'

It was almost patronizing, Yvette's attitude to her, but Jennifer did not mind at all, for she did it so sweetly it became a delightful thing.

Forgoing the issue of her shyness, Jennifer asked Yvette how long she and Robert had been going out with each other.

'Wee-er not love-ers,' answered Yvette, somewhat surprised at the assumption.

'Oh,' said Jennifer, feeling a little stupid and unhip.

'Mah boyfwend's called Peter. Eee's at work tonight.'

Jennifer began saying how she had broken up with her own boyfriend the night before, and that was mostly why she had come to London. But the cab had now stopped, and Jennifer could hardly believe it: they were apparently already at their destination.

Yvette and Robert opened their doors, Robert then paying the driver.

Jennifer spoke with amazement. 'We could have walked this in three minutes!'

'But I can drink a beer in three minutes,' said Robert with a smirk, taking the lead as they strolled to the bar door behind a young couple.

A dark-haired, narrow-faced waitress of masculine appearance (although also heavily pregnant), was standing just inside the door. She stepped prohibitively in front of the couple. 'Sorry, no tables free,' she said indifferently, her voice deep and husky, her accent recognisably continental.

The disappointed couple turned around and left.

'Hello, Robert,' said the waitress when she saw him, standing aside so that he could enter. 'Trevor's been in looking for you.'

Robert showed great interest in this intelligence. 'Really?'

'About an hour ago,' said the waitress, about to turn Yvette and Jennifer away, until Robert intervened.

'No. These two are with me,' said Robert.

The waitress stood aside, discreetly allowing Robert's companions entry, like she was granting a privilege not really hers to permit. 'Trevor left something for you behind the bar,' she said in a low voice. 'Ask Danny for it.'

'Excellent,' rumbled Robert quietly as he walked past.

Approaching the bar, Robert explained to Jennifer that the licence here only allowed for drinking to be done with a meal, but that he knew all the staff.

There were indeed no tables free, observed Jennifer, also observing that this place was like no place in Richmond. She had been expecting a pub, but this was like a lively restaurant for getting drunk in. It was quite small and very crowded, but some standing space was available at the drinks bar, and that is where they stood.

Lighting was minimal. Candles burned on each table. Loud Latin music played, matching the establishment's obvious Mexican theme.

Drinks were ordered by Robert, and soon Jennifer had a bottle of Mexican beer in her hand, her third beer of the evening.

'I used to be shy,' said Robert unexpectedly, necessarily leaning close to talk in her ear above the music. 'Want to know how I got over it?'

'How?' shouted Jennifer.

'By telling myself that in any gathering I might be in, no one was anywhere near as clever as me. Just think of the other people as mere children compared to yourself, then you'll never feel shy again.'

'I'll try,' said Jennifer.

An hour later, they were moving on again, to a bar in Soho this time. Robert had paid the whole of the bill in the Mexican bar, despite both Yvette's and Jennifer's insistence on sharing it, and was now telling a cab driver that they wished to be taken to Greek Street.

Tipsy with beer, excited to have been taken under the wing of such kind, warm, loveable people, speeding off to yet another bar, Jennifer felt like she was beginning to live life like it should be lived. Everything and everyone she had seen today had been new and different.

Robert and Yvette began clowning around, and Jennifer smiled at their buffoonery.

The ride was filled with spirited talk about nothing in particular.

A partner in a publishing company. When asked, Robert said he was a partner in publishing company. 'Nothing interesting. Just business titles,' he explained. 'We're based in Harley Street.'

'And ee earns lots of money,' added Yvette proudly. 'And ee's the most wonderful person ah know.'

'I earn it so I can give it away,' said Robert, lighting a cigarette, perhaps his tenth of the evening so far.

Jennifer had earlier decided that he was probably a rock musician, and was a little disappointed to learn he wasn't.

'I was a musician before I moved to London,' Robert went on to say. 'I came down here about five years ago, but the music didn't come off, so I moved into publishing.'

Soon the streets became narrow and winding, thronged with young people.

'Just over here, thanks,' said Robert to the driver.

This bar was an exclusive place, explained Robert to Jennifer. Paul McCartney had held a party here recently.

A beefy doorman with short, gelled ginger hair was on duty. Entering the establishment with lofty confidence, Robert nodded to him in passing.

Sophisticated is the word which immediately entered Jennifer's mind. It was a plush place.

Ignoring a long, glittering bar just inside the door, Robert led his companions up a wide, ornate staircase.

Yvette and Jennifer were the reason why a number of men made discreet upward glances.

Twenty-three carpeted steps later, they were in the smaller upstairs lounge, furnished with its own corner bar. A half-dozen or so low tables with small, two-seater sofas placed either side were positioned around the floor space of this high-ceilinged room. Some of these sofas supported reclining patrons.

Yvette immediately placed herself down on a sofa as if she were tired out, blowing her wayward hair away from her face through comically twisted lips. Smiling, she patted the cushion beside her, playfully enticing Jennifer to sit next to her.

Taking off his coat, which smelled heavily of stale smoke, Robert, smiling euphorically, sat opposite his companions.

A waitress came over to take their drinks order. Robert asked for a double brandy, insisting that the brandy be *Rene Martin*. 'The best brandy in the world,' he explained to Jennifer. 'Put it all on my tab here,' he called out after the waitress had written down the orders and walked away.

'Hello, Robert,' said a young man alone at the bar after turning on his stool. His tone was cheerless. 'Hello, Yvette.'

'Ello,' said Yvette, her return tone approaching very close to suspicion.

'Hello, Mark,' said Robert, as if mildly surprised to see him sat there.

'Don't sound surprised,' returned Mark, 'you know I'm here most nights.'

And then he turned around again.

Yvette pulled a twisty face in response to Mark's unsocial attitude.

'Try working with him,' said Robert, just so low as not to be heard by Mark. 'It's like having a rain cloud in the room with you all day long.' Looking at Jennifer, he explained in a somewhat deprecating but forthright manner, 'One of my partners. King of the barbed comment.'

Jennifer glanced Mark's way. He was taller than Robert — but then so were most people — with a saturnine face and weak chin. He wore a light-coloured jacket, inside which he seemed to be holding his shoulders in a lasting shrug, and his straight, collar-length brown hair was swept back.

Now watching Robert draw on his cigarette, Jennifer was struck by the thought that if he wasn't so nice, she might have described him as ugly.

'Here's to Jennifer in London,' said Robert, picking up his drink.

'Yes!' said Yvette with approving, childlike enthusiasm.

Clinking glasses, they all three drank to her.

After the toast, Jennifer observed that Mark had gone.

2.16
Maximum Cunning

Tonight Pross was going to pull what to him felt like a merry prank.

And he *had* debated the morality of this prank with himself before deciding to really do it, concluding that since Simon, Mick and Phil were already mad, they had nothing to lose.

And anyway, it was their fault for kidnapping him.

After having taken a solitary, robed walk in the grounds until complete darkness fell, necessarily thinking of that muddy pool several times, Pross returned indoors to execute his plan's master stroke.

Of course it made no sense. But it didn't have to, it was a matter of faith to Simon. Crystals were magic to him and his ilk, like crosses to Christians. Except that tonight, *his* cross was really going to bestow blessings. Pross would see to that.

'Anyone got any *sellotape*?' asked Pross, explaining that he needed it to tape crystal fragments in strategic places.

Mick said he kept some in his cab and went to get it.

'I can't allow it,' said Pross, some minutes later, 'it's the most powerful science on Earth.' Phil was lamenting Pross's instructions that his followers should leave the house while he placed the crystal fragments in their positions. 'If this knowledge were to fall into the hands of evil, it could be used to spread hate around the world just as easily as love, or liberate enough zero point energy to destroy the whole solar system.'

'He's right,' decided Simon, sensibly considering the issue. 'That's why we're not allowed to see inside the prayer batteries. The technology's too powerful.'

'Precisely,' said Pross.

'How will you know th'where to put the crystals without measuring?' asked Phil.

This would have been an awkward question had Pross not anticipated it.

Although initially annoyed that Phil was questioning Pross's methods, Simon also wanted to know the answer and endorsed the question with a noise.

'I don't have to measure the angles and lengths,' explained Pross patiently. 'I just understand the pattern. It's like a bird migrating: instinct. The extraterrestrials didn't tell me the figures, they infused the shape into my mind. I *comprehend* the shape.'

'Amazing,' breathed Simon.

And soon Pross was alone, walking to and fro, upstairs and downstairs, actually placing crystal fragments in various locations just in case he was being glimpsed through the windows.

In ten minutes it was done, and he beckoned his followers, one torch between them, back inside from the near total darkness of the grounds.

He gathered them together for a lecture before the fire, now blazing with burning logs.

'What happens now is that I stand at the activation node...'

'Th'where's that?' interrupted Phil.

'I can't tell you. If any of you were tempted to pray at that spot, you would flood the house with unbalanced energy. Only my energy is balanced enough to create New Age consciousness.'

'Amazing,' breathed Simon.

Pross continued. 'While I pray at the activation node, my spiritual energy should excite the crystals, which will slowly begin to resonate. It'll be like an echo growing louder, except there'll be nothing to hear. But, if it works, you'll gradually begin to feel my bliss, until you're saturated. That's *if* it works.'

'Th'why mightn't it work?' asked Phil.

'Quartz is a crude crystal and the fragments aren't pyramids,' explained Pross. 'We just have to hope.' Giving Simon a supplicating look, he said, 'Please don't be deterred if it doesn't. It's not as precise as the device will be.'

But bliss was not quite yet ready to come, for it had earlier been suggested by Pross that Phil should cook supper first.

Later, visiting Phil in the kitchen, watching him cut a chicken into pieces, Pross said that his appetite wasn't really up to a full meal, but he'd welcome another cheese sandwich or two.

'Sure you don't th'want any?' lisped Phil. He was upset. He really wanted Pross to eat his food.

'Sure. Anyway, I don't eat meat any more.'

Gushing apologies for not asking before if he was vegetarian, Phil set about cutting the cheese for Pross.

And behind his back, Pross surreptitiously introduced the contents of two of his three remaining ecstasy capsules into the pasta sauce just prepared, figuring two between three to be enough — besides, he wanted to keep one for himself.

Receiving the sandwiches, Pross took them upstairs to eat while washing the previous night's bonfire out of his hair.

'I hope you like them,' said Phil as Pross took them away, then calling after him, 'I'm going to grow my hair like yours. I'll th'start tomorrow morning.'

And while Pross was upstairs, the meal was presented. A small, rickety table had been brought out and positioned in front of the fire in the big room, still lit only by candles. Upon this table, Phil set two plates of his cooking — pasta with a sauce made from fried chicken, canned chopped tomatoes, peas, carrots, sweetcorn, fried peppers, and a shot of tabasco. They had all contributed equally to the purchasing of these ingredients — Simon had seen to that.

Mick ate like he was trying to remember the rules of etiquette.

Phil ate separately, preferring to sit alone in the shadows. His white robe was rucked up to his waist and his plate was balanced on his bony legs. He did not speak at all while eating, and if anyone had remembered to look at him, they would have seen that he devoured his meal in much the same way he'd devoured the Mars Bar that morning — like his was worried to show his teeth, or be seen eating at all.

His teeth were tiny and pointy.

But no one looked at him. Mick was too busy remembering not to use his knife to pick food up with, and Simon was fast becoming like someone about to undergo an operation: he knew it was necessary and that it would do him good, but the sense of trepidation was huge and growing with every minute.

Both Simon and Mick felt that Phil had used too much salt in the sauce. Phil thought that too, and was perplexed: he hadn't used any salt at all.

Coming downstairs with hair lank with water, two books hidden under his robe, Pross knelt before the fire to dry himself out, happily seeing that all plates had been cleaned.

'When do we start?' asked Simon, greatly subdued.

'It already has,' answered Pross, seeing from Simon's wristwatch that it was now just past nine o'clock. 'I prayed at the activation node a few minutes ago. My spiritual energy should begin to build up, then echo for a while around the house before fading.'

Now staring into the fire's flames, Simon asked, 'What'll it feel like?'

'It might be a little unpleasant at first,' admitted Pross.

'Why's that?' asked Simon, continuing to stare into the fire.

'Quartz is not so pure a crystal as diamond. The energy might become a little distorted. It's like plucking a guitar string. The string mainly sounds the fundamental note, but overtones will be present that might cause some side effects, especially at first until your own spiritual vibrations become attuned to it. You might feel lightheaded. Nauseous, even.'

'Will it hurt?' asked Simon, ashamed of himself.

Seeing that Simon was fearful, Pross sought to reassure him. 'No, it won't hurt.' Speaking louder for the others, he said, 'And don't worry. Eventually you should begin to become sympathetically balanced to the fundamental spiritual vibration. Don't worry about the overtones, just enjoy the bliss of New Age consciousness while it lasts — it'll soon come. The bliss should last for hours. The quartz should be able to resonate that long without being primed again.'

Simon looked at Pross and forced a smile.

Pross placed a hand on his shoulder and said, 'Peace be with you very soon.' Then, looking at Mick, he said, 'Please tell me your poem again.'

Apparently nervous at first, by fire and candlelight, Mick began reciting his finest work:

> *'Ere I woke before the dawn*
> *I dreamed I was in some distant clime*
> *Where as I lay in state forlorn*
> *I felt Aileen's gentle 'and touch mine.*
>
> *A maiden and she is wondrous fair*
> *Elegant, wise and kind,*
> *An angel with long, long 'air*
> *Who is always on my mind*
>
> *Gazing at 'er all the time,*
> *I began to feel as one blest;*
> *But then she sighed a name that was not mine*
> *As she lay 'er sleepy 'ead upon my breast.*
> *Then I realised with un'appy light*
> *That she'd mistook me for 'er lover in the dead of the night.'*

His own poetry seemed to have transported Mick somewhere else entirely.

'That was beautiful,' said Pross, deciding that his hair was dry enough to go out with.

'Thanks,' said Mick, leaving Memory Lane.

'Can I borrow your cab for the evening.'

Mick blanched. 'Can't. Not insured for you. It's me livelihood. I would but...'

'OK. Understood,' cut in Pross placatingly, standing up, not about to insist or pull rank (he was the Messiah, after all). But he still wanted to go to the pub, and most definitely didn't want to be around when his followers came up on the E, in case they tried to hug him or something.

'Where you going? I'll drive you,' offered Mick.

'No thanks,' said Pross, thinking that Mick on drugs in charge of a vehicle would be just a little too much.

'You can borrow my bike,' spouted Phil excitedly from the shadows. 'Can you ride a bike?'

'Where are you going?' asked Simon anxiously, rising to his feet.

'I can't tell you. To a sacred site,' answered Pross, also telling Phil that he could indeed ride a bike, although he was debating with himself whether or not he should use it — it was getting bloody cold out. Sod it, he only wanted to go to the pub he'd seen a few miles down the road. He could even keep his robe on until almost there, no one would see him in this isolated area. 'I'll be back later on tonight,' he assured Simon as he was handed the motorbike key by Phil. He also received the key to the gates from Mick.

'Please stay,' said Simon to Pross.

'Can't,' said Pross. 'I've been told to be at a special place at ten o'clock.'

Phil picked up a candle. 'I'll get you my helmet from my room,' he said, taking the candle away with him because many of the house's light fittings were without bulbs.

Simon became filled with mystic astonishment. 'The extraterrestrials?' he guessed in awe and wonder.

Pross nodded his head and said in a low voice, 'Yes, Simon, the extraterrestrials.'

'Why?'

'I don't know. I don't at all know.'

'I feel strange,' said Simon, looking perturbed, and Pross discerned that Simon was coming up, and probably had been for some minutes. He hadn't expected it to happen so soon. He looked at Mick. Mick, too, seemed to be experiencing something perturbing.

'It's working,' said Pross. 'Don't worry about the overtones, just enjoy the New Age.' Touching Simon on the arm, he said, 'Tell Phil I'm outside with the bike.'

And, taking the torch with him, he left them to it.

2.17
Hysterical Paralysis & Serene Guilt

It was an old MZ. A bizarre, East European, two-stroke, oil burning, noisy old MZ. But what the hell: it would get him to the pub and out of his drugged followers' way for the better part of the evening.

Five minutes of torchlight investigation was required before he discovered where to stick the key — under a flip-back plastic shield on top of the headlight. Another five minutes of kick-starting followed. But eventually the bike was rattling away bravely. All he needed now was the helmet. But, leaving the bike running and walking up to the window, peering through, only Mick and Simon were in the large room. Simon was wandering around, shifting his weight between legs. Mick was looking twitchy by the fire... but he was *grinning!* And Simon also seemed to be moving halfway to a smile. But there was no Phil. Probably found a mouse dropping somewhere, thought Pross, and decided to head off without the helmet, estimating the chances of encountering a police car thereabouts as virtually nil.

Muddy pool. Muddy pool.

Leaving the torch on the ground, Pross hitched up his robe and straddled the small machine. Jerkily at first, he set off down the private road through the wood, the headlight being just about adequate. Reaching the gates, he unlocked them, and was soon zipping along the narrow, winding road that led to the village. Unfortunately, as soon as any incline was encountered, the bike's engine proved sadly lacking, first gear having to be employed often. But it was fun, and the thick robe kept the worst of the wind off him.

He started weaving and swerving around for the joy of it.

Shit, a car was coming along from the other way. Pross looked straight ahead and concentrated on riding sensibly. Becoming fainthearted, he decided he ought to take off his robe in case it attracted unwanted attention. So, just after the car had passed, he pulled up and disrobed, stuffing it behind a fence to collect on the way back.

Simon and Mick had come up on the crystal energy differently. Simon had been the first to feel the effects, only a few minutes or so after finishing his meal. And by the time Pross had come down to dry his hair by the fire, Simon's natural anxieties were being artificially magnified. Although bliss had been promised, he was now uneasy about being the subject of a scientific experiment, especially one which he was now learning could have side effects. It was just so daunting, the house being swamped with spiritual energy.

He was waiting for it to start to take effect, unaware that it already had.

'It might be a little unpleasant at first,' said Pross.

Say something. Say something. Think of something. 'Why's that?' said Simon, continuing to stare into the fire.

'Quartz is not so pure a crystal as diamond. The energy might become a little distorted. It's like plucking a guitar string — the string mainly sounds the fundamental note, but overtones will be present that could cause some side effects, especially at first until you become accustomed to it. You might feel lightheaded. Nauseous, even.'

As Pross continued to talk, Simon began, for the first time in his whole life, to see things differently. Here was a man who had never even been drunk once in his life, but now reality seemed to be becoming a little distant, yet he still didn't realise that his mind was already being changed.

Worry.

'Will it hurt?'

No, it wouldn't hurt. And not to worry — he said it will be all right in the end. But he didn't feel all right now. He felt scared and lonely. He looked at Pross and forced a smile.

Pross placed a welcomed hand on his shoulder.

Energy was zipping through him. Mick could actually feel the crystal energy zipping through him. It was amazing. He wanted to laugh, but was suddenly hit hard emotionally:

'Please tell me your poem again.'

Suddenly feeling like he'd been caught doing something filthy, Mick stopped enjoying the energy. But he kept a grip on himself and, after a debate with himself about whether or not Prospero had actually asked him to recite his poem, he decided he had and began. And when he finished, he was emotionally back in school again, passing Aileen in a corridor; she, laughing with friends, the centre of attention; he, ashamed of his cheap blazer, the cheapest in the school... 'Can't. Not insured for you. It's me livelihood.' These things he'd blurted without feeling he'd said them himself. 'You can borrow my bike,' said Phil, and the drama all seemed to swing mercifully away from him.

He's going! He's going! Simon was floored. He was scared, and wanted Prospero there. 'Where are you going? Please stay.' But he was forgetting what it was all about: the extraterrestrials. And he was scared because he was affected. He hadn't realised it until now, but he was definitely affected — the crystal resonance experiment was working. Extraterrestrial science was at work on him. 'I feel strange.'

'It's working,' said Pross, touching his arm.

And then suddenly Prospero was gone. But somehow, once he'd gone, it didn't matter. Everything was, or was promising to be very soon, exactly as it should be. He reminded himself that he was in the hands of a great scientist using extraterrestrial knowledge to give him a taste of New Age consciousness. He'd felt a bit strange at first, but now it all seemed to be levelling out, just as Prospero had said it would.

He heard the motorbike start up.

Energy. He was jazzing with energy again. 'Can you feel it?' Mick said to Simon. 'How you feeling?'

Simon looked at him and felt that any answer he could give in mere words could not describe it.

'Never felt anything like this,' said Mick, who couldn't keep still, fidgeting and shifting himself on his chair by the fire.

And then Simon, having braved the dangerous crags, stepped on to the pristine plateau and looked about himself, and all was calm and still and beautiful and untrodden. The candles glowed warmly, oozing divine light, rich in reds and yellows. The room, with its log fire, was the cosiest room he had ever known. The shadows were things of wonder. Mick was smiling, and he felt a smile come to his own face.

He was in the New Age.

Pulling up outside the pub, an old man walked past Pross on his way inside. 'Shouldn't thou be wearing a helmet?' the man said.

'Don't need one. I've got a really strong aura.'

'Humph,' the old man muttered.

While Pross was putting the bike up on its stand, the old man reversed his steps. Peering at him, he said, 'You're wun that came t' look at 'ouse, aren't y'?'

Pross now recognised him. He was the gatekeeper.

'That's right.'

'Was't you that bought it then?'

'Not me.'

'One of those other wuns up there now then?'

'That's right. Simon.'

'Humph.'

And he went inside, ahead of Pross.

'I feel fackin' great,' grinned Mick manically. But that's as far as it got with him. No deep thoughts about thoughts. No introspective insights. Simon, on the other hand, was filled with the true glory of it all. He was in the New Age, and the New Age was beautiful, and it was Prospero Pi-Meson's magic that had made it all happen. Prospero Pi-Meson truly was the Expected One, and all the Expected One needed to spread his bliss around the world was a few diamonds.

'Imagine,' he said in awed tones to Mick, 'this is what it'll be like all the time in the New Age. Everyone will feel like this.'

'I feel fackin' great,' said Mick again, looking jerkily around the room.

Faltering in a sincere attempt to describe how *he* felt, Simon finally settled for the word *hallowed*. And then his eyes juddered, and a wave of bliss washed over him. 'Amazing,' he breathed.

He knelt down near the fire and imagined he could actually see Prospero's spiritual energy streaming through the room. It was dark pink and tenuous.

Wispy. Ethereal. 'Amazing,' he breathed.

He closed his eyes and began to drift away with the expanded wonder of it all.

'Where's Phil?' jabbered Mick. 'Ain't he s'posed to be getting 'is 'elmet?'

That was a point — where *was* Phil? And how long had he been gone? Simon looked out of the window and saw, under a newly-risen, waning half-moon, that Phil's bike was gone. But Phil definitely hadn't come back from his excursion to his room, or had he?

After a muddled discussion, Mick and Simon went to investigate, each taking a candle that oozed wonderful light.

The floorboards creaked loudly beneath their feet as they passed down the corridor leading to Phil's room, Simon in the lead.

Candlelight was seeping mellifluously from Phil's room.

'Phil?' called Mick. 'Where are ya?'

There was no return call.

They reached his door, which, being half open, allowed the scene within to be viewed. Phil was sat hunched on his helmet, fingers gripping the hem of his robe. His bony legs were drawn up to his waist but turned to the side, so that he appeared to be trying to ride the helmet side-saddle.

He looked scared.

Very scared.

He rolled his eyes towards the doorway, and neither Simon or Mick had ever seen a more terrified expression on anyone before. Someone about to be disembowelled alive might have appeared more sanguine than Phil at this moment. But there was more to it than fear. There was a haunted, hunted look to Phil. 'It's not th'working,' he insisted weakly, trying to sound confident.

'What's not working?' asked Mick.

'The energy. It's not th'working,' Phil said.

'What's the fackin' matter wiv ya?' asked Mick harshly, stepping into the room.

Simon, perplexed, followed Mick.

'Look at his fackin' eyes!' said Mick.

'It's not th'working,' said Phil, still clutching his robe's hem.

He had not as yet moved, or even relaxed, a muscle.

'Why didn't you bring Pross the helmet?' asked Simon. 'He's gone without one now.'

'It's not th'working,' said Phil again.

'Don't talk stupid. Of course it's working.'

There was no improvement in Phil's countenance.

Viewing him sympathetically, Simon said, 'It must be the overtones. Maybe the energy's purer in the big room.'

Phil's eyes seemed to show that he was torn between seeing Simon and Mick as comforting friends and seeing them as people about to do him some great harm. Those desperate eyes would not let them out of his sight. Mick, especially.

'Come into the big room,' said Simon.

No response from Phil.

'Cam on,' said Mick.

Phil confessed he couldn't move.

'Whad'ya mean?' asked Mick.

'I can't th'stand up,' said Phil quietly. Embarrassedly. 'My legs th'won't work.'

And they could see Phil wasn't joking.

'Let's carry him,' said Mick.

'No!' pleaded Phil. 'Leave me here.'

But they didn't, and he remained rigid all the way, like a twisted spastic. He was put down on a chair near the fire.

'You should be all right here,' said Simon. 'The energy's purer in here.'

'It's not th'working,' said Phil again.

'It is,' said Simon. 'We're in the New Age.'

'I feel fackin' great,' said Mick.

And Simon sat on the floor and closed his eyes again, wallowing in the comfort of knowing that the Golden Millennium was his to buy.

He meditated.

Mick didn't. But soon he had the idea of getting a cassette from his room so they could have music.

He put on *Stairway to Heaven* and began swaying.

And then dancing.

He closed his eyes and danced.

And for the next half an hour, Phil could not let Mick and his jerky motions out of his petrified sight... until later when Simon stirred, breathed deeply a number of times, then stood up.

Perceiving he was about to leave the room, Phil looked at him and pathetically said, 'Th'where are you going?'

'The toilet,' answered Simon.

'Don't be long.'

Simon looked at him and wondered.

And when Simon returned from the toilet and Phil quietly said, 'I missed you,' to him, Simon wondered a lot more.

A finger moved. Phil definitely felt a finger move. Then it moved again, under his control this time. The sense of relief was beyond words. He felt like he was waking from a nightmare, and knew that he could lift his whole arm if he really tried. So he began concentrating on doing that great thing... but, dancing uncoordinatedly, Mick stumbled towards him, knocking into him, almost displacing him from his seat.

Abruptly, Mick opened his eyes, looking sharply and defensively at Phil, almost, at first, as if believing *Phil* had been the one to bump *him*. But then Mick relaxed and was about to say sorry when Phil suddenly blurted, 'It's not th'working.'

'Of course it's working,' said Simon. 'Prospero said it would, didn't he?'

'It's not th'working. It's not.'

'Course it's fackin' working,' argued Mick. 'I feel great.' And then Mick could hardly believe what he was seeing: 'He's pissing himself!' he observed loudly.

And Simon saw that Phil was indeed pissing himself, urine streaming off the chair on to the floor.

'It's not th'working,' said Phil through taut lips.

All at once, Simon remembered the Truth, as written in the scriptures he poured over each day: *All who do not heed his words must be removed from the Earth*.

'He must be evil,' breathed Simon.

That realisation hit Simon like a true afflatus. Phil must be evil, otherwise the goodly energy would not have reacted badly with him. And was it not written that evil would try to stop the New Age from coming? It *was* so written, knew Simon.

So Simon said, 'Kill him.'

The room froze.

Mick looked at Simon.

Simon looked at Mick.

'We have to kill him,' said Simon again. 'He's evil. He'll try to stop the New Age, like the scriptures say.'

Phil rolled his incredulous, terrified eyes to Mick and squealed like a slit pig when he saw Mick's fist raised against him. Mick rained a frenzy of blows down on to his head and body, knocking him off the chair. Lying sideways on the floor in a pool of his own urine, still twisted with hysterical paralysis, still gripping the robe, Phil squealed louder and louder. Soon Mick began stomping his victim over and over again, who cried, wailed, whimpered and sobbed... but would not die.

Almost exhausted, about stomp again, Mick slipped on Phil's blood and urine and fell to the floor, ending up on all fours beside his victim, panting like a dog.

Blood seeped from Phil's smashed face as he lay groaning, his flooded airways bubbling with each laboured breath. One glancing stomp had ripped the flesh from his broken jaw so that it lay as a bloodied, bearded flap for his own astonished eyes to see.

When those eyes rolled up to view Simon, as if searching for an explanation, they saw him again say, 'Kill him.'

And Mick did next time.

The *Lorimer's Arms* was a farmer's pub.

Shabby old men.

Shabby young men dressed like shabby old men.

Grey old dogs lying bored and arthritic under scuffed chairs.

A fire.

Polished brass and black leather horse tackle on whitewashed, unevenly plastered walls.

And everyone looked like they owned at least one shotgun.

Pross felt like a target.

But no one so much as looked at him.

Standing at the bar waiting to be served, he observed the gatekeeper sat on a stool over to his left.

His eyes were watery and spent.

Prevailing over the initial currency suspicion his reconstituted five pound note had raised, Pross bought a pint and found a corner to sit in, reading an Atherius Society booklet.

Ten minutes later, he was bored.

He got to reflecting.

Twenty-four hours, that's all it was. Twenty-four hours since he'd taken his E trip. He could hardly believe it. And strictly speaking, it was still the same day in which he'd sat, haunched and tearful, by the dying fire. The same day he'd listened a second time to Jennifer's message, desolate and guilt ridden. The same day he'd set off, most heavy of heart and light of pocket, to redeem himself somehow in the eyes of those he felt he'd hurt or ruined.

He remembered how *enthusiastic* he'd felt at the beginning of his trip, before all his Jennifer grief. That had felt so good. Enthusiasm was the thing most absent in his normal make up.

He still had a capsule of enthusiasm left.

He got the urge to enthuse again.

Taking an E now might be a beautiful thing to do, he thought. He could sit happily in the pub for two hours or more, and then maybe later he could ride the bike to the top of the hills if he wished. Sod the danger and the lack of helmet. This was frontier land as far as he was concerned. The ordinary rules of the highway didn't matter up here where so little traffic buzzed around. No one would see him up here. And he was in a much better frame of mind than the one he'd been in in the morning. And he could hardly be destroyed over losing Jennifer again, since he'd already come to terms with that. Anyway, things were going right for him. He just *knew* that his scam was going to work. Everything felt right about it.

Yes, he would take the remaining ecstasy.

He dared.

He did.

And he waited, sipping beer slowly, reading.

It seemed only ten or so minutes later when he began to experience tummy-fluttering excitement, and knew he was coming up.

Elusive, almost comical anxieties.

Fleeting nausea.

And then hallowed clarity and stillness.

But be buggered if he could read. He just couldn't focus his eyes that near. But he didn't care, he was all right just sitting sipping his drink, the conversations around him being like a lulling murmur. Thoughts drifted through his mind, but they didn't hurt. Even the thoughts of Jennifer didn't hurt *too* much.

Thirty hours, that's all. It was about thirty hours since he'd last seen her.

He wished so much she were with him.

With some pain, he wondered where she was now, and who she was with, if anyone.

He admitted that if it wasn't for that tiny, saving thought that he would surely be with her again, he would be in tears again now. He knew that thought was just an aspect of the inherent, necessary, universal, religious belief that all will be right in the end, but it bloody helped.

Sometimes he wished he could have more of that help. Sometimes he wished he could turn off his reasoning and just praise the Lord, or reincarnation, or Allah, or Golden Millenniums, or whatever else people praised. That would be such an escape. Be more like Simon — beguiled into happiness. Ignorance *was* bliss.

He wondered how *Simon* was getting on with the E.

Poor Simon. Just carried away with the innate comfort that things will be better, that's all. And he, Pross, with a mind unfairly cunning, was going to exploit it for his own benefit. That wasn't nice, really. Wasn't nice at all, really.

Thinking about it now, he could hardly believe what he'd done — fucked with some peoples' minds just for laughs and the chance of a few million or so.

Gradually it stopped being a silly game and became a callous crime. He was being a bastard. Simon's foolishness wasn't hurting anyone. If people wanted to believe rubbish, then let them — why ruin their comfort? In fact, as far as Pross could tell from reading the Aetherius literature, the founder of the society had perhaps set out to unify disparate religions, adding a strong karma code for a better world. Of course it was nonsense, but was it not laudable nonsense? It was certainly more laudable than exploiting religious longing to steal a few million quid.

Bugger. What a bastard time to develop religious sympathies, thought Pross to himself. What an irony.

And then he began imagining how Jennifer, if she were here, would react to knowing he was planning to break Simon's heart and take his money.

Annoyed and angry, that's what she'd be. Annoyed that he was being such a fraud.

Anyone viewing Pross would have seen his face become very serious at this point, and this was also the point when the gatekeeper, coming from the gents, loped shakily up to him. Standing above him, looking down at him, he said, 'You're with wuns that bought it, though?'

'I know them,' admitted Pross.

'Humph,' reacted the gatekeeper, then shuffling disconsolately away.

But he shuffled disconsolately back. 'What's going t' come of me, then, lad?' he said, making it sound like an accusation.

'Pardon?' said Pross.

'Six weeks,' muttered the gatekeeper in angry, bewildered resentment. 'Six weeks t' leave. Forty-three years lived there. Six weeks t' leave.'

And then he went away again, placing himself on what was probably *his* stool at the end of the short bar.

He looked so unhappy, so very unhappy to Pross.

Rent free is how Lilith had described his status on the estate, in exchange for watching over the property and maintaining the grounds. His status under Simon had evidently changed for the worse.

Pross wanted to help him. Christ! the man had probably fought nazis in the war — why should he lose his home because of a silly story some cocky youngster had written about a physicist?

Simon. He actually wanted to help Simon too. Pross reminded himself that he didn't need to steal the money, after all. He could try to reclaim his lottery win instead, like he'd resolved to when on E the previous day. He could get a solicitor on to the case, or something.

In his druggy state, it was all becoming clear to him: he would never again do anything that would add to his not inconsiderable guilt baggage.

This hit him like a true afflatus.

Guilt. Pross was beginning to feel guilt about most everything in his life. From turning a blind eye to his mother's suicide attempts, to losing Ron his job.

Sod evolutionary psychology, *that* was how he would live from now on. Like a saint. There was nothing noble about it, he just wanted to be able to take drugs without getting bogged down with shame. And since he'd come to the conclusion that he wasn't likely to get round to killing himself for quite some time yet, not at least until he started to go bald, a guilt-free conscience seemed a highly desirable life-enhancement asset. It certainly seemed desirable at this druggy juncture.

But what could he do about Simon? If he just buggered off now, Simon would spend the rest of his misguided life looking for him. No, the best thing would be to tell Simon the truth, especially about putting ecstasy in the food. That might actually convince him that he was not the Expected One.

Yes, that's what he'd do. The cruel fraud had gone far enough. He would bring it to an end now while he was in a proper frame of mind.

Drink soon finished, he was off back to the house, intensely proud of himself for listening to his conscience and not his haughty logic, hugely amplified by drugs though that niggling conscience was.

2.18
Big Trouble

It was just like when he'd left the Arts Centre to join Jennifer at Ron's party. It was the same feeling of a weight having been lifted from him.

He felt emotionally exhilarated.

He also felt bloody chilly.

The half-moonlit motorbike seemed strangely cartoon like. Like it had its own quirky, innocent character.

It was no big deal riding on E, or so he felt. It was certainly easier than climbing that fence at Ron's mother's place had been. He naturally slowed for the twisting corners, braked when he should and accelerated when it was wise. Maybe, he reckoned, it was something to do with the incredible danger that riding presented — minds just aren't going to let you seriously fuck up, no matter what you've taken.

And he even remembered where he'd stashed his robe.

He collected it and put it on. It was a good wind-cheater.

A thought occurred: a powerful thought. He should go and see his mother soon, now languishing mentally ill in some institution somewhere, according to reports. It was seven years since he'd last seen her, or made any contact. She occasionally wrote to him, but he never read a word — garbled nonsense about persecuting devils, according to Ron, who found the letters fascinating. Going to see her was the thing Pross feared most in the world.

But he always felt the guilt of having turned away.

But now he felt strong. Now he felt like he could do it, and take the disturbing sight of her on the chin. He might even be able to touch her. Hold her bony, cold hand and offer some comfort, pointless for her though he knew it would be. He should do it for *himself*, if not for her.

Yes, he would go to see her soon.

Engrossed in the two-wheel experience too much, he didn't stop at the gates, but purposefully rode straight past, staying loyal to the twisting road as it snaked upward, discovering that, after passing but a few dwellings and farm entrances, it turned from tarmac to rutted earth. Here he stopped.

The air was beautiful and fresh.

He felt reborn.

Looking back the way he'd come, now from on high, in the weak moonlight he could see the mansion amid its shielding woods. Behind him, sheep faintly speckled the high fell.

But he really had to be getting back.

The suitcase had become like a magic symbol. It was as if if it were looked at long enough, the mystery of where he was would be revealed, or he would somehow be lured back.

It was still where it had been left yesterday afternoon, on the floor of Melanie's living room.

Ron and Sarah had been searching for Pross since she'd returned from her Aunt's, two hours earlier.

Her Aunt had cursed Pross's name.

No one had heard or seen anything of Pross all day. He didn't have a wide circle of friends, and that circle had been traced, visited or telephoned. But no Pross. All there was was a heart-rending, desperate letter. And Melanie confirmed that he had no money, just as Ron had suspected.

Now back at Melanie's, Ron, pressured by Sarah, eventually telephoned the police. Not to report him as missing, but just to check if any unidentified corpses bearing a likeness had turned up.

One apparently had.

Ron volunteered to identify the body at the hospital.

A police officer took him into the mortuary, pulled the drawer out, then lifted the shroud.

'No. That's not him,' said Ron, strangely disappointed.

He didn't know it, but the corpse was what was left of Moaning Joe. He had died after accidentally crashing his borrowed motorbike into a tree while on E.

Putting the bike back where it belonged, Pross realised he was getting cold feet about telling the truth. But he had seen so *clearly* that it was a good idea, he *had* to do it.

Into the house he went.

Lifting the large, cold iron latch on the heavy front door, then stepping into the small porch, he was met by Simon, bearing a candle.

Simon was aglow with emotion. 'What did the extraterrestrials want?'

'What?' asked Pross, forgetting the yarn he'd spun to excuse his visit to the pub, surprised to hear music coming from within.

Passing Simon and entering the main room, Pross sat himself down on the nearest suitable object, which was a wooden box, on top of which was a cassette player, quietly playing music.

He looked at Simon.

Simon looked at him.

About to speak, Pross was pre-empted. 'I'm in the New Age,' breathed Simon ecstatically. 'Master, you're magic *is* greater than all others.' He then took on a more pragmatic attitude. 'How much money will you need for the diamonds? Godfrey made you win two-and-a-half million, so that's how much they'll probably cost. But then this house would have cost you nearly half a million, wouldn't it? So two million should be enough, shouldn't it? Or should we get the biggest diamond pyramids we can afford? Will that make the device work better? I've got over seven million pounds we can use.'

Pross turned off the cassette.

Fuck. It had all worked. The plan had worked. He could rob him of seven million if he wanted. What a waste of an opportunity. It was a crime to waste such an opportunity.

Now looking very glum, Pross asked, 'Where's Mick and Phil? I want to tell you all something.'

'Mick's in the kitchen, and Phil's over by the fire. He's dead.'

'Dead?' queried Pross.

'He was evil.'

'That's right,' confirmed the voice of Mick, coming into the room, feeding a sausage roll into his mouth. 'I feel fackin' great. D'you still want to lend me cab? The keys are under the driver's seat if you want it.'

But Pross wasn't listening. He was looking over towards the fire, before which lay Phil, his robe, stained in parts with darkness, glowing warmly in its light. Curled almost foetal like, he wasn't moving. He wasn't moving at all.

The ability to react appropriately was simply not there, and he disturbingly knew it. He knew he should be rushing over to Phil, or screaming "who did it?" but everything seemed muted. Everything seemed to happen silently in his head, and only there. It seemed a long time. Or was it? He didn't know. Then he consciously thought of how strange it was that he should be wondering about subjective time frames when there lay a bloodied corpse in the room. There *was* a body in the room, wasn't there? Or was this some crazy hallucination. Had he gone mad? Ron always said he would one day.

'We'll never grow old,' realised Simon in awe as Pross starkly regarded the bloodied corpse.

It was a living nightmare. A druggy, living nightmare. In fact, so bizarre was it all, he actually thought it *might* be a nightmare. *Must* be a nightmare. He'd had dreams before where he'd been fully aware he was dreaming — lucid dreams — and this felt like one now.

But it wasn't.
This *was* happening.
Phil *was* lying on the floor.
He slowly approached the corpse.
'Fackin' 'ell, you're right,' realised Mick.
'Or get sick,' added Simon, tagging along beside Pross.

A spill of dark, viscous, congealed blood surrounded the pummelled head of Phil. His hands were gripping the hem of his stained robe. His face was battered and shattered. His jaw was greatly dislocated. His hair was sticky and matted. Some bearded flesh was torn away from a cheek, attached only by a thread of tissue. His teeth, some dislocated, had cut through his own lips and cheeks and were shining white amid red pulp.

Only his sunken, bewildered, betrayed eyes seemed unscathed.
'Who did this?' murmured Pross.
'Mick,' said Simon.
'That's right,' agreed Mick.

Turning in mute astonishment to them, Pross saw that the lower parts of Mick's white robe were stained with evidence.

'It's all right,' assured Simon. 'We discovered he was evil. He didn't agree with us.'

'That's right,' said Mick. 'We had to do it.'
Pross collapsed to the floor.

Or at least he fantasised he did. Fantasised he should have, that is. But he was still standing within the living nightmare. He didn't know what to do. What could he do? Call the police? There wasn't even a telephone here. Maybe Phil was still alive... no, surely not. Half his head was smashed in, and his eyes were staring, accusing, dead man's eyes.

'Don't worry,' said Simon, 'there's some spades in the outbuilding. We'll bury him now. No one'll find him. We didn't want to do it earlier because the crystal energy doesn't extended beyond the house, does it?'

'That's right,' chirped Mick. 'It's great stuff, ain't it?'

And before Pross's eyes, they began pulling Phil by his feet towards the door. His battered head leaving a dark, sticky trail. His loose flap of skin snagging on the floorboards and coming away.

Simon picked it up in his hand. 'Won't be long,' he said, 'and don't worry.'

Out with Phil's carcass they went.

Alone. Pross was now alone in the room. The vast, empty, silent, candle-lit room with it's lofty ceiling, flaking plaster, gothic adornments and lurking shadows. The stillness was killing. He should be doing something. But all he could think of doing was sitting down. Moving back over to the box, his feet seemed to stick.

Murder. There had been a gruesome murder. It was unbelievable. It was staggering. It was crazy. It was surreal. But most of all it was numbing.

He slowly sat down, then just as slowly arranged his robe for comfort and appearance. Minutes, maybe, passed without a single tangible thought arising. He was just blown away, gazing brain-dead towards his hands. Upon looking back to the fire, as if still unconvinced about the reality of the happening, he saw a set of bloody footprints leading directly to him. He stared in sudden horror at the testimony. Yes, he had killed Phil himself, or as good as. And not only that, he was in trouble.

Big trouble.

Him.

'Maybe he's in some kind of trouble?' feared Sarah.

'Such as?' asked Ron, in a tone which dismissed the notion.

No one could think of any kind of trouble he might be in.

Suddenly Pross's drugged mind began a riot of self-defence and panic.

And that's when it started — a gripping, empty feeling in the pit of his stomach. A contained panic. An inhibited anxiety. One second it wasn't there, the very next second it was.

And it didn't go even a little bit away as he tried to reason his way out of trouble.

He couldn't tell the police. Couldn't. He could go to prison for his part in the murder. No, he *would* go to prison. At the very least he'd be charged with administering and possessing a controlled drug. And they'd throw the book at him for it. It was life maximum, wasn't it? supplying a hard drug.

He had to get away. Far away. Run. But where could he go? Not back to Durham — he had nowhere to stay. Should he go? Maybe he could conceal everything. Nobody knew he was here. Nobody at all... only Simon and Mick. Maybe he should kill and bury *them, then* run away? No, the gatekeeper had seen him. The gatekeeper would tell the police, who would find him out through Lilith's estate agency. Maybe he should kill the gatekeeper too?

No, he was being crazy. He wasn't going to kill anyone, and anyway, the more disappearances, the more chance of investigations.

He had to stay calm. Use his cunning. This was happening. This was *really* happening. What he had to do was think of a way to make sure the *one* murder never came to light.

'It's done,' said Simon, coming into the room. 'He's three feet down in the woods. No one will ever find him.'

'No way,' said Mick. 'Gawd, I feel fackin' great.'

'You shouldn't swear,' said Simon to Mick. 'Not here. Not in front of the Master.'

'You're right,' agreed Mick sensibly. 'Sorry.'

It was bizarre. They had no sense of horror or guilt at all. Pross looked at them in bewilderment. 'Why?' he mouthed.

'We had to,' said Simon. 'It's in the scriptures.'

'He went all weird in your energy,' reported Mick. 'You should've seen it.'

'That proved it,' said Simon.

'Proved what?' asked Pross with muted desperation.

'That he was evil,' explained Simon. 'If you'd been here, you would have seen it too. It was like he was negative and the energy was positive.'

Mick then gave a demonstration of how Phil had been.

'For ages he was like that,' said Simon, who then began to quote his scriptures. '*And all who do not heed his words must be removed from the Earth.*'

'Whose words?' asked Pross.

'The Expected One's,' said Simon, as if the fact were obvious. 'Your words.'

Pross sank his face into his hands.

'Don't worry,' said Simon sympathetically. 'No one will know. And once you start the Golden Millennium everything will be different.'

Mumbling through his hands, Pross said, 'He'll be reported missing by friends before that.'

He was ashamed to hear himself discussing a cover up.

'He doesn't have any friends,' answered Simon.

'Family,' muttered Pross. 'His family will look for him.'

'I'm his family,' said Simon. 'He was my younger brother.'

'It's wearing off now,' said Mick, disappointed.

After thinking for a few seconds, Simon decided that Mick was right. 'You said it would, though, didn't you, Master? You said that the crystals would stop echoing after a while. Should we see about getting the diamonds tomorrow?'

'Can you get the energy going again?' asked Mick.

Pross was still sat with his face in his hands, drowning in the sheer incredulity of it all. Thirty minutes earlier, he had been high on the resolution to divest himself of guilt, now he had killed someone. Could he ever win? Could he ever fucking win? Again he began thinking that he was in the hands of some sinister supernatural agent bent on breaking him with irony, disappointment and frustration.

He forced the thought away, was angry at himself for even thinking it. He would overcome this. It was a test, that's what it was. No. Don't be stupid. Don't be fucking stupid. How could it be a test? Who could be doing the testing? God? No, it wasn't a test. It just was.

That's all. It just was.

Simon sat next to him. 'Don't worry, Master. We had to do it. Everything's going to be all right.'

'What about the energy?' jabbered Mick again. 'Can we 'ave some more?'

Pross lifted his head. Saying nothing for a while, he eventually muttered, with undertones of resentment and anger, 'No more energy. Clean all the blood away. Clean everything. I'm going to bed.'

And to his bedroom he went, like he somehow expected the grotesque nightmare to pass once he was on his own upstairs.

'See you tomorrow, Master,' called Simon.

'G'night, guv,' called Mick.

'Don't worry,' called Simon.

And then they set about the cleaning, with eyes rapidly becoming tired.

After switching on the bedroom light, Pross closed the door behind him like he was closing out madness. Like it would be all right once he were hidden away in his bedroom.

After taking a sputtering piss in the room's basin, having to roll his robe up to his waist, he fell down on to the bed and stared at the ceiling.

Alone, shut away, he felt more at ease, despite there being no let-up in the feeling of tightness in his stomach.

The room was cold, so he kept the robe on.

It occurred to him that once the drug wore off more with Simon and Mick, they would realise the horror of their deed... and that would be dangerous for him.

Better that they never understand.

The morning. The morning, when they awoke, would also be when reality would dawn. In the morning, Simon might understand that he had murdered his own brother. Anything could happen then. There would be chaos in the morning.

Turning on to his side, he lay in one position for what seemed a long time, staring in growing mental remoteness at the floor beside the bed. For a long time, just staring.

He heard Simon and Mick going to bed downstairs.

The E was wearing off for him now. It was like he was waking up, and he wished he could just sleep for real now, but knew it would be hours yet before his eyelids fell, if they fell at all. Many hours. Many lonely hours shut into a strange little room that was like a penitential cell.

He sat up, then got up and began wandering around the small room, frustrated and pent-up. He felt trapped. Crazily trapped. He had to do something to occupy himself. Anything to keep his mind distracted.

Time was a cruel enemy tonight. A slow torturer.

He quickly found himself back on the bed, back on the bed wondering how it had all gone so helter-skelter wrong. It was so ironic. Twelve hours earlier, he had been on this very bed wondering how he had come to be regarded as a saviour, now he was wondering how he had become a killer.

Unexpectedly, he became angry with himself. No, he wasn't a killer. *Wasn't*. He'd been cavalier, that's all. Fuck it, he wasn't going to let this pull him down. It wasn't going to end *this* way. He wasn't going to be defeated by irony. He'd been right downstairs: he had to *think* his way out of this. *Had* to. He would get out of this *somehow*. He didn't have to wonder how it had gone wrong, he had to *calculate* it. Working out what had gone wrong might be some of the problem of how to throw a smoke screen over the event solved.

He hadn't been the killer. *Religious mania* had been the killer. He'd inadvertently stirred up some kind of religious mania and Phil had copped for a vicious death, that's all. It was misadventure.

Scriptures were the big problem with religion, realised Pross starkly. Mad scriptures giving crazy people all the scope for interpretation they need to carry out their insanities. If only all the bibles and korans and everything elses in the world could be replaced with a simple thing too short ever to be twisted, then peace and goodwill might stand a chance. Something like: *Forget gods and Messiahs. They can't be hurt. You can even crucify your Messiahs if you want. Worship mankind instead, then heaven will be on Earth.*

He had to think and plot. Every available second he had to think and plot. He would put his sleeplessness to use.

And so for much of the rest of the night, Pross became desperately saturated in the problem of how to escape. Half-glimpsed answers sometimes seemed to surface, only to be sunk by an obvious flaw.

With the dawn approaching, no true solution had he yet found, and he resigned himself to failure: soon Simon would wake and realise his crime. And with this resignation, it was as if he was then given permission to sleep himself.

He closed his bleary, exhausted eyes, and arranged for sleep his limbs, limbs grown weak and feeble from two consecutive nights of tripping.

But there was as yet no let up in the feeling of anxiety in the pit of his stomach, and he still figured that when Simon awoke, the real hell would begin.

But he also realised that part of him was making him remain at the scene of the crime to face the consequences.

He was waiting to give himself up.

2.19
Her First Line

She seemed a little changed. From the moment he arrived, she seemed just a little changed, and Jennifer noticed it.

From the bar in Greek Street, Yvette had telephoned Peter, who worked late. She had said where she was, and he had said he would come to meet her. 'Mah boyfwend's coming later,' she had then said to Jennifer.

Later turned out to be a little after eleven o'clock, by which time Jennifer was more drunk than she had ever been. A little before eleven o'clock, one of the Rolling Stones had come upstairs, alone. Just after the hushed flurry of his appearance settled down, Robert said he was going to the bar to get a light. Requesting a book of matches, Robert was now stood beside the illustrious gentleman, who was standing with his drink. A few moments later, both he and Robert disappeared downstairs together, causing much confusion and excitement with Yvette, excitement she conferred to Jennifer.

But then Peter arrived, and Yvette changed.

Peter was maybe a little older than Yvette, reckoned Jennifer, now that she knew Yvette's true age. When earlier she had asked this fact, she had been surprised to hear that Yvette was only twenty-one. Not because she really looked old, but because she appeared so worldly in Jennifer's inexperienced eyes. Peter, a good-looking, slim six-footer, had very long, straight dark-brown hair which was drawn into a tight ponytail. He was half English, half French, and spoke both with seeming fluidity, his English being flawed only by him occasionally stressing the wrong syllable, Jennifer having first noticed it when he'd idiosyncratically expressed the word sca-*van*-ger.

But Yvette was changed with Peter around, noted Jennifer. Gone was a little of her interactive exuberance, it seemed.

Upon arrival, noting that Jennifer was a stranger, Peter politely shook her hand and asked her about herself, but it was Yvette who answered first. 'She's called Jennifer, and...'

Peter looked at Yvette. 'I was asking *her*.'

'Sorry,' said Yvette, deferring her comments.

After Jennifer divulged the required information herself, Yvette entered the conversation unchallenged, telling Peter in low, conspiratorial, but excited tones that Robert had gone off somewhere with a Rolling Stone.

But then Robert came up the stairs, alone, smiling easily.

Upon seeing Peter, Robert opened his arms, and the two hugged heartily, like soul brothers long separated by time and adventure.

They all wanted to know what Robert had been doing with the Rolling Stone.

Answer: a line of cocaine. Robert had offered him a line of cocaine.

'He's like a hoover,' smiled Robert. 'Good job Trevor sorted me out today.' Looking at Jennifer, he asked, 'Do you want a line? It's really good stuff.'

'For once,' sniped Peter, but also laughing.

Five minutes later, after having been persuaded, cajoled and finally dubiously convinced, Jennifer was in the ladies with Yvette, nervously doing her first ever line of coke, indeed, her first ever drug. Doing it with the rolled up fifty pound note that Robert had passed to her. Although worried about having to physically snort a powder up her nose, she felt secretly thrilled and glamorous. But surely it would hurt? Or at least make her sneeze for hours?

It did not hurt, or make her sneeze. In fact, physically, it was almost pleasant.

And soon it seemed to clear her woozy head, for which she was very grateful.

'You've gone all quiet again,' noted Robert a little later, back upstairs.

She *had* gone all quiet, she realised. Distant is what she'd become. Distant and sad. She was back in that deserted banqueting hall, treading alone. She couldn't account for it. She'd been all right earlier. She wasn't thinking of anything sad in particular, but sadness had overcome her. She'd become withdrawn, and strangely irked by the others' attempts to lure her into conversations she now found oppressive. And minutes after taking her second line, she realised what it was. 'It's the cocaine,' she said to Robert. 'I think it's making me feel depressed.'

From Yvette there was an immediate reaction of dismissive amusement to Jennifer's observation. 'Of course eets not the cocaine,' she said, trying to coax a smile from Jennifer, who was looking terribly serious now.

'Cocaine's a stimulant,' said Peter, as if he were a pharmacologist. 'It activates the brain.'

Yvette did a little dancing motion for Jennifer to support Peter's assertion.

But Robert was more empathic. His eyes expressing concern, briefly holding Jennifer's hand over the table, he said, 'No, listen to her. Coke's a very subtle drug. It swings you whichever way you're naturally inclined to go.'

'That's right,' said Peter immediately, now sharing Robert's seriousness.

'Yeah,' said Yvette, dropping the register of her voice and taking Jennifer's arm to give friendly comfort. 'Are you all right?'

'I'm all right,' said Jennifer self-consciously. 'Just tired. I think I'd better be going back to my hotel now.'

'No,' protested Yvette, supported by Peter.

'We're going to a club later,' said Peter. 'Come along with us. Do an E.'

'Yeah,' enthused Yvette.

Strongly Jennifer felt the dispiriting effect she was having on her new friends, and part of the reason she wanted to leave was that she was now being a damper.

She stood up, having fully decided to depart, despite having become shy about knowing she would have to engage in some kind of effusive parting ceremony. 'Will I be able to get a taxi outside?'

'Oh, you're not go-een!' cried Yvette. 'You can't.'

'Let me come along with you,' said Robert chivalrously, standing with her.

Yvette also stood, putting her arms around Jennifer. 'Call mee tomorrow,' she said. 'Robert will geeve you mah number.'

Jennifer promised she would.

On the other side of the table, Peter also stood, kissing both Jennifer's cheeks goodnight. 'Nice meeting you. Very sorry the coke made you unhappy.'

'That's all right,' said Jennifer.

Yvette kissed Robert goodnight, and Peter threw his arms around him even more enthusiastically than he had done earlier. And after this, Robert and Peter vigorously shook hands.

Jennifer smiled at Yvette and Peter as Robert led her down the stairs. 'Tomorrow. I promise,' she called back.

2.20
The Curious Mutuality

In the cab, Robert had said that they would pass his office, where he also lived, in Harley Street, and asked Jennifer if she would prefer to come back there with him for a while until she felt better, it being only a few minutes walk from her hotel.

She was not at all averse to the idea, for she had no fear or suspicion concerning his motives. He was sensitive and kind, and very comforting company, and Jennifer admitted to herself that she didn't really want to be completely alone just yet. She was a person who enjoyed the company of a friend, but not a crowd.

'All right,' she said, and that was that. There was nothing more to it at all.

Along the way, Robert explained how his office was in one large room of his two-room, second-floor flat. The other, even larger, room was his own private room. 'Nearly big enough to play tennis in,' he said. 'I should know, I've tried.'

But Jennifer remained much in her withdrawn state, finding herself having to consciously make returns to Robert's utterances. She hated being like this.

Harley Street was deserted when they arrived, the cab stopping directly outside Robert's door. Four storeys high was the long terrace of elegant houses. Robert explained that every other business in Harley Street was medical — had to be by law — but he had tricked the landlord to get the prestigious address from which to run his own business.

High black railings fronted the house. Below, stairs led down to a basement where a dental technician had his workshop. The front door, only just off the pavement, was raised two steps and was large and imposing, also painted black.

For possible future use, Robert showed Jennifer which intercom bell was for him. It was marked *Chesterford Publishing*.

The door opened to a lofty, plushly carpeted hall.

A world-famous gynaecologist had his private surgery on this floor, said Robert. Royalty sometimes visited here for consultations, often entering the building through the basement, as if thinking that ruse sufficient to throw a smoke screen around their visit's purpose.

Pressing the timer lights, Robert led Jennifer up flights of stairs, then into his office.

It was not what she had been expecting.

What Jennifer *had* been expecting was an organised, modern work place. What she saw was a messy, untidy living room, littered with pieces of paper. Some half-eaten pizzas and empty sweet wrappers lay around. A sunken old sofa was in one corner. In the room's centre was a tubular kitchen table with two telephones on it. The only things that really looked like office items were a computer and a fax machine, both resting on what looked like a school dining table, near to a window that had torn, dirty curtains hanging from it.

The room smelled faintly of old socks.

'Sorry about the mess,' said Robert. 'Mark doesn't tidy up any more.'

Jennifer didn't know whether he was joking or not.

The computer was of the same make that she used to use at the veterinary surgery for generating invoices and writing letters. When she told Robert this throwaway fact, he became quite curious and impressed. Looking around the room, she asked, 'How many people work here?'

Leading her into his own room, Robert answered, 'Just three. Me, Jeremy and Mark.'

Robert's own room was much more pleasant. Rectangular in shape, the door was at one corner, with a futon being in the adjacent corner. A large, uncluttered expanse of deep-piled, light-green carpet extended to two bay windows, set side by side at the other end of the room. Below each window were placed small, identical sofas. Two enormous, expensive-looking black hi-fi speakers on black metal stands sandwiched these sofas. Along one long wall, painted white with a hint of pink, ran a series of fitted closets and mirrors, the opposite long wall having art prints displayed on it. Save for the television, a white chest of drawers, a crammed, black bookshelf and two low, black, square tables in front of the sofas, that was everything.

Looking at the tables, Jennifer saw that they were both faintly dusted with white powder.

A few brandy bottles, some empty, were lying around.

'Do you feel any better now?' asked Robert with great consideration while lighting some candles.

Before Jennifer could answer, Robert burnt his finger, reacting in a comical, childish way, falling around the room in pain.

Jennifer laughed.

'Bastards!' laughed Robert excruciatingly, showing Jennifer his wound. 'Look, mum.'

Jennifer gave his finger a little kiss. 'All better.'

'It's bloody not,' contradicted Robert, returning his attention to the candles, walking over to the other end of the room. 'Take your coat off, for Christ's sake!' he suddenly demanded in a comically exasperated way.

Robert had a tongue-in-cheek, but caring manner that was very easy to get along with, and he was very attentive to other people's emotions. Watching him, it was strange, but he somehow reminded Jennifer of Pross. Some strange how.

She began taking off her coat, placing it out of the way on the floor near the bookshelf. She caught the titles of some books. *Healing the Inner Child*, was one title. The *Tibetan Book of the Dead*, was another.

Coat removed, now sitting on the floor with her back supported by one of the sofas, Jennifer wondered just why he should remind her of her last lover. Maybe the similarity came from their almost equal capacity to clown around? Or say things to deliberately make themselves look daft? The capacity was equal, but the method was different. Pross's was a more intellectualised, clever silliness, but Robert's was an endearing, warm silliness. He made people smile when he clowned.

And Robert had something Pross was wholly lacking in, or at least refused ever to show: charm. Robert had oodles of charm.

But then Jennifer figured what it was: it was femininity. They were both a little feminine in their motions, their long hair adding to the impression. Not camp. Not at all camp. Just not particulary keen to appear tough and manly when they walked or sat down or stood or spoke. That was it. That was the curious mutuality.

'I feel drunk again,' lamented Jennifer as Robert came back over to her side of the room, putting a cd of classical music on.

'You should do another line. Coke's great for sobering you up. You'll be all right here. If you get depressed, just have a cry. I'll join in, if my finger's still hurting.'

Robert immediately began setting out two lines on one of the low tables, carefully chopping the crystals with a razor blade.

'How much does coke cost?' asked Jennifer.

'About fifty a gram,' said Robert, waving the tiny, inch-long paper envelope for her to know how much a gram was. Before snorting his line, becoming more serious in his tone, he asked, 'Why do you think you got depressed on the coke? Are you unhappy about something?'

He looked at her, his face showing sympathy and promising help.

Through the small hours, Robert had gently encouraged Jennifer to talk about herself. She had been drawn into saying things about her reservedness and almost perpetual sense of loneliness that she had never even really said to herself before, let alone a virtual stranger. Eventually, she talked about how she knew she had changed since the death of her parents: how she often felt numb and distant.

Always Robert was sympathetic and encouraging. In turn, he told Jennifer things about how he himself had come from a broken home and had learned to overcome its legacy. There had been nights when he'd cried like a child in his ex-girlfriend's arms, he said. Poured out his locked up pain.

The only thing Jennifer didn't talk about was Pross. Somehow that seemed both discourteous to him and annoyingly pointless to her, for she was coming to the opinion that Pross had been a strange mistake. An abberation. Someone without a real heart. A cold person who had played at being warm and won her affections.

And also, after a time, she realised that she didn't want Robert to know that just two nights earlier she had slept with someone else, even though she did not find Robert physically attractive and had no intention or expectation of ever sleeping with him. He looked too old and rough.

About forty, she thought he must be.

Thirty, she found out he was.

Before they had begun talking, Jennifer had risked another line of coke, mostly because it seemed to please Robert to have his generosity accepted. But soon after she found her herself automatically taking more lines whenever Robert laid them out for her, a strange solace in the routine to be had. Whatever effect it was having on her now, she found hard to tell. The room felt more intimate and cosy, perhaps, and the candlelight seemed particular rich, but that was it as far as she could tell. It wasn't the elated experience she'd associated with cocaine from things she'd read, but it wasn't the depression — the anguished loneliness — she'd experienced earlier.

Robert was drinking much brandy, but showed no signs of drunkenness.

'Why did Mark leave tonight?' asked Jennifer out of the blue.

'He gets weird sometimes,' returned Robert, then, half joking, adding, 'Come to think of it, he's weird most times.'

'Was it to do with Yvette?'

For a moment, Jennifer thought that Robert was acting like he had been put on the spot. There was a hesitation before his return.

'Why d'you ask that?'

'It was the way they spoke to each other.'

'He's wild about her,' revealed Robert, adding, 'in his own sulky, dismal, adolescent way, that is.' He began laying out another line. 'What were you doing in Camden, today, anyway?'

After a pensive moment, Jennifer talked about how she had wanted to visit the place her parents had first met, and that restaurant had maybe been it.

'Really?' said Robert with deep interest. 'It's good that you did it. You have to explore who you are and know where you came from. We're all on a journey to find ourselves.'

But Jennifer hardly heard him. Suddenly, with the hour approaching four, she became filled with emotion. 'I visited their grave yesterday. It made me so sad. I'd never been before, not even for the funeral. I was sick that day. It was so sad. So sad.'

Hiding her face in her hands, she sobbed quietly. Robert comforted her in his arms, embracing her feminine frailty.

'This is healthy,' said Robert gently. 'You need to grieve for them. You haven't let yourself openly grieve yet. You haven't really accepted that they're gone. That's been you're problem. That's why you never went to their grave, because unconsciously you didn't want to admit their death. That might even be why you were sick for the funeral. You've been clinging on to something that's not there any more. Grieve for them now, then get on with your life. It's what they'd want you to do.'

Returning Robert's embrace, Jennifer sobbed harder.

2.21
Ghosts

A tap on the door, and he awoke bolt-upright.

'Breakfast, Master,' said Simon's voice.

'Down soon,' blurted Pross automatically. Nervously.

'It's outside the door.'

'OK.'

'Before it gets cold. It's two o'clock, by the way.'

Simon's footsteps departed.

Pross lay his head back down and realised it was just the same. The tenseness in his stomach was still there, unchanged.

And Phil was still dead.

Yes, Phil was still dead... and he was still an accessory to his murder.

But Simon had sounded no different. That was astonishing. That was utterly astonishing.

His mind began churning on this unexpected situation.

He quickly got up, still clothed in the robe which was now greatly creased. He needed a bath, and his ordinary clothes underneath the robe needed changing. He calculated that he hadn't been out of them for almost fifty hours straight. But he didn't have any other clothes with him. He would either have to go back to Durham to collect his belongings from Melanie's, or somehow acquire a change of clothes. He didn't want to go back to Durham. He was in an even worse position than when he'd left: his reasons for leaving were now compounded with accessory to a murder.

Then he remembered that there was a washing machine in the kitchen. He could simply wash the clothes he had on and wear only the robe while he waited for them to dry. Put them in front of the fire, maybe.

That's what he'd do.

Opening the door, he found his breakfast on a tray: toast with fried eggs and mushrooms, and a cup of tea. A large envelope was beside the tray.

The envelope was weighty.

He took everything into his room, and despite the previous night's events, found he had no lack of appetite.

After eating, he opened the envelope, discovering it to contain a quantity of money — slim bundles of fifty pound notes, each having a paper wrapper. Printed on each wrapper was the figure £1,000.

There were ten bundles.

A hand-written note was included. It read: *for the engineering equipment you will need*. A bank receipt also fell out. The receipt bore the day's date, and was stamped by a Bishop Auckland branch.

Sitting on the bed, he stared at the money. Ten thousand pounds was enough to flee the country with, he realised. But that's not what he wanted. He wanted mostly to escape the crime, not just the law. He placed the money aside and washed his face in the basin. He wanted to brush his teeth, but couldn't. Moving back to the bed again, he was about to lie down, but felt himself becoming excited, curiously excited, for no clear reason at first.

And then the reason started to become known.

It was not something he was consciously calculating, it was just happening. It was surely the pay-off for all the thinking he'd done last night. He'd thought harder last night than ever before.

Once he'd read a definition of the creative process as being one of *saturation, incubation, illumination.* And he'd so often found that to be the case himself. So many times he'd thought about a problem for hours, or even days, only to give up on it, only to have the solution simply pop into his head unexpectedly some time later. Without being aware of it, peoples' brains undeniably continue work silently on problems that have defeated their conscious abilities. Pross tended to liken conscious thoughts to visible surface motions swelling up from a vast and deep sea of activity. The whole *mental* sea of activity conspires to convey surface swells. People only ever hear the crashing of their waves, never the vast, undulating, unfathomably deep, relentless, dark body of computations that powers them.

Last night had been the saturation period here, he realised, and the incubation had been his sleep time.

And now he had true *illumination*.

He now actually seemed able to plot a clear escape from his nightmare. For every problem, a cunning solution appeared to make sure the murder would never come to light.

Religion would save him.

And so much the better that Simon still believed in him, that would make it even more watertight.

First of all, he would tell Simon he had seen Phil's ghost.

Simon was a trainee spiritualist — he believed in ghosts.

2.22
History Now

His erect penis was pressing hard and insistent into the small of her back when the sound of someone coming into the next room awoke her. He was snoring badly, as he had done through most of the night.

A tap sounded on the closed door. 'Robert,' said a dissatisfied male voice. 'It's past eleven o'clock.'

Turning over, politely distancing herself from his erection, Jennifer gently shook him. 'Robert, wake up. Someone's in the office.'

He would not be woken, even when shaken.

She heard another person arrive next door.

Sitting up, being naked except for her knickers, she protectively covered her breasts. Looking around in the dim light, she located her clothes and made a scurry for them.

Quickly getting dressed, she again tried to wake Robert, but still he would not stir. Never had she known anyone slumber so deeply.

Arranging herself as best she could, she steeled herself in preparation to meet the people. Mark, sat behind the computer, she recognised from last night. The other person, sitting on the dingy sofa, eating a pastry item, she assumed to be Jeremy.

The person who was perhaps Jeremy was tall and athletic-looking. He was in his late twenties, supposed Jennifer, with collar-length sandy hair which often fell over his eyes as he ate, seeming to bemuse him equally each time.

His eyes seemed a little lost.

'Morning,' politely said the person eating when he saw Jennifer.

'Morning,' said Jennifer, standing half in one room, half in the other.

Hearing a female voice, Mark looked over his shoulder and also said, 'Morning,' except he said it like it had a secret cynicism attached to it.

'I'm Jeremy,' said the eater.

'Jennifer.'

Mark said nothing, seemingly engaged in typing something.

'Is Robert up yet?' asked Jeremy, his speaking manner purposeful but plodding; cultured, but without any mercurial element.

'I can't wake him,' admitted Jennifer, whereupon Jeremy sprung to his feet like a Boy Scout leader setting off on an expedition. He came over to where Jennifer was standing and tapped loudly upon the half-open door.

'Robert,' called Jeremy, attempting an authoritative, displeased voice. 'Robert.'

Merely a groan came from within.

'We're supposed to be starting the new sales campaign today.'

Another groan. A groan which with one syllable said: *I'm doing my bloody best, aren't I?*

Stepping into the office, Jennifer said to Jeremy, 'Mind if I use the bathroom?'

'Go ahead,' said Mark, since Jeremy was mentally fixed on getting Robert out of bed.

'Come on, Robert, get up. I'll make a you a cappuccino.'

While she was in the bathroom, Jeremy tapped on the door and offered her a cappuccino too.

And when she came out, face freshened, Robert was in the office, sitting with Jeremy at the table, barefoot and dirty toe-nailed.

Mark, at the computer, had his back turned.

'Here's your cappuccino,' said Jeremy kindly, indicating the cup next to Robert's.

Robert smiled broadly at her. 'How are you today?' he said in a voice deeper than his usual.

'Better,' said Jennifer, smiling a little. 'Got a bit of a hangover, though.'

'It's just starting,' muttered Mark.

Both Robert and Jeremy seemed to react to Mark's comment with a fleeting look of restrained annoyance.

Robert went into the bathroom while Jeremy made polite, caring conversation with Jennifer, asking how she knew Robert. In answering, Jennifer was very conscious that Mark and Jeremy would be assuming that she and Robert had had sex. They had not. It having become very late, and with her being upset and tearful, he had offered to let her share his bed for the night if she liked, and that had been it. He had even turned all the lights off to allow her some modesty when undressing.

'Should we go out for some breakfast?' asked Robert coming out of the bathroom, stubbly face looking fresher, 'and let Mark think his negative thoughts alone?'

'No, you can't,' blurted Jeremy, losing his composure a little, but still very much keeping it. 'We have to start the new campaign today.'

Robert seemed to be coming to life now. Going sprightly back into his room, he called out, 'We'll start in the afternoon. One o'clock. Big push at one o'clock. Promise.'

A few moments later, he was back, dressed exactly as he had been the night before, except for the addition of an expensive black hat, of the sort that Zorro wore.

'See you at one,' said Robert as he and Jennifer left together, Jennifer saying a general goodbye.

'One o'clock,' insisted Jeremy.

'See you tomorrow,' said Mark without turning around.

It had obviously rained much in the night, but the sky was clear as they emerged into Harley Street. It was cold, and Jennifer was glad of her coat.

'What did you think of Jeremy?' asked Robert, struggling to keep his hat on in the breeze.

'He very courteous,' said Jennifer, not knowing what opinion she was supposed to have formed.

'Jeremy's the most fantastic person I know,' gushed Robert. 'He's so honest and loyal, really in touch with his own feelings and energy. I really love him.'

A further five minutes of walking alongside Robert brought Jennifer to what was described to her as a "tapas bar and restaurant" in Paddington Street. The establishment was in the cellar of a row of shops and offices, accessed directly from the street. Robert pointed out that they were now right opposite Nottingham Street, where her hotel was.

The ceiling was low, and the space cramped. The walls were finished in a dark wood. The lighting was subdued. A small bar was in one corner, unmanned at present, but two extraordinarily pretty girls were in attendance as table waitresses. Both had long, black hair, pale skin and deep eyes. One was tall and slim, the other shorter and more rounded. Both wore identical short black skirts and white blouses.

Both girls smiled a greeting to Robert as he came into the bar.

'Hello, Robert. How are you?' asked the shorter girl in slow foreign tones.

'Thirsty,' answered Robert, kissing her cheek before he took a table, many being free.

The girls smiled at Jennifer as they placed cutlery and menus before her.

'Anna and Denise,' said Robert, introducing the waitresses to Jennifer as they arranged the table.

They both smiled.

'Jennifer,' said Jennifer.

Observing them later, she saw that the shorter girl, Denise, smiled all the time.

Denise was Brazilian, and Anna, Portuguese.

A basket of sliced French bread was set out on the table, but the first thing to pass Robert's lips was beer.

'What exactly do you do at work?' asked Jennifer while they were waiting for the ordered meals to arrive.

'We publish business reviews,' said Robert.

'I don't know what that means.'

'We'll,' explained Robert, 'we work on behalf of various organisations. Like, say, the Regional Health Authorities, and we publish yearbooks for them. The books are distributed free, and we make our profits out of the advertising in them.'

A short, denim-clad man with a long, curly blonde perm entered the restaurant. Seeing Robert, he came over to him. 'All right, Robert?'

He had a strong Geordie accent.

'All right, Colin,' said Robert enthusiastically, standing up to shake his hand.

Colin didn't stay with them long. He was merely looking for someone, and left after Denise explained that that someone had already been and gone.

While Robert had been talking to Colin, Robert's accent had become very northern, and when Jennifer pointed this out to him later, he simply said that he unconsciously slipped back into his native tongue whenever it was being spoken around him.

Colin, explained Robert in his usual voice, was a tour manager in the music business. He had just done a David Bowie gig in Brixton.

Over the meal, of which Jennifer ate as much as she could stomach after the previous night's drinking, she and Robert talked about what she planned to do in London. With some awkwardness, Jennifer admitted that she had no real plans at all.

Robert ate very little of his meal, but drank a further two beers after they had both had coffee.

'Am I right in guessing you've split with a boyfriend recently?' asked Robert out of the blue.

Jennifer hesitated before saying, 'Saturday.'

'That recently?' mused Robert.

'How did you know?'

'I didn't know. I just sensed it from the way you are. I can tell you've had a lot of energy drained from you recently. You need to build that energy back up. What happened, if you don't mind me asking?'

'I don't know what happened,' confessed Jennifer.

'What sort of person was he?'

'I don't know that, either. We weren't together long.'

'Did you leave him or did he leave you?'

Their conversation was ended by the appearance of Jeremy.

'It half past one,' said Jeremy, standing behind Jennifer. 'You said you'd be back at one.'

'I was coming soon,' said Robert earnestly, without any indignation.

'Mark wants to know if you've got the cheque book. He needs to pay some bills.'

Patting various pockets, Robert said that he thought he indeed did have the cheque book somewhere. In an inside pocket, he found it, folded tightly, and he handed it to Jeremy. 'I'll be along as soon as I've finished this beer.'

Jeremy left.

'He can be a bit of a mother hen at times,' explained Robert with a smile.

A man came over to Robert, and Robert introduced him to Jennifer as being Mike, the restaurant owner. He looked to Jennifer as being a person who might wake up each morning and be immediately sad that he was so unattractive. He *was* a sorry-looking person. He had a lazy, shiftless body, with short, black curly hair, and a face fat and pig-like. He had thick-rimmed, black spectacles, and was approaching middle-age.

He spoke in Robert's ear about something which he obviously did not wish to have overheard.

True to his word, Robert did leave after his beer. Jennifer insisted on paying the bill, and was permitted to.

'Call me later if you need some company,' said Robert as they parted, giving her his telephone number.

She now remembered to ask him for Yvette's number. Two numbers she received, one for her home and one for the shop in Camden where she worked making silk prints.

Before going off in different directions, Jennifer quickly kissed him on the lips and thanked him for a wonderful time. 'I'll ring you,' she said.

She smiled as she walked the short distance to her hotel. Smiled with delight at her life suddenly having become so rich and varied. She could never have guessed when she'd set off two nights ago that she'd have landed on her feet so soon. Meeting Robert and Yvette was the most wonderful thing that had ever happened to her. She was really living now.

Back in her hotel room, she slept for an hour or so, then, after taking a shower, she plucked up the little courage she needed to ring Yvette at her workplace.

Yvette was as warm as she'd been the day before and immediately organised a rendezvous in Camden for when she was finished work.

Then Jennifer rang Robert, and he said he would join them in Camden too.

And so, at six o'clock, taking the tube this time, Jennifer was once again in Camden, sitting in wait at a table in the same restaurant in which she had first met Yvette. Yvette was only a little late, for which she greatly apologised.

Sharing Jennifer's pot of tea, Yvette asked her how she had got on with Robert after they had left together the previous night, as if she expected a romance to have developed in the cab.

'I don't like him that way,' said Jennifer, not mentioning that they had shared a bed.

'Ow long eese it since you separated from your boyfwend? The one you mentioned last night?'

'Did I mention him last night?' asked Jennifer.

'Yes. Before the Mexican bar,' stated Yvette, in the endearing, burnt-tongue-tip way she had of talking and finding her English words.

'Not long,' said Jennifer, not wanting to think about sad things.

To Jennifer, Pross was history now.

But the conversation soon moved away from that subject. Indeed, so far away it was soon after agreed that Jennifer should stay at Yvette's and not in an expensive hotel, at least until she found a place of her own. 'Ah ope you like cats,' said Yvette. 'Ah've got one theese big!' And she flung her arms out wide to show its enormity, her bracelets jangling.

Jennifer laughed.

2.23
Thanking Nature

Robert did not arrive. Two hours they waited, and four telephone messages they left.

'Ee as so many fwends ee sometimes forgets where ee as to be,' explained Yvette in a remorseful way that sounded almost as if she were taking the blame on to herself. 'Don't worry, you'll see eem soon.'

And so, at nine o'clock, Jennifer and Yvette left the restaurant to make their way by tube to Yvette's flat on the Holloway Road. Walking down the street, Yvette linked her arm with Jennifer's.

They talked about their families along the way. Jennifer told her story and Yvette told hers. Yvette was the daughter of a designer, well known in France, who had split from her mother when she was fourteen, and she hadn't seen him since, but he did send her money each month.

Above a dry cleaner's was Yvette's flat. Outside, even at this late hour, shops remained open and the street was lively. Inside, although quite spacious, the flat had a cosy feel. Printed fabrics and rugs hung from walls and across corners. There was only one bedroom, but the sofa was large and comfortable enough for Jennifer to sleep on until she found a place of her own. Jennifer did not mind this arrangement at all.

The woman who lived upstairs was mad, said Yvette, and she would often jump up and down on the ceiling if she heard too much noise, or sometimes any at all.

Jennifer decided to telephone her sister now to say that she was safe and settled with new friends. Yvette's big tom cat appeared and jumped into her lap when she sat down.

'Pross has disappeared,' said Sarah after Jennifer had explained and apologised for her own disappearance. 'He's got no money and he's left all his things at Melanie's. Everything. He hasn't got anything with him.'

'When?'

'The morning after the bonfire party. He was really upset that you weren't there. No one's seen him since.'

'Why?' asked Jennifer, thoroughly bewildered. 'He left *me*.'

'He left a letter for you. Do you want me to read it to you?'

'No,' said Jennifer immediately. 'I don't want to hear it. It's over. I don't want to think about things past.'

'I think you should hear it.'

But Jennifer was adamant and Sarah soon deferred to her wish.

'Let me speak to er,' said Yvette soon after, and Jennifer passed her the phone. Yvette reassured Sarah that Jennifer was in safe hands and enjoying herself very much, and that she would be staying with her for a while.

Prompted by Jennifer, Yvette gave Sarah the address and telephone number.

Seeing that Jennifer was a little upset by the call, Yvette suggested they go to a nearby club together for a few hours. Do half an E each. Just enough to get them relaxed.

Yvette was amazed to discover that Jennifer had never taken E, or been to a club. 'Oh, you merst!' she said. 'Eet ees *so* beautiful. Don't worry, eet's not like coke. You won't feel bad. Ah'll be weeth you. We can come back eef you don't like eet.'

Although apprehensive, Jennifer soon agreed. What actually worried her most was that she had never danced before.

'You can't wear those clothes. You'll av to wear something looser,' said Yvette, and she began finding things for Jennifer to wear.

While they were both getting ready, Jennifer noticed a two inch long scar on Yvette's hip.

'How did you do that?'

Twisting round to look at it herself, Yvette said, 'Mah boyfwend deed eet with glass.'

There seemed to be an element of pride in what she said.

'Why?' asked Jennifer.

'We were so much een love. We cut each other and mixed our blood.'

Jennifer found the idea insane, and said as much. It was such a deep cut, for one thing. 'How could he do it to you? One thing I know for sure about Pross was that he would have fought to the death for me if anyone so much as hurt my finger.'

She was surprised to have evoked the name of Pross, but stood by the claim with herself.

Yvette responded to the criticism curiously. She did not argue, but rather she became almost sullen in her aspect. Even more insane to Jennifer, she mumbled, 'Eeet's just Peter. Eee as a thing about glass and knives.'

The telephone rang.

It was Robert.

Discovering that Jennifer was there, Robert particularly wished to speak with her.

'I'm sorry. I'm so sorry,' he immediately gushed. 'I was delayed. I went to the restaurant, but you'd left by then.'

'That's all right,' said Jennifer.

'We're going to a club soon,' shouted Yvette.

Robert said he would meet them at the club.

She hated it. The moment she walked in, she hated it. It was hot. The thumping music was loud, repetitive, oppressive and spiritless, and it was already driving her crazy by the time Yvette had scored an E from a dealer she said would be operating within the club. Jennifer wanted to leave. Wanted desperately to leave. Wanted to go and get her coat straightaway but stayed because she didn't want to let Yvette down.

She could barely hear herself talking, and that she hated most of all.

Jennifer had never been to such a place before, although she supposed that the clubs in the larger northern towns many miles from Richmond must be pretty much like this one.

The only club she'd ever been to herself before had been a dismal, local disco affair.

One thing she did like was the cosmopolitan mix of people. She couldn't think of a single black person living in her home town, but here things were excitingly multi-cultural.

The dance floor was sunk below where they were now standing, on a circular balcony furnished with easy-chairs and sofas. Down below, it was teeming with young people, most gyrating and jerking without grace or indeed rhythm. Many faces were as if hypnotised. Drugged senseless on E, she figured, although all she *really* knew about ecstasy was the warnings her aunt had raved to her over Sunday lunches.

They had bought a bottled beer each from the bar, which was in another area, and now Jennifer watched with trepidation as Yvette snapped a small white tablet, swilling half down.

Yvette handed over the other half.

'Go on, eet's beautiful.'
Jennifer took it.

They sat together on a small sofa, waiting for the effects, Jennifer becoming greatly, but secretly, anxious about what might happen.

For some reason, Yvette decided to tie Jennifer's hair back while they waited, hair almost the same colour as the baggy silk shirt loaned to her for the night.

'Ah'm coming up now,' shouted Yvette into Jennifer's ear a short while later, smiling and doing the same little dance with her gangling arms that she had done the previous night to portray the effects of cocaine. She was wearing a sleeveless, loose black top and black leather trousers. Her long hair was thrown back and full of body. A large, rectangular, rough metal jewellery piece was hung around her neck by a thin leather thong, so that when she leaned back its weight pressed down the fabric of her top, divulging the shape of her breasts.

Something was happening with Jennifer, too. She began to feel anxious. She found herself looking around at the people near her. But everyone was smiling. No one seemed concerned to avoid making eye contact. And she realised that *she* was making lingering eye contact too, not thinking anything of it all.

She felt good, she quickly decided.

Things were becoming brighter and fresher. Then, in an almost magical moment of discovery of transubstantiation, she realised that the music had ceased being an annoyance, becoming perfectly complementary to the new experience. Perfectly part of it. Enhancing it, like it was actually helping to make her feel even better, taking her further into it all.

'Ow do you feel?' shouted Yvette, smiling.

Gauging her state with misty surprise, Jennifer returned, 'Beautiful.'

'Let's dance,' shouted Yvette, standing.

'No, not yet.'

'Yes, now,' insisted Yvette, taking Jennifer's hand and trying to pull her up.

'No, not yet,' repeated Jennifer, remaining rooted.

Yvette affected a chiding, sulky expression, but returned to her seat beside Jennifer, quickly smiling and squeezing her arm to demonstrate her forgiveness.

Jennifer would have been happy just to sit for a few hours then go home were it not for her being very conscious of being a disappointment to Yvette.

'Yvette!' sounded a sugary voice from nearby. 'Jennifer!'

It was Robert.

Yvette stood and flung her arms around him.

And Jennifer found herself doing the same thing.

'Come on, let's dance!' he screeched comically, as if it were a life or death issue.

'Jennifer doesn't want to,' said Yvette, sounding both sympathetic and displeased. 'She's shy.'

'What!' shouted Robert. 'She bloody well will!'

And, brooking no resistance, affecting a determined expression and stance, he gripped Jennifer's wrist and pulled her down to the dance floor, quickly aided by Yvette, who pushed from behind.

Though very self-consciously at first, Jennifer danced alongside Robert and Yvette, soon not caring what she must look like. Not even thinking about it. The music and lights overwhelmed and entered her, and before long she consciously thanked nature for the use of her limbs.

Two hours later, they had to pull her away.

She was sweating much, and her shirt had turned transparent where it was wet, her contours adhering to the fabric. 'You have a very beautiful body,' said Robert into her ear as they were collecting their coats. But he said it in a congratulatory way more than anything else.

'Deed you enjoy yourself?' asked Yvette.

Jennifer just grinned and nodded her head.

Yvette seemed so pleased, and took Jennifer's arm in hers.

2.24
Someone New

She woke as she had done the day before, with the sound of someone coming into the office next door.

Twelve o'clock: she had to clear her things from the hotel by that time today or she would be charged for another day. Looking at the clock beside Robert's bed, she saw that she had less than an hour to spare.

Lying in bed, she felt unsanitary. Her period had started yesterday, but she had made love regardless. Robert's sofa and carpet, and no doubt now his bed, were stained with her menstrual blood.

It had been unexpected and not especially desired. After sharing a cab together back from the club, she had returned with Robert to his room to borrow a self-hypnosis tape he had spoken to her about, a tape which offered to give its listeners' confidence.

Entering his room, she encountered surprises, each with a little note attached. There were French chocolates, which he explained were the most expensive brand available. There was a teddy bear. There were flowers.

For an amusing hour or so he communicated his admiration and appreciation of her, saying how amazingly in love with her he had fallen. 'You're the sweetest, most wonderful person I've ever met. I'd even give up coke for you,' he declared. And later, after they'd both done a line, he had taken her hand and placed it on his crotch.

That is how their unprotected and unabashed sex session had begun.

Now she did not try to awaken him. Instead, she put on her clothes, picked up her presents and went into the office.

It was as it had been the day before. Jeremy was eating a croissant, and Mark was at the computer.

'Morning,' said Jeremy. 'Nice teddy bear.'

'Morning,' returned Jennifer. 'He's still asleep.'

Mark looked at her. 'Second night lucky?' he said, then returned his attention to his screen.

The remark both puzzled and irritated Jennifer, even though she knew not what he was referring to. Was he referring to the sex she had had? she wondered as she went to the bathroom.

She did not remain long. She had to make her way back to the hotel otherwise it would cost her money. After checking out, she brought her cases by cab to Yvette's flat. Yvette would be at work, but she could let herself in with the key given to her the previous night.

But Yvette was not at work. Jennifer found Yvette huddled under a duvet on her sofa. She looked distraught. 'What's the matter?' she asked, it being evident that Yvette had been crying.

'Peter deedn't come back last night,' returned Yvette, looking to Jennifer with hurt eyes. 'Eet's the third time.'

Jennifer put her bags down and embraced Yvette. Soon the cat jumped up and began to cuddle itself in between them, which made Yvette smile through her tears.

They talked for a long time.

Peter, it transpired, was having an affair. He had first slept with the other woman while Yvette had been in hospital. Carefully encouraged by Jennifer, Yvette resolved to finally end her relationship.

A little before three o'clock, Yvette's telephone rang. It was Robert. He wanted to speak to Jennifer. 'Mark's left the company,' he immediately said to her. 'You've got to come and help us.'

'Me?'

'You know how to work computers.'

'Barely.'

Not knowing at all how she could, she nevertheless promised to go straight along to the office to try and help.

When told of the news, Yvette cursed Mark's name.

Having quickly responded to Robert's call, on the doorstep of the office, pressing the intercom bell, Jennifer noticed that someone had made *Chesterford Publishing* read *Chesterfraud Publishing*.

Jeremy was sitting at the table, a picture of controlled distress, his fingers running through his hair. Robert was standing in the middle of the room. He smiled a worried smile and thanked Jennifer for coming so soon.

Then he quickly kissed her on the lips.

He smelled of spirits and cigarettes.

Beneath his mask of composure, Robert was lost and scared, Jennifer could easily tell that.

'Why did he leave?' she asked, standing beside Robert.

'He had an argument with Robert,' said Jeremy plainly.

'What about?'

'About you, apparently. I wasn't here. I was getting a croissant.'

'What about me?' she asked Robert.

Robert cleared his throat. 'It was nothing. He's just weird and jealous. It freaked him that you'd stayed overnight.'

Jeremy looked at her, saying in his quiet, genuine way, 'Do you think you'll be able to help us?'

Jennifer was baffled. 'I don't know what you think I can do. I don't know anything about business.'

'You know how to work the computer though,' said Jeremy, pointing to it. 'Can you show us so that we can do it ourselves?'

Jeremy got up and walked over to the enigmatic machine, which was turned off. Robert also moved towards it. But neither of them seemed confident enough to take the seat behind it.

Robert spoke in a formal, yet humble voice. 'Ideally, that's what would happen. I'm useless with computers, but Jeremy could learn what needs to be learned.'

'That's right,' said Jeremy more hopefully.

All three of them were now staring at the blank screen.

'How does it switch on?' asked Jeremy.

'The on button,' said Jennifer, finding their helplessness incredulous.

'We're making progress already,' said Robert, tongue bravely in cheek.

Taking the plunge, Jennifer sat down and switched the computer on. While waiting for it to boot up, she expressed an idea. 'Why don't you employ someone from an agency to come in and work things out?'

After clearing his throat, Robert said, 'It's not as easy as that.'

'Why not?'

After a pause, he said, 'The business isn't completely legal.'

'Yes it is,' countered Jeremy as if he meant it.

'No it isn't, Jeremy,' returned Robert.

Jennifer was intrigued. 'What's illegal about it?'

'We exaggerate a lot of the things we tell people to get them to advertise in our books, that's all.'

'No we don't,' said Jeremy.

'Yes we do,' said Robert, like he was telling him for the very first time.

'But no worse than other companies, like you always say.'

The computer was ready, but Jennifer wasn't. 'I don't know where to start,' she confessed.

Neither did Jeremy or Robert.

No one knew what to do until Jennifer thought of asking, 'Well, what does Mark use the computer for?'

'He keeps customer records in a database,' offered Jeremy.

'That's right,' said Robert. 'And he desktop publishes the books we publish. And there's some sort of link to the factoring company and the bank.'

But Jennifer was still no wiser about what she should do. At her old place of work she'd had a software routine explained to her and had never had the inclination or the permission to wander further afield.

'I can't even find the customer database,' admitted Jennifer after a while. 'Why can't you ask Mark to show you things?'

'Because he's gone,' returned Robert, sitting down on a chair he'd dragged near to Jennifer. 'Can you find out how much money we can draw out of the bank today?'

Jeremy seemed mildly vexed. 'We agreed we wouldn't draw any more money out this week,' he said, a comment ignored by Robert.

After a discussion and several attempts, Jennifer answered that she could not. 'You're going to have to get someone else to help you.'

Robert wandered over to the other side of the room. He cleared his throat again. 'We don't know anyone else. No one we can trust, anyway.'

Jennifer felt she'd done all she could and switched the computer off.

A pall hung over Jeremy and Robert as they considered their position. Very soon, however, they were lifted by a thought of Jeremy's, and the thought was *Penny* — she might be able to help. 'Penny knows all about computers and business,' said Jeremy.

Penny was an ex-girlfriend of Jeremy's.

'And she knows about *our* business,' added Robert, immediately encouraging Jeremy to telephone her.

But Penny was away for a few days, they discovered. However, they were told she would be back by the end of the week, and the prospect of enlisting her help seemed to bolster Jeremy considerably, but Robert remained much in his brooding state.

'Don't worry, Robert,' said Jeremy, 'We'll survive. We can start the new sales campaign when Penny's back. And we'll be all right for wages once the *pro formas* start coming in.'

Robert began putting on his coat and hat.

He quickly left without saying where he was going or inviting Jennifer along.

Jeremy apologised for Robert's behaviour, saying how much stress he was under.

Jennifer heard nothing more from Robert that day. When she returned to Yvette's, Peter was there, collecting his things. She didn't probe, but what she gathered was that he had already decided to leave, and had not been ordered out.

Yvette and Peter had lived together for two years.

That night, Yvette and Jennifer went out to Camden, and Yvette met someone new in a bar. It was as simple as that.

2.25
A Changed Person

Phil's ghost had caused fear. Subtly led by Pross, Simon had come to the conclusion that Phil's evil spirit was intent on destroying the Golden Millennium project from beyond the grave.

Pross put his mind at rest by saying that he could keep Phil's spirit at bay while he was building the Empathy Device by adapting extraterrestrial know-how to generate a force field that would repel all negative spiritual energies around his bedroom, which he would use as the workshop.

But as well as keeping Phil's ghost at bay, this force would be harmful to Simon and Mick, since their own energies were not completely pure, and would not be until the device changed them and the world.

Only he, Prospero Pi-Meson, the Expected One, with thoughts as pure as snow, could survive unaffected within this force field.

Simon had thought this to be a brilliant idea.

So Pross's bedroom became conveniently out of bounds during the Empathy Device construction period. And once the device *was* constructed, it would have its own internal shielding to repel negative spirituality. Once operating, it would be spiritually unassailable.

He was walking in the woods now.

He knew for almost certain he was set soon to become fantastically rich, but he dwelled upon it not, for he was no longer the same person. Now everything he did felt like he was just going through the motions. It was like some reserve, automatic part of his mind had taken over, and the clamouring remainder had been quelled. When he thought, it was without personal involvement. When he ate, it was without relish. When he walked, it was without vigour.

But the gnawing anguish in his stomach was still there, unchanged.

Drifting through the woods within the grounds, Pross came upon what he immediately knew to be Phil's grave. Some earth had recently been turned, and made a bulge. He flattened the bulge as best he could with his feet and dragged a broken branch over it.

Then he piled and trampled leaves over the whole area.

It was Wednesday today — he had to work that out by counting. Yesterday, Simon had gone to London to buy diamond pyramids. He was going to spend five million pounds of his money on them.

And Pross had almost finished making the Empathy Device in his out-of-bounds bedroom, acquiring welding skills along the way.

Only once had he left the house or its grounds since the death of Phil. Yesterday, he had instructed Mick to drive him into Darlington where he had bought spare clothes and all the tools and materials necessary for the great project.

He'd also bought a reliable car, driving it back himself.

After the purchases, he had over six thousand pounds in cash left over, cash which Simon had not asked to be returned.

He drifted back into the house to continue his job.

2.26
Out To Lunch

Steven had a friend with him who'd tried to gain the affections of Jennifer, but had failed and gone home alone.

Steven had gone home with Yvette.

Jennifer heard them making love through the small hours.

Presumedly taking the day off work, Yvette was still in bed with her new lover when Jennifer left the flat at around eleven o'clock. Her intentions were to call on Robert, then go shopping in Camden for clothes.

She had telephoned the office earlier, but the phone had been engaged each time she had tried.

Robert was a worry to her. He was so sweet and kind, and had been such a help to her that she wanted to help him in return, and that help seemed to extend to sleeping with him, although she didn't think of him as a lover.

Arriving in Harley Street, she found Robert to have only just risen from his bed, and the atmosphere the same as when she had left the day before: an oppressive stagnation.

The telephone was off the hook.

Robert smiled his smile when she came in, and Jeremy, sitting at the table, said his polite greetings.

'How are you?' asked Robert, briefly putting his arm around her.

Jennifer soon told Robert about Yvette and Peter, but he didn't seem too interested, so she dropped the subject. What he was interested in was how "the company", as he called it, was going to survive financially until *pro forma* payments from the next sales campaign came through. It was agreed between him and Jeremy that twenty thousand pounds would be needed.

'What do you normally do?' asked Jennifer.

'We arrange an overdraft,' said Jeremy.

'Well, do that again.'

Robert cleared his throat. 'We can't. Mark did all that stuff with the bank. When the sales campaign starts, we'll pull in thirty grand in *pro formas*, and a lot more from the factoring company when the book's out, but there's no money left now.'

Jennifer did not know what *pro forma* payments were, or what a factoring company was, or indeed exactly what their business was, but she believed Robert. 'I can lend you enough money,' she said.

Jeremy sat up straight. 'Twenty thousand pounds?'

Robert cleared his throat. 'Where will you get it from?'

'It's in my account already. I inherited it.'

The cloud immediately lifted. 'This is amazing,' said Robert, displaying the very essence of motivation. 'We'll be able to start the new sales campaign as soon as Penny comes back, and we'll make a killing, like we did on the first one. Hundred and fifty grand target.'

In his own restrained, slow way, Jeremy was sharing Robert's positivity. 'And it'll be so much better not having Mark in the room with us. He was such a negative influence.'

'Listen,' said Robert earnestly to Jennifer, looking into her eyes, 'we'll pay you back thirty grand within three months. It can't fail. We've been doing this for three years now, and we've made over half a million so far.'

'That's right,' said Jeremy.

Jennifer simply took out her cheque book. It pleased her to do so.

Jeremy and Robert insisted on taking Jennifer out to lunch, a Japanese restaurant on Baker Street being the chosen place.

Jennifer ate with chopsticks for the first time, and they finished lunch with champagne.

Spirits were high.

Afterwards, Robert went to Camden with Jennifer to accompany her around the shops and market stalls.

With her credit card, Jennifer bought clothes more like the things Yvette wore, Robert passing judgement on each item.

After half an hour, he passed her a rose he'd bought behind her back.

After an hour, he asked if she wouldn't mind much if he left her to finish shopping alone, saying he had to see someone on business matters.

They arranged to meet again in the evening.

After shopping, although laden with bags, Jennifer decided to take the tube back to Holloway Road rather than pay for a cab.

She gave a wino five pounds, and he blessed her.

Nearing the entrance to her new home, Jennifer saw that Yvette's cat was at the door on the busy street. It was nervous, crouching whenever anyone walked past, which was every few seconds. Since the flat was on the first floor, it had no hope of getting in.

Jennifer could not imagine how it come to be there, since Yvette had told her that it was never allowed out.

It bolted inside when Jennifer opened the door, she struggling up the stairs after it with her carrier bags.

At the flat's private door, Jennifer let herself in with her own key, and the cat ran in in front of her.

'No!' cried Yvette, 'Eet can't come eeen!'

The cat hid.

'Why not?'

'Because Ah'm seek of eet.'

After seeing the look of incredulity and reproach she was getting from Jennifer, Yvette seemed to relent, or resign, and the cat was allowed peace.

'Deed you see Robert?' Yvette asked.

Jennifer told Yvette all that had happened, and Yvette praised her for loaning the money. 'Don't worry, you'll get eet back. They earn lots of money.'

Then Yvette told Jennifer that Steven was the man for her.

She would see him again on Friday.

Later, before going out to meet Robert, Jennifer fed the cat, since Yvette didn't want to bother.

That night, she slept with Robert again.

2.27
Three Hundred Trillion Possibilities

Each one worth four hundred thousand pounds... and he had just been handed thirteen of them.

Simon had done the business. At a jewellers in Hatton Garden, London, he'd ordered thirteen diamond pyramids to be cut, a request which had cost him more than five million pounds.

Everything was done secretly. No one was told what they were for. That was Pross's order, for evil would try to stop the project if it could.

Secrecy was going to save Pross's skin and make him rich.

Stood at the window in his bedroom, he regarded the glittering jewels in his possession without any sense of accomplishment or excitement. The horror he had seen on Sunday had sunk deep.

He had dreamed of that horror last night.

And the night before.

And the night before that.

In last night's dream, Phil, holding out the patch of flesh torn from his cheek, had implored him with a look never to be forgotten to return it to his bloodied face. Suddenly finding the flesh in his own hand, Pross could think of nothing but microsurgery, but the *Yellow Pages* he frantically thumbed had no listing for such a service.

He tried to cut the glass of his window with a pyramid, and easily succeeded in making a scratch.

No mark was to be seen on the jewel.

Pross knew it was the hardest substance known. Thermal conductivity six times greater than copper. Many times lighter and stronger than steel. It really would be the substance of the future, once its artificial creation was perfected.

He also knew that nanotechnology vaguely promised to deliver that perfection.

As well as being defended from Phil's malignant ghost, the diamonds, or so Simon was told, had to be decontaminated of all the negative spiritual energies they would have picked up when being handled by others. No one was allowed near the diamonds now. Only *his* spiritual energy was pure enough. Any contamination would endanger the project, corrupt the output of the Empathy Device.

He had told Simon that the Empathy Device generated a special spiritual shield which would protect the pyramids from outside contamination once inserted and sealed within. Even ghosts could not penetrate this shield. But opening the device would bathe the pyramids with impure energy, rendering it dangerous to use, for it would amplify unbalanced energy, inducing imperfect mind waves in the population.

So it was forbidden, strictly forbidden, to ever force the box open, even if Phil's ghost were laid to rest.

Simon understood this like he understood he should never attempt to look inside his prayer battery.

Pross's device itself was well crafted. Metal sheeting had been welded to create a vessel the size of a shoe box. Surfaces had been painstakingly smoothed and enamelled. An antenna was fixed to the rear to receive spiritual energy for its initial charging.

Pross had told Simon that the advanced extraterrestrial electronics within could capture enough of his perfectly balanced spiritual energy in a one hour prayer session to trickle a sufficiently strong signal into the device's crystal amplification circuitry for a full thousand years.

Another antennae was in front for directing the amplified output, the energy drawn from the unlimited zero point source.

The Golden Millennium depended only on the device being prayer-charged then left working over the ley pole in the garden, where Pross had built a small stone shelter to house it for its proposed millennium of use.

For a thousand years it would broadcast his spiritual energy to the world, creating peace and enlightenment.

Thirteen small metal rods protruded from the device at random angles, like the swords running through a magician's box. Each metal rod was free to move to any one of thirteen marked positions, supposedly moving a pyramid inside with it.

This was so that only someone who knew the right positions could operate the device. If any one rod were set incorrectly, then so would be the diamonds, and the device would be inert. The geometry would not be sacred.

If someone *were* to break it open, unless the rods were already set correctly, they could not know the secret crystal geometry, the geometry that could supposedly unleash unlimited energy if fully tapped. A geometry that could annihilate the planet, or even the whole solar system.

All thirteen positions had to be known.

A switch to supposedly irreversibly disable the receiving antenna was also present, so that it would not be able to accept further spiritual energy once charged by Pross.

A *real* electrical circuit was built into the device. This battery-operated circuit made a pyramid pattern of light-emitting diodes on the top activate when the rods were set in what were supposed to be the right positions. This would show that the device was working. Simon would see these lights work only once, unless he lived for nine million years, trying a different combination of rod positions every second, day and night.

Thirteen variable positions on thirteen different rods gave three hundred trillion possible alignment combinations.

Already he had welded the device shut and smoothed the last surface.

The diamonds he would later hide under the seat of his car.

It was becoming dark. A lone blackbird, out of season, was singing somewhere in the murky distance as he returned through drizzle to the house after secreting the diamonds.

He had told Simon he had something wondrous to tell him.

In the large room, as Simon and Mick stood by the fire over the place where Phil had been slain, Pross, robed as ever, presented the device to them.

Although not exactly a thing of perfect beauty and grace, it was sturdy and certainly better made than the prayer battery Simon lugged around.

'Amazing,' breathed Simon when he first beheld it, moving in for a closer look.

'Not yet,' said Pross, speaking in an even, almost drab, tone, staying Simon's advance then walking back a little.

An even, almost drab tone seemed to be about all he was capable of now.

Explaining his purpose, he went on to say, 'The spiritual shielding isn't at full strength yet, so you can't get too close to it for another few hours at least. You'll be able to touch it after I charge it with my spiritual energy. It's empty now.'

Simon accepted this.

'It's fantastic,' said Mick. 'What are all those rods?'

Pross said what the rods were. That they were effectively a combination lock disallowing others to operate it, or know its secret internal geometry.

'What's the combination?'

'I'll tell you soon. Remember, it's not to be activated until the return of the Third Satellite, and as you know, the next date for that is February the first. But when the right combination is selected, these lights glow to show that it's working.'

Unknown to his followers, Pross had set twelve of the rods correctly, leaving only one needing to be moved to activate the light diodes. He had kept Simon at bay so that he could not glean the correct position of any of the rods. 'This is what it will look like when correctly set.'

Moving the final rod produced a triangle of dim red light on the top of the box as the internal battery was connected up.

'Amazing,' breathed Simon.

Becoming stern, Pross reiterated an earlier warning. 'No one must ever try to open it.'

He pushed all the rods to their base positions.

'I understand,' said Simon immediately, pushing his glasses up the way he always did at such serious moments, 'Doing that would let unbalanced energy inside.'

'When it works proper, will it feel like the energy on Sunday?' Mick wanted to know.

'Purer. There'll be no side effects. No physical effects at all. Just peace and bliss for a thousand years.'

'Amazing,' breathed Simon.

'All you need to know, Simon,' said Pross, 'is the right combination for the rods and then it will work. When the time comes, that's all you'll have to do. Place the device over the ley pole, then set the rods.'

Concern showed itself on Simon's face. 'You'll be doing it yourself, won't you?'

'No, Simon, I won't,' answered Pross plainly. 'I'm going away forever. I'm going away tonight.'

Concern giving way to anxiety, Simon made a little step closer to Pross. 'Where are you going, Master?'

'On Sunday, when I went out alone, I was going to meet the extraterrestrials. I went aboard their ship, and they asked me if I would represent Earth at the Interplanetary Parliament.' Looking into Simon's eyes, Pross said, 'I agreed, Simon. They're picking me up from their secret landing site tonight to take me to another planet. I can never return. I am no longer of this world. I have changed.'

Wonder and dismay both gripped Simon as he gazed at Pross.

Mick was pretty stunned too, once he'd worked out what was going on.

Turning, Pross said, 'I have to go upstairs to charge the device with my energy now. As you know, you must not come up.'

With falling features, Simon watched him ascend.

A tear emerged.

2.28
Another Apology

Thursday began badly for Robert.

'Robert,' called Jeremy, tapping loudly on the bedroom door.

Robert woke, but in stretching sleepily over Jennifer to reach his clock, which was so small he had to hold it close to read, his fingers accidentally brought with them an open coke packet.

With Robert stretching over her, Jennifer stirred also, sitting up as Jeremy put his head into the room. When she realised her breasts were bare, she began to pull the duvet up, but Robert dropped the best part of a gram of coke over her chest first.

'Penny's turned us down,' said Jeremy with palpable dismay, ignoring Robert's crisis and Jennifer's exposure.

'Fuck,' said Robert upon noticing that he'd spilled his coke, pulling the duvet down in opposition to Jennifer's inclination to modesty. 'No!' he said in desperate voice, 'you'll lose it.'

'Robert!' complained Jennifer when he began trying to accumulate the spilled drug from her bare breasts. 'Wait till Jeremy's gone.'

Jeremy and Jennifer were to be ignored while Robert rescued what he could. But Jennifer became annoyed. Twisting round, she tipped what she could into her hand, then put it into Robert's before getting out of bed, walking naked to her dressing gown.

Robert was frantic for a while during this procedure.

Jeremy repeated his news. 'She's turned us down, Robert.'

'Who?'

'Penny.'

'Did you tell her how much we'd pay her?'

'Yes,' returned Jeremy in his slow, plodding, slightly downward inflecting way, 'she said she's not interested at any price. I just don't understand it. She was really sardonic as well.'

'We'll think of something,' said Robert, laying out a line of the rescued coke, chopping the crystals fine with a blade. 'D'you want a line, Jen?'

'Course I don't. It's morning.'

'So?'

'Can't you go five minutes without it?'

'I'd rather not.'

Robert ignored her, so she made for the bathroom.

Ten minutes later, they were all three sat at the table in the fusty office, Jeremy and Robert pondering the day's batch of enigmatic letters, only half of which they opened.

Finally, Jennifer's idea that an employment agency should be contacted seemed the only solution. Over the telephone, questions asked led to the agency saying that at least a separate bookkeeper, secretary, desktop publisher and administrator would be required. Four people minimum at up to fourteen pounds an hour each.

And the tax would have to be legal.

Jeremy thought it could be done, but Robert thought otherwise.

Jennifer began to worry about the safety of her money, the cheque having already been deposited into the Chesterford account.

After his morning coffee, Robert put his hat and coat on, smiled and said he was going around the corner to get some cigarettes.

He did not return that day.

Later, Jeremy again apologised for Robert, citing worry as the cause.

Having waited all afternoon in the office, Jennifer finally went back to Yvette's flat at five o'clock, much troubled.

The cat was outside again.

When she entered the flat, she found Yvette with her wrap-skirt lifted high, examining the red scar on her milky hip.

'Ello, Jennifer,' she smiled, kissing her cheeks. 'No!' she shouted at the cat when she saw it, it having been let in by Jennifer.

'Why not?' argued Jennifer. 'You can't just throw it out.'

'Steven doesn't like cats,' was Yvette's reply.

Jennifer could hardly believe what she had heard. 'He's not even here now!'

Yvette produced the same face she had produced when Jennifer had expressed horror at the scar's story. A sullen, resentful, but nevertheless yielding look.

The cat was allowed peace as Yvette returned her sullen attention to her scar, the legacy of a broken relationship. 'Ah'm going to av a tattoo over eet tomorrow,' she said.

Jennifer passed no comment.

They stayed in together the rest of the evening, watching television.

Yvette spoke often of Steven.

Robert did not phone.

2.29
Revenge

A full moon glowed weakly behind thin, softly weeping clouds.

But many earthly tears emerged as Simon said his goodbyes to Pross.

Before stepping out into the drizzle, Pross hugged him, and then Mick.

Except for that disconcerting feeling in the pit of his stomach, Pross felt nothing, not even impatience.

Through his tears, Simon disclosed a comforting thought. 'We'll see each other again, though, won't we, Prospero? When the Golden Millennium begins, old age will be conquered, and eventually I'll graduate to other planets as the same person I am now, won't I?'

'That's right, Simon. If you do your work here first, one day, maybe a million years from now, we will meet again. And you too, Mick.'

He started to walk away. 'I have to be gone. There's little time to spare. The spaceship will arrive in an hour. It won't wait for me, and it's over half an hour's drive away where they land in the Lake District.'

Blending with the darkness, Pross progressed towards his car.

'What about the combination?' called Simon anxiously.

Pross stopped and turned around, saying, 'It's written in an envelope hidden inside your mattress, Simon. Don't lose it. The Golden Millennium depends on you doing my work.'

'I won't lose it, Master.'

'Activate the device when the Third Satellite is in orbit. If anything goes wrong and you miss the date, wait for the next date. You know the dates for the next thousand years, so don't worry. Never tell anyone about the device, or the project, or me. You two are the only people who can ever know. The technology's too powerful to be revealed.'

Mick, too, was crying. 'Goodbye, Master,' he called.

'Goodbye, Mick.'

Simon could contain his emotion no longer and ran to Pross. 'Don't go, Master. Please don't go. I love you.'

Mick came to him too.

They both knelt at his feet, sobbing, and he placed a hand on each head. Again, he told them, 'I have to leave. I'm no longer of this world. I have changed. My time here has come to an end. Even if the Golden Millennium were never to arrive, I could not stay, my spirit has seen too much.'

That much he believed. It was another irony — just as he'd got used to being himself, he had to go and change.

Pross turned away from them. Three steps later he was beside his car. As a last word, he said to Simon, 'Don't ever let the gatekeeper leave. He's spiritually linked to this site. I can't explain more, it's too complicated. Let him live in his cottage as long as he likes. But don't ever let him in the grounds, he might find the body.'

His lights shone, the engine started, and then the gravel crunched.

Through the woods he drove, Mick and Simon watching until no glint of light was left to be seen.

Overcome, neither of them felt inclined to return to the house for many minutes.

Once back inside, Simon, vision blurred with tears, made his way to his own bedroom. Examining his mattress revealed a slit in the side. Opening the slit revealed an envelope. Opening the envelope revealed sabotage.

Thirteen small holes were burnt into the single piece of paper contained within the envelope. Each hole had evidently destroyed a written number. What appeared to have originally been a diagram was also burnt beyond comprehension.

Below the burns, singed into the paper was the message: *revenge from beyond the grave you put me in.*

Find him. Catch him up before the extraterrestrials took him away forever. That's all they could think of doing. To the cab they ran, flogging the sluggish diesel engine as best Mick could.

He'd had a good ten minutes head start on them, and they weren't even sure which way he was likely to have gone.

For an hour, they sped through the drizzle, over the Pennines and on into the Lake District, but his car they did not encounter.

Eventually, knowing that Pross would be in space by now, Simon called the search off, and he and Mick returned to the house, utterly despondent.

Upon returning, Simon began trying combinations, first at random, then to a system. Slowly, as night became day, he realised what a task he had before him: he began to comprehend the enormity of three hundred trillion possibilities.

He wept with despair as the sun came up.

Pross had not gone to the Lake District. He had gone east, not west. With his computer's hard disk bearing all his writing in one pocket, thirteen diamond pyramids in another, and thousands in cash in a third, he'd headed towards Durham to return to his friends and give Ron his due.

Somehow, now that he was rich, he could face seeing them again.

It was nearly midnight when he pulled into the short drive of Melanie's new-private-estate, slightly out of town, slightly detached two-bedroom house.

He parked behind Ron's Car, who was apparently visiting.

Opening the house door, which was unlocked, he walked into the living room.

He was still wearing his robe.

He could smell dope.

In the room, Melanie, Ron and Sarah were all sat on the sofa, vaguely looking at Pross's suitcase, for it seemed to have replaced the television as a point of focus.

Tony was sitting *on* the suitcase, watching the television, back to the room.

All heads except Tony's turned slowly to look at whoever had come into the house.

Ron was the first to speak, observing dryly, 'So you're still alive then? Wrong again, Sarah.'

'Why shouldn't I be?' returned Pross blankly.

Sarah and Melanie were too thrown by the sight of Pross in a golden robe to say anything at first.

Seeing Sarah, Pross, unsure how she would react to him, gave her a little twiddly finger wave.

After a moment, she twiddled her fingers back. 'I was worried you might have topped yourself,' she said, perplexed by his outfit, 'that's why. You're supposed to be brokenhearted after all.'

'Yeah, living one,' said Ron accusingly, 'deem yourself a poet?'

'I am brokenhearted,' said Pross, standing by the door. 'I've just learned to live with it.'

'Shallow,' gibed Ron, surveying the robe.

'Quick learner,' returned Pross slowly.

Tony turned around briefly. 'Hello, Pross.'

'Hello, Tony.'

Tony looked at the tv again.

Ron said, 'You've turned gay, though, haven't you?'

Pross found Ron's comment unfathomable, and his face showed it.

'The dress,' explained Ron.

The dress. He'd become so used to, and was so preoccupied, he'd not even realised he was still wearing it. Or rather he did know he was wearing it, but it didn't seem important or unusual.

He looked down at it.

'It's my uniform,' he said. 'I've got a job.'

The job claim clinched it: Melanie perceived that Pross was not quite his usual self. 'Are you all right?' she asked.

'No. I've got a feeling that won't go away.'

'That's your gayness,' stated Ron, receiving an elbow in the ribs from both Melanie and Sarah.

'I'm not gay. I've got a job, that's all.'

'Vicar?' wondered Ron.

'Higher,' said Pross.

'Bishop?'

'Higher. Much higher.'

'Pope?'

'Higher.'

Ron couldn't think of any transvestite job in the world higher up the career ladder than pope. For a number of seconds, he viewed his friend, dressed in a golden robe, stood framed in the doorway. 'You've flipped, haven't you?' he said, delighted. 'It was those drugs. You've finally gone wacko. Told you it would happen one day soon.'

'I'm not mad. I've got a job, that's all.'

Ron stood up. 'Come on, we'll take you to the mental hospital. Put you in the gay ward.'

Melanie pulled Ron back down, then sought to raise her psychiatrist husband's interest. 'Tony,' she said petulantly, 'we think Pross has gone mad.'

Tony reluctantly turned around. Regarding Pross for a few seconds, he concluded, 'Yep. Total nutter. Take him to my hospital. Put him in the gay ward.'

'I'm not gay,' said Pross. 'I've just got a job, that's all. I'm not mad, either.'

Ron leaned over to reach a telephone. Pretending to dial a number, he said into the receiver, discreetly, but not *too* discreetly, 'Hello, Gay Helpline? It's about a friend of mine. He's acting really suspicious.... What's that?.. Yes, all the signs are there... Yes, that too. Long and golden it is... You'll send someone over to take him away?.. That's good?... Ten minutes?.. Right. Thanks. Be careful, he's whacko with it.'

He put the phone down.

Sarah went over to Pross. 'Are you all right?'

'Where's my lottery money?' said Ron, suddenly remembering.

Pross ignored Ron and looked at Sarah. 'Any word from Jenny? Is she all right?'

'She's all right. She phoned. She's in London. She's living in a girl's flat.'

'I'm sorry. I'm so sorry.'

Sarah hugged him.

Ron pitched his oar in. 'Don't blame yourself,' he said plainly.

'Why not? It was my fault,' said Pross back, talking over the shoulder of Sarah.

'I know it was,' agreed Ron immediately. 'I meant don't blame yourself when there's other people who can blame you a lot better. Jenny's aunt, for instance. She wants to kill you. I said I'll help. But now you've turned gay, she could probably do it herself.'

'What about Sarah?' asked Pross, numbly grim, expecting the worst, talking about her even though she was actually hugging him at the time, to which he seemed oblivious.

'She was more worried about you than about Jenny. That's her, by the way, hugging you. Recognise?'

'Come over here,' said Melanie, pushing Ron off the sofa.

Sarah began leading Pross over to Melanie. Smiling a concerned smile, Melanie sat him down beside her, and Sarah sat the other side of him.

'You're acting a bit weird, Pross,' Melanie said. 'Are you all right?'

'No. Never felt worse.'

'What's the matter?'

'I've got a feeling that won't go away. I'm not mad though. You'd have this feeling too if you'd done what I've done.'

'Why've you got a dress on?'

'I'm not gay. I've got a job.'

Ron, now sitting in an armchair, lighting a joint, piped up. 'Ever thought of doing it competitively?'

'Doing what?' asked Pross.

'Being gay. You could win medals, you. Represent the country.'

'I'm not gay.'

'You are. Just admit it, then you'll feel so much better. Isn't that right, Tony?'

'Certainly is,' answered Tony without turning around. 'Repressing all that intense gayness must be doing him damage most everywhere.'

Ron was not finished yet. 'You're deluding yourself because of your madness. You think you're wearing a butch lumberjack shirt, sat between two gorgeous chicks who are worried about you, when in fact you're alone, wearing a dress. You've got a stupid pudding basin haircut too. We all meant to tell you about that before, but we didn't have the heart.'

Looking at Ron, Pross said, 'Thanks for bolstering me. Anyone else want to stick the bolster in?'

Tony put his hand up to say something, but Ron beat him to it. 'You're ugly too.'

'Do you want this or not?' asked Pross, holding out a diamond.

'What?'

Pross tossed it over to Ron. 'It's your redundancy payment,' he said. 'It's worth around four hundred thousand pounds.'

Melanie and Sarah scurried over to examine it with Ron.

About an hour. That's how long it took Pross to convince Ron that the jewel was genuine. In that giddy hour, Pross felt his usual self return a little, and the tenseness in his stomach began easing.

He was getting better.

The diamond staggered Ron. Utterly staggered him. 'One hundred and fifty three years' unemployment benefit,' he kept saying.

Melanie was staggered too.

And Sarah.

And Tony.

They were even more staggered when Pross gave them each a diamond of their own.

He gave Melanie two, actually. One for Lilith.

But he refused to say how he'd come by them. 'Don't worry. They're not hot. Never will be. They were acquired with maximum cunning. There's reasons why I can't tell you more, but the rip-off won't be discovered for at least nine million years. Trust me.'

They all agreed that they actually did trust him on this.

Ron produced a pipe, and Pross accepted the gift that was passed to him, drawing deep on the psychoactive smoke.

Just short moments later, amid talk of holidays and mortgage settlements, the anguished feeling inside of him that had begun to diminish suddenly became overwhelming and acute. Frightening. And that feeling began showing on the outside, for halfway through a sentence, he dried up, as, within a pattern of shadows in the simulated coal fire he was gazing into, he began clearly visualising the smashed, bloodied face of Phil. And then he felt his own face burn red with guilt and shame.

Everyone noticed.

'What's the matter?' asked Melanie. 'Why are you blushing?'

But Pross did not answer. He was now listening in astonished shock to the cd player. A Beatles song was playing quietly. Pross had suddenly begun interpreting each line of lyric so that it became a contemptible condemnation of him. Not only the full lines, but elements of the lines too. It was all a perfect analysis and judgement, stunningly clever. He wasn't hearing things that weren't being sung, just finding new meaning in the familiar words. And there was no effort or time delay involved: in a literal instant, his mind was twisting what it was hearing to make attacks upon itself. Some of the interpretations even relied on cryptic references and word play more cunning than a Times crossword.

Part of his mind had turned traitor. A powerful part.

'Pross, what's the matter?'

'Someone died because of me,' murmured Pross to Melanie, feeling more afraid and disturbed than he could ever have believed himself capable.

And he realised he could not bring himself to look directly at Melanie.

Tony came near and looked into guilty eyes until Pross reddened with shame and turned away.

Tony then diagnosed, 'A genuine cannabis psychosis — cool.'

'Told you he was gay,' said Ron.

2.30
Bender

A letter arrived for Jennifer.

Today was a work day for Yvette, and she was up early, trying to be quiet as she got herself ready, for Jennifer was still asleep on the sofa, despite the noise of traffic below.

But Jennifer awoke when Yvette picked up, and accidentally clinked, two mugs from the floor near the sofa.

'Good morning,' said Yvette brightly and musically when she saw Jennifer's eyes open.

'Morning,' smiled Jennifer sleepily.

'A letter's come for you.'

When handed the letter by Yvette, Jennifer recognised the writing as belonging to her sister.

She would open it later.

Sitting up, yawning, she slipped her feet into sandals and shuffled to the bathroom.

A little later, she was making toast and marmalade for Yvette and herself, and putting food out for the cat, which had slept at her feet most of the night.

'What should we do tonight?' asked Yvette.

'Can we go dancing again?'

Yvette erupted into a grin. 'Of course we can,' she answered, then did her endearing little gangling arms dance again.

A personal triumph is how Yvette looked upon Jennifer's transformation, in only five days, from demure to joy-seeking. 'Ah av to see Steven first. Let's meet een the same club at nine.'

It was agreed: Jennifer would meet Yvette and Steven in the club at nine.

After Yvette left for work, Jennifer took a bath, then sat down with a cup of coffee to read her letter.

The envelope from Sarah contained Pross's letter, forwarded to her unsolicited. When she realised this, she was annoyed at the liberty taken by her sister. She'd moved on now. She was with new, open, caring people, and didn't want to have to think about the complicated mystery which he had been.

But she read it anyway.

Like it had her sister, it made her tearful too, and much of that complicated mystery was now solved for her. And like Sarah, she, too, regretted many of the misgivings she had had about Pross.

She was especially moved to learn of the bad time he had had on his first E trip because he could not find her. She could imagine how upset *she* could have felt if something emotionally wounding had happened to her on *her* first trip.

But there was no thought of going back. When reading the letter, she was moved by sympathy, not yearning. Of course it crossed her mind that things could have turned out different if she'd gone to Ron's party, but the past was the past, she decided, and the two weeks with him had not been long enough for her to have invested much in the relationship. She had said she was growing to love him, but it hadn't worked out, and she'd moved on — that was her attitude, and she would be stupid having any other.

She did worry about his disappearance, though.

But Robert's disappearance was a more immediate worry to Jennifer. After telephoning, she discovered from Jeremy that Robert had been on a hideous bender. He'd been drinking without rest all day yesterday and all night too, fortified by cocaine. The inevitable crash had come when he'd returned to the office that morning.

He was now effectively unconscious on the floor.

Jennifer hastened to be with him.

Not only was Jennifer concerned for her new friend, she was also concerned for her own money. Still not very clear what it actually was that Robert did *to* earn his living, she knew he couldn't do it if he was lying drunk on the floor, which he wasn't by the time she arrived in the office. By that time he was in the kitchen.

Jeremy was on the telephone.

Seeing Jennifer, Robert smiled a smile that was not far from lunacy, then put his arms around her. 'How are you doing, Jenny?' he drawled, grinning a wet grin.

He smelled of booze, fags and staleness.

'Better than you,' returned Jennifer with an edge.

Adopting the voice of a drunk Dudley Moore, Robert protested his sobriety. 'I've only 'ad one little'un. That's all. Just one... thirty big'uns, but just one little'un.'

Jennifer was not amused.

Robert seemed oblivious to her disapproval, and he returned his attention to doing whatever it was he'd been doing when she'd arrived.

Whatever that whatever was, it involved bicarbonate of soda.

A few moments later, it involved cocaine too.

'What are you doing, Robert?'

'Washing some coke. It makes it purer.'

'Please don't take any more. Go to bed. Can't you see what's happening to you?'

Robert deliberately ignored her, so Jennifer became resigned to watching him do whatever he was doing.

Jeremy came into the kitchen. 'Robert,' he said, 'we've got to start selling on the new book soon.'

'We can't,' returned Robert, continuing with his task. 'Not until we replace Mark.'

'We can. We can make a start at least. We can write the sales pitch.'

'Did you manage to speak to Mark?'

Jennifer suspected that Robert's enquiry was simply to divert Jeremy from disturbing him.

'No. He doesn't answer his phone or return my messages... What are you doing?'

'Washing the coke. It makes it purer. Trevor showed me how to do it. It gives an amazing hit. It's like a mental orgasm.'

'You're making crack, that's what you're doing.'

'No I'm not, I'm just washing it. Do you want some?' he asked, holding out a pipe made of silver paper.

Jeremy suddenly knocked it out of his hand, and it fell at Jennifer's feet.

'What did you do that for?' cried Robert in a high voice, immediately getting down on the floor to rescue what he could.

Jeremy was angry, even though he didn't suit it. 'It's crack, Robert, you fucker. The most addictive drug there is.'

'It's not. I'm just washing it.'

Jennifer made one more effort to reach Robert. 'Please, don't take any more.'

Robert pushed her foot away so he could reach his spilled desire.

Having seen enough, Jennifer left.

Robert let her go without a word or a look.

On the tube back to Holloway Road, she again read Pross's letter.

2.31

Containment

All night he'd tried combinations, randomly at first, then systematically. But by the time the sky lightened, hardly a dent seemed to have been made in the total he would have to explore.

Months, or even years, he'd then vaguely realised it might take to run though them all.

Now despairing, fatigue forced him to rest.

But upon waking in the afternoon, a resolve overcame Simon. If years were needed, then years he would give, he decided. He would give over years of his life, if necessary, to trying combinations on the Empathy Device. And Mick pledged to help him too. It was their sacred duty to Godfrey.

Shifts. They would do it in shifts. While one rested, the other would work. And this pattern would not be broken until those lights came on, as they had done for Prospero, to show that the combination was right.

And they would pray as well. Pray always for help and guidance.

There would be no centre for New Age studies yet. Simon had no time to spare. Only he and Mick were allowed knowledge of the device by Prospero's wise order, so it was up to them alone.

Alone, unknown by the world, they would endure tedium in the name of Prospero and the Golden Millennium.

They were a match for it, they vowed.

And so Simon drew up a rota, and began the first four hour shift, not knowing that nine million years at a different combination a second was needed to cover all.

2.32
Still Mad

It was early Friday morning. Melanie and Tony were having breakfast in their pine kitchen. Pross was still in the living room. He hadn't slept or ate all night. He had gone ga-ga after the dope. And when the dope wore off, he'd remained ga-ga.

He couldn't look people in the eye.

'Bollocks to him,' said Tony to Melanie. 'I used to offer to help him, but he just took the piss.' Melanie threw Tony a look which elicited a more considerate and professional attitude. 'He's having some kind of guilt crisis. The lid's been taken off.'

'Why does he keep saying someone died because of him?'

'How should I know? The mind's a fucking funny thing. The state he's in at the moment, he'd admit to starting World War Two.' Tony's hand went up to his chin, which he began kneading. 'I think it's probably the culmination of years of repressed guilt over his mother and her suicide attempts. That's what it'll be. He feels he's as good as killed her, and while under the influence of cannabis, invented a death to release his guilt upon. The mind *is* a fucking funny thing.'

'His mother? What do you know about his mother?'

'She my patient,' revealed Tony. 'Has been for years. She's in my hospital.'

Melanie was astounded. 'You've never told me. Why didn't you ever tell me?'

'Because you would have told Pross,' he said simply, 'and I don't think Pross wants to know.'

Melanie was inclined to be angry at first, but held herself in check.

'Help him.'

'He doesn't need my help. Going mad's the sanest thing he's ever done.'

Now she *was* angry.

'Tony,' she snapped.

'Oh, don't worry about him,' grumbled Tony. 'He'll think his way out of it on his own. It might take him months, or years, but he'll pull through. He's not like the feckless cases I see in the hospital every day. He ought to be pleased, really. Once he gets this out of the way, he'll be a better person. It can be a privilege to go mad. He's in the hidden rooms at the moment, having a good look around.'

Melanie was not entirely convinced. 'Haven't you seen him in there? He's tortured.'

'I know that. I could prescribe him sledgehammers, but I don't want to. He knows he's gone loopy. He's not going to go out and do crazy things, like think he can paint the Forth Bridge or something. He's going to stay in and work everything out.'

Tony went into the living room. 'Aye up, nutter,' he said jauntily to Pross.

Melanie followed.

'Aye up, Tony,' returned Pross mutely, sat on the sofa, looking at the floor.

'Still mad?'

Pross nodded his head a little to confirm his sorry condition. 'Loco. The Beatles have been sticking the boot into me all night.'

'Bastards,' said Melanie.

'Don't blame them,' he droned, 'I deserve it.' Then he had an idea. 'Put that Paul Simon cd on over there. See if he hates me too.'

Melanie put on *Graceland*. 'How's that?'

'Not good,' admitted Pross cheerlessly. 'Maybe we ought to try an instrumental.'

'Hey, Pross,' said Tony, pulling his briefcase out from behind the sofa, 'if you stop being mad at any time today, could you fix our fridge? It keeps making the milk freeze over.'

'I'll try.'

Tony kissed a worried Melanie and went off to work.

Melanie went to work on Pross, who was still staring at the floor.

'Come on, take that dress off,' she ordered.

Pross took it off, all the while looking downward.

'Now, for the first time ever, tell me honestly and properly how much you love me.'

'I can't tell you,' droned Pross to the floor. 'It's a curse being loved by me. It'll bring horrors. Cramps too.'

Melanie drew her fist back and hit him right in the mouth.

'You mad bitch,' he complained with a groan shortly after employing a defensive cringe to protect himself, then patting his lips to check for blood. 'What did you do that for? I'm supposed to be the nutty one.'

There *was* blood.

'Tell me honestly that you love me or I'll hit you again,' threatened Melanie.

Pross told her honestly. 'I love you, Melanie. I really do love you. But I'd love you even more if you weren't hitting me.'

'Now look me in the eyes and tell me again.'

From his cringing position, he looked her in the eyes and told her again, but his face began burning with shame.

'And I love you too,' said Melanie plainly. 'Now go upstairs and get some sleep.'

'Someone died because of me.'

'I don't care. He probably deserved it... it was a he, wasn't it?'

'He didn't deserve it.'

'All men deserve it.'

Then Melanie had a shocking thought. 'It wasn't that bloke who bought you a drink, was it? The one you were jealous of? The one Lilith told you you'd have to kill?'

'No. Not him. He's better than ever these days.'

'Did someone really die because of you? Tell me truthfully, Pross.'

'Someone did,' said Pross to the floor.

'Who?'

'Can't tell you,' he said, beginning to stammer a little. 'Don't worry, no one will ever know. Your diamonds aren't really part of it. They were given to me. Trust me.'

Melanie looked at Pross sympathetically. 'Go upstairs, please. Get some sleep.'

Pross went upstairs to bed but lay in a feeble, drifting state all day long. The anguish inside was worse than ever. He wondered if he'd ever be able to eat again.

It seemed that every bad thing he'd ever done in his life was coming back to haunt him now. His mind teemed with incidents long forgotten: kids bullied; harsh words spoken; people thumped.

And Spock: he began torturing himself over Spock. A cat had died because of him — would his conscience ever forgive him for that? Maybe he should devote the rest of his life to cat welfare?

A young girl began screeching in the street outside. It anguished Pross. Tore through him. It sounded to him just like the prolonged, agonised, diminuendo scream his mother had made after placing an electric fire into her bath water.

It was he that had unplugged her, already supposing she was dead.

And then he'd gone out to play football.

Throughout the long day, he heard people visiting. Lilith was now downstairs, he knew.

Lilith. He had to apologise to Lilith. He began formulating the things he needed to say to her when he heard someone coming up the stairs.

A tap sounded on the door.

He froze.

The door eventually opened, and Lilith came in.

Pross tried to speak, to gush his sentiments, but found himself barley able to utter a word.

And then he burned with shame.

He pulled the duvet over him and hid like a tortoise, hunching up in the centre of the bed.

'Thanks for the diamond, Pross,' said Lilith, sitting on the bed.

'You're welcome,' he returned, finding it easier to speak when concealed. 'Don't shout about it. Sell it discreetly.'

'I hear you've gone mad.'

'Demented.'

'What's it like?'

'Interesting... and scary. Maybe I'll be mad for the rest of my life. That wouldn't be any picnic.'

'Come downstairs,' said Lilith.

'Not yet.'

Lilith patted the hump that was Pross, and gently repeated, 'Come downstairs.'

Then she left him alone.

Remaining under the duvet, Pross soon began worrying that he should be fixing the fridge for Tony. It was surely just a thermostat problem. When he heard Tony return later in the evening, he steeled himself, then got out of bed to see to it.

2.33
Reunion

The money began preying on her mind. Twenty thousand pounds of hers was invested in Robert, almost half her inheritance.

At first, he had charmed her, but today he had maddened her. She had wanted to shake him.

But she still worried about him.

The hours alone in the flat dragged for Jennifer, until near to the time when she was due to go out to the club to meet Yvette and her new man. When this time approached, she found that she had to hurry all of a sudden to get ready.

She wore the new clothes she'd bought in Camden. Tight, pink, patterned velour leggings and a garish, tight purple top.

She fed the cat before she left.

The club was a short walk down the busy Holloway Road. Along the way, she closely followed a group of girls she guessed were heading for the same venue, and she was proved right.

She joined a small, high-spirited queue outside the club, which diminished quickly.

She paid her ten pounds entrance fee and left her coat with the attendant.

Hovering around the circular balcony, she kept an eye out for Yvette, but Yvette was not to be seen.

Later, Jennifer decided to score some E herself, and she asked around for the dealer.

As before, she only took half a tablet, keeping the remainder for Yvette, should she arrive.

By ten o'clock, Jennifer was coming up.

A minute later, she was dancing alone. Liberated.

Very soon, through a seething wall of faces, she saw Yvette coming to her, smiling hugely and hurrying with outstretched arms to greet her.

Jennifer returned the greeting.

Steven was lagging a little behind Yvette. He was a tall man in his middle twenties with shoulder-length streaked blonde hair. He smiled little, and never made a joke.

He made Jennifer uneasy. Even now, though on E, she was reluctant to become familiar with him.

After saying hello to her, Steven began dancing a serious little dance.

'I've got the E for you already,' shouted Jennifer into Yvette's ear as she too began to dance, almost at once bumping and grinding with Steven.

Yvette shook her head disapprovingly. 'No, Ah don't do that any more,' she shouted, like she was telling a child off, 'eet's bad. You shouldn't need eet to av a good time.'

Steven made an expression of cynical rejection to Jennifer.

Had this scene not had precursors, Jennifer might have been dumbfounded. As it was, the explanation was arrived at easily by her: Steven disapproved, and therefore so did Yvette. Yvette had even been turned against her own pet by Steven.

And Yvette had even let herself be slashed with glass because a boyfriend had wanted it.

Jennifer began disliking Steven, and as a protest against him, she defiantly swallowed Yvette's half of the E while he was watching. Soon she found she could no longer bear being near him, and moved away to dance alone.

Then she left the club, without telling Yvette.

Outside, she knew not what to do, or where to go. The E was at its height, and she was in no mood for going back to the flat, especially since Yvette and Steven might soon arrive there.

The traffic and pedestrians had a kind of stillness about them.

Jennifer wanted to be with Robert. She wanted to be with Robert when Robert was like he'd been when she'd first met him less than a week earlier.

She began wishing she hadn't left him in the afternoon.

Quickly finding a telephone, she rang him, but he was not at home.

She had been surprised by how faint and remote the dialling tone had sounded to her drugged ear.

Hailing a cab, she went looking for comfort. First, she tried the Mexican bar. Then the French restaurant. Then the tapas bar in Paddington Street.

Twenty pounds in fares altogether.

At the tapas bar, she sojourned, pleased to see the smiling face of Denise, the Brazilian waitress.

'Hello,' said Denise very nicely to Jennifer, 'How are you?'

'Have you seen Robert?' was Jennifer's first, almost desperate, utterance.

Denise made a butterfly in flight gesture. 'Here before, but gone now. Where, I do not know.'

The diners' talk sounded like a lulling hum to Jennifer, and she wanted to stay, stay where she knew at least one person's name.

She sat on a stool at the bar, and Denise served her a white wine.

Jennifer was captivated by Denise's warm beauty and the softness of her motions, and found herself gazing at her often.

Sometimes Denise would catch her eye and dedicate a smile to her.

'Looking for Robert, I hear,' said a voice behind her. It was Mike, the bar's owner with the harried, pig-like face. He looked like he hadn't slept for days. He was opening a bottle of wine for a customer, his white shirt wet with sweat under the arms.

Jennifer confirmed that she was indeed looking for Robert.

'He's gone to a private bar in Brewer Street,' said Mike in a matter of fact way.

'Where's that?'

'Off there myself soon. Come in the cab with me if you want.'

Jennifer agreed to this.

'Give me five minutes,' said Mike, going behind the bar to speak with Denise.

Five minutes later, Jennifer was standing on the street with Mike, waiting for a cab to appear. She felt awkward, like she was stood with one of her schoolteachers.

A cab was soon commissioned.

In the cab, at first Mike spoke about the pressures of owning a bar, until he asked, 'Have you done an E tonight?'

He had recognised the look in her eyes.

'An hour ago.'

'Good?'

'Fine.'

'You're very beautiful.'

'Thanks,' returned Jennifer plainly.

Mike's hand found its way on to Jennifer's thigh, and he turned to bring his face nearer to hers.

'Get off me,' said Jennifer, pushing him away.

'Come on, where's the harm?' said Mike. 'You're so beautiful. I can't help myself. You've done an E, I've done some coke. Let's enjoy ourselves.'

He forced his hand further up, and in between, her now squeezed-tight thighs.

'NO!' screamed Jennifer. 'Driver, stop.'

The alarmed driver stopped and looked at his passenger. 'What's up, love?'

'He is,' said Jennifer, and she got out.

Mike started to follow her, but she screeched at the top of her voice, 'Piss off!'

It was a narrow, busy street in the West End. Dozens of people turned to look at the scene.

Mike returned to the cab.

Once around a corner, Jennifer began to cry a little. All she wanted was a friend tonight. She wanted to hold and be held by a friend.

Although tearful, she continued walking. Walking nowhere in particular. So lonely was she, she began to feel jealous of the couples she was seeing. Thousands of couples. But then, at first not realising why she was struck with a feeling of familiarity, she happened upon the bar where she'd seen the Rolling Stone.

She went straight in, hoping that Robert might be there.

She looked all around downstairs, and saw him not. Saw only strangers. Then she proceeded upstairs, and as the room rose into view, she saw not Robert, but Mark.

He was sat at a table, looking morose and talking to a young woman with short ginger hair.

Avoiding being seen, she returned downstairs.

She didn't know what to do.

Out into the busy street she went. It was chaotic with traffic and people, but not oppressive. She was becoming frantic, but not confused.

A moment later, she had a thought, and the thought was this: she could ask Mark to help Jeremy and Robert. After all, the argument that had led to his leaving had apparently been over her.

The onerous procedure made easier by the drug, she returned to the bar and approached Mark.

Looking up from his low sofa, he recognised her at once. 'Hello, Jennifer,' he said in a descending tone, like she might be bad news, his worried, moon-like face becoming serious.

'Hello, Mark.'

Pulling his hair back over his head with both hands, Mark looked gloomily around the room, resignedly sighing, 'So where's Robert?'

'He's not with me. Can I ask you something?'

'You can ask me anything you want, Jennifer. It doesn't matter now.'

Jennifer came straight out with it. 'Will you help me help Robert? Teach me how to run the business?'

Mark balked. 'What? Are you mad? Tell them to find someone else, then run for your life.'

'They tried someone else. A girl called Penny.'

Mark pointed across the table, and said, 'This is Penny.'

Amused, Penny smiled and said, 'Hi, Jennifer.'

At first thrown, Jennifer then felt stupid. Felt like there was something going on she should understand, but couldn't. 'But it's my fault,' she suddenly blurted to Mark.

'What?' asked Mark, nervously amused by her passion.

'Why you left. You had an argument with Robert about me coming into the office.'

Mark drew in a deep, stressful breath and leant back in his seat, putting his hands behind his head for a few moments. 'That's not strictly true. It wasn't even an argument. I'd just had enough of him. It was the last straw.'

'What was wrong with me staying overnight? It's his room.'

'Nothing was wrong with you staying overnight,' countered Mark, 'but I had to listen while he took slimy Mike on a triumphant tour of your menstrual stains on the carpet and the bed. It's the not the crudeness, it's the hypocrisy and duplicity of the bloke.'

Jennifer was slowly struck with horror: Robert had been boasting of his conquest to the man who'd just assaulted her, triumphantly showing him where her period blood had stained during the sex they had had. 'Mike who owns the bar?' she asked with muted incredulity.

'He doesn't own it,' corrected Mark, 'he manages it. And he's going to be sacked soon, I happen to know.'

Seeing that Jennifer was deeply wounded, Penny took hold of her arm. 'Sit down,' she said sympathetically.

Jennifer did sit down, looking across the table into Mark's eyes, hurt and confused.

'Don't worry, you're not the first,' muttered Mark. 'Most every week he finds some lost soul and does a cheap emotional guru job on them. Never fucks them the first night, so they think he's a saint. A few weeks later he's tossed them away, and they come running to me to find out what he's really like. Sometimes they end up back with him again for a while, and they tell him what I said about him. I'd had enough of all that, thank you.'

An emotional nightmare, that's what it felt like to Jennifer. She did feel like she was dreaming. She felt disassociated. She began picturing Robert's face with her drugged mind's eye. His smiling, charming face. How could she have been so wrong about him? So taken in? 'How did I let him fool me?' she murmured painfully. She was so disturbed, she began to feel physically sick.

'Forget him,' said Penny, picking her jacket up from the floor. 'When I knew him, he'd argue black is white and white is black, and think he had such an aura about him you'd believe it.'

Penny said goodbye to Mark, and expressed her regret to Jennifer.

After Penny left, Jennifer starkly revealed, 'I've lent him twenty thousand pounds.'

Mark nearly fell off his sofa.

'What for?' he said in a high voice.

'For his business.'

'It's collapsing! I kept telling them that. They owe money all over the place. Forty grand's owed to the V.A.T. alone. They won't last another month before the bank pulls out. Even if they manage to start a new title without me, it's still hopeless. They're a lost cause.'

After some questions from Jennifer, Mark revealed secrets. He told her exactly what the Chesterford business was.

It was this:

When he was sober and undrugged, Robert was a particularly effective telesales agent. He could lie wonderfully over the phone. Lie on his feet. Jeremy was also good, but only because in his woolly-minded way, he had been half convinced by Robert that what they were doing was worthy. Mark had set the business up. At first, fraud had not been an intention, but had become inescapable as things got out of hand, which included Robert's cocaine addiction. What Robert and Jeremy did was to telephone companies, pretending to represent an official body, such as the Regional Health Authority, and say to the contacted company that they had been selected to appear in a forthcoming official review book where they could describe their product or service for the benefit of Health Authority specifiers. They would then sting the company for print fees of a few thousand pounds, promising that the books would be sent to every doctor and health service specifier in the country.

A stethoscope manufacturer would think that their stethoscopes would be seen by tens of thousands of doctors.

Alas, to save printing and distribution costs, what few books *were* printed never went anywhere, except to the advertisers.

'I'd had enough of that too,' said Mark finally. 'I'd rather be poor than go on doing that.'

He seemed very resentful, and even ashamed.

Battered is what Jennifer felt. Emotionally battered and betrayed. Even Yvette had become a disappointment. What did Yvette see in Robert? Surely she must have seen his true side by now. She broached this subject with Mark, but the very mention of her name seemed to hurt him.

'He likes to keep her fooled,' said Mark, 'if just to win one over on me. She's his big redemption too. So long as he keeps her fooled, he can still convince himself he's an angel.' He paused, then grumbled, 'Keeping Yvette fooled wouldn't be hard.'

Jennifer felt emotion welling up inside her. Everything that had seemed so wonderful had turned sour. It was all too much, and she became engulfed in distress, hardly able to utter a word.

Moved by her plight, Mark said he'd get her home, and helped her out on to the street to find a cab.

'Come with me,' pleaded Jennifer quietly when a cab drew near. 'I don't want to be alone yet. I've done some E.'

Mark did go with her.

He didn't know Jennifer was living with Yvette.

The telephone was ringing as Jennifer, her equanimity largely recovered, let herself into Yvette's flat.

Before she could answer it, it ceased.

Yvette was not yet back — that's if she intended to return at all. Maybe she would be staying overnight at Steven's? Jennifer did not know either way and had not thought about it at all.

Invited, Mark came in with her, wandering around the living room in an unsettled manner, unsure of what to say to Jennifer. Jennifer herself had already decided she didn't want to stay with Yvette any more, and had already began packing her things to take away at once to find a hotel for the night. As she worked, Mark regarded a photograph on a sideboard.

The photograph was of Yvette and Peter.

'Whose flat is this?'

'Yvette's,' said Jennifer, at first forgetting that Mark was reputedly in love with her... but then she remembered. 'Oh, I'm sorry. I should have told you.'

And she really did look sorry.

'Not as sorry as me,' muttered Mark, looking at the photo. 'I had to go and meet the one I couldn't forget, didn't I? Might as well have died the day I first saw Yvette.'

Pausing in her task, Jennifer asked, 'Don't you have a girlfriend?'

Mark shrugged. 'I'd only be lying to her if I did. I don't want to do that. I've told enough lies in my life.'

A key entered the door lock — Yvette was returning.

And Steven was with her.

Yvette's face became angry when she saw Mark standing in her own flat. 'What are you doing eer?' she said brutally.

'Leaving,' returned Mark.

'I asked him in,' said Jennifer. 'I'm leaving too.'

'Get eem out,' said Yvette to Steven. 'He's weird.'

Mark did not wait to be got out by anyone, and walked to the door, past Yvette and Steven, who were hand in hand.

Something about seeing Yvette with a new boyfriend wounded Mark deeply. He knew it made no real difference, but it hurt badly nevertheless. So badly.

Steven glared at Mark, although he knew him not, and closed the door with an aggressive conclusion about the action when he'd gone.

With Mark gone, Yvette turned her attention to Jennifer. 'Where are you go-een?'

'I don't know,' smouldered Jennifer. 'I've had enough of Robert, that's for sure. The bastard.'

Yvette was outraged. 'Ow can you say that about Robert? Eee's so sweet.'

'Oh, open your eyes, will you?' said Jennifer, picking her case up. Even though it was well past midnight, she intended standing by the road until a cab came along.

Suddenly, Yvette shrieked. 'No! The cat's een!'

Steven became angry. 'I told you to get rid of that fucking thing.'

'I did,' protested Yvette, trying to catch it.

'Leave it!' shouted Jennifer, so loud that both Yvette and Steven were jolted.

The woman upstairs began banging on the ceiling. Jumping, it sounded like.

And she *kept on* jumping.

Tires screeched outside, punctuated by a thud.

Then screams.

An accident had occurred.

The woman upstairs was still jumping.

They all moved to the window, and saw Mark in the road below, mangled and broken.

A lorry had hit him.

He was under its high bumper, bent backwards double, his feet beside his own head.

Jennifer turned pale with fear, and felt also that it was her own fault that this had happened. She had brought Mark here.

'Shit!' said Steven, almost seeming to be thrilled by the accident.

Yvette and Jennifer found themselves looking at each other. Aghast at first, Yvette then acquired her sullen look, a look which spoke her resentful awareness of self-fault.

She moved away from the window, acting as if nothing of importance had happened.

Then she went into the kitchen and put the kettle on.

Steven, saying nothing, opened the window to get a better view of the accident.

Starkly, Jennifer moved away, slumping to the floor.

The woman upstairs kept on jumping, so hard the ceiling could be heard cracking.

Steven saw the cat in the room and caught it, dropping it out of the first floor window.

Jennifer could only watch in dumb horror as he did this. She felt she was losing her mind, or would do soon in this insane asylum.

The woman upstairs was still pounding on the ceiling.

Police sirens began to wail.

The telephone in the room rang. Yvette came in from the kitchen to answer it as Jennifer sat adrift in horror and confusion.

'Ello?.. Yes, she ees.'

Face twisted, she proffered the receiver to Jennifer, saying nothing. Jennifer found herself reaching to accept it.

'Hello?' said Jennifer, so strangely that Sarah, the caller, immediately suspected that all was not well.

The sirens grew louder. The woman upstairs tired not.

'Jenny? Is there something wrong? What's all that noise?'

Pross was sat in a corner. Simply Red were criticising and judging him while he stared at his diminished collection of diamonds, laid out on the carpet before him. The gems appeared to him now like some taunting, mocking irony, placed in his possession only because they were of no use to him, or rather he was of no use to them. He was of no use to anyone, least of all himself.

He was clutching the little velvet pouch he'd made from the curtains in his bedroom up on the moors to keep the diamonds in. The pouch was damp, he realised. Since going mad, his hands had begun sweating so much that he left drops of fluid on the things he touched. He constantly wondered if he would have been all right if he hadn't drawn on that pipe last night. Would he have gone ga-ga the very next time he got stoned? Or was it because things were so fresh in his mind? Or was he simply due to go ga-ga anyway, never mind the dope? He would never know. Never know. And would he ever feel comfortable again? It couldn't end like this. Not like this. If it was going to end, it was going to end the way *he* wanted it to.

When he heard Sarah say Jennifer's name, and he realised who it was she was calling, he began trembling.

'Someone just died because of me,' Jennifer murmured.

'What?'

'Someone just died because of me,' repeated Jennifer.

Now Sarah thought it was all a joke. She thought that someone else had told her about Pross first, and that she was mimicking him. 'Leave Pross alone, he's a bit fragile at the moment.'

Amid the swirling madness, the utterance of that name seemed like a raft of sanity to cling to. 'Pross has come back? Is he back? Is Pross back?'

'You know he's back. He's with me now. I'm at Melanie's. He's sat in the corner counting diamonds. Listen, something wonderful's happened, Pross has...'

'Put him on,' cut in Jennifer sharply. 'Put him on now.'

There was a worrying desperation in her voice which now told Sarah that things were genuinely bad with her sister. 'Are you all right? Jennifer? What's going on?'

'Put Pross on. Please.'

Sarah asked Pross to come to the phone, whereupon his trembling became a visible shaking. She called him again, but he could not come, or even look. So Sarah brought the phone to him, making him hold the receiver and lifting it up to his ear.

'Jenny?' inquired Pross tremulously.

'I want you here,' implored Jennifer straightaway.

Even Pross, disturbed though *he* was, could sense Jennifer's state.

And he forgot his own condition a little.

'Are you all right? Jenny, what's wrong?'

'Please, I want you here.'

'Really?'

'Really.'

'Little problem,' admitted Pross. 'I've gone mad.'

'I want you here. Please hurry.'

'You don't understand. I've really gone ga-ga.'

'I don't care. Pross, please. Come to me. Borrow the money from Sarah. Please come.'

'I can't.'

'Please,' implored Jennifer, beginning to sob. 'Please. I need you here. Something terrible's happened.'

Pross fell silent. Horrified. Thinking how impossible it would be for him to even leave the house, let alone make it all the way to London. It was out of the question. He was with the fallen.

But Jennifer continued to cry to him. Cry anguished sobs.

'Four hours,' decided Pross, 'I can be with you in four hours.'